# Praise for Caravan

"Caravan is a standard setting masterpiece."

*Wagon Magazine*

"A book that stole my breath, defied my expectations, and was impossible to put down."

*Minute Magazine*

"Caravan is an absorbing story that keeps you enthralled with every turn of the page. Adam De Collibus takes readers on an intriguing journey of one man's persistent quest for self-discovery."

*Natasha Ganes, Cofounding Editor of TreeHouse Arts Magazine*

"A bewitching tale of one man's struggle to find his place in the world."

*Paragon Journal*

"Few contemporary writers conjure up atmosphere and adventure as well as De Collibus has in this fascinating history."

*Tessa Arlen, Author of The Lady Montfort Mystery series*

"Photographer William Abney seems a quiet soul; rootless—like so many—at the end of the Great War. Embarking on a mysterious quest in Morocco he is soon drawn into a colorful and disturbing world. Joining a desert caravan William slowly becomes aware of the intrigue and violence all around him. The author's travel experiences shine through—De Collibus has clearly enjoyed crafting every dangerous step of William's Saharan journey."

*Lucy Adlington, Author of The Red Ribbon.*


"A delightfully simple, yet awe-inspiring fable."

*Roxana Nastase, Chief Editor of the Scarlet Leaf Review*

# Caravan

# Caravan

a novel

Adam De Collibus

Third Lion Publishing

ISBN: 978-0-999085-0-3
Library of Congress Control Number: 2018903900

Any references to historical events, real people, or real places are used fictitiously. Names, characters, and places are products of the author's imagination.

Cover design by Arbëresh Dalipi
Cover layout by James Taylor
Book design by Allyson Wendt
Editing and layout design by Vanya Drumchiyska

Third Lion Publishing
P.O. Box 928
Paso Robles, CA 93446

All men dream, but not equally. Those who dream by night in the dusty recesses of their minds, wake in the day to find that it was vanity: but the dreamers of the day are dangerous men, for they may act on their dreams with open eyes, to make them possible.

*T.E. Lawrence*

*For Julian*

# 1

IT WAS LIKE EVERY LONDON MORNING since the beginning of time. Foggy and wet. To all but a few, today seemed as though it was just another unadventurous happening. In his opinion, William belonged to the majority, and his stare out the coach window reflected his own bored confidence at life's repetition, though inside he craved for the Fates to intervene.

The cobblestone street was empty and lined with lampposts glowing yellow in the fog. Over the roofs, long tongues of smoke emitted from industrial factories added to the gray in the sky. The coach came to a gradual stop on the left side of the street. William, a slender man wearing an earthy brown suit, stepped out of the coach and walked to the driver.

"How much do I owe you?" William asked.

"Thirteen pounds, sir," the driver replied.

"Very well, let me see," William said in a cheery voice as he reached into the right pocket of his trousers and rummaged around. William drew a fist out of his pocket and opened it. "I'm afraid two is all I've got. I am terribly sorry," he said, looking up from his hand, slightly afraid the driver might become angry.

"Going through a bit of a rough patch?" the man asked.

William gave a disheartened nod.

"Well if that's all you got, I'll take it," the driver said, barely satisfied, while lowering an opened hand to William. As the money traded palms, an automobile purred past the coach and disappeared farther down the street. The taxi driver tipped his top hat and sent the coach rolling forward in a sudden jolt. Now penniless, William watched as the coach carried his last two pounds down the street. He had earned the money taking a baby portrait, which had hurt his ears more than his ego. As far as he was concerned, not starving to death was more important than his honor.

1

William turned toward the building to his left. In front of him was a small set of stairs that led up to a massive black door. He reached into the front pocket of his coat and took out a piece of paper that opened to reveal an odd triangular shape. Scribbled in the center in blue ink was a simple note: *London Dove. Reginald Helee.* William looked up from the paper. Above the door was a white plaque, reading, "The Office of the *London Dove*," in a tangle of black paint.

A sigh of determination filled the misty air.

William walked up the steps. The sound of faintly clattering typewriters came through the door. He tapped the knocker several times and waited, taking a step back toward the handrail. While waiting for the door to open he turned away and looked down the street. *My last two pounds*, William thought, his mind too focused on his money to notice a low, dull chime sounding in the distance. It was seven o'clock in the morning.

A loud sequence of clicks sounded from the door and William turned around to a man smoking a cigarette. The man's hair was slicked back, and he had a thin mustache. "How can I help you?" he asked in a drowsy voice, the sound of a hundred typewriters clattering and dinging behind him.

"I am here for an appointment with Mr. Reginald Helee," William said.

"Your name?"

"Abney, William Abney." He smiled sadly as he stepped closer to the door.

"Abney?" the man said, frowning, and William's heartbeat fastened for fear that something was wrong. "Oh, Abney. You're here to take pictures," the man stated, recognition brightening his eyes.

"That's right," William nodded, feeling relieved that his name had not been lost in the pile of candidates who had responded to the newspaper's simple advertisement: "Photographer wanted."

"Come on in. Mr. Helee is expecting you," the man said as he stepped back, releasing the full roar of the typewriters. William walked through the door, and the man closed it behind him. The room was plain and crammed wall to wall with wooden desks. Behind them sat young men with black vests and rolled-up sleeves, punching away at typewriters like their lives depended on it. Second to the clattering that filled the air was a cloud of cigarette smoke that hung just below the ceiling. The atmosphere in the room was so noisy and busy that William had forgotten about the man standing next to him.

"Your coat?" the man asked.

"Ah, forgive me," William said handing over the coat, and the man hung it among a long line of overcoats and hats.

"Come this way," the man said, walking past William through the rows of desks. William followed. They turned right and entered a narrow hall that led away from the main room. Flanking the narrow hallway were the doors to other offices. At the end of the hall, a wooden staircase twisted up to the second story, a single naked bulb the only source of light. The man started up the stairs and William followed him.

"You can wait here," the man said, looking down on William as if he were unworthy to ascend the steps.

William stepped down and the man continued marching up alone. William took a seat on the stairs and looked up at the ceiling. As he listened to the echoing footsteps, they became fainter as they reached the lofty gloom coming from the light bulb above. Then came a knocking, followed by the muffled sound of a relaxed voice.

William assumed the voice belonged to the man he was there to see. He leaned back in the staircase, the fingernails of his right hand thoughtfully hovering near his lips. From his position, he couldn't see much of the second floor, only the top half of the man walking through an open door before disappearing behind it.

The secretary walked in the office and had he not seen the room's lavish décor every day for years, he would've been awestruck. The room was decorated wall-to-wall with red embroidered fabric and illuminated by several lamps. The secretary sighed, hesitant to speak to the director who was shielding his face and upper body with a newspaper at a desk situated near the windows. Behind him, white shutters covered the panes, allowing only four sharp rays of light to slip through the seams and enter the room.

"What is it?" a lethargic voice asked. The director was in his mid-fifties and his dark hair had receded from the top of his head and looked slightly disheveled; brandy and caviar had gotten the better of his health. Below his round nose sat a mustache that the secretary could only aspire to brandish.

"There is a man here to see you, sir." The secretary straightened his spine and lifted his eyes to the shutters above the director's barely visible head.

"So?" the director continued closing and opening the newspaper.

"He is currently waiting downstairs," the secretary explained, shifting on his feet.

"Tell him to go shear a sheep," the director declared and straightened the newspaper in a rustling jolt.

The secretary, used to the director's moods, cleared his throat insistently. "The man is William Abney, sir."

The director slammed the newspaper down and rose to his feet. "Why, for God's sake, man, why didn't you say so? Bring him in at once," he barked, unaware he was still wearing his red morning robe over his usual dress shirt, a habit he had formed on sleepless nights. The secretary darted out of the room and closed the door, fearing a desk decoration or a jar of ink would be hurled at him.

Reginald Helee, the director of the *London Dove* continued to stand behind the desk for several moments, slightly confused about what had happened.

His eyes wandered to the newspaper then slowly to the pants he wore, which happened to match his robe. Reginald suddenly rushed from behind the desk and toward the door where a coat hanger stood, his slippers shuffling on the carpet. In quick succession, he slipped out of his robe, snatched a black coat, and started heading back.

Coming around the desk, he frantically buttoned the coat over his white shirt and retook his seat. Just in time too, as the secretary was opening the door, William Abney in tow.

As William was led to the armchairs, he thought the man behind the desk looked as though he were the essence of masculine authority. The secretary was about to speak, but the man spoke first.

"William, m'boy. Glad you're here this fine morning. I'm Reginald Helee and I own this establishment."

"Thank you for having me, sir," William said, his voice sounding delicate in comparison to Reginald's baritone. When William reached the desk, he and Reginald shook hands.

"Call me Reginald, and please, take a seat." Reginald pointed to one of the chairs.

"Don't you think it's a little bit dark in here, sir?" asked the secretary, motioning toward the windows.

"Why, now that you mention it, yes, it is." Reginald began to rise from his seat to open the shutters but froze, reminded as he looked down that he was still wearing his red pants. "Why don't you open them for me," Reginald said, making his movement look like he was adjusting himself in his seat much like a man nearly caught pretending to be a cripple.

"Of course, sir."

The secretary opened the shutters and a flood of silvery light shot into the lavish office, shaming the lamps with its brightness. William squinted and looked away slightly while Reginald stared at him with an inquisitive gaze. As William's eyes adjusted to the brightness—and to the pair of eyes intently looking at him—the secretary took his leave, softly closing the door to the director's office.

Reginald's dark brown eyes stayed locked on William for a moment longer and then, as if announcing himself to be a breathing being, he said, "Do you know why you are here?" The suspicious tone in Reginald's voice was enough to make William doubt his whole existence and what came out of his mouth was a cross between self-doubt and self-consciousness.

"I'm here for an interview?" William asked, confused by the question because every person who ever went to an interview, especially if they were desperate for money, knew why they were there.

"No. You're here to get hired," Reginald corrected.

There was a short silence in which Reginald waited for a reply while William's eyes said that he was beginning to have his doubts about this interview.

"I must say, William," Reginald continued, clearly measuring William with his words, "I am quite impressed with your history."

"I beg your pardon?" This interview was not going at all how William had imagined. He was beginning to think Reginald Helee had mistaken him as a war hero.

"Don't be ridiculous, William. Any man who arms himself with a camera instead of a rifle in the trenches should be awarded a medal. I can have it arranged if you like." Reginald's low and lively voice reeked with a boastful resonance.

"No, thank you," William said, trying to keep the revulsion from his voice and face.

"Kill any Germans?" Reginald asked, and William saw an unrestrained excitement in the man's features that caused wrinkles to appear on his forehead. Only a man who had never been to war could be excited by the prospect of it.

The memories softened the look in William's eyes with a touch of grief, and the enthusiasm drained from Reginald's face. "Shame. Well, whether you want a medal or not, consider yourself as now working for the *London Dove*," Reginald stated, leaning to his right and rattling open a stubborn drawer.

William was surprised—and slightly suspicious—of how suddenly he was hired. This whole affair reeked badly but he couldn't pinpoint the exact reason why.

Reginald slapped a fat envelope on top of the newspaper that lay on his desk, and then carefully aligned a sheet of paper and a pen next to it. From the microscopic letters on the paper and the line at the bottom William knew what role the paper played, but the envelope was a bundle of hidden opportunities. William looked hesitantly at Reginald, then at the envelope.

"Go on, take it," Reginald cooed with the kind of assurance that would make a rabbit willingly hop into a cage.

"What is that?" William asked, looking briefly up at Reginald and trying to hide his excitement about the contents of the envelope.

"It's everything you'll need to get to where I am sending you," Reginald said.

"Sending me?" William asked.

"Inside is a boat ticket. You leave at midnight tonight for a port town on the coast of Morocco. Nador? I believe it's call. I don't know, I can never get the pronunciation quite right." This raised William's interest. He took the envelope, opened it and looked at the contents. A thick stack of green and pink Moroccan dirhams, along with the boat ticket, were neatly stashed inside.

"Since our soldiers returned from fighting the Turks, bringing the spoils of war with them, anything from that part of the world has become the new sensation in London. Even I've fallen prey to it." Reginald stopped and nodded to a Persian rug on the floor. "And our paper would benefit greatly if the people knew more about the environment where these desired items were made. Also, your boat will arrive in Nador three weeks from today, and when you get there, you are going to receive a letter from me containing very important instructions that must be followed to the letter."

"What will I be doing once I get to Morocco?" William asked, still unsure what he was being hired to do.

"You will cross the Sahara by caravan to Yemen, taking photographs of the culture and the desert, as well as the local people along the way. It's essential that you photograph only what catches your eye, because if it catches your eye, it will catch any other Englishman's eye, and that is what sells more papers. When you reach Yemen, you will take a boat back to London to deliver the pictures you've taken—only if you accept my offer, of course." The smile that lit Reginald's face turned predatory as his eyes pointed to the contract.

William considered the offer, and though a hundred suspicious thoughts crossed his mind, he decided to take this chance and see what life had in store for him. Opportunities like this didn't come knocking often—if at all. "I accept," he said solemnly, then leaned forward and scratched his name on the line at the bottom, cautious of Reginald who kept a careful eye on the trembling tip of the pen.

When the pen made a soft thud on the paper, the director gave a cheerful, "Good, good," and extended a hand to William without rising from his chair. William, though, rose to his feet and shook Reginald's hand.

"Thank you. I am very grateful" William said.

"Think nothing of it. And if I were you, I'd pack my things and leave at once; the boat waits for no one."

William nodded. "I will leave right away, sir," he said, taking several brisk steps toward the door with the envelope in hand. As he reached the door, William turned around to face Reginald.

"How much will I be paid?" he asked in an honest yet cautious tone.

"Ten thousand pounds when you return from your journey. If you return," Reginald added, his voice shaken by an amused chuckle.

The thought of ten thousand pounds made William a bit light-headed. He had nothing in his pocket right now—but those ten thousand pounds? He'd live like a king for the rest of his life...

"If?" William asked softly, finally realizing that he might have just signed away his life.

"Well, you see, William, being a photographer is no cake walk—especially if you work for one of the most read and respected papers in England. I've lost many photographers during my years here. One of them had his head beaten in by a savage's club during the wars with the Zulu, another man was murdered by gypsies in Romania, and many have fallen so much in love with the land or the women that they decide to stay indefinitely, wasting the money I gave them on wine, women, and song." Reginald sounded full of contempt retelling these stories. He also seemed to feel pleasure from torturing William with them.

"Oh God, tell me you're not one of those pathetic sympathizers. Are you, William?" Reginald asked in a sneer of disgust as he leaned over his desk.

William shook his head solemnly.

"Good. From the moment I laid eyes on you I knew you were the kind of man who holds his duty to king and country first," Reginald declared.

The newest *London Dove* photographer remained silent where he stood by the door, wondering if Reginald will finally reveal what this whole sermon was about. He was curious, yes, but his intuition told him he might be better off not knowing.

"On one incident, a year or so after the French built that tower, I had a photographer achieve something just short of a miracle while in Paris. Have you heard of the story?" William shook his head. "A shame. Anyway, the man managed to fly nine hundred and eighty-four feet without wings. You see, the night before he'd gotten as drunk as a weasel on the best cognac he could get his sticky little fingers on. Yet in the morning, he had been determined to do his duty and take a picture from the top of the tower as I'd requested. Sadly, because the effects of cognac don't wear off easily—it's strong stuff, you know," Reginald smiled, smacking his lips delightedly, "he fell backwards over the handrail, splattering every drop of cognac on the ground on impact."

The director suddenly clapped his hands together to demonstrate the force of impact before returning them to their folded position on the desk. He fell silent for a moment, his dark head bowed over his interlaced fingers. "Damn shame it is; the French make such fine cognac," he added with a sigh.

William didn't know what to make of this story. Was Reginald testing him? If he had been in better circumstances, William would have simply walked away, contract or not. But he was as desperate as desperation went, and he was determined to hold onto this job, return home even if half-dead, and get his ten thousand pounds.

He turned to the door, hand on the brass knob.

"Oh, and one more thing, William," Reginald's voice came, and William turned to look at the now dark silhouette behind the desk. "Don't forget that if something were to happen to you, or you don't return in six months, you'll be presumed dead and our arrangement will be canceled."

"I understand," William replied, though he was beginning to wonder why all these terms weren't mentioned before he'd signed that contract. He was fair to admit, at least to himself, that he would've signed even if he'd known the terms.

"Do you take to the bottle, William?" Reginald asked as he stood, and William shook his head. "I recommend you try it sometime. I can't get enough of the bloody stuff." William felt slightly uneasy, not because of this conversation—though that too—but because he now noticed Reginald's mismatched clothes. *Obviously*, he thought, nodded absently, and stepped out of the office, leaving the silhouette of his new employer basking in the light behind the desk.

Now on the other side of that door, William looked at the envelope. Sure, he had his fears about this assignment, but what an opportunity this was for him. A small smile budded on his lips, and he hurried to get out of the building and into London's damp air. He rushed down the stairs and through the noisy room filled with typists until he reached the front door, where William grabbed his coat and walked out.

As his feet landed on the cold sidewalk, William allowed the excitement to wash over him and he smiled so widely that his cheeks began to ache. Other than getting shipped off to France during the war, William had never left England, and now he couldn't help but wonder how his world would soon change.

The street was quiet at this early hour, and the cobblestones were beginning to glisten from a light mist. With no coaches in sight, William decided to walk instead of waiting for one to appear. By the time he had turned the corner, the mist had become a torrential downpour, forming streams in the gutters and puddles in the cobblestones.

Only the memory from his early morning coach ride guided William back to his apartment. When he spotted his apartment building, the rain had already soaked every inch of his suit, but he still leapt up the set of stairs as if that would somehow save him from the downpour. He stepped inside the door and closed it softly, trying not to give a sign of his presence. A narrow hallway lead to a tall window that filtered in a beam of gray light—the only sign of life in the house.

William's apartment was upstairs. With a slight smile, he headed toward the wooden staircase to the left, walking past a line of coats and hats hanging on the flower-papered wall. He took the stairs at a painfully slow pace, making every creak and croak come to life in the deathly silent building.

At the top, another narrow hall awaited, a door housed on either side. Smile gone, William walked toward his apartment on the right, giving a dreaded stare at the other door. He held his breath and listened.

All was not silent. Drops ticked on the tiles near his shoes creating a cacophony of noise in the otherwise quiet hall. He took the key out of his pocket and placed it into the lock, then turned it slowly until the lock gave way and a loud clap echoed in the hallway.

With the door wide open, William stumbled into the safety of his apartment, closed the door behind him, and sighed. He stood there with his eyes closed, as the rain pummeled the windows and a motor car splashed through the flooded streets. Finally, he locked the door and walked through a small hallway that opened up into a room.

This was his apartment. He stopped and looked around, thinking that after midnight tonight this cozy little room would live only in his memory. He would miss the two large windows overlooking the street, and the small tea table where a lonely vase sat, housing a single white iris. It was difficult to call this room cozy, but to William it was home.

The floor creaked beneath his feet as he walked to the table and sat in the loveseat, leaning forward to get a closer look at the flower. The gloomy room only made it appear brighter and otherworldly; its petals glowing like the eye of a newborn baby. William lifted his hand and touched the lowest hanging petal—it was so soft and breakable. He felt its fuzzy surface tickle him as he moved his thumb to pet it delicately.

Not a moment later, a burst of knocks came from the door. At first, William jumped startled, his first instinct urging him to answer, but he stopped himself and sat down again, looking over his shoulder at the dark hallway. Several seconds passed in silence. Another burst thundered against the door. "Come on, I know you're in there. I saw you. Don't play hide and seek with me, Mr. Abney," he recognized the elderly landlady whose voice sounded like the taunting sneer of a little sister out for revenge. *How'd she see me go in?*

"If you don't come out, I'll get the constable," Mrs. Eldrich threatened, which got William's attention. This wasn't an empty threat—not this time.

The race was on.

Hurrying to his wardrobe, William rose to the tips of his toes, pulled down a dusty brown leather suitcase, and laid it on the bed. The latches were a little rusty at first but surrendered after a minute of fumbling over them with cold-stiff fingers. He opened the wardrobe without caring about the noise he was making and started frantically emptying its contents into the suitcase, as if disposing of a lethal disease.

The nervous rattling on the door suddenly stopped. *She's gone to get the constable.* This made him hurry all the more. Snapping out of his momentary distraction, William continued collecting his belongings—most important of which was his camera, a Seneca Competitor—and placing them in the suitcase. A moment later, he thought he could hear the jingling of keys coming from the hallway.

Short on time, William realized he had only a minute to gather his belongings before the landlady and the constable entered his apartment. He reached high into the right corner of the wardrobe and pulled down the narrow bag containing his camera tripod, then slung it over his shoulder.

A loud click came from the door, quickly followed by a second one. William pulled the lid of the suitcase over the clothes, trying to force it shut, but little corners of cloth kept popping out. The apartment door opened just as he managed to click the locks into place, and short footsteps marched in.

Suitcase in hand, William started walking toward the small hallway when he saw the grayish blue eyes of his elderly landlady looking up at him. Below them, a pair of wet-looking lips puckered up at him in anger.

"I knew it—trying to leave, are we?" the woman shouted.

"Mrs. Eldrich..." William said, calmly preparing to explain the situation.

"Don't you 'Mrs. Eldrich' me," she shouted, pointing a wrinkly finger at him. "You owe me two weeks' rent and I want to have it. Right now," the landlady said, whipping her hand back to her side.

"I don't have the money," William said.

"Don't have the money?" she shouted. "You better tell me you got robbed or I'll call the constable on you. Now where is it?" she demanded.

"I spent my last pound on a taxicab," William replied.

"You did what?" The woman's eyes widened in disbelief.

"Let me explain, Mrs. Eldrich," William started, speaking quickly because he knew he had little time. "You are in luck."

The woman grimaced in suspicion.

"I have just been hired to do a job and I have to go away for some time," William said, fully aware that some time usually meant much longer. He was about to go on when she interrupted.

"That's it, I've had enough of your lies. I am going to get the coppers," Mrs. Eldrich said as she began to move toward the door.

"Mrs. Eldrich, when have I lied to you?" William pleaded. "You know I keep my word, so let me give it to you." The elderly woman stopped and turned around with a thoughtful look in her eyes. "I'm telling the truth," William added, seeing he had her attention.

"All right, then, let's have it," Mrs. Eldrich said. Her voice had softened a little, but the fists on her hips were a sure sign this was William's last chance.

He chose his words carefully, taking a step closer. "I just signed a contract that will earn me some money—enough to pay what I owe you, and perhaps a little extra—the moment I get back in six months."

"This is true—you promise?" she demanded, sharp eyes probing for any lies she couldn't otherwise detect.

"I give you my word that the very moment I set foot in London I will not rest until you get paid," William said.

"Alright," Mrs. Eldrich said after a short silence. "But if you set foot in London and don't come running here, I will have you arrested."

"I suppose that's fair. Now, I must leave quickly, otherwise I might miss my boat. Goodbye and farewell," William said. He quickly put his hands on her shoulders and kissed her forehead before she could protest.

As she was processing his sudden show of affection, William had already left the apartment and descended halfway down the stairs to the ground floor. William's echoing steps brought Mrs. Eldrich back to her senses and the smile that had appeared on her lips quickly vanished.

"What do you mean, your boat?" Mrs. Eldrich growled from the lofty heights of the stairwell, where she'd nearly run to get a last glimpse of her tenant.

"Yes, a boat," William said, almost daring her to run after him.

"Where in the devil are you going?" Mrs. Eldrich demanded.

"To Morocco," William said as he opened the door.

"Don't you have anyone to tell about your... um... being gone?" she asked, a note of concern seeping in.

"No. Just you!" William shouted as he stepped into the pouring rain. Silence filled the staircase when the door closed behind him.

"To Morocco?" Mrs. Eldrich said to herself, moving slowly away from the handrail. She glanced at William's room and scurried down the hall to get a last glimpse of him through the windows that looked down on the street.

When her face got close to the glass, she wiped away the fog that had settled there and leaned in against the window. William was standing near a lamppost, suitcase in hand, getting drenched by the rain. He looked left, then right, as if figuring out which direction to go, then started walking down the street and vanished silently around the corner.

And that was it.

She could now start counting the minutes till he returned. When the landlady realized the lonesome burden she would have to bear, she took a deep breath and moved away from the window. Mrs. Eldrich glanced at the white iris on the table, sadness filling her soul because she was going to miss the kindhearted William Abney. Finally, she closed the door, leaving the room empty, with the sound of the rain ticking gently against the window.

# 2

A STEAMBOAT'S WHISTLE SHRILLED over the shouts of the crowd standing on the docks below. The passengers of the SS Dorset, a steam vessel that had seen this voyage countless times, stood lined front to back, slowly descending an iron gangplank. The pier they stepped onto was overflowing with frenzied merchants yelling out the prices of spices and fine cloth; their roar creating an unpretentious, unrestrained welcome to the prudish passengers, who had become too accustomed to the tea-time life aboard. The merchants' foreheads glistened with sweat, something that the foreigners weren't used to but experienced nonetheless due to the Moroccan heat. Dusty air thick with the sharp smell of rotting seaweed completed the picture, enough to turn a soft stomach.

The men that descended the boat wore plain suits kept to tidy perfection, and even the warm sun could not tempt them from removing their coats. Their gentler counterparts sashayed in lavish dresses and hats, dozens of feet of fabric folded over in layers like rose petals.

As the passengers spilled from the gangplank, a hundred caddie boys eager to earn a penny hefted luggage down their own special walkways, piling bags on the sides of the dock before running back for more. They were young and wore the same black uniform, which made them look a lot like an army of ants gathering their food in disorganized heaps. The whole place was engulfed in chaos as passengers scrambled to get their suitcases while the roaring merchants tried to sell their wares.

William was standing on the gangplank among the last of the passengers, watching the cacophony of people mingling like pigeons around a morsel of bread. The ticket Reginald had given him wasn't exactly first class, and William was sure the rat that had shared his room had come to the same realization. Along the voyage, William had studied his roommate so well that he felt he could write an entire tome on the behavior of rodents. The idea teased a smirk on his face, but he knew that his most effective language was not words but photographs.

Overwhelmed by the sudden onslaught of the heat, the smell of seaweed, and the noise, William thought he was close to fainting. He swallowed, taking shallow breaths so as not to feel the stench too much. The other men around him seemed adamant to stick to their guns, but William had already broken the silent code and had taken off his coat and rolled up his sleeves, the better to adjust to the heat. It helped, but only a little.

William lifted his gaze from the pier toward the city that spilled down the mountainside behind the docks. The dirt streets of Nador seemed darkened by windowless structures that were, for the most part, unpainted. Closer to the docks, however, the story was much different. The buildings were either bright red, orange, or blue. Some of them even had signs in English and French.

The passengers began to move steadily down the gangplank and William followed them. When he stepped on the pier, he was absorbed into the crowd and carried away as the passengers hurried toward the streets where the more scrupulous merchants waited for the foreigners to arrive. The shoulder-to-shoulder jostling made William hold his suitcase just a little tighter as the crowd swept him closer to the city. The envelope he'd stashed inside held five hundred dirhams and he wasn't about to lose a single one. He'd counted the money nearly a thousand times, and though he sensed a fear of being robbed, that wasn't what bothered him—not ultimately. Indeed, there was something else, an invisible unease masked behind the newness of everything around him, that frightened him more.

As he neared the edge of the dock and the narrow pier that led him to an open area overlooked by the colorful buildings, William squeezed his way out of the crowd. The further he moved away, the softer the joyful chatter became. Finally on his own, he leaned against a wall where the boulder-scattered shore descended into the bluish green water. He could feel his nerves beginning to calm and was even more relieved when a sudden breeze chilled his sweat as a wave crashed on the rocks below him, sending mist in the air. William set his suitcase down and laid his useless coat over it. He pulled out a handkerchief, wiped away the sweat and dust from his forehead and looked with revulsion at the smudge of dust. He was going to have to get used to the dirt and sand— he wouldn't last in the desert otherwise. He whisked the handkerchief into his shirt pocket, shifting his focus on what still had to be done before the real journey began.

Looking away from the water, William's gaze found the Nador crowds. He couldn't fail to observe that people dressed in the finery of dukes and duchesses walked alongside people wearing dirty robes, some of whom leading a goat or a camel behind them, others carrying pots on their heads. This was a new world that welcomed him, a world that frightened him and fascinated him all at the same time. William scanned the narrow streets in front of him, wondering which shadowy path would take him to a post office the quickest. A faint sound, possibly music, echoed off the walls to his right and moved towards the shore like a breathy whisper. The street there was crowded but appeared safe and William started in that direction, his suitcase in one hand and his coat in the other.

The street funneled into a path so narrow the sunlight couldn't reach the heads of even the tallest people, creating a world of dream-like quality that brought a feeling of unease. A turbaned man lead a camel past William, the strange creature catching his attention and making him consider how much he stands out amidst the locals. He came from a country of typewriters, automobiles, and factories into this city that was busy playing catch up with the rest of the world. The Arabic women wore long hooded dresses that left only their faces exposed and walked together in small numbers, and children had yet to make an appearance. The men wore caps or turbans and long white robes that appeared light and comfortable. The buildings on either side of the street were covered in thousands of blue, white, and green tiles, creating a sea of color. Curious people leaned out of lofty windows, watching with curiosity the new wave of foreigners enter the city. Many boats had come and gone, bringing wealthy tourists to their city. Very few newcomers stayed, but over the years, things had changed, and it now seemed that for every Arab in Nador there was a European.

William sensed hidden resentment in the eyes of the locals, and he remembered the stories he had overheard aboard the SS Dorset. The locals felt dependent on the Europeans much like slaves depended on their masters. The entire Nador economy was structured around the foreigners' curiosity and the money they brought in, so if the wealthy Europeans stopped coming, the Arabs would need to find other means to provide food on their tables—a premise few were willing to consider.

William looked at the crammed street ahead of him. The cool air began to carry new scents—the stench of animals mixed with the aroma of spiced lamb kabobs and sweet teas from restaurants ready to serve the foreigners. The buildings, the voices, and the still-elusive music made his feet carry him into the shade of the street. A lone tambourine was rattling over the crowd and William poked his head above the people to see where the sound was coming from. He knew he was getting closer, but his eyes couldn't see anything in the river of bodies and animals that flowed freely in the narrow street. Then, he caught a glimpse of a delicate hand shaking a tambourine and moved closer lead by his curiosity.

When he jostled his way out of the crowd, William saw the hand belonged to a woman who was dancing as seductively as she was dressed. She swayed and spun to her own music, never moving away from the glowing fabric shop behind her. William found himself staring at the woman until his eyes landed on a tough man, probably the owner of the shop, who was leaning against the doorway with his arms crossed over his chest in a miserable attempt to look casual. William didn't like the thought that formed in his mind, but he felt it was true. The people here used all kinds of tactics to make the foreigners spend their money—even on things they didn't want or need. With this new awareness, William continued walking.

The further he moved down the street, the more he realized his observation had been true. There were small shops and colorful stalls that sold merchandise of every kind. Hundreds of displays offered row after row of food, spices, fine cloth, and anything exotic that could catch the attention of the newcomers. Each shop was unique and easily distinguishable from the hundred others in the crammed street. William had made a promise that not a single Moroccan dirham would leave his pocket except for lodging, but looking and listening were for free, and he enjoyed the beauty of the city by observation alone.

But though he would look at the fine fabrics and catch the occasional sniff of expensive oils, William most enjoyed the animals. Small monkeys dressed in suits and caps, enormous elephants, and snakes draped over the shoulders of short, bright-eyed men provided passersby with the right amount of bizarre and sometimes dangerous sights that they were sure to leave a coin or two behind.

The farther William walked down the street, the shabbier the shops looked, and the displays became less appealing to the eye, selling only the essential foods and spices. Looking around, he noticed he was the only foreigner who'd remained, though the crowd was still dense and uncomfortably choking. The shop owners stared at him from behind the displays, hungry for his money, but lacking the colorful enchantment that usually grabbed the attention. To William, this change of scenery was a curiosity. His eyes were busy gazing at the barren walls, the narrow length of blue over his head, and the robed men that walked past him. At this point he felt his stomach grumble. He hadn't eaten a thing all day and it was long past noon. Despite the hunger pangs, he decided that until he found the post office he would not look for food.

It wasn't long after William followed the directions of a shop owner that he approached a doorway of a building that looked especially bland. He walked closer and noticed a plain sign that hung above the door, an Arabic inscription on it. Underneath were French and English translations, one of them barely readable.

"Post office," William said to himself.

He walked closer and stopped just inside the doorway. To his left were several wooden benches, and to his right, a long counter divided the room nearly in half and continued all the way to the end, with small arched doors situated every four or five feet. A skinny, barred cage descended from the ceiling down to the top of the counter. It seemed like this had once, a long time ago, been a busy place. Behind the counter was an open doorway that revealed only a glimpse of a wall covered in blue light.

The whole room was empty and quiet. William saw a cheap bell on the counter, reached out for it, and rang it, creating a dry clacking noise. A moment later, he heard a shuffling sound that grew louder until a white robed man stepped tiredly into the doorway. He stared at William in expectation.

"Umm, good day. I am here to collect a letter," William said, hoping he hadn't misread the sign.

"Name?" the man said in a thick accent.

"Abney, William Abney," replied William as he brought a hand up to his neck and began twisting a button with his fingers. The post office clerk hmphed and stepped back into the room he'd come from, leaving William open-mouthed with the beginning of an explanation of the importance of that letter. Left on his own, William stepped closer to the bars wishing he could see behind the wall into the backroom where the clerk had disappeared.

Just when William's thoughts had started wandering in directions of doubt and betrayal, a faint crash came from the back room. He turned toward the doorway not knowing what to expect—had the man found the letter?

There was a lull, then the commotion suddenly started again, accompanied by a mumbling voice. Then the noise ceased and footsteps, along with loudening grumbles, neared the doorway. The man appeared a second time, holding an envelope in front of his stomach, his eyes looking down at the paper's wrinkled surface.

He walked up to the counter, still mumbling, and slid the envelope underneath an arch in the bars where William could reach it. After shooting him a loathing glance, the man turned around and shuffled back to the inner room. William stared at his robed silhouette until it disappeared in the doorway, then picked up the envelope making sure it was addressed to him. He started to open it but then stopped, because the hunger pangs in his stomach were becoming more insistent. Stashing the envelope inside his coat pocket, William walked out into the street, his ears listening for the clinking of utensils and the warm chatter of a restaurant.

In front of him were three narrow lanes. The one to his right led back to the coast where he'd come from. The one to the left led farther up the mountain, and the one straight ahead seemed to hold a greater risk of being robbed than finding a restaurant.

He took the left street. The light was scarce here, and unlike the crammed street he'd walked before, now he was the only passerby. From a few open windows, he could hear people shouting or laughing, but there was no other sign of life. The farther he walked, the more he realized that the chance of finding a restaurant was becoming slimmer.

Oddly, he didn't care. His mind was pleased and calmed by the serenity of this homey part of Nador. He liked it so much that he almost forgot about his hunger. Old women carrying pots on their heads and children circling their feet were the only people he met. Even though the streets were dirtier and less appealing to the eyes, William found something that made him feel different from the other foreigners: joy in simplicity. He felt content.

The street continued to lead William further up the mountain, no restaurant in sight. He was just about to head back to the docks when he smelled the sweet aroma of baked bread. He breathed fully, and the scent filled him, awakening his hunger. All afternoon he'd wandered around leisurely, but now he followed the scent at a brisk pace. At last, his senses were bombarded as he came around a bend and spotted a small doorway. A bright light made the doorway glow in the twilight, sending a warm invitation to all who were desperate to fill their bellies. William wasn't sure if this was a restaurant since no signs faced the street, but he couldn't turn back now. When he reached the doorway, he stopped.

The place was empty, the floor covered in white plaster tiles painted in blue and yellow designs. The glowing light that poured into the street came from a humble lantern hanging from the ceiling. A door further back was the only other entrance. As William was wondering what to do, the inner door crashed open and a short bald man rushed out, unaware of the hungry customer. The short man was about to clean a table when he noticed William. A look of joyful surprise brightened his face.

As if William was a good friend, the man smiled widely, plumping up his thick cheeks in delight. William hadn't expected the stranger's warm welcome, but at that moment, he didn't stop and consider it. His body was weak with hunger and he felt that he might actually faint if he didn't eat something soon. The man, very possibly the owner himself, spoke happily in Arabic as he walked over, but William's unaffected expression made his short steps come to a stop and he frowned. The man scratched the side of his head and looked at the floor as if trying to remember something important. "Français?" he said cautiously, putting a great effort to push past his thick accent.

"English," William replied, finally stepping inside the doorway.

"My friend," the man said as he neared the door, nervously wiping his hands on his white apron. "Welcome to my humble restaurant; please come." Then, as if startled by a sudden thought, the man jerked his head to the inner door and yelled something in Arabic. A second man came bursting out and walked toward William at a forced pace. He took William's suitcase and coat and placed them with gentle care near an empty table positioned at an open window facing the street.

"Here, my friend, have a seat," the owner said, leading William by the arm toward the table.

William was both surprised and entertained at being treated like he was the sole patron at this establishment. He also thought this was probably true most of the time since the restaurant was situated in an area too remote for foreign tourists to wander into. When William and the restaurant owner reached the table, they took seats opposite each other. The other man, who'd watched the proceedings from the nearby wall, walked back into what William thought was the kitchen. A moment later, a skinny young man, more a boy with a whisper of a mustache, came out carrying a small tray at his waist. He gently placed the tray on the table and unloaded two small cups and a silver teapot right in front of William. The waiter bowed and was just turning to leave when the restaurant owner grabbed him by the elbow.

"My friend," the man said to William, all the while pulling the young waiter back to the table, "let me to introduce this boy—my son Waseem—the most great cook from the Mediterranean." He leaned forward and pretended to whisper with uncovered excitement, "Or even the world!" The boy smiled as he stood proudly at his father's side.

"My pleasure," William said with a smile, while his stomach grumbled. He appreciated these people's hospitality, but also felt a little wary and vulnerable.

"I am blessed to have my son with many talents in the arts of food, what I enjoy most," the owner said, chuckling heartily and landing a pat on his son's back.

William chuckled a little as well, memories of his own father surfacing. He shook his head as if to shoo them away. That was a time in the past he didn't want to revisit. Instead, he turned to analyzing his host and much as he wanted to think that the man was only after his money—any foreigner's money—William actually found he didn't believe this to be so. The man, and his son, appeared genuine and their hospitality—sincere, and William decided he could be more open and appreciative.

The owner spoke to his son in Arabic, a language that sounded strangely interesting to William. At once, the boy rushed toward the kitchen, leaving the two men alone, and William decided this was a good time to introduce himself.

"My name is..." he started.

"Ah, talking can wait, my friend, but not tea," the man interrupted before taking one of the cups and lifting the teapot. Golden brown tea swirled inside as first he filled William's cup and then his own. The only sound in the restaurant came from the fizzing bubbles popping in the tea. The ritual was ready to begin.

The restaurant owner picked up his cup and took a long sip. William watched the man, hesitant to do the same, until he realized there was no plot to poison him—only hospitality at the hands of strangers. He looked down at his cup then brought it to his mouth. At first, he took a small sip, then gulped down the full cup, his whole body welcoming the drink. The owner followed his guest's movements with expectation, and finally, delight, as William's sigh of appreciation confirmed the quality of the tea. The tea, which tasted strongly of sweet mint, was different from anything William had ever tasted in England.

A good kind of different.

"It's delicious," William said as he lowered the cup.

The man nodded. "Thank you. Now, we can talk," he said, wiping his hands on his apron. "My name is Gabriel. This is my shop" He proceeded to stretch his hand over the table to William who shook it briefly, introduced himself, and leaned back in his seat.

"So, my friend, what brings you my country? Business or pleasure?" Gabriel asked as he grabbed the teapot and refilled the cups.

"Business," William replied.

"Ah, you have made an excellent choice to do business here. To see Morocco is to see the world," Gabriel stated and drank his tea, then set the empty cup back on the table. Suddenly, a thought brightened Gabriel's eyes. He lifted his index finger in a universal sign, rose from his seat and rushed toward the door in the back, disappearing from William's watchful gaze.

The Englishman stared at the door for a moment, then turned to explore the restaurant. The place was clean with bright tapestries covering the white stone walls. It wasn't good enough to host a duke, but it was cozy and William liked it. He picked up his second cup of tea and waited for Gabriel to return.

Soon enough, the door opened and in came Gabriel, carrying a delicately carved wooden box in his hands, along with the scent of sizzling lamb. A smile brightened his eyes as he neared the table.

"Now, you are an Englishman, no?" Gabriel said as he slowly took his seat.

"I am," William replied, wondering what his host had in store now.

"And, are you a man who appreciates tobacco?" Gabriel inquired, placing the rectangular box on the table in front of him.

William had taken to smoking cigars, but he only did it sparingly. "Occasionally, yes," he nodded.

"Then, I will be happy to show my collection of tobacco. Some is gift, some I traded with the foreigners who came in my restaurant," Gabriel said, glancing up at William then back at the box as he opened the lid. William leaned closer and the smell of tobacco filled his lungs. The Arab turned the box around, showing its contents like a proud owner. Inside were seven little troughs, six of which contained a different type of tobacco. The seventh was empty.

"Here," Gabriel said pointing at the far right compartment, "is tobacco I bought from a Turkish soldier many years ago. I am saving it for a special occasion. Maybe when Waseem gets married."

He moved his finger down the compartments, explaining how each type of tobacco was grown and how he'd acquired them. William was impressed by Gabriel's collection, but was mostly unsure of why he was doing this. His stomach rumbled, reminding him that food was yet to come. The Arab was explaining the origin of the sixth type of tobacco, when his son came in, carrying two plates piled with freshly cooked food.

Falafel, pita bread, hummus, and a small cut of lamb made for a glorious sight. As the boy set down the plates, a fork speared into the meat, Gabriel quickly closed the box of tobacco and moved it aside to make room. William was eager to fill his belly with hot lamb but decided it wouldn't be polite to jump on the meal before his host. When Gabriel's son left, the two men ate in silence, enjoying the young cook's obvious talent with every bite of the meal.

William preferred to eat slowly, so he was only halfway finished when Gabriel pushed an empty plate aside and brought the tobacco box back to the center of the table. "Mr. William, I think you a smart man, and you probably recognized my one weakness: I like things to be... complete." Gabriel made this confession with a tense expression, his fingertips resting on the top of the tobacco box.

That explained everything in William's mind—the tea, the food, and the hospitality.

"And you would like for me to sell you some English tobacco?"

"Exactly—buying tobacco from an Englishman would be an honor, no matter its origin," Gabriel stated, his tension dissolving into a smile.

"I'll tell you what," William said, setting down his fork. "I'll trade you a cigar for this meal."

Gabriel's expression turned thoughtful. "That sounds fair to me," he concluded after a moment, happy to see his hospitality paying off. William reached into the pocket of his coat and took out a small rectangular box that had been a gift from his father from before the war. It had gone unopened, waiting for an occasion cheery enough to require a cigar. The cigar had become a good luck charm William always carried with him. He didn't mind parting with it now—it would find a better home with Gabriel anyway. The Arab's eyes studied the box from left to right.

"Take it," William nodded. "It's yours." Gabriel's eyes darted up to William's face then returned to the cigar's case.

Slowly, he took the box and opened it. Inside was a small brown cigar, a red print on the band marking it as a "Montecristo." William smiled, happy to complete Gabriel's collection and get a delicious meal at the same time, all without a dirham leaving his suitcase.

"What a trade," Gabriel exclaimed as he carefully removed the cigar from its box and stared at it with unwavering fascination.

To William, there were more important things to think about—like where he would spend the night, and the possible contents of that envelope. Would he have time to photograph this beautiful Moroccan city, or would Reginald demand him to move along right away? He was dreaming of roaming the city and revisiting the shops when Gabriel spoke to him.

"So, my friend, how long are you here in Nador?" He placed the cigar with delicate care into his own tobacco collection.

"I don't know yet," William said frankly. He hadn't read the letter.

"Long enough to see the festival?" Gabriel asked as he closed the box.

William frowned. A festival sounded like a good opportunity to take pictures before he had to leave for Yemen. "What is this festival?" William asked as he cut a piece of lamb.

"It's the celebration of Amadi Hamed," Gabriel said, probably hoping the name would mean something to his guest. William shook his head as he chewed on a piece of meat, and Gabriel shifted eagerly in his seat. "The festival is only held in Nador. Here Amadi Hamed is considered to be a..." Gabriel paused, searching for the right word. "A very good man."

"A saint?" William supplied.

"Yes, that is it. A saint," Gabriel agreed. "He was the son of sea merchant who lived before many years. He was very poor but traveled to nearly every city in the Mediterranean." Gabriel frowned, then scratched his head. "Umm... I don't remember the story well, but Amadi Hamed became the ruler of this city turning Nador from a small fishing village one great city in the Mediterranean. He brought wealth to the people," Gabriel continued, his insufficient English making him talk slowly and carefully. "To show our gratitude to King Hamed, we take a day off work and have a celebration with dancers and music. Very beautiful, you must see it."

"When is it?" William asked, hoping the instructions in the letter would give him enough time to document the festival.

"Tomorrow. It will be magnificent," Gabriel said, bringing his hands to his sides to show exactly how magnificent. Then he reached into his pocket and pulled out a small silver watch.

"It's seven-thirty and I am afraid it is time to close my shop. It was good meeting you, Mr. William, and I hope to see you again at the celebration tomorrow." With that, Gabriel rose from his seat, bowed, and walked off to the kitchen.

With Gabriel gone, the restaurant became silent. William looked out the window, noticing that darkness had arrived. He stood, picked up his suitcase and coat, and walked outside. The street was dark, the light from the restaurant the only source of brightness in sight. Looking to his right and left, William wondered which direction would take him to a place where he could spend the night. He wished he had asked Gabriel, but it was too late now. From his left he could hear the sounds of people dining and enjoying themselves by the docks. And there, past the distant lights, he could see the sea, dark and eternal. William sighed and turned in that direction, hoping to find a decent hotel where he could take a much-needed rest. In the morning, when his mind was clear, he would open the letter.

# 3

A CLANKY COW BELL BROKE the morning silence. William slowly opened his eyes and looked at the tall yellow grass as it swayed, giving him glimpses of the mountain that surrounded him. He gradually pushed his stiff body upright and saw a herd of cows chewing on the grass at various locations around him, without paying him much attention. He frowned, scratching behind his ear as memories of the night before flooded in—he'd visited all the hotels near the docs, but none had had vacancies. Then, he remembered wandering onto the hillside in the middle of the night, tired and frustrated.

Now the sun had risen, but the early morning chill still loomed like the salty smell of the sea. From this side of the mountain, he could see the whole city, poured down in front of him all the way to the shore. Beyond the maze of buildings, the minuscule masts of fishing boats mixed together in the calm waters, while the city was already radiating liveliness that could mean only one thing—the celebration had begun.

William picked up his coat and suitcase and started walking down the slope toward the city, listening to the ever-growing noise of the festival.

Today was going to be a very busy day. Upon reaching the city, William took a turn down a wide street where he noticed a group of children playing with an orange kitten that was rubbing its sides on their short legs, purring with squinted eyes. Laughter echoed all around him, unrestrained and pure.

With a smile on his lips, William walked past the children, realizing the streets were even more crowded than the day before. The closer he got to the docks, the more dancers and musicians he saw, all of them performing in the street, entertaining the sea of people. Behind the crowd, the watery abyss looked a greenish blue that faded over the horizon. William liked that color, but there was nothing more spectacular than the sea's unconquerable vastness, something he never got to enjoy back in London.

The musicians were competing now, each performing complex tunes for the joyful crowd, and the dancers followed them, stepping lightly and swaying like delicate shoots in the wind. The tambourine dancer, like the day before, was dancing to lure, though her rattling tambourine couldn't compete with the strange symphony of the street performers who used various types of flutes, drums, and stringed instruments.

William's gaze darted from a veiled woman, who was spitting balls of fire in great, warm gusts of flame, to an old man with a spotted snake draped across his shoulders like a shawl. In the gutters, games of wit and sleight of hand took place and, with a little luck, a few dirhams or a pocket watch were won in the process.

Past the dancers, a little boy was the lone entertainer, juggling swords above his head while balancing on a chair that was tilted so only one leg touched the ground. This performance marked the outer edge of the festival and beyond it, the street was mostly empty. William thought the dancers were beautiful and lively, but the boy on the chair would make the perfect picture. Still, he only had a little length of film and didn't want to waste it for just any shot. For all he knew, a grander opportunity might await behind the corner.

He knew he was getting close to the shore when the pungent smell of gutted fish and drying seaweed filled the air. For the first time, he welcomed it. The festivities, along with the restless night he'd spent on the mountain, made his head pound, and now he only wanted to find a place where he could read Reginald's letter in peace. Then he would look for a room and plan the next days of this adventure.

With these thoughts in mind, William spotted an open restaurant in a building that overlooked the shore, and stepped inside. The white-washed, stone walls were decorated with the much-desired rugs that were popular in the homes of the London upper class. On the tables, silver utensils and China plates awaited hungry customers. The room was square, with large open windows that revealed the inside of the restaurant from the street.

Most tables, William noted, were occupied by the same crowd he'd traveled with on the SS Dorset, all of them eating and talking cheerfully among themselves—perhaps discussing the food, or the festival. This restaurant, like many others, was owned by some Arab who wanted to make a quick fortune off the pockets of the foreigners. But there was another faction of Moroccans who resented selling their culture to the Europeans. To them, this equated treachery to their history and lineage.

William walked to a corner in the room where the restaurant was the quietest and the shadows obscured him from the noisy street. He set his suitcase and coat close to the wall and sat down, content that no one had noticed him. He reached down, took the letter from his coat pocket, and briefly looked at the front of the envelope before tearing it open. A single piece of paper was folded neatly inside, scribbly handwriting covering it on both sides in a dozen uneven lines. Reginald had probably written it the same day William left England—he wouldn't be surprised. The scratchy blue ink read:

*Dear William,*

*You will receive this letter on the day you arrive in Nador.*
*You are to start taking photographs as soon as possible.*
*You are to stay in Nador for two days, during which time*
*you will take pictures of the city and its people and find a*
*caravan to take you across the Sahara. When you reach*
*Yemen, find a city capable of harboring a steamboat back*
*to England and board it. Document your journey by taking*
*pictures of the caravan and the desert as you travel, taking*
*at least one a day. And most importantly, William, don't*
*get yourself killed. I want my photographs and you want*
*your money. I have faith in your ability to deliver, even*
*though you are a bit green.*

The note wasn't signed, but the wording spoke for itself—there was no doubt it was crafted by Reginald's cognac-shaken hand. William looked up from the paper imagining the director saying to him, "even though you are a bit green," his silhouette contrasting against the white light coming from the window behind him.

That image gave William an odd feeling, but he couldn't decipher its meaning because an outburst of laughter shattered his concentration. He eyed the source of disruption, a crowded table across the restaurant, then placed the ripped envelope and the letter inside his coat and stood up. Uncertain of his destination, William thought it would be best to ask for direction this time, so he doesn't end up on the same hill as the previous night. Taking his belongings, he walked to the back of the restaurant where a bartender in a black suit kept a busy counter. Behind the bartender a tall mirror reflected the restaurant's crammed interior, and happily chatting customers.

"Excuse me, can you tell me where I might find a hotel?" William asked the bartender, a well-built, dark-skinned man who, at that moment, was mixing a martini.

"Yes, I know just the right place," the bartender replied with a grin and started walking along the counter toward the open doorway.

William followed the man until they were at the door, but when he looked outside, he was surprised to find the street had gotten more crowded than before. The bartender leaned close to William and pointed down a side street that led away from the noise and celebration.

"Go down that street and you will find what you are seeking," he said nodding to William then walked back inside the restaurant.

Now that he had a direction to follow, William hurried through the crowd, maneuvering around the camels, the streams of people, and the numerous performers. When he emerged on the other side, he started down an empty lane where the air was calmer and colder. After a slow bend to the right, the voices and music gradually faded away. William didn't remember coming to this part of Nador the night before, though he'd been certain he'd checked all possible hotels.

The few locals he passed looked malnourished: skinny bodies with bony faces. The robes that hung over their skeletal figures were stained and filthy, exposing bare feet and dry skin. The street bore a grim air that was disproportionally magnified by the magnificent celebrations happening just on the other side of the buildings.

No colorful awnings adorned the walls here; every building's facade had chipped paint and many were covered in mud. On one side of the street, an elderly woman sat on a stone threshold, the head covering of her dark blue robe hanging just over her gray eyes. Her arms were folded on her knees in silent observation. They were a mother's arms, strong and wrinkled from holding an infant, feeding a child, and hugging a man goodbye.

William noticed her staring at him, and in those eyes he saw grief so deep, he had no heart to ignore it. The closer he walked, the stronger his compassion pounded inside his chest. When he thought of his own mother he stopped and set down his suitcase. He took the torn envelope and the letter out of his coat and stashed them in the right pocket of his trousers—the woman following his every move with silent curiosity. Then he slowly walked toward her. When he was but a few feet away, William placed his hands around the collar of his coat and reaching the doorstep, he leaned close to the woman and whisked the coat over her shoulders before stepping away. A smile appeared on her beautiful wrinkled face as she pulled the collar tight around her shoulders.

A moment later, as William was lifting his suitcase off the dusty street, he took a last look at the woman and saw in her eyes that she was smiling with gratitude. He smiled back and continued walking down the street, unsure whether he wanted to explore the feeling that compelled him to give up his coat. Why had this woman reminded him of his mother? Was it because he felt regret for leaving his mother to go to war? Or did he simply have a compassionate soul? Whatever the case, William didn't want to start prodding for emotional cavities.

The past was the past. Now, almost a decade later, he was in a foreign country, searching for a hotel on a beat dirt street that screamed of poverty and abandonment.

He'd left the old woman behind a while ago and was now wondering whether he'd somehow gotten lost. He hadn't taken any turns, but the street wasn't exactly straight either, and the buildings looked all the same— white washed stones and no paint. He reached a crossroads some time later and noticed a taller building to his left standing higher than the other ghostly structures.

The sun caught on its front, the shiny red-painted facade radiating a globe of pure light. It was the first colorful building William saw since he'd left the main street. He stared at it, marveling at the simple, yet beautiful structure, wondering if this had once been the rich part of the city where merchants and government officials had lived before the desire for European money had changed history.

William was not a superstitious man, but he trusted his instincts and they were leading him toward the red building. He walked closer and upon reaching the entrance, looked around, noticing the hinges that had once held massive doors, now missing. A hallway stretched beyond, a single source of light inside.

A wooden sign was still visible above the entrance, the writing in Arabic, no translations. What had appeared as a shiny red facade from afar, from up close was chipped paint that revealed a pearl white plaster underneath.

Despite the windswept appearance, William decided to check out the place and see if he could find a room to stay the night. He stepped through the arched entrance, his heart pounding in the dimness beyond. The lobby, a vast circular room with a dusty floor that might've been made of marble, reminded William of the post office he'd visited the day before—lifeless, weathered, and left to its own devices. To his right, a staircase led to the upper floors, and to his left, a man, probably in his early fifties, sat behind a tall desk. For a moment they stared at each other, then William stepped forward and cleared his throat.

"Excuse me. Is this a hotel?" he inquired, motioning with arms to encompass the building.

"Yes. Want room?" the man asked. His English was poor, but William sighed in relief. At least the man knew some words even if his grammar wasn't that good.

"Yes, please," William nodded, happy that his intuition had been right. "Do you have any available rooms?" he asked, hoping this time he wouldn't be rejected.

"All room," the old man replied calmly.

"All of them... are taken?" William asked hesitantly, unable to read the man's expression in the semi-darkness.

"No, all room empty. Want room or not?" the man demanded, scrunching his brows.

"Yes, yes I do. But... Can I have a look first?"

The man mumbled something in Arabic, then waived a hand and said, "Follow me." He rattled a thick metal ring of keys from the desk and headed for the stairs. William walked behind him toward the end of hall and up several flights of stairs, wondering if he could stay in this place for the next two nights before he had to leave for Yemen. At that thought, he also remembered he had yet to find a caravan to get him across the desert.

"Do you know of any caravans going to Yemen?" William asked the old man after they had climbed two flights of stairs in silence.

"Yes. One coming after today and leaving to Yemen day after," the old man replied as they arrived at the top of the third flight. He took a step further but suddenly stopped and looked down at William who was a couple steps below. "Why want to know this?" the man asked, frowning.

"I am traveling to Yemen for business," William answered, unsure what could be the matter. He was certain lots of people took caravans to Yemen; it wasn't an exotic destination anymore.

"*You* want cross the Sahara?" the old man smirked, eyeing William head to toe.

"Yes, I do," William said, but the words tasted weird coming out of his mouth.

"Ha!" the man exclaimed as he turned around and continued up the stairs, leaving William standing at the bottom, confused and slightly insulted.

William watched the man shake his head and chuckle, expecting some kind of explanation. "What do you find so amusing?" he asked and hurried up the stairs to catch up.

"You," a lofty voice echoed from above, followed by even more dry chuckles.

"What about me?"

"You are English, no?" the man asked as he continued climbing yet another flight of stairs.

"What does that have to do with anything?" William asked, finally catching up.

"You see the desert before?"

"No, I haven't, but..." William started to say.

"That explain everything," the old man stated, grunting as he took the final step and turned to face William who had stopped three-quarters of the way. "You not know the desert, English. The sun burn your skin and steal your strength. Sandstorm scrape your skin. Night is cold and scorpion and snake creep in your bed. You get lost with no water or food, you die. Every day, you see the sun rise, but you not know you live to see it set."

William didn't know if the man's words were true, but he hoped they weren't. He had read about the desert, short, random accounts of people who'd come to Morocco. But he had read nothing about crossing the Sahara. Was it really so dangerous?

"Ah, we arrive," the man said as he led William along the hall at the top of the stairs to a door near a window overlooking the street.

He was placing the key in the oval-shaped hole when William asked, "Have you lived in the desert?"

"Yes, I was young," the man replied, turning the key inside the lock three times. Before he opened the door, the man turned to William with a deep frown above his piercing eyes. "You are ordinary man; we are. Flesh and blood. Nothing more. Ordinary men not like the desert. It burn every man, and none leave the same. If I was you," he motioned from William to himself, "I stay far away from the desert." Then the warning disappeared from the man's eyes, "But you choose to die in the desert, I not stop you."

"Where would be the fun in that?" William mumbled more to himself than as a response.

"Do as you wish," the man said then pushed on the handle. The lock made a loud snap and opened. "Room is thirty dirhams for night," the man said, knowing the price was way too high for this part of Nador.

The room was no larger than a prison cell, and even though William had considered his London apartment plain and simple, this was another level of plainness altogether. Nothing adorned the walls, not even a picture frame, and the only furniture consisted of a spring bed with short legs and a yellowish looking mattress. The only source of light was a square window that was about shoulder width through which he could see a sliver of the sea. There was an overall, claustrophobic tightness that made it hard to breathe.

"Do you have anything larger?" William asked.

"No. All same. Please, look for yourself," the old man prompted, stepping aside from the door to let William enter. William thought he caught a string of nervousness in the man's voice and went in cautiously. In one corner, he spotted a crack that wriggled its way up several inches from the floor. He stared at it for several moments, wondering whether going back to the nicer district would bring him better luck than the night before. *What if there's a fire and the door is stuck? You will have nowhere to run; you will be trapped. Burnt alive.*

For a moment, William thought the walls were closing in around him. He glanced from one corner of the ceiling to the other, telling himself that he was going to sleep in this room whether he felt afraid or not. He wasn't spending another night out on the cold mountain, and he wasn't going to sleep where his countrymen found shelter. This was it.

"Well?" the man asked as he leaned into the doorway, his face fluctuating between a smile and a twitchy frown. William stood with his back to the door and stared at the crack in the wall as he thought about his answer. He could sense his host was growing anxious but couldn't tell what it was hinting at.

"I'll take it," he said at last, putting his suitcase on the bed.

"Good choice. How long you stay?" the man asked.

"Just two nights," William replied, sitting down to test the bed.

"Good. You pay now and I get the key." With arms crossed before his chest, the man seemed adamant.

"All right, give me a moment." William turned his attention to his suitcase where he'd safely packed his travel money. He took the envelope and counted out sixty dirhams then passed them onto his host. The man looked at William with a mixture of surprise and suspicion, then took the money and handed over the rusty key. A moment later, he was already on his way down the stairs, happy to have landed a customer for two nights.

William closed the door and walked back to the bed from where he could see the street below. A lone, scrawny dog sniffing the gutter was the only sign of life. The small room, now brightened by the rays of the early afternoon sun, seemed slightly more tolerable to William, especially since he had an unobstructed view of the sea. The music of the festival came from several streets over, a little muffled and mixed with the chattering of the crowds.

William thought it would be a good idea to take some photographs while the celebration lasted. He took two hundred dirhams and placed it safely inside his pocket. With his camera over his shoulder, William went off to take the perfect picture—and to buy a meal. After all, being a photographer was hungry business.

# 4

WILLIAM WALKED DOWN A STREET in search of a shop selling paper and ink so he could take notes of his experiences when he travelled across the Sahara, a habit he'd picked up during his time in France. It was a way to help him make sense of things that didn't make much sense.

The streets looked completely different from the day before when he had had the chance to take three photographs of performers and musicians. Ahead of him, the people were going about their day with the same numbness that fills the mind when an activity is repeated day after day, leaving you unaware of the beauty of being alive. Some led sheep and goats to the butcher's shop; others carried bags of barley over their shoulders on their way to the market.

William had been walking for nearly two hours now and in that time had learned only one thing: not a single shop in the whole of Nador sold writing supplies. As the thought began to dawn on him, he noticed a small, secluded square to his right, enclosed on three sides by tall buildings, and stopped to consider whether it was worth exploring. The crowd continued walking past him, blissfully unaware of the little square that escaped the excitement. William made his way out of the street and into the entrance of the square, welcoming a moment of silence after the day's fruitless search.

A small dog hurried past his legs and out of the square in search of a curious scent. When it was gone, a peaceful silence filled the air, nearly making William forget about the items he'd come to look for. In the center of the square was a stone fountain with a tall pillar rising from its calm pool of water. William walked closer to get a better look, because this was the first fountain he saw in Morocco. Carved out of the stone were four heads of bearded men, each spitting a stream of water that splashed in the blue and white tiled pool below. William took a seat on the edge of the fountain and combed his fingers back and forth on the water's surface, wondering if this little square classified as picture material with its fountain, chipped-paint buildings all around, and the laundry-lines stretched above. As he came to think of it, he wasn't even sure what counted as picture material for Reginald. What he knew was that he wanted to get paid, which meant, he'd have to do as good a job as he could. Feeling slightly discouraged, William lowered his head and watched his fingers sweeping the cold surface of the water, leaving small wrinkles behind them.

He thought of the old man at the hotel who'd warned him about journeying through the desert. The man had shared he'd lived in the desert in his youth, but whatever hardships he may have faced seemed irrelevant. Those warning words had only made William daydream about the desert ever since that conversation. The sound of the trickling water urged William to close his eyes, and he obeyed. *What if the heat proves too much and I die? What if I become sick? What if I get lost?* Thoughts like these swirled in his mind, much like the water did around his fingers, chilling but harmless. His mind calmed when it focused on the silence. The splashing of the water. The murmuring voices that came from the street. The silence was sweet to the taste buds of his mind.

From the top of the mountain overlooking Nador, a horn sounded, its faint echo interrupting the silence like a loud whisper. William opened his eyes, unaware of the time he'd blissfully spent in the quiet square, and turned around to look at the street and the flow of people sweeping past on their way toward the mountain. The joyful murmur on the street grew louder with each resonant blast of the horn, arousing William's curiosity.

He rose from the edge of the fountain and joined the crowd which quickly swept him away. Looking around, William realized that every man, woman, and child, foreign and Moroccan, was heading toward the mountaintop at an eager pace. He wondered if there was a continuation of the festival which the friendly restaurant owner, Gabriel, hadn't told him about, but he doubted it. Unlike the day before, there were no street performers and dancers anywhere in sight. William felt a bump against his side and turned to see a short Arab walking next to him, eyes carefully set on the mountain top.

"What's happening? Why is everybody running?" William asked. The man spoke briskly in Arabic while pointing to the mountain with a look of excitement in his eyes. Then, without another word, he stepped away from William and disappeared. William hadn't understood anything, but he'd picked up on the man's excitement and that made him even more curious to find out. As he neared the edge of the city, William saw that the top of the mountain was lined with a forest of people standing shoulder to shoulder with their backs to the sea, their murmuring voices turning into a deafening roar.

Slowly, he jostled his way to the front of the crowd wondering what he would find there. In front of him was a hilly stretch of open land, barren but for a few boulders scattered amongst the hills. Rising from behind one hill was a pillar of dust that spiraled into the air. William looked to his right along the row of people and was surprised to see Gabriel standing near the remnants of a tree that had long since been uprooted by a strong wind. He hurried to his Arab friend in hopes of finding out what was going on.

"What is happening, Gabriel? Why the rush to get here?" he panted out, his lungs expanding as if he'd sprinted up the mountain.

Gabriel looked at William and recognition lightened his sweaty face. He patted William on the back then pointed at the hills.

"My friend, a caravan is coming from the east. We've been waiting for it several months," Gabriel said as he leaned closer to William, his voice full of barely contained excitement. That was all William needed to know. He faced the hill where the pillar of dust rose. Would he be welcomed in the same way when he reached Yemen? For a fleeting moment he imagined himself riding into the city on a camel's back, face darkened by the sun, the tested look of desert eyes on his face. It almost made him smile.

William was shocked back to reality when the crowd around him burst into a sudden uproar. A speck of black appeared over the edge of the hill halfway to the horizon and slowly grew longer as it crawled toward the mountain. A sudden, high-pitched wavering yell sounded as though it came from an instrument than from a human voice almost punctured William's eardrums. To his right, a handful of European men mimicked him, covering their ears. He traced the sound of the yell to a group of black-robed women standing near the highest point on the mountain. Several more women joined in the keen yell that had a strange, harmonious ring to it.

"What are they doing?" William asked Gabriel, his eyes on the women. The Arab looked at William and followed the direction of his gaze.

"They rejoice the arriving of the caravan," Gabriel said. A frown appeared on his face as he turned back to William. "Women do not do this in your country?" he asked slightly bewildered.

"No, it's not customary," William said with a bit of a smirk, imagining the average English woman deafening nearly half the audience at a horse race before being rushed into a stray jacket.

"I see," Gabriel said in voice that seemed to say he did not see at all. When he turned back to the hills, William did the same. The small black speck had turned into a long trail of people, animals, and wagons that continued to make their way toward Nador.

Slowly, and to most of the Europeans' relief, the wavering yell of celebrating women began to soften until only the voice of the crowd remained. As the excitement dwindled, part of the crowd turned back toward the city, while the other part, comprised of locals, walked down the mountain to greet the caravan.

As the caravan drew nearer, William began to distinguish the individual people and animals. He even spotted a few people on one side of the caravan walking alongside a camel that carried large baskets and bags. He couldn't be sure of the contents, but he'd read somewhere that many caravans carried goods to trade for supplies while crossing the desert. Looking from above, it seemed as if a crack in the ground was spilling forth hundreds of people and animals, if not thousands, their only goal to reach the mountain at Nador.

In an hour's time the whole caravan had gathered at the base of the mountain. Many people of the city went to welcome them and to see their fares, though the large crowds had already gone back to their businesses and homes, including Gabriel who had slipped away unnoticed. But William's attention was on the newcomers—Arabs unlike the ones who lived in Morocco. The people were dark and looked worn, their robes faded and covered with a whitish dust that resembled flour. Now that they'd arrived at their destination, the caravan made good time erecting dome-shaped tents that speckled the base of the mountain in a collage of color.

William couldn't take his eyes away from them, but he didn't have to. On the contrary, he observed them carefully, taking mental notes that he hoped he could one day write on paper and send to Reginald. He didn't usually make a habit of carrying his camera around, but today he had it on him—just in case.

And the case was spectacular. But he was not in the right position.

Looking around, William realized the best shot could only be taken from the highest point of the mountain as that would give him a view of the entire camp while the sun would be in the exact position he needed it—behind his back. To get there, however, he had to climb up a narrow ridge that was steep on either side. One wrong step and he, along with hundreds of boulders, could end up tumbling down the mountain.

Taking his time, William reached the peak of the mountain after no less than half hour, but the hiking was worth it. Now he had a full view of the hills that stretched up to the horizon and the busy caravan camp right below him. He positioned himself beside a large boulder that looked down on the camp, took his camera out of its case, and positioned it on a flat rock. Kneeling behind the camera, William looked into the clear lens that blocked out everything but the camp. He carefully adjusted the frame so the caravan sat neatly inside of it, and waited until the moment was just right. When he took the first picture, the camera winked at him.

William snapped a couple more shots, looking at the caravan through his magnified camera lens like a spy that needed to collect important information. All the while, he felt the desert pulling him in, calling his name, shouting over the boisterous distractions of life, and making it impossible to be ignored. He didn't know whether to succumb to this call or run back to England and face a country that was no less ruthless than the desert. At least here he had a chance of adventure.

Sitting back, he took the lens away from his sweaty face and looked down at the fully developed camp. He was getting thirsty, and the heat of the sun was making the experience more potent by the minute. William took his handkerchief out of his chest pocket and patted away the sweat and some of the dust that had gathered on his forehead.

The hotel keeper's words came back to him. *Would I last on this trip? What if I perish in the desert like the hundreds of other people who've tried to cross it and failed?* If he was going to accomplish his assignment William knew he would have to endure the same difficulties as the people who lived in the desert. He looked at his now dirtier handkerchief—a useless thing on a journey such as this—and left it on the flat rock, a sign of initiation into a new world that he didn't belong to but was eager to meet.

Walking down the same narrow ridge he'd climbed up earlier, William decided it was time to meet the caravan's leader and pay the price needed to join them. Having made that decision, he felt a freeing sensation grow in his chest, and a smile bloomed on his lips.

The camp looked like an invading army, its tents covering a ground William could not begin to estimate. When he reached the outer edge, a tall bearded man walked past him.

"Excuse me, where can I find your leader?" William asked, hoping the man spoke his language. The Arab examined William slowly, then nodded toward the center of camp before continuing on his way. Unsure of this vague communication, William had no option but to follow the man's directions and see whether he would end up where he needed to go. On every side, colorful tents surrounded him—from black, red, and green to intricate patterns woven with several different colors—and curious Arab and Africans faces met his own intrigued gaze. Perhaps they had never seen a European, let alone one walking through their camp.

William was beginning to near the center of the camp when he noticed a tent that stood taller and wider than the others. It was made of blue and white sheets of thick cloth held down by ropes and pegs. Two guards dressed in blue robes stood underneath an awning that extended from the entrance, each with a rifle slung over his shoulder and a sword on his hip. William was pretty certain this was the leader's tent and needed no further direction. He walked forward with a strange, lingering pace, unsure how to approach the guards and gain their favor. Armed with the camera on his hip, he cautiously neared the awning and stood before the guards, who moved their hands on the hilts of their swords.

They said something in Arabic, but seeing William's perplexed expression, turned to horridly accented English. "Why are you here?" demanded the guard on the right.

"I am here to join your caravan," he responded frankly. The two men frowned at each other and traded several quiet words in Arabic, glancing at William as they conversed.

The guard who'd spoken to William turned back to him and ordered, "Stay." He then proceeded to walk into the tent, giving William a glimpse of the dark, shadowy interior, the only item worth noticing being a colorful rug stretched out on the floor. The guard who remained outside looked at

William with a mixture of distaste and curiosity, perhaps wondering why a foreigner like him would want to travel with the caravan in the first place.

A moment later, the first guard ambled out, an unreadable expression on his dark face. "You cannot join caravan," he said as he walked closer to William, stopping but a foot away.

"Why not? I need to travel through the desert to Yemen," William began explaining, hoping the men would understand and allow him to join them. Besides, he didn't want to wait until another caravan came to Nador, especially as that seemed to happen once in a very long while.

"This caravan is full. We have no room for more people," the guard said, smirking at William's misfortune.

"No room? But I don't take up much space—it's just me," William motioned to himself, hoping that would change the matters. Then a sudden thought formed in his mind. "I really must take this caravan to Yemen. I'll pay any amount necessary," he said and reached into his pocket wondering how much the journey could cost.

"You try to bribe?" the guard roared, wild fires lightening his eyes as he stepped closer, his companion close behind.

"I am not trying to bribe you, please. I was trying to say that I..." William's voice was interrupted when the guard's rifle rattled against the left side of his head. He landed on his side, his hands shaking near his ears. His whole head felt like it had been split open with a chisel. One of his hands touched the wound and pain seared the side of his skull. When his trembling fingers moved in front of his eyes, he saw they were covered in blood.

A pair of strong hands grabbed him by the shoulders and jolted him to his feet. "Go now and don't come back," the guard growled in his face before shoving William onto the ground outside the awning. He rolled several times and landed flat on his stomach, where he lay for a few moments, feeling the paralyzing pain in his head. The guard who'd struck him kneeled and picked up the money that fell out of William's hand, tucking it in his robe as he rose. Then the two men resumed their posts, leaving William to writhe in pain in the dust.

William felt two kinds of ache pulsing in his head, one from being struck by the stock of a rifle and the other being the strongest feeling of mistreatment he'd ever experienced.

He didn't want to push himself up—lying there in the dirt felt like what he deserved for being foolish enough to come to Nador—but he couldn't lie there forever. Slowly, he struggled to his elbows and knees, then staggered to his feet, feeling a trail of blood trickling down the left side of his head. William dared a look at the man who'd struck him but quickly turned away like a dog that's been kicked repeatedly. The guards could—and probably would—kill him if he tried to get his money back, and no one would think to question them. This was Africa, not England—what had he been thinking?

He had no choice but to leave, without his money or his dignity.

William stumbled away from the tent, keeping his eyes to the ground and hoping his camera was still intact in its case. He hadn't fallen on it, thank God, or it would have been smashed to pieces. All the while, he only dared look up to see where he was going, catching a perplexed glimpse from a person who noticed the gash on the side of his head.

By the time he walked out of the camp, the wound had stopped bleeding and he had regained enough of his strength to attempt the walk back to Nador. As he hiked up the mountain, he gently examined the side of his head and decided it wasn't as bad as it felt. He even briefly considered reporting the guards to the police, imagining himself and several of the local officers marching back to the caravan to arrest the man who had struck him. And to get his money back.

For a moment the idea felt liberating, but reality hardly worked out that way. In fact, now that he thought of it, chances were much higher that he might end up under arrest himself because he was the foreigner here. Who would believe him? He couldn't speak a word in Arabic, had no money to hire an interpreter, and would most probably be left to rot somewhere, never to be found again. No, going to the police wouldn't solve the matter. Besides, right now he had a bigger problem.

The caravan wasn't going to take him with them. And he'd botched his chances further being so insistent with those guards. What was he going to do now? He certainly didn't feel the same determination to explore the sands of the Sahara. What had he been thinking, really? Feeling the call of the desert—what nonsense.

On his way down the slope of the mountain his gaze found the sea with its glistening, deep waters. That peaceful picture and the dark silhouettes of the buildings below brought him a little comfort, and he kept his eyes on the sea until he descended into the cold streets of the city. For the most part, he went unnoticed by the women and children he occasionally passed—perhaps they thought he was a drunk—but the loud music and thundering voices ahead were a sure promise that he'd soon be entering the livelier streets. He wanted to avoid the main streets where the excitement blossomed, but he was sure he would get lost looking for his grimy old hotel, and the side streets weren't safe.

Keeping to the shadier side of the street, William walked as fast as he could through the crowds, until he found the side street he was looking for and ducked in. When he reached his hotel, he expected to be greeted by the old man and had even prepared an explanation for the gash on his head, but the man wasn't there. Hollow silence filled the hotel, a sure sign that the place had died along with its once opulent history. The only thing he wanted now was a night of deep sleep, to awake up to a new day when he could start again, and properly sort things out. After standing in the entrance for a moment, William calmly walked up the four flights of stairs, his footsteps echoing in the stairwell. He couldn't help but wonder why the hotel keeper wasn't at his post, but perhaps he'd had business to attend to.

William's feet dragged as he walked along the hallway to his room, today's events replaying in his mind like a silent film. If all had been a film though, perhaps he would've laughed at his own foolishness and naivete. He did not feel like laughing now. His head was heavy, but he managed to lift it up, then stopped dead in his tracks. The door to his room was wide open, even though he'd closed and locked it before leaving that morning. With a cautious step, he neared the open door, the ancient floorboards croaking threateningly under his feet. A moment later, William stood in the doorway, absolutely still, his face too tired to express his horror.

The room was covered in the orange light of the setting sun, a picture that would have been beautiful to behold. Except his suitcase lay on his bed wide open, and his clothes, once neatly packed, covered the bed and floor in heaps. He rushed into the room, as if the building was about to collapse, and stopped mid-stride, considering the suitcase. It was almost empty. The thought of the last of his money being stolen made William's breath shaky.

He moved the few items in the suitcase around, his eyes searching for the envelope. It wasn't there. His chest began to tighten, considering who could have even known to look for his money in that envelope. William groaned internally and began rubbing his forehead. The hotel keeper knew, that's who—he'd seen the money when William was paying for his two-nights' stay. And now the old man was gone with the money.

With a hand on the wall, William panted his frustration out into the room. Why hadn't he taken his money with him—though, wait, he *had* taken part of it and now he didn't have that either. How could he have been so blind? How was he going to manage his assignment without any money? And most importantly, how was he going to even survive in these circumstances?

For a short while, William sat there on the bed, staring at the clothes that covered the floor.

He realized that since he didn't have any money, he would have to earn it by working at the local shops, sweeping floors and washing dishes until the next caravan arrived, months from now. William didn't like that prospect at all. He wanted to finish his assignment and get the payment he was promised as reward for a job well done. Now, he couldn't be sure he would actually survive this "adventure," let alone live to tell the story.

Another option was stealing, but William was no thief and found the idea repulsive. He wouldn't let himself put a man in the same situation he was in now.

But before despair could set into his soul, a third option rose in his mind. His three days in Nador had taught him an important lesson he could use to his advantage. On a journey through the desert, he wouldn't need a suitcase full of shirts and trousers. He'd need food and water, the clothes on his back, a tent and blankets. Money would be nice too.

Considering what he had brought with him from England, William realized he could probably sell most of his belongings for a good price and get the items that he actually needed. Picking carefully the clothes he was going to keep, he placed them—along with a blanket he found underneath the bed pad—neatly in his suitcase. The rest of his belongings William stashed in a makeshift bag he created out of the old bed sheet. He was ready to make a trade.

Somewhere from the deep recesses of his mind, an old proverb resurfaced. "He who wants a rose must respect the thorn," he whispered to himself as a tentative smile brightened his face. *If I sell my belongings, I can still make it. If I can't join the caravan, I can follow them. And if I follow them, I will still be able to cross the Sahara and reach Yemen with all the photographs I could ever want.* As soon as the thought entered his mind, excitement and relief followed because he wouldn't need to wait for months before going on his intended journey.

His mind was set on that decision, and neither cold nor blazing heat would stop him. With the suitcase in hand, William marched out of the room, wondering which shop owner would be eager to buy his wares. When he stepped into the street, it was cold and dark, but he was determined to conclude the day with a wad of dirhams in his pocket. He took one last look at the red wall of the ghostly hotel before walking briskly toward the main street where the echoes of music and laughter would serenade the long night ahead.

# 5

A CROW CAWED AND CLOTH FLAPPED gently in the wind. These were the first
sounds William heard when his eyes opened the next morning. He looked
at the ceiling of his tent—an old contraption he'd managed to acquire in
exchange for a linen shirt and a pair of trousers—swaying under a gentle
breeze. His back felt like a board and his neck was as stiff as the dead tree
outside. The memory of competing with the cold and dark of night as he
attempted to pitch his tent near the fallen tree sent a small shiver up his
spine. He brought his hands to his face and pressed his palms softly against
his eyes, letting out a sigh of exhaustion as he did.

Taking a minute to stretch his body, William rolled over on his stomach
and crawled out on all fours. His feet came out first, followed by his legs and
torso. When his head peeked out, he stopped and looked at the sea to his left.
The sun had not yet risen but the darkness was beginning to lift.

William rose to his feet, patting the dust off his clothes as he did. He
looked at the buildings scattered around the mountain. They looked more
like the creations of nature than manmade structures, colorless and bland,
compared to those near the shore. In that maze of stone and mud buildings,
a blue-domed mosque complemented the brilliant color of the sea. Its walls
seemed to emanate a holy light, not unlike a lighthouse that would direct lost
ships away from danger in the dark sea. It was the only building in Nador that
didn't draw you in with its colors alone. Rather, what was inside pulled you
in, much like the scent of food had taken William to Gabriel's restaurant.

Turning around, William looked down the other side of the mountain.
Riddling the hills below were more specks of color than he could count. The
caravan camp. Each tent seemed to emanate the same kind of holy light as
the mosque, pulling him in with a strength more powerful than anything he'd
ever felt, yet rejecting him when he got too close. The sight of the camp filled

William with a bittersweet desire. He stood a few feet from the dead tree where he had spoken with Gabriel the previous day and where he had made his tent, admiring the caravan from a distance, something he knew he would be doing often for the next couple of months.

It was then that he noticed something moving up the mountainside below him. Looking closer, he saw a man in a brown robe hiking steadily in his direction, a rifle hanging on his shoulder. William shivered. Did the caravan leader send this guard to warn William off? Had his tent been noticed already? He wanted to hurry up and collect his things then run as fast as his feet would carry him, but he knew the man would reach him before he could even close his suitcase.

Having no other options, William sat on the tree, the better to control his instinct to run, and waited for the man to hike the slope and reach his small, overnight camp. In what seemed like a matter of seconds, the brown-robed man stood before William, examining every bit of him with the trained eye of someone who lived in the wild.

William did the same, though more cautiously than he would've liked. The man had nearly black skin and Arab features. His clothing consisted of a dusty brown robe that had seen better days and light, strapped shoes. A curved knife was tucked in his belt, along with a pistol and some rope.

"Our leader wants to speak with you," the man said in a low, blank voice.

"And who is your leader?"

"He wishes to speak to you. Please come," the man repeated. William got the vague feeling he was trying to be polite the best he could.

William considered his options. He could no longer think of following the caravan at a safe distance now that they were aware of his presence. But he could go down, see what the leader had to say, and negotiate a safe passage to Yemen. There was, of course, a chance that he might get killed.

"May I gather my things?" William asked, motioning to his tent.

"No," came the brisk answer. "Come."

William thought about leaving his belongings there. Would he get to return and collect them? He didn't know, but decided to take his camera, carefully strapping it over his head, just in case.

"I'm ready," William said, looking at the man whose expression remained stone-cold.

He expected his Arab escort to turn around and lead the way down the mountain, but he didn't. He simply motioned with his head for William to move on ahead of him. William frequently turned back to look at the Arab and was surprised that the man didn't follow him so close that William would feel threatened. In fact, there was a comfortable, respectable distance. He couldn't believe he actually felt safe. But when he turned back to look at his escort again, William saw the rifle was now in the man's hands, not on his shoulder, and the feeling of safety vanished. He now felt like a sheep being herded to graze with the others or, God forbid, to be slaughtered.

The camp appeared empty at this hour. Either everyone was still sound asleep, or they had already ventured into Nador to buy last-minute provisions in preparation for departure. Whatever the case, William felt even more threatened, seeing that no one was present to defend him should things go badly. He walked between the tents at a brisk pace, with no guidance from his escort. He remembered the path to the center of the camp and found the big tent easily. When he reached it, William stopped right outside the blue awning, noticing that no guards were positioned at the entrance.

"Wait here," the Arab said as he walked past William and into the leader's tent. William had heard those exact words the day before and resented them now. The memory they brought was a nuisance he wanted to forget but the pain of his wound made it impossible.

He looked at the mountain where he had spent the night. It, too, was beginning to wake up. A row of sunbeams outlined its ridge, shining into the air above the camp. A moment later, the sea breeze brought a man's prayerful voice from the direction of the city. William stood listening to the strange but eerily beautiful song, wondering what the words meant. He felt like praying too, to anyone who would listen and help him with his journey.

The sound of cloth shifting broke his thoughts, and looking to his left, William saw his escort standing at the tent's entrance, holding it open for him. The man motioned for William to enter, and he carefully strolled inside.

In his mind, William had pictured the leader as a severe man sitting on a throne, half a dozen servants bowing down to worship at his feet. So, when he saw an average-looking man in his late forties sitting on the ground with his legs crossed, William frowned.

The leader wore an average blue robe, and a headdress was secured around his head by a round roll of black cloth. His hands laid relaxed on his knees, maintaining a posture that was upright but natural. His calm face curiously radiated an aura any monk would envy.

William didn't dare go closer but freely roamed the tent with his eyes. It looked simple yet comfortable, with Persian rugs and soft pillows situated in various locations. A small table held a teapot and some fruit, along with some scattered papers and a map of the Sahara. Nothing out of the ordinary or opulent caught his eye. While William was looking at the leader's private world, the man said nothing, performing a mental evaluation of his own.

"What is your name?" he asked a moment later. William said nothing, fully intending to stand his ground this time. A lengthy silence stretched between them, but the leader took it comfortably. "I am Hakeem el Almin. I lead this caravan." The Arab placed a hand over his heart as he spoke and bowed his head in respect, then looked back at his guest.

"My name is William Abney."

"Please, sit," Hakeem invited as he motioned to a pillow a few feet in front of him.

"I will stand, thank you," William replied defiantly. He didn't want to feel comfortable in this man's presence. For all he knew, this could all be staged so that they would kill him this time.

"Then I shall stand as well," Hakeem said before leaning forward and smoothly rising to his feet. "I did not order my men to mistreat you," the leader told William, placing his hands behind his back.

"And yet, while I was getting beaten and robbed, you did nothing," William countered, his tense voice showing he did not take the injustice lightly.

"You are wrong," Hakeem said and turned around.

He walked to the small table William had already noticed and took something from it before walking to stand before his guest. William's money was right there in his hand, folded in half at the man's chest. William looked down at the money then up at Hakeem, his eyes shining like bright hazel embers.

"My men lied to you," Hakeem explained. "There are never too many people in the caravan. I had both of them beaten and thrown into the city streets to beg." And though that seemed a bit harsh, William actually found it appropriate punishment for what he'd suffered at their hand.

"Why then, didn't they just take my money and let me in? Why hit and threaten me?" William asked.

"You are English, and they had both fought for the Turks against your countrymen. They bore scars that would never heal. To them you were still their enemy. And I considered it a test, so I made an oath: If you returned, I would consider you worthy to join the caravan, but if you did not, well, that was up to you."

With an extended arm, Hakeem offered the money to William who took it, speechless and dumbstruck. In the short moment of silence that followed, William counted the money, unable to believe his eyes and the dignity of the man before him. Not a single dirham was missing.

"I want to go to Yemen," William said simply, glancing up from the folded money, his defiance long forgotten.

"A reasonable request. But you will need to take your own tent," Hakeem said and walked back to the table.

"That won't be a problem," William chuckled, unable to believe the turn of his luck as he carefully tucked the money in his pocket. Hakeem lifted a teapot from the table and poured steaming liquid into a small cup, then looked up at William.

"We will begin to pack the tents once the last of the people have said their prayers. Be ready to leave when they are finished," Hakeem instructed, nodding in the direction of the mountain.

"I will," William promised with a smile.

Hakeem showed a toothy grin, then placed his hand on his chest and bowed. William followed suit, but just before he turned to leave, he looked at the leader with curiosity. "You do not pray?"

"Only when it is necessary," Hakeem replied, toasting him with his cup of tea.

"I see," William said softly, finding that curious. He had thought all Arabs prayed with dedication, three times a day. But the leader was an odd man indeed.

William stepped out of the tent feeling grateful that he had met Hakeem. Now he had his money along with a passage to Yemen. What could be better?

He rushed out of the camp and toward the top of the mountain at the speed of an avid explorer venturing up a secluded mountain pass. As he reached his overnight camp, William saw the sun was already hovering above the sea, full and fiery. Everything it touched with its light was coated in strands of liquid gold.

After disassembling his tent, William folded it neatly and placed it inside an improvised parcel bag he'd created out of the old bed sheets. The rest of his belongings—clothes, water, and some bread—he stashed in his suitcase and so, with the sheet parcel in one hand and the suitcase in the other, he was ready to go meet the desert. Before he started descending, and seeing that the caravan was still in the early stages of preparation, William decided to take a last look at Nador, a city he will always remember. He hiked back to the ridge and simply sat there.

Below him, Nador stretched over part of the mountainside, coated in golden light. The sea that lay beyond was crowded with the black silhouettes of sailing boats. Together, the city and sea silenced William's mind and captured his eyes the way a beautiful woman does.

A horn sounded behind him, and William turned around to see a large gathering of people, camels, and other livestock slowly drifting toward the hills that led away from the coast. He shot one last glance at the sea behind him and realized he was standing on the border of two completely different worlds. Behind him lay the city that thrived with excitement, luxury, and the cocktail blend of Europeans and Africans. Ahead awaited real adventure— the path of the nomad that had gone unchanged ever since the first man with a restless heart ventured into the desert.

William belonged to neither world. He was just a guest paying a short visit.

Now that the caravan was packed up and ready to start its journey through the desert, William saw no reason to lag behind. He ran down the mountainside as quickly as he could, making his way around boulders and over fallen trees, while being careful that he didn't fall or otherwise injure himself. His heart was racing in his chest as William caught up with the wagons at the back. The whole caravan was already moving over the small hills, leaving a trail of flattened grass behind.

He found a smaller wagon with barely enough space to accommodate him and his things, but it seemed sturdy enough. William tossed his suitcase and the tent inside before lithely jumping up after them. From his place in the wagon, William watched the mountain, and Nador, slowly getting farther away.

Several hours had passed, and the caravan was already far enough away from the coast that the mountain had become just a speck on the horizon and the sweet smell of salt was replaced with dust that stuck to the tongue. The terrain here was rocky, and the wagons bumped so much that William jumped off the wagon and left everything behind except his camera. He thought now would be an ideal time to capture the caravan, strung out in a long procession of people and animals, in his lens.

William made his way out of the procession, and, walking at a brisk pace, started looking for a good spot where he could set up his camera and work undisturbed. When he decided he had walked far enough out that he could capture the entire caravan in his lens, he ran along the side of a hill to get ahead of everyone. On the hillside, William found a blocky cluster of boulders and set his camera up on one that gave him a good view of the land. He took several pictures of the caravan as it moved past, relocating as needed.

He spent several hours alone with the camera, the wind whispering in the golden grass around him while the caravan stood still in his lens. Even though he wouldn't see the photographs until he returned to London, he enjoyed taking every one of them. With each click, the image of the caravan was burned into his memory.

The people below looked like miniature chess pieces while the necks of the camels towered over the sea of dusty robes that crawled along the rocky ground. William's finger crept closer to the camera's release button and his left eye squinted. He was preparing his next shot when he noticed a distant cloud of dust drawing closer from the stretch of land ahead of the caravan.

Reluctantly, William took his eye away from the camera and saw a small group of riders carrying square banners colored green, white, and black. They rode past the front of the caravan before circling back and reaching the front again. A screeching horn filled the air and the procession crawled to a halt.

Everyone remained in their respective places, though their raised voices told William they, like him, were wondering what was happening. At the front of the caravan, the riders dismounted their horses and several ant-sized men walked to meet them. William recognized Hakeem's blue robe as well and wondered if it was normal around these places for a handful of riders to demand a caravan's attention. *What for?* He thought. After several minutes of talking with Hakeem, the riders rode away, creating a cloud of dust in their wake. When they disappeared over a hill William realized he forgot to photograph the riders and shortly after the caravan started moving again.

William spent the rest of the day with his camera, certain that the handful of shots he had snapped would turn into grand pictures in Reginald's paper. As evening fell, he walked back to his wagon and decided to stay with it until they stopped to make camp for the night. The caravan was drawing near a mountain range that crept out behind the horizon and dwarfed the surrounding landscape with its sheer size, making the caravan look like an army of insects carrying disproportionate crumbs on their backs. With the fading daylight, the caravan arrived at the foot of the mountains, a bay-like area which appeared perfect for making camp. Upon Hakeem's signal, every pair of hands became busy unloading the supplies that would be used for the night, pitching tents, and starting fires.

Along with everyone else, William unloaded supplies and helped build several tents, inspired by the cheerful hustle and bustle all around him. He noticed that several people gave him a look of strange recognition—perhaps they remembered his bloody face as he stumbled out of the camp the day before. As darkness fell, the camp was nearly set, and William decided it was time to start on his own tent, especially because gusts of cold wind were beginning to swell in the camp. He was certain he wasn't going to live through another night of shivering.

By helping a few people set up their tents, an art form alien to William, he realized he'd pitched his travel home wrong the night before. He'd been missing a middle post and some pegs that had to stabilize the cloth from being blown every which way—or away into the night. He had none of these.

After asking around and receiving lengthy explanations in Arabic, with the added bonus of vehement hand gestures, William came across a man who had the necessary items. Happy that he'd found what he needed, he offered the man some money, but instead of taking it the Arab laughed heartily, shaking his head. He gave the post and pegs to William and, still chuckling, waved him off.

Grateful for his luck, William walked to a spot near the edge of the camp and decided that he was going to set his tent there. He had a good view of the camp and perhaps could take an early photograph as the sun broke the horizon.

But setting up his own tent turned out to be more difficult than he'd imagined. After what seemed like an hour of grunting, hammering, and pulling fabric, William managed to do a decent job, to the amusement of others, though if he had to be honest with himself, it was nowhere as good as he'd imagined.

After pounding in the last peg, William stood at the entrance of the tent and wiped a few drops of sweat from his forehead. Cold was beginning to set in, and he hoped the tent, which looked crooked and tortured, didn't fall on him in the middle of the night. Behind him, the other tents looked three times as large and sturdy as his own. The smile of pride faltered as William realized it would probably take him many shivering nights to master the skill of tent setting.

A little distance to his left he saw the silhouette of a man sitting on a short stool, a warm fire crackling nearby. At the man's feet was a chessboard with small black and white pieces. A thorough examination of the man made William frown—his hair was the same bright orange as the fire and his clothes even looked similar to William's. *A European? What's he doing in the desert? Perhaps he's a lost fool or a madman looking for adventure. But no. He's neither. Fools don't play chess and madmen don't sit quietly by themselves. That makes me wonder...*

William started walking toward the man, glad that he wasn't the only foreigner in the caravan. As he neared the man, he noticed that his hair and beard were carefully trimmed and brushed to near perfection.

"May I?" William asked, standing by a second stool, this one positioned across from the man. The European answered by opening and closing the hand in which he held his chin. William sat down and leaned forward. The few black and white pieces remaining on the board had wandered to places far away from where they belonged.

The nearby fire was playing a crackly song that shadows danced to. William looked up from the chessboard, but the man was still frowning. William's eyes returned to the pieces a second time and he saw it.

William's king was in checkmate while the one across was safely castled. As if noticing this at the same moment William did, the man brought his hand from underneath his chin and scratched the side of his beard which parted as a row of white teeth appeared in a smile.

"Who did you beat?" William asked, smirking.

"Oh, no one important. Just the man who claimed to be the chess champion of the caravan, that's all," the European said as he straightened his back, his German accent masking the sarcasm in his casual tone.

"Ah, I see. And now you are the champion of the caravan?" William said.

"That is correct," the man answered with a note of superiority.

"Not a bad achievement, but may I make a suggestion?" The German nodded solemnly, his earlier smile forgotten. "Prepare to have your title ripped from right under your nose," William warned as he leaned forward and began moving the black pieces to his side of the board.

"You won't be the first person to challenge me," the German said cheerfully while collecting the white pieces. A moment later, as if suddenly remembering something important, he stopped and leaned away from the chessboard. "Before we begin, I would like to know who I'm playing," he said, extending a hand to William.

"I'm William," William said as he shook the man's hand.

"Hans Drachman, Germany's greatest chess champion," The man seemed to be looking for a reaction of recognition but William had never heard the name before. Obviously, Hans was no fool, but his sanity was yet to be proven.

William noticed Hans frowning at the scab on the left side of his head, and his heart started pounding in a different rhythm. "I fell down the stairs," he lied, looking away. Hans nodded, apparently accepting that unlikely explanation, then looked back at the chessboard.

"So what is a chess champion like yourself doing in a caravan heading to Yemen?" William inquired as he and Hans set up their armies opposite each other.

"I have a man to prove wrong," Hans replied, a teasing smile on his face.

"Wrong? About what?"

"The man claims he can beat any chess player brave enough to travel to Yemen and challenge him. I think he hasn't played anyone above the age of five," Hans stated with a smirk.

"So you're on a bit of a crusade then," William said as the last pieces took their places on the board.

"That's right." With all the pieces set up, a short silence followed as each player contemplated their first move.

"Tell me, Hans," William broke the focused silence, "what do you know about the men who rode up to the caravan earlier?"

"Didn't you hear?" Hans sounded surprised as he moved a pawn to the center of the board.

"No, I was busy. What do you know?"

"The riders were Bedouin warriors, nomads who wander the desert. Apparently, a man from their tribe killed another man in an argument and fled. The criminal had been hiding in the desert for about a month when a shepherd boy found him half dead near a well," Hans recited.

"If he was found, why are they looking here?" William asked leaning forward and moving his knight.

"Because when they captured the man and brought him back to their camp, he killed several warriors and rode back into the desert. The Bedouin leader placed a bounty on the murderer's head and it has yet to be paid."

"And they did not bother to look in Nador? What if their man has been hiding there?" William asked bewildered. If he were looking for a criminal, he'd definitely search the city.

"What if their man has been hiding in the caravan?" Hans suggested as he made his move.

"The caravan?" William shouted in surprise.

"It's not impossible," Hans answered calmly. He was right, too.

"Does anyone know what the murderer looks like?" William asked as he moved his next piece.

"Yes. Hakeem has allowed several of the tribe's warriors to join the caravan for a few weeks. If the murderer is not found, they will look for him elsewhere, maybe in Nador."

"Do you think it is possible that the warriors will find him before we reach the desert?" William asked, a feeling of fear creeping into his chest. Perhaps joining this caravan had been a bad idea after all. Maybe he should've waited for the next one?

"I don't know. We shall see," came Hans' simple answer. There was a short silence between the two of them as they considered the position of the chess pieces. "Honestly, I think it's brilliant," Hans said at last, looking up at William.

"Brilliant? What is?" William asked with a confused expression, his focus clearly on the game.

"How the criminal managed to hide in plain sight," Hans said.

"What kind of man would do that?" William asked, once again shifting his thinking.

"A man who has nothing to lose. The kind of man who is not afraid to kill. Dangerous and bold—a bad mix. But we can't do anything, can we? The warriors were sent to do a job and we can only hope the murderer doesn't get wind of it. If he decides to stay here and hide, then his days with the caravan will be the longest days in his life," Hans said, his voice bearing a slight tone of empathy for the murderer.

As silence settled, Hans and William fully committed their attention to the game. At first, the pieces seemed passive, but that all changed when Hans' queen took both of William's knights in two swift moves. One after the other, William's figures fell, and Hans' forces began to corner William's king, cutting off all escape routes.

Hans took William's last piece and only the black king remained, pushed into the far corner. The figure had nowhere left to run. Hans moved his bishop so that it controlled a square near William's king, but when it was William's turn, he realized he didn't have anywhere to move. Still, he wasn't in check.

"The devil? Is that stalemate?" William asked as he looked up at Hans.

"Impossible," the German gasped as he leaned away from the board. William began to chuckle, knowing luck had saved him from handing Hans an easy win. "Fluke," Hans exclaimed, his voice almost sounding angry. "Nothing but a coincidence. I am the best and I'll prove it," Hans said while pointing at William.

Hans turned around at the sound of someone approaching. "Alexander, take a look at this," he said. A tall man dressed in a black shirt and brown pants stepped into the light. He had dark hair but was going bald, though a small peninsula of hair still remained above his forehead.

"Ah, playing chess, are we?" Alexander noted in an English accent then bent over to get a better look at the board. William couldn't believe his luck. He was't going to be the sole foreigner on this journey after all.

As Alexander examined the pieces, a smile started pulling the forest of his beard closer to his eyes. "Looks like you met your match, Hans," he said, crossing his thick, club-like arms in front of his chest.

"Match?" Hans obviously disagreed, sounding insulted. "This was just a qualifying round to test his skill. To see if he is worthy for a real game, and by the skin of his teeth, he passed," Hans declared, making up an excuse to play William and beat him this time.

"How about it? Are you going to play again?" Alexander asked William, an enthusiastic smile in his eyes.

"I hate to disappoint you, kind chaps, but it's time for me to get some sleep," William said as he slapped his knees and rose from his stool.

"I think I smell fear in the air," Hans taunted, exchanging a sly look with Alexander.

"I agree. I think he's chicken," Alexander said, nodding at William.

"I'm very tired," William waved them off with a yawn.

"I told you," Hans said in a victorious tone and began putting away the chess pieces.

"We'll play some other time, when my wits are at full strength, and then you'll have to earn your stalemate. I promise," William said in a sigh as he moved away from the fire.

"Right, another time," Hans snorted.

"Sleep well," William heard Alexander say. He turned and waved to the pair, hoping Alexander's words would come true. In his shabby tent, he hoped he would be able to dream, uninterrupted, of the desert.

# 6

AT DAYBREAK, THE MORNING HORN split the silence, sending an almost deafening echo through the surrounding mountains and creating a feeling that somehow the day would be difficult to forget. The night before, William had gone to bed early so he would be among the first to rise and be ready to help with loading the supplies. By the time the horn declared that a new day had arrived, William had already taken down his tent, folded the cloth, and gathered all his belongings, something that he was getting better at with each repetition.

All around him, people were walking out of their tents, ready to start packing. In a matter of minutes, the camp had become crowded as tents were being disassembled and wagons were being loaded with merchandise and supplies.

William left his belongings at the spot where his tent had been pitched and walked into the camp, knowing help would be needed. It had been a week since they left Nador, and already William felt he was adjusting to the way of the caravan. In that uneventful week they had traversed through the dense mountain range where William first met Hans and Alexander. Now they were packing their things to leave the mountains for the flatter—but no less difficult—terrain ahead.

As usual, people were busy in preparations, but one thing made today more special—the silent excitement at the closeness of the desert which everyone seemed to feel, but no one spoke about.

After helping several people nearby, William walked through the camp to see if anyone else needed assistance but quickly got swept down one of the narrow pathways by swarms of busy people. In the frenzy of movement he caught a glimpse of a woman dressed more like a gypsy than an Arab. She wore a blue and green dress and a head covering decorated with small beads. She looked at him and William noticed her eyes were also different—a dark mossy green that was forever imprinted in his memory.

William helped in disassembling the camp until the last piece of cargo was safely stuffed in a wagon or placed over a camel. A few people recognized him and, through gestures and the small amount of Arabic he'd learned, they spoke to him about their families and why they were traveling to Yemen. Every time he shared he was from England, a string of nostalgia pulled at his heart. He missed home, even with its cold and humid weather.

Some time later the caravan appeared about ready to move, and William went off to gather his belongings and find a wagon that he would stay with until making camp again. A second horn blasted just as he was loading his things in a wagon pulled by two donkeys.

Slowly, the caravan began moving away from the mountain range. Walking among the throngs of people and animals, William's mind turned to the gypsy woman with the dark green eyes. He'd never been to the jungle, but he'd read stories written by people who'd spent years there. Their description of the jungle undergrowth, untouched for millennia by human hand, matched what he saw in those eyes.

He wondered if he should have spoken to her or taken her picture. But no. Such beauty was sacred and did not belong in photographs. Better leave her alone than feeling forever guilty for ruining something so otherworldly.

William wanted to believe he'd taken more than enough photos of the caravan on the first day, but he wasn't keen on missing a good opportunity, so he always kept his camera close and a healthy stock of extra film he purchased from a caravan merchant. A couple of mornings ago he'd taken a photo of the still asleep camp, just as the sun was beginning to rise, and last night he'd found a bright fire to capture on film for the British audience. Reginald should be happy.

Because William always kept to the back of the caravan, it didn't take long for his new acquaintances, Hans and Alexander, to find him.

"Hallo, William," Hans said in greeting as he and Alexander strutted along.

William smiled and gave them a cheerful, "Hello, boys," happy to have finally found them. He hadn't seen either of them in nearly a week and was curious to learn if Hans had been able to find a solution to the latest chess conundrum.

The German yawned loudly.

"Tired?" William asked with a slight smirk.

"Tired?" Hans shook his head while Alexander followed with a yawn of his own. "I don't think I've been this exhausted in all my life."

"I'll have to agree with you. I wasn't able to get a wink of sleep after I heard footsteps running past my tent and thought it might have been the murderer," Alexander chimed in, his cautious voice complementing his words.

"Footsteps?" Hans asked in evident fear and disbelief.

"That's right. I thought someone must have been in a hurry to get to bed, but when I looked out, I saw several men chasing someone down the path outside my tent," Alexander added with a nod.

"Did they catch him?" inquired the German. Suddenly, he didn't look so tired anymore. Gossip seemed to be his morning coffee.

Alexander shrugged. "I don't know. But I heard this morning that the murderer was among the best warriors in his tribe."

"That's a story. What about you," Hans turned to William. "Did *you* hear any news about the murderer?"

"Not a word," William replied, disappointed he didn't have any news to share regarding the criminal.

"So, our boy Alexander here is the only one enlightened. And since he's got some things common with our wanted man..." Hans said in a chuckle as he elbowed Alexander.

"Stop that, will you? I have nothing in common with that man," Alexander snapped and William saw a momentary sadness pass through his eyes.

"What did you mean by that?" William turned to Hans, hoping to be included in what appeared to be an inside joke, but the German lost the cheery look and chose to examine the ground instead. However, the silence made William wonder if this was a joke at all, and the smirk faded from his face. "You don't mean to say that he's a... you're a..." William started with a nervous laugh that died off when no protest arose from the other two.

Alexander sighed, but a quiet anger was simmering in his posture. Clearly, there was more to this story. "This idiot has no idea what he's talking about," he said, looking irritably at his Germain friend.

"You know I didn't mean it," Hans said as an apology. Then he turned to William, "Can you keep a secret?"

"I... Yes, yes, I can," William stammered hungry to know more.

With a theatrical voice, Hans stated: "Alexander over here is a wanted man in your part of the world."

"Why?" William asked, prompted by curiosity.

"Well... He might have murdered his wife," Hans said as if delivering the punch line to a joke.

Alexander punched him on the shoulder. "You just can't help it, can you?" Turning to William, he explained, "I didn't kill her. I was framed in the most humiliating manner."

William had no idea what was going on, but he thought it was best not to interfere or ask any questions. Patience was known to be a most prized quality.

"Oh fine, you don't like my version of the story, then tell him yourself," Hans said and stepped out of the way, so Alexander could walk next to William.

"You ever heard of the Clavert Steel Company?" Alexander asked, leaning closer to William.

"Umm, no, I don't think I have."

"Well, it's a steel company my family has owned for three generations. For my twenty-fifth birthday my father placed his newest factory in my management and told me I could own it if I did a good job running it. Within a few years, the factory was beginning to build a reputation, and I got a client from America saying that he wanted to build a franchise of our factories in New York. To do the negotiating, he sent his daughter who knew the steel business well. She was beautiful, smart, and as strong-willed as the country she came from. A year later, I made her my wife, but was beginning to see less of her with each passing day." Hans seemed to find all this amusing because William heard him chuckling. After slapping Hans on the back of the head, Alexander continued.

"As I returned home from a trip to France, two policemen intercepted me at the door, saying I needed to go with them to the station, where my wife was waiting for me. That was the only reason I agreed to go in their coach, but we didn't head for the police station. We were clearly going to the port. I can't believe I was so stupid back then, but I trusted those officers until we reached a secluded part of the port and I saw my wife smiling slyly from a second coach that was already waiting there.

"I didn't understand what was going on. This couldn't have been a secret welcome she had planned. She didn't come to greet me. Instead, the officers threw me out and made me kneel. One of them drew his pistol and placed it at the side of my head. I glanced at the second coach and saw my wife's victorious face staring at me through the glass window.

"It was then I realized what was happening—her ambition had gotten the best of her and she had found a way to get rid of me and retain my factory and my money for herself. I got so angry, the blood pumped in my veins, taking away the fear and confusion. I wasn't scared of death, I wanted justice. Seizing the pistol pointed at my head, I ran. Shots were fired at me but I was lucky to get away with just a scratch.

"I went to look for help at the police station, hoping they would catch that viper so she wouldn't go about ruining anyone else's life. What were the odds that I would be marked a criminal without court of justice? The whole station was up and about looking for me. Nowhere was safe. I hid in the slums for several days, until I saw a newspaper story of a steel baron's wife getting murdered.

"This was no coincidence. Obviously, she had faked her death somehow, becoming the martyr and making me out to be a murderer. I couldn't go to my family and make them a part of this whole mess, nor could I leave them worry sick about me. I knew my mother wouldn't handle not knowing the truth, so I sneaked them a letter explaining what had happened and warning them not to look for me until I thought it safe to return.

"Since then, I have been in hiding. I knew I couldn't stay in England much longer, so I looked for a ship to take me far away. Keeping to dark alleys and constantly looking over my shoulder, I was able to purchase a ticket to Portugal. I lived there for several month, doing whatever work I could find so I could save some money and journey even further from home. That's where I met Hans, a coincidence really, and decided to go with him. Perhaps, whatever spies my wife sent after me would lose my tracks as I left Europe. We joined this caravan and have been here since leaving Nador."

"Wow. That's quite a story, Alexander," William said, trying to get his head around the mess in his countryman's life. "What are you going to do when you get to Yemen?"

"I'm hoping enough time would have passed and I'll be able to sail back to England. I will telegraph my father and ask him if it's safe for me to return under different alias. I miss my family and I'd like to start a new—"

"Life as a sheepherder," Hans interrupted, a smug smile on his face. Obviously, the German was trying to lighten the mood, and William chuckled along. He couldn't believe anyone's life could turn out so miserable, especially since Alexander really seemed to be an honorable man. But then again, fate was a peculiar thing.

"I believe you understand this is a serious matter? I'm in hiding and don't need anyone else knowing my story," Alexander said, looking at William with intense, searching eyes.

"I understand. You can be sure I won't tell a soul," William promised, shaking the hand Alexander had extended to him.

The trio continued walking, but soon the conversation began to dwindle to where no topic could last for more than a sentence or two. Each man seemed to have his own thoughts in mind, or perhaps Hans and Alexander were too exhausted from lack of sleep. This went on for some time as the endless line of wagons, camels, and people slithered in the distance ahead.

Having nothing better to do, William turned his attention to their surroundings. One thing in particular was pretty interesting—the ground beneath his feet. It had somehow changed from the rocky, grainy soil of the mountains to something softer, finer, and light in color. It seemed to find creative ways to get inside the soles of his shoes, and each step he took had his feet sinking a little deeper.

William stopped walking, his full attention on the ground, the moving caravan completely forgotten. Vaguely, he heard Hans and Alexander ask what he was doing, but he let that slip too. He was too busy wondering if they had reached the desert. Lowering a hand to the ground, William scooped up a small mound of soil. He'd always thought the sand in the desert would be exactly like what they had at home, only a lot more.

This sand, however, felt like powdered dough, and he tilted his head as he smiled in fascination. Rising to his feet, William continued observing the small mound of sand in his hand. He poked it softly and saw it powdered the tip of his finger.

# De Collibus

When a faint shout finally broke his concentration, William looked up and found himself all alone in a sea of white. He squinted up in the distance and saw the caravan appearing like a black river flowing over the horizon. Rippling in the heatwaves, the two figures of Hans and Alexander were waving at him and good thing too. He could've easily gotten lost.

William waved back, a smile splitting his face, and started walking slowly after them while toying with the handful of soil in his palm. He took his time to enjoy the comforting silence around him—something that is difficult, if not impossible, to accomplish when traveling with so many people.

As he caught up with the caravan, William wondered how after only one week of travel the soil already looked more like fine sand. For a moment longer, he studied what was left of his scoop of soil, then let it slip through his fingers, a little at a time, until his hand was empty.

When William caught up with the wagon carrying his things, Hans and Alexander were nowhere to be found, probably having left to rejoin their own belongings.

When the mountains turned into vague outlines behind them and the cool of the evening began to settle over the desert, the caravan stopped to make camp for the night. Hakeem had chosen a strategic open plain surrounded by a few white hills covered in shrubs. The area was large enough to hold everyone and still provide protection from the wind that would sometimes haunt the desert. As the tents and animals were all set, numerous fires were started, their light illuminating the camp and calling the people to warm themselves as evening turned into night.

William didn't take long to set up his tent. After a week of doing it, his skills had improved noticeably, and now the sides didn't sag anymore, and the central post was aimed directly at the sky of tiny diamonds that glimmered from thousands of kilometers away. Standing outside his humble abode, he smiled with the pride of a child who had just learned how to tie his shoes. This time, the tent actually looked sturdy, and the soft glow of the large candle he'd bought after spending a very dark first night with the caravan made him feel like a first-rate genius.

Hans and Alexander would probably look for him for a night of chess or gossip, but for their own good, William decided it would be best to disappoint them. They'd both looked exhausted in the morning, and after the day's journey, he reckoned they would be incapable of standing on their feet or holding their eyes open. Besides, he didn't want Hans using exhaustion as an excuse for getting decimated.

The cold air outside made William shiver and think about the coat he'd given to the old woman back in Nador. Surprisingly, despite his own discomfort, he didn't regret that act of generosity. Now, being determined to adapt to the severe conditions in the Sahara, William was committed to spend some time in the cold each night, so he would get used to it over time. A quarter of an hour later, he decided to call it a night.

He gave one last glance at the camp and walked inside his tent where the candle, underneath its glass dome, gave off a nice warmth that put some feeling back into his fingertips. A cozy blanket he'd bought from a cloth merchant was spread on the ground in front of him. It seemed more welcoming than ever after standing out in the cold for so long. Snuffing the candle, William felt the thick of darkness cover him. He tucked himself in the blanket with arms folded behind his head and closed his eyes.

His mind was occupied by thoughts that slowly drifted into dreams of traveling with the caravan and reaching the desert. That filled him with an odd warmth that kept him asleep for a couple of hours. Just as he was about to pick up a handful of white sand and observe it drifting through his fingers like water, William heard people talking loudly outside his tent. He was about to dismiss the noise as part of the dream, but even though the men spoke in Arabic, he could clearly distinguish their panic. He lifted his head and cracked open one eye slowly coming to consciousness. The cloth of his tent was covered in dark silhouettes of people running, some waving their hands wildly in the air.

Something was wrong.

Curious to find out what was causing the commotion, William rose to his feet and staggered outside where he found himself surrounded by people talking loudly. Some of them had torches that cast grotesque shadows on the surrounding tents and on others' sleepy faces. The camp was usually a quiet place at night, but one wouldn't know it by all the noise. Everyone looked tired, and yet it was obvious that there would be no getting back to sleep until the matter, whatever it was, was settled.

Somewhere ahead of him the crowd started to part, and William stood on the tips of his toes to see if he could follow the action. It was no use—his average height and the dense crowd made that impossible. Shouts and what sounded like insults were added to the noise when the crowd split and a small group of men came into the circle of light. They were armed guards who were dragging a dirty looking man down the path between the tents. His arms were tied behind his back, but he must have been very strong, because four men couldn't hold him still.

One of the guards gave a sudden roar of pain when the struggling man bit him on the shoulder, drawing blood even through the cloth of his robe. The scream summoned more guards to help lead the prisoner someplace safe where he wouldn't cause more trouble.

William's foggy brain, now fully awake, was able to put two and two together. Such fuss could be caused only by the murderer everyone had been looking for. The man was wild and dangerous, maybe mad too. No wonder all he was driven to do was kill. The crowd followed the guards and William went along until they stopped at a large open area near the center of the camp. Even though he was thrashing like a beast, the guards led the prisoner to a sturdy-looking post and tied him there while the crowd created a circle around him and some started spitting on him in disgust.

William squeezed his way to the front of the crowd without taking his eyes away from the murderer. He didn't join the spitting rain, but he didn't hide his contempt either.

As the prisoner strained against the ropes, sweat began to darken the dust covering his face and clothes. A wild beard hid the lower half of his face, and his eyes burned with the fire of a man driven to the edge of his moral borders. One of the guards, a tribesman William recognized seeing in the camp, stepped closer to the post, and the criminal stopped wriggling and exposed his throat in a silent dare. The Bedouin said something to the prisoner and spit in his face, but he wasn't finished. With one swift motion, the guard grabbed the man's robe near the collar and gave it a sudden tug, tearing it down to the waist.

Suddenly, the man's dirty skin was revealed, and though William knew nothing of the Arabic customs, he was almost sure this was a testament of guilt. Having done his job, the tribesman stepped away from the post and rejoined his people who had observed the whole procedure from a couple of feet away. And the criminal, having recognized that justice had come upon him, bowed his head and his body relaxed on the ropes that bound him. Then he started weeping; a sad song of strange sounds that probably made sense only to him.

William was bewildered by what he saw. He turned to a short youth to his right and asked, "What does this mean?"

The man seemed confused for a moment, then looked around and motioned for William to repeat the question.

When he did so, the lad replied slowly, "Warrior have honor and strength. Kill brother, no honor. Break robe, take strength. Man very guilty and Bedu want remove everything. He is nothing." Then the lad spit on the ground as if to demonstrate how strongly he felt on the matter.

Another moment passed, then the people across from William suddenly stepped aside as Hakeem and four of his personal armed guards stepped into the circle and toward the group of tribesmen who were quietly speaking on one side of the criminal. A conversation ensued between the two parties, and Hakeem patted one tribesman on the shoulder as if to congratulate him on a job well done. Then Hakeem turned to one of his men and seemed to give him instructions because the guard nodded briskly then walked away with a purposeful stride. A moment later, William heard a horse galloping away from the assembled group, and he was dying to know what had just happened.

After the rider left, Hakeem seemed to dismiss the crowd, but no one felt prepared to leave the scene just yet. Everyone was curious to see what would happen next. Apparently, nothing more was planned for the night, because Hakeem left two of his guards to stay with the tribesmen and motioned the other one to follow him.

William didn't know what to do. He, too, wanted to see the resolution to this spectacle, but as the crowd began to thin, he headed to his own empty tent. For a while, he stood at the entrance, staring blankly at the blanket at his feet, then collapsed on the ground in hopes to get some sleep. Unfortunately, squeezing his eyes shut and rolling around didn't help to put his mind at ease. He kept thinking of the murderer and how quickly one's life can become disastrous when giving in to primal instincts.

Unable to find sleep, William stepped outside, hoping to get some peace of mind by walking it out. He hadn't seen Hans and Alexander in the crowd, but then, he hadn't been looking for them. A few people sat around a fire, boiling water for early tea. He nodded curtly, but didn't stop to join them.

In the distance to his left, William saw the dark outline of a hill and thought it made for a great observation spot. Perhaps he should have taken his camera as well, except he didn't feel like shooting pictures. He wanted to look down at the camp and memorize it just as it were. As he walked between the tents, he soon found himself at the very edge of the camp, his destination just before him. A narrow path to his right seemed to be leading exactly where he wanted to go, and he was more than eager to follow it.

The sky was turning brighter the further he walked up the hillside, reminding him that a new day was coming. What would this day bring? Would it be more peaceful now that the criminal was found? Would the caravan travel safely through the desert?

When he reached the top of the hill, the sun had almost broken the horizon. William looked down at the camp, a scattering of colorful specks that could've made any painter jealous. From up here, the camp easily fit in the palm of his hand. He walked around the shrub-scattered summit, looking for a place to sit and watch the sun rise. A large boulder that stuck out of the hillside like a half-built bridge seemed like the best spot. He pulled himself up easily, and sat there, his legs dangling over the side, facing a flat stretch of land where the sky bore a soft red tinge.

As he watched the sun peek over the horizon, William wondered whether the caravan would resume travel to its next stop or if they were going to stay here until the prisoner was brought to justice. His thoughts then wandered from the caravan to the desert and what it would be like to stand on top of a dune, completely alone. Completely separated from the rest of the world, surrounded by dunes so numerous that the whole world appeared a desert planet, a pleasantly inescapable one. He wanted to know what it was like to hear silence. Real silence. To feel nothing but his own heartbeat and the scorching sun on his face. To be king of a boundless kingdom ruled and inhabited only by him.

The sun rose brilliantly over the hills, bringing the promise of a warm, dry day. William watched it climb up the sky for a bit longer, then started on his way back. Halfway down the hill, he spotted a small company of riders and horses drawing closer to the camp and guessed that the Bedouin had sent them to pick up their men and the prisoner. Soon, crowds from the caravan had gathered at the edge of the camp to see the arriving company. Everyone seemed excited about this new development and cheers could be heard in the warm morning air.

William quickened his pace so as not to miss anything. The crowd of spectators had quadrupled by the time he reached the camp, making it difficult to get closer to the front. Thanks to his perseverance, however, and a little weaving skill, William found a spot that gave him a great view of the ensuing scene. What he saw was Hakeem, followed by two of his men who held the prisoner, walking toward the dismounting tribesmen ahead. The prisoner's shoulders were slumped forward in a posture of defeat. It seemed like the fight had left him and he was now succumbing to his fate. Behind the guards walked the four tribesmen who were responsible for catching the criminal the previous night.

As the procession moved forward, a man dressed all in white with a red turban covering his head and a matching sash around his waist dismounted and walked on to meet them. The man's posture and the hushed voices around him told William this was the Bedouin Sheik. Hakeem and his men stopped and bowed as the high-ranking tribesman approached them. He hugged and kissed Hakeem and patted him on the back. Then his gaze turned to the criminal.

The grateful look in his eyes slowly drained until a scowl of hatred took its place. From his place in the crowd, William could see the leader's lips moving as he spoke to the criminal, but he felt grateful that he couldn't hear or understand them. As if being crushed by a boulder, the prisoner lowered his head and began to weep. At first silently, then uncontrollably. The leader turned back to Hakeem and nodded silently. This time he wasn't smiling.

He spoke a command and Hakeem's men, together with the four tribesmen, dragged the criminal toward the horses where six more warriors were waiting. It was at the exact moment of exchange when the criminal wriggled his hands free from the ropes and pulled a sword from a guard's belt. He made a mad dash for the Bedouin leader before anyone could even recognize the threat and react.

William felt his stomach turn when the crowd shouted in shock and fear. *The warriors must catch him*, he thought, but despite being tied to a pole all night, the prisoner seemed light on his feet. And he had a purpose.

Hakeem and the leader looked at the crowd, unaware of the threat, until they turned around and saw the mad man running right at them, sword at the ready. With the tribesmen getting swiftly outrun, the crowd roared in outrage. But what could they do?

William felt a sudden surge of energy come over him. He couldn't watch such a vile act take place right before his eyes and do nothing to stop it.

Without thinking, he bolted out of the crowd, with a few men following close behind him. The soft sand made running difficult, but if the prisoner could do it, William could as well.

Finally realizing that the criminal was on the loose and coming at them, Hakeem pulled the tribe leader behind him, but the man stumbled and fell. He was still struggling to get to his feet when the criminal reached them, shouted something indistinguishable, and raised the stolen sword over his head like an executioner. Hakeem drew his sword, a last, desperate line of defense that would do nothing but postpone the inevitable.

With no one in his way, the mad man gave a victorious cry and the blade slashed down. One strike would've took the leader's head, but William reached the man just in time and tackled the murderer to the ground, pinning his sword hand with all his weight. The criminal was rightfully among the best warriors of the Bedouin, and William felt the truth of it with each strike the man delivered to his body in attempts to free his arm.

The murderer's face was covered in sweat, contorted in a grotesque expression, and his eyes were dark and furious. In his craze, he could've killed William with bare hands had the guards and warriors reached them a moment too late.

Someone pried the sword from the man's grasp while the others grabbed a hold of his legs and arms and lay across his torso to keep him from moving. He thrashed in the sand, perhaps realizing he'd fumbled his only chance for revenge. This time the tribesmen didn't take any chances. Tying the man's hands and feet securely, the warriors carried him off like a carpet and plopped him in the sand by the horses.

William, feeling exhausted and aching all over his torso, was gently propped up by a dozen hands. Slowly, he stood up and watched as the man was taken away. His stomach felt hollow and his lungs quivered to suck in air. A strong hand gripped his shoulder and William turned to see who it was. Hakeem stood a little to the side while the Bedouin Sheik placed a hand over his heart, a look of solemn regard on his face. Stepping away, he nodded and turned to Hakeem, saying something in Arabic.

After the exchange, Hakeem turned to William, a small smile playing on his lips. "The Sheik has asked me to thank you for saving his life, since he does not speak English."

William placed his hands over his heart and bowed his head slowly, mimicking the gesture Hakeem had made when they first met. The Bedouin looked at William curiously, then said something to Hakeem who shrugged and smiled. Observing the exchange, William was most surprised when the Sheik bowed to him in the same manner.

Speaking in Arabic, the Bedouin motioned for William to raise his hand. "The Sheik would like to show his gratitude with a special gift," Hakeem explained while the crowd around them cheered. William didn't want any gifts, he was just glad the whole ordeal was over and that everyone was now safe. He did want to show disrespect, though, so when the Emir twisted a gold ring from his little finger and placed it on one of William's fingers, William eagerly bowed again. "This ring carries the sign of the Bedouin and will grant you safe passage through the Maghreb territories if you ever find yourself in these lands again," Hakeem announced.

William looked down at his hand, now adorned with a gold ring. A blue oval stone was fixed in its center and a few Arabic symbols were engraved on the side of the gold band.

Looking the elderly man in the eyes, William said, "Please tell him I am honored to receive his gift and that I was happy to help," then watched Hakeem relay his words.

"The Sheik is glad you accept his gift. He will never forget what you have done today, for him and his tribe," Hakeem translated, then, as an afterthought, he added, "You must be the first Englishman to ever receive such respect."

William didn't know what to think of that. "I will not forget this encounter either," he said, unable to hold back his smile and the three bowed a final time. Having accomplished his mission, the Bedouin chieftain patted Hakeem on the shoulder and walked back to his warriors who had already hefted their prisoner up on one of the spare horses. As the small group mounted their horses, the crowd cheered and waved, shouting blessings and goodbyes. Then they rode off, leaving a cloud of dust in their wake.

The crowd suddenly swarmed him, patting William on the back and shaking his hand as if he had saved each of their lives. He smiled and nodded to the people, urging them to get a move toward the camp. They had yet to pack, he felt exhausted and his body ached all over.

After everyone had dispersed, which had taken quite some time, William found his tent and stepped inside. A wave of dizziness came over him and he grabbed hold of the center post to steady himself. The events of the morning were like a fairy tale dream that shouldn't be real. But he felt the ring on his finger.

It had been real. All of it.

Some time later, after he got his balance back, William gathered his things and took down his tent. The caravan was, once again, on the move, ready to face the next day of travel.

# 7

WILLIAM SAT FORWARD ON A SMALL STOOL as his right hand played with the side of his forehead to satisfy an illusive itch caused by the nightmare at his feet. Opposite him Hans had assumed the position of a mind hard at work. Alexander sat on the ground with his legs crossed, occasionally glancing at Hans and William, but mostly he kept his eyes on the chessboard between them.

They had been playing for a half hour, and small grains of sand had been swept onto the board as the wind picked up a little with the arrival of evening. They were too focused on each other's kings to notice, let alone care, about the sand. It was Hans' move in this battle of the minds, but he remained indecisive. He shifted on his stool and William took note of his quirky movements, quickly returning his focus to the board.

Hans took his hand away from his chin and pinched the top of his queen piece, moving it to William's side of the board. After making his move, Hans crossed his arms as if to say, "What do you think about that?"

Despite the German's careful thinking the move had a flaw. After Hans leaned back in his stool, William slowly moved his hand down to the chessboard, getting Hans' full attention, picked up Hans' queen, and replaced it with one of his own pieces that had been sitting neglected on the edge of board. Hans' eyes lost their glow, though his face bore the stiffness of a statue, and kept its confident smirk. William glanced at Alexander, but the Englishman looked as clueless as he was.

When William's eyes returned to Hans, he saw the German's face begin to morph into an angry scowl, but before the scowl fully appeared Hans pulled a mask of confidence over his anger and straightened his back. The game continued, but with Hans at a great disadvantage. Occasionally, a piece from either William's or Hans' side would be dropped into the pile of discarded pieces. Slowly but surely the two rivals' pieces left the board until Hans ran out of pieces first and his king was the first to be alone on the board. William's situation wasn't much brighter; he had lost his queen to a foolish blunder and all he had left, other than his king, was a pawn. A race began for William to get back his queen, but Hans reached the pawn first.

In the excitement of the race to victory, Hans took the pawn and placed it on the ground to the side of the board. There was a short silence.

"Oh, not again," William groaned as he covered his eyes with his palms.

"What's the matter?" Alexander asked, surprised because thoughts of returning to England had distracted him from the game.

"See for yourself," Hans said with a disappointed groan as he pointed to the board. When Alexander leaned forward to take a better look, Hans turned away. This second stalemate was too much for him to stomach. "It's a stalemate," Hans explained to Alexander, his eyes still gazing out over William's shoulder.

"Again? The two of you are quite strange. Can't one of you win, for God's sake?" Alexander observed, as if he had placed a bet on them. William started to chuckle at how fate seemed to be rewarding him with flukes and punishing Hans by having him tie with someone less skilled than he was.

"And what are you laughing about?" Hans asked in a mocking tone. Alexander joined William's contagious laughter, which continued until their bellies started to hurt.

Hans couldn't stand it. While his friends were laughing at his expense, he was blaming himself for making the silly mistake of moving his queen, which began the downward spiral to this second stalemate. Hans stood suddenly and shoved William off his stool.

William's back hit the ground and his laughter only increased. Hans looked to his left and then to his right to see if anyone had seen him. Luckily, the passages around their meeting place were empty. He looked back at William and Alexander and frowned. Both of them were lying on their backs with their hands curled over their chests like poisoned rats. Hans realized he was making a fool of himself and sat back down.

Still chuckling, William weakly returned to his stool, and Alexander pushed himself back up, shaking his head in amusement. As he looked up, William saw Hans sitting across from him collecting the chess pieces inside a small leather pouch.

"And here I was, thinking you were going to beg me for a rematch," William gloated.

"I was going to, but seeing that you lost, there's no reason to keep this up," Hans replied, looking at the leather bag.

"Hold on a second, he didn't lose. You said yourself it was a stalemate," Alexander spoke in William's defense.

Hans' hand froze and he stared into the pouch for several moments but couldn't think of anything to say that would make him in the right.

"Well, the least a man can do is try, right?" Hans replied with a bit of a smirk.

"I suppose so," Alexander said as he stood, a chuckle sounding in his voice. William rose from his stool. As Hans picked up the chessboard and clamped it under his arm, William folded the small stools and passed them to Alexander. There was a nearly silent exchange of half hugs and handshakes, their minds exhausted from the day's travel and ready for a good night's sleep.

"Don't think too hard about your loss, William. I'm sure you'll recover," Hans taunted, smiling as he walked toward the closest path. William smiled back and watched as Hans and Alexander disappeared into the sea of tents.

Left on his own, William looked at the camp around him. The sun was already setting behind the hills, turning the sky a bright orange and the earth an impenetrable black, void of color or shape except for the tips of the tents that pointed toward the stars. There was still a little while before darkness settled, and William thought it would be a good idea to end the day by taking a walk around the camp to get his evening dose of cold.

He took off toward the perimeter, which seemed abandoned compared to the camp's usually lively atmosphere. The tents around him began to dwindle and the paths between them were wide and open, creating a grand view of the horizon that lured him with its host of colors. When he emerged from the scattered tents and walked into the open plain, there was nothing standing between him and the horizon, and the glow of the dying ember behind the hills captured his mind in a whirlwind of emotions. Almost instantly, William was hit by a gust of fresh air, which carried with it some heat from the desert. The breeze ruffled his sleeves as it stormed into the camp.

The warm breeze conjured up images of the desert in his mind and one in particular floated to the surface. He closed his eyes and opened them up to another world. He was standing all alone, overlooking a desert as empty as he felt. Empty inside except for what was pure and beautiful.

He was the king and no one and no thing could judge or oppose him. Neither could time, because here it didn't exist. William looked up. The sun's glare nearly dominated the blinding sky. Its cleansing heat made him feel lightheaded, like he was staring up at the gates of heaven from the depths of hell.

But the dream didn't last. He was woken when the wind in his sleeves turned cold. His eyes opened and William was back at the edge of the camp. Ahead, the sky was glowing orange over a pitch-black horizon. He tucked his hands into his pockets and pushed his elbows closer to his sides to evade the cold.

For the past day, since he had saved the Bedouin Sheik and word about it spread around the caravan, William had been congratulated by almost every person he met during the day. Which is why solitude made him especially happy.

The desert sands were about to recapture his eyes when his attention was suddenly attracted to a dark silhouette appearing to his right. He looked to see who had joined him at this lonely part of the camp. It was a woman, admiring the hills and the setting sun. She wore a dress of green, burgundy, and blue that the wind swept behind her like the banners of an army waiting for the command to charge.

William froze. Could it be her? The design of her dress looked similar to what he saw the woman with the beautiful green eyes wear the day before. But there was something else as well. It was the way she carried herself: her shoulders back and her chin up as if the sun was setting for her. Something about her made her look more like a warrior queen than the other women around the camp, quiet and shrouded in cloth.

William turned around, determined to walk back to his tent, but his feet refused to move while his eyes were glued to the woman. He stood motionless, while a strange feeling of nervousness took over him. Part of his mind told him to go talk to the woman and see if she really was the one he had seen the day before.

That thought spiked up the nervous feeling, because he was afraid that he would just stand there looking at her eyes, his mind completely blank. Or perhaps she would slap him for thinking that just because he had saved a man's life he was entitled to a kiss from a pretty girl. William thought it best to avoid the risk, after all, what good would that be?

He remained where he stood, hoping that she wouldn't notice him. After a moment of silence, William realized that going back was no longer an option. Neither was standing where he was. Finally, he made up his mind and started walking towards her with what felt like the charm of a prince in his stride.

In reality, all William managed to do was turn in her direction and plant one foot several inches short of a full step in front of him like an unskilled acrobat balancing on a tightrope. To William's relief, the woman continued staring straight ahead, not noticing his puppet-like attempt to walk to her or that he was even there.

Looking to his right, William sought the comfort of the camp, perhaps that would give him strength to meet the woman. For a moment he considered forsaking his own rules, but he knew he couldn't. He had made up his mind and couldn't turn back now. His back foot moved forward hesitantly, almost dragging on the dirt, and stopped when it passed his other foot. Moving more quickly, William took another step and then another, and before he knew it he was actually walking toward the woman, hesitantly, as if she might run away in fright, but walking.

As William neared the woman, he began to feel more comfortable and the nervousness from a few moments earlier was starting to lose its hold on him as a peaceful bliss filled his mind.

"Beautiful, isn't it?" William asked as he neared the woman, his words sounding to his ears, like they came from someone else. She turned toward him, a slight smile appearing on her face. Was she happy to have company?

"Yes, it is," she replied, her voice soft and accented, and turned back to the horizon. He stopped walking a safe distance from her and faced the horizon. The fear of not knowing what to say next crept back into his stomach. "You are a foreigner?" the woman asked curiously, a hint of doubt on her face since foreigners, were a rare sight in the caravan.

"Yes," William replied, looking slightly worried, insecurity bringing a dead and uncertain smile to his face.

"Oh," she said, her eyes returning to the sight ahead.

"What's the matter?" William asked as he stepped closer to this intriguing creature of the desert.

"You know this caravan is going through the Sahara?" she asked, lifting her eyebrows and pointing to the ground at her feet, her fingers covered in small brass rings decorated with patterns of flowers and birds.

"I do," William replied, thinking he was about to receive yet another sermon on why the desert was no place for foreigners.

"Then you are a strange foreigner," she concluded with an unexpected giggle.

"You think I am strange?" William asked perplexed. The giggle in her voice was as infectious as malaria in the jungle—and it was his first time dealing with mosquitos.

"No. I think you are dumb," she said jokingly, her bright green eyes glancing up at him to see if he was offended.

"Stupid people can only count up to three," William said as if reminding her of a common fact.

"How high can you count?" she asked.

"Four," William said, proudly raising three fingers.

"I can teach you to count higher if you like," she said.

"You teach?"

"Yes. I teach the children in the evening," she said.

"What do you teach them?" William asked intrigued.

"Everything. How to read, write, draw, and count," she explained, a kind of happiness filling her words. "Telling them stories is my favorite thing," she added.

As she spoke, a different kind of feeling entered William. He didn't know quite what it was or what it meant, but he knew that whatever it was, it felt right. Like how living was supposed to feel.

"Are you going to Yemen?" William thought to ask.

"Sadly, no. I am visiting my grandfather who lives in a village near Yemen. He is getting old and my mother and I wanted to see him before he dies," she replied and quickly looked at the ground as if this was the first time she said this out loud. There was a short silence but she quickly brought the conversation back to life.

"And you? Why are you going to Yemen?" she asked, looking up from her feet where her eyes had wandered at the thought of why she was telling a stranger something she hadn't told anyone else.

"A newspaper in London sent me to take pictures of the desert and your people," William answered simply, not feeling as proud as he usually did when explaining why he was here.

"Ah. So, coming to the desert was not your own idea?" she concluded with a smile as if she had finally determined his character.

"No, but it was my choice, if that makes a difference," William replied.

Just as she was about to speak, another woman, dressed similarly but slightly older, emerged out of the tents, a worried look on her face. His companion noticed William looking over her shoulder and quickly turned around to see what had captured his attention.

"She is my mother and is looking for me. I have to go now. It was good to meet you," Without giving William a chance to speak, she said, "Goodbye" and ran over to her mother, her dress ruffled by the growing wind.

As William watched her leave, he felt like he was being shaken from a beautiful dream, the covers being pulled out of his slumber-weary hands and a pitcher of cold water getting poured on his face. When the two women met, he thought he heard them arguing. She's probably getting scolded for not returning to her tent after sunset, William thought. Would she be punished for talking with a man, a foreign man?

William watched the women argue, then noticed the younger woman's shoulders slump in defeat. Suddenly, her mother grabbed her by the wrist and started pulling her back toward the tents. Then, as if realizing her daughter is old enough to walk unassisted, the older woman let go and disappeared behind the tents. Just then, William remembered something important.

"What's your name?" he yelled, hoping that the wind wouldn't steal his voice before she was out of site. The woman stopped walking and turned in his direction.

"Nadia," a voice made faint by both the distance and the wind reached him. With a sudden tug, she disappeared behind the closest tent.

William smiled and turned toward the sky behind him. It was almost completely dark with small traces of soft green light remaining just at the stretch of the horizon.

Suddenly, his mind was taken away from Nadia when something caught his eye, something that would have been impossible for him to see earlier, now revealed by the darkness. Far in the distance, a light as small as the tip of needle flickered yellow in the hills below the horizon. At first, William thought it was a brightly shining star, but as he looked on, he realized it came from a campfire, contained and probably small enough to warm only one person.

Something felt strange about this fire. It flickered in a sinister way, as if it belonged to an evil sorcerer standing hunched over a cauldron while stirring a bubbling green stew. William didn't believe in the supernatural, but the fire was convincing enough to make him think of the stories he had heard as a child that frightened him from wandering the woods at night.

William shook his head. That fire must belong to a lone traveler who unknowingly camped near the caravan for the night. He quickly turned back toward the camp, his head still facing the open horizon where the fire flickered.

After a final glance, William tucked his hands inside the pockets of his trousers to keep them warm from the desert cold while he made the long journey across the camp to his tent. With each step he took, the unusual campfire was replaced with thoughts of his conversation with Nadia and the forest green color of her eyes.

When he walked inside his tent, William laid down on the ground since the day had been long and eventful. He rested his head on his suitcase, even though it wasn't exactly soft. The wind outside made the tent creak softly like a cradle being rocked, gently soothing him to sleep.


When William woke up the next morning, he stepped outside of his tent to stretch his body from spending yet another night on the cold ground with only a blanket for warmth. A wide yawn stretched his mouth, and William thought it was going to break his jaw while summoning a conversation with the nearest camel. It took him a moment to realize that he had overslept.

The sky was much brighter than it normally was for the tents to still be standing and the empty paths were a disturbing sign. William didn't remember hearing the horn, which was also odd, and he began to wonder what was going on. He saw movement far down the path and started walking in that direction. As he neared, he realized that a small crowd had gathered at an intersection, most of it concealed by the side of a tent.

William quickened his pace toward the crowd hoping to see what had kept the caravan from leaving. From up close the crowd appeared much larger and probably included every person in the caravan. Men, women, children, and soldiers were all mixed together, gathering around something in the center, where the loudest voices came from.

When he entered the crowd, a few people walked away from the center with theirs hands covering their mouths like they had seen the mangled victim of a gruesome murder. The terror in their eyes made William consider it a possibility. As he moved through the crowd, peeking over people's shoulders to get a better look, William made out the figures of four men among the jostling heads of the crowd standing in a circle at the very center.

A man William had never seen before was crouched at the side of a figure that lay deathly still on the ground, while two others stood right behind him, waiting. William stepped near the front of the crowd and recognized Hakeem along with one of his personal guards. The crouched man perhaps served as a physician, seeing how he was examining the dead man before him.

Two diagonal slashes were cut into the man's body, exposing his mangled chest for all to see. The cuts looked as if they had been made by a curved sword and with expert precision. It didn't take William long to realize that the man belonged to the group of Bedouin warriors who had helped capture the criminal.

The physician slowly rose to his feet, his eyes still fixed on the dead man before him. Then he turned to Hakeem and shook his head. Murmurs spread through the crowd like the ripple in the center of a pond. Hakeem's expression was a mixture of disbelief, disgust, worry, and determination as he walked over to the dead warrior and looked down at him.

The murmurs began to quiet as people waited to hear what Hakeem would say about the present situation. He waved a hand, and a couple of his men walked through the crowd toward him. One of them grabbed the dead tribesman by his legs and the other from under his arms. They picked him up and carried him out of the crowd, the eyes of the people following the silent procession.

Once the body was taken away, Hakeem looked into the faces of the crowd around him, turning slowly in a circle to encompass everyone.

"This man was a warrior of the Bedouin who came to us asking for our help, and today we find that he wandered into our camp and died in an ambush." Hakeem paused to let his words sink into the minds of the people. Although Hakeem spoke in Arabic, William was able to understand a good portion of what he said.

"Was this the doing of another tribe?" a man asked deep within the crowd, his voice loud but carrying no tone.

"If this was the work of another tribe, then the caravan will be caught in the middle of a blood war." Hakeem's words sent the crowd into an uproar of shock that deafened the unprepared ear. The people quarreled and Hakeem stood silently, his hands behind his back and a look of ease on his face as he waited for everyone to calm.

Seeing that the voices wouldn't settle without intervention, Hakeem raised a hand. The crowd became silent. "The caravan is going to stay here for the day, while my men and I ride in search of any survivors of the ambush. Anyone who wants to come with us is welcome."

When Hakeem finished, he and his guards began walking out of the crowd so that anyone who wanted to ride with them could talk to him. William pushed his way through the murmuring crowd and followed behind them. Once the crowd began to disperse, William moved quickly toward Hakeem, who was already surrounded by a group of men eager to join the party.

"Do you want to come with us?" Hakeem asked when he saw William's face among the other men following him.

"Yes, but I don't have a horse or a camel," he replied, fearing he would have to stay while they went into the desert.

"I will have one ready for you," Hakeem said briefly before turning to the eager men around him and answering their questions as the group started walking to his tent. Everyone seemed in an awful hurry and William struggled to keep up with them.

"What time do we leave?" William finally managed to ask so that he would know how much time he had to prepare.

"We will meet in one hour where the warrior was found. The sooner we get out into the desert the better. The Sheik's life may depend on it. The lives of our people depend on it," Hakeem said as the group walked down the path.

"I will see you then," William said as he branched away and continued down a path that would lead him to his tent. He passed the place where an hour later he would meet Hakeem. Most of the people had dispersed around the camp in small groups talking quietly with each other.

When William reached his tent, he grabbed his suitcase and opened it. He searched to see if there was anything that he might need to take with him. He decided to take his camera so that he could capture the perfect picture of the desert. He snatched his camera and a small loaf of bread he had purchased the day before, stepped outside his tent, and walked toward the meeting place. Once there, he stood in the shade created by the tip of a tall tent and waited for Hakeem and the others.

Thoughts of the desert flooded his mind until he saw someone moving toward him. Hakeem and eight of his men were walking in his direction. Behind them were seven others who had decided to join them in the search. Hakeem's men brought along rifles. Some had muskets, but most carried the standard British army rifle that was often distributed among the uniting Arab tribes that aided the British in fighting the Turks. They were very accurate and durable rifles; durable being the feature most respected by the Arabs.

Crossing each man's chest were ammunition belts that overlapped at the center of the chest and held several clips each in small pouches, providing each man with his own supply of ammunition. The men looked as if they were massing to fight the Turks for a second time, as some among them had actually done. They were an intimidating force, their quick pace making them appear even more ferocious and determined.

William began walking over to Hakeem, who led the group to the center of the open area. When Hakeem saw William, he called something out and motioned to one of his men. A moment later the man came from the rear of the group leading a black horse behind him, and handed the horse's reins to Hakeem before walking back to the group to prepare to leave.

"Here, this is your horse," Hakeem said, passing the reins over to William. "Do you have everything you need?" he asked before William could thank him.

"Yes," William replied as the horse stepped closer to him.

"Good. We will leave soon," Hakeem explained. He turned to the group of men standing among their horses and camels and spoke loudly as he called for their attention. "The group who ambushed the Sheik might still be somewhere in the desert waiting to ambush any others who would go looking for him. If we do not keep our eyes open and our ears listening, we will be food for the vultures." Hakeem pointed to both of his eyes and to his ears to make his message perfectly clear. The men's faces sobered and their backs straightened. Hakeem surveyed their eyes. They looked cold and ready to begin the journey. He nodded in respect, then turned around and climbed onto the saddle of a camel that sat a few feet behind him.

Once the group mounted their horses and camels, they followed Hakeem to the edge of the caravan. As William rode he felt a rush of excitement fill his chest and a slight smile appeared on his face, despite the danger they were accepting. The people who saw them leaving the camp cheered for them as they rode past, hoping for a safe, quick return with the Sheik along with them, alive and well.

# 8

WILLIAM WATCHED AS ONE OF THE RIDERS walked away from him and the others. The soft crunching of the sand beneath his feet only strengthened the silence and the men's curiosity. He stopped and knelt. On the ground, a man lay on his chest, his eyes staring blankly at the sand near his left shoulder. Dust covered his robe and a circle of blood wet the center of his back. Slowly, the rider's eyes followed the trail of blood to the tribesman's back. An arrow lodged deep into the man's back pointed to the sky.

"Short bow, powerful strings," the rider observed. "Perfect for shooting from horseback."

He brushed the fletching of the arrow, the black and glossy feathers of a crow, with his fingers. His dark face bore a curious yet slightly disgusted frown that tugged at his upper lip. The rider put one hand on the dead man's back and with the other he gripped the shaft of the arrow. He gave a strong tug and pulled the barbed tip of the arrow out of the dead man's back. The rider gave a sigh of dismay and rose to his feet with the arrow in his hands. He gave the Bedouin's body a last look and started walking back to the group waiting a little distance away, silent and curious. William watched as the man arrived at the side of Hakeem's camel and handed the arrow up to him.

"He died running less than an hour ago, I am sure of it," the tracker stated as Hakeem took the arrow with the same frown of disgust. Hakeem inspected the arrow by spinning it slowly in his hands.

Some of the animals shifted on their feet from the heat in the dusty white sky. The land was flat and barren like the fields of Carthage sown with salt. They were near the edge of the Sahara, the cause of silence in the group. William could feel the difference in temperature from just a half a day's travel, and the slight rise in the heat resurrected an uncomfortable question in his mind. If this was just the border of the desert, how would he survive the unbearable heat of the Sahara? Every bead of sweat that dripped down his cheek he wiped away, disgusted by his own weakness. He gave half of his attention to Hakeem as he glanced around them, searching for a dune in the distance even though he knew it wouldn't be that easy.

"From the markings on this arrow, do you know which tribe it belongs to?" Hakeem asked.

"It does not belong to any tribe I know. Most likely a band of thieves, but I am not sure," the tracker replied, hoping to calm the men's worries about impending war. Hakeem looked away from the arrow and stared at the flat stretch of land to his right in disappointment. "I do not know who killed this man, but I do know one thing," the rider continued. Hakeem looked at him with eyes held hostage by the possibility of an answer. "Whoever shot this arrow was an excellent archer and horseman, because the arrow pierced the heart. My father was a doctor in Tangier," the rider said.

"You grew up in the city?" Hakeem asked with disdain.

"Like I said, I do not know what tribe that arrow belongs to," the rider said quietly while lowering his head in sudden embarrassment.

Hakeem looked over his shoulder at the group behind him, his eyes asking if anyone recognized the arrow. A few men shook their heads and the rest stayed quiet. He turned around and looked at the arrow's black fletching. He stroked the feathers with his fingers and watched them pop back in place, his eyes blank as he searched in the recesses of his mind for a tribe known to use crow's feathers.

The tracker looked up at the sun with squinted eyes. The big ball of light was going to be setting in just about six hours' time, barely enough time to make it back to the caravan before dark. The man lowered his eyes to look at Hakeem, whose mind, as the stillness in his body suggested, was burning up shovels of coal with a hungry appetite.

"It will be dark soon and if we don't go back, the people will start to wonder what is keeping us. What shall we do?" the tracker asked. Hakeem looked at him, annoyed by the interruption. But the question was relevant and he carefully considered his response.

"Ride back to the caravan and tell the people that we are going to search for the Sheik or any other survivors until they are found, dead or alive," he said, a new determination in his voice.

There was a slight chill in the bellies of the men, because most had brought only enough food for two days—if they rationed it—and would need more sustenance to travel farther away from the caravan. The faces of the men remained calm at the change in plan, and none protested outwardly, though some tension remained. Hakeem turned around in his cross-legged position on the camel's back and faced the riders.

"He who wishes to ride back to the caravan with this man is free to go and will not be judged, but if you decide to leave it will be as if you did not come at all." The choices were posed. Any man who had fear in his heart or was too exhausted from riding in the heat could return to the comfort of the caravan, but he would receive no honor should the Sheik be found.

A few riders, all men from the caravan, looked about to see how the group would be divided, trying to decide which party to join. William saw several men dismount and lead their camels and horses over to Hakeem's camel. No words were exchanged as those with too weak a stomach to continue the search left them for the shade of their tents and the cold water of the well. William counted the men who were going back: eight men had chosen to leave. Every man in the remaining group had seen the Sahara and their eyes bore the tested squint of true heat, all except William.

Despite his rising doubts, he felt reassured by the thought that he was in the good hands of desert men and as long as he didn't do anything foolish, he knew he would be all right. When the men who were leaving had gathered, Hakeem gave them permission to leave and they did. William and the rest of the men watched the riders disappear in the cloud of dust they stirred, When they were gone, Hakeem motioned for the men to gather around. They obeyed quietly, willing to endure whatever lay ahead.

"Now that there are fewer of us we need to change the way we search," Hakeem said as he turned his camel around to face the group. "Look at us," he urged, trying to make a point. William took a quick glance at the riders on either side of him and, other than being reminded of how few their numbers were, he couldn't see what Hakeem was trying to show them. The others looked back to Hakeem with clueless eyes.

"We are all bunched together," he explained. "We need to spread out and cover more ground. Half of you will ride west as far as you can without losing sight of the rider next to you," Hakeem said, pointing to the left. "The rest of you I want to ride east. If you find something, alert us with one shot from your rifle and we will ride to you. If you find anyone, alive or dead, fire two shots instead of one. Now go." Hakeem's voice came out as a loud shout as he finished and urged his camel forward.


Once more the group was split in half, each party riding in its assigned direction. William rode to Hakeem's left. He could feel himself shrinking quickly in the emptiness that entered the air. After riding west for around five minutes, he brought his horse to a stop, becoming the rider farthest on the left wing. He looked to his right to make sure he hadn't lost sight of the man linking him to the rest of the company and spent the next couple of seconds searching until he spotted the man and his camel looking like a dark speck standing on the edge of a tan earth and dusty sky.

Almost perfect for a picture. He resisted taking out his camera, because he had promised himself that his next picture would be of the dunes and he would not break that promise. William pointed his horse in the direction they were riding before the group separated and waited for the man to his right to start moving.

Even though Hakeem and the others were not far away from him, fear pulsed in William's stomach every time he thought of losing sight of the rider. He looked down at the rifle on his saddle and hoped he wouldn't have to use it, especially on a person. To calm his fear of getting lost, William thought about the caravan, a thought that always had a calming effect on his mind. He imagined its colorful tents and happy people walking in its maze of paths.

Nadia floated to his mind along with the memories of talking with her. He thought it strange that she hadn't mentioned his rescue of the Sheik and oddly enough this elevated her in his mind to a higher status. She didn't dress like the other caravan women and she didn't think like them either. The more he thought about her, the more he wanted to see her again when they returned.

Even though various thoughts chased around his mind, William kept his eyes on the rider to his right, and when the man began to crawl forward, William started out as well, slowly and alone. As William rode on, he couldn't stop paying attention to the almost overwhelming silence, something he hadn't experienced in England. The longer he rode in silence, the more he realized that his whole journey had been a constant symphony of unfamiliar noises. This deep silence seemed strange and almost ominous to him. Not even the breeze sang its whistling tune. Only the horse's hooves sinking into the sand as one fell after the other and the booming of distant winds made him sure he hadn't gone deaf. He kept his eyes open for anything that might stand out, but the desert remained as plain as it had been.

Every few minutes he looked right to make sure that he wasn't wandering away from the rider on the wavy horizon.

The silence stretched on, deeper than he had ever experienced, but after a while he became comfortable with it and, to his surprise, seemed to like it a little. The silence had a strange quality too; it made every sound that revealed itself sharper and more distinct. Up until that point in the search, there had been no sign of anyone else, dead or alive. And the silence produced a new feel in the air, one belonging to the mysterious or even the supernatural. Having no trail of the Sheik or his attackers made William think of ghosts wandering the desert—a strange thought encouraged by the silence and heat of the desert.

His train of thought was broken when he heard a soft crack in the distance to his right. William stopped his horse so he could listen better. He looked up and saw that the rider was gone. He had vanished from the dusty horizon and into the mirage behind it. William's heart thumped in his chest as he sat still, his eyes wide and tense. A bead of sweat trickled down the side of his head and off his chin.

When his stare failed to pull the rider out of the heatwaves, William spun his horse around to look, thinking he had ridden in the wrong direction. He changed his direction once more, thinking he would find the man, but he wasn't there, either.

The land was so featureless he couldn't remember which way he had been riding, and after completing the scan of the horizon he had lost any sense of direction he may have had. The feeling of peace he sought in the silence quickly became a nightmare he couldn't escape. William stopped searching and stared in the direction where he thought the rider was most likely to be. When he was sure he was on the right track, the silence offered him a miracle. Another soft crack sounded from behind him.

He turned his horse around and began riding quickly in the direction the noise came from. As he rode, a breeze swept over the desert and thundered in his ears, deafening him for a moment. William kept his eyes focused on the land he was approaching, searching for any sign of Hakeem and his men. He continued to ride, but still there was not a single track in the sand for him to follow. The group had become as elusive as the Sheik.

It was beginning to dawn on him that he was lost when William caught a glimpse of something far ahead. He squinted. What he saw confused him, though it filled him with a little hope. Two vertical shapes separated by a blurry mirage on the horizon revealed themselves to him, the bottom dot looking like a reflection. He changed his direction and rode toward the specks which slowly united and formed the wavering figure of a man and his camel. As William rode closer, he noticed that the rider was looking at something black at his feet.

When he got within a stone's throw from the man, William dismounted. He stopped in his tracks when he noticed a dead man sprawled on the ground at the rider's feet, an arrow lodged in his back pointing at the sky. William grabbed the reins of his horse and walked toward Hakeem's man.

The rider's bearded face looked like it had been frozen permanently in a painful squint that wrinkled his nose and pulled at the corners of his fat lips. William stopped walking when the rider knelt at the tribesman's side and swiftly plucked out the arrow. The rider glanced at William with a hollow look in his eyes, then looked over his shoulder.

William followed his gaze and saw Hakeem and the rest of the men riding toward them, still a good distance away. He looked back at the rider when he saw him sling his rifle over his shoulder and pull the tribesman on his side. For a moment, the man bent over the tribesman and stared into the man's face, tilting his head a little to one side to look right at him as if searching for something in his dead gaze. Then he examined the man's clothes and reached for a dagger held in a pearl colored sheath at the man's waist.

"Don't!" William yelled, knowing that the rider was going to take the dagger as plunder. The rider's hand stopped. He looked at William with a square grin that pulled the top of his curly beard just below his eyes, gave a disdainful sniff, and took the dagger anyway. The man stood and tucked the dagger into his belt as he walked back to his camel. William thought that what the man did was wrong, a breaking of the code that any man who respects the dead has. He wanted to call him out as a thief when Hakeem arrived, but he didn't want to slow down the search for the Sheik just because of a petty theft of something that didn't belong to him.

His thoughts of justice were interrupted when Hakeem and the others joined them around the dead man. The rider who took the dagger glanced at William with a smile on his face before walking closer to Hakeem to share what he'd found. William watched as the man handed the arrow up to Hakeem, who was eager to listen to what he had to say. As the rider recounted what he'd found Hakeem brought the arrow up to his eyes and spun it back and forth with the tips of his fingers as he had done with the first arrow, carefully digesting the new information.

When the rider finished giving his report, Hakeem placed the arrow in a bag at the camel's side where he had probably put the first arrow. William started walking toward the riders, his horse following behind him, feeling frustrated he couldn't do anything about the theft of the dagger. To keep his sanity, he decided let go of, but not forget, what he had seen.

"What do we do now?" the rider asked Hakeem.

"We will camp here for the night," Hakeem said, and tapped his camel on the shoulder so it would kneel.

"Here?" the rider asked, glancing at the dead man behind him while the rest of the riders dismounted.

"He's dead, Fudail, there is no need to worry," Hakeem replied in a calming voice that aroused a slight round of chuckles from the other men, and slid off the camel's side onto the ground.

Seeing that there was work to be done, everyone began setting up camp for the night as best they could with what they had brought. Four of the men were assigned to burying the tribesman while the other four, including William, were assigned to making fires and rounding up the camels and horses for the night. When night fell and all the tasks were completed, there were three small fires crackling beneath the stars. Some of the men had begun cooking a late dinner over the fire, since they hadn't eaten during their day's search, and kept each other awake by talking in soft voices. The light from the fire threw shadows on their faces, making their dark figures look ghostly and frightening.

William sat alone by the side of a fire, surviving off a sparse pile of twigs placed in a small pit he had dug with his hands. Because the fire offered little heat, William sat with his arms hugging his legs close to his chest to keep himself from shivering. He stared at a small mound of sand just outside the reach of his fire's light. He kept himself entertained with the thought that several feet beneath the mound lay a man who had been just as capable of breathing and feeling as him.

He looked across the small camp at the other riders. They were talking normally as they ate the meal they cooked for themselves, the cold appearing not to have an effect on them. The flames of their fire flickered above the ground whereas William's had the warmth of a matchstick, but it was his and that was all that mattered to him. In his mind, the cold was nearly as unbearable as the heat, and he knew he had a long way to go before he became as accustomed to both as the other men. The idea of moving to the warmer fires tempted him a little, but he convinced himself to stay where he was and hugged his legs a little closer to his chest.

After having eaten, the men did not have to be told to go to sleep. In a moment's time, the camp came alive with a wide variety of snores that differed in tone and tempo as much as the instruments of the festival in Nador. All but one of the riders contributed to snores that spooked the animals lying around them in a protective circle.

William sat awake by his fire, staring into its modest flames. The excuse of staying up to get better at withstanding the cold was keeping him awake, and he knew that he would pay the price in drowsiness the next day. He stared blankly at the flames, remembering that day in London when the rain had poured down like a flood while he was walking back to his small apartment, unaware that he had probably made the best decision in his life.

He thought about how quickly his life had changed from the blandness of England to the excitement he experienced now. He looked up at the stars. They were scattered in the cold sky, no lights from the city stopping them from shining as they were meant to. He watched them for a long time while the group snored all around him until he heard soft footsteps behind him. William looked over his shoulder and saw Hakeem stepping into the fire's light, a small loaf of bread in one hand and a sheepskin of water in the other.

"Looks like I am not the only one who can't sleep," Hakeem observed with a sigh as he sat down next to William and crossed his legs, obviously coming to talk rather than for the warmth of William's fire. Hakeem rubbed his hands together before holding out his palms to the smoldering twigs to warm them. As he studied the man, William realized that the suspicion he had about him was true. Hakeem was different from most men with power.

He didn't use his position as a way to separate or elevate himself above his men but instead used it to become closer to those who followed him, to earn their respect instead of demanding it. William saw Hakeem as the kind of leader who, if he were a general, would walk through the camp of his army to congratulate the men after a hard day of fighting and thank the wounded for their suffering.

Hakeem took the loaf of bread that was resting on his knee, tore off a small piece, and extended it to William. William smiled, slightly surprised by Hakeem's generosity, and took the piece with gratitude. He ate it happily since he had finished his bread much earlier than he expected. Hakeem tore another piece for himself and ate it.

"Do you think there are any survivors?" William asked as he put a fluffy piece of bread in his mouth. Hakeem's shadowy face turned to him then back to the fire.

"It is possible, but the way things are going, I do not think we will find any," Hakeem said before bringing the sheepskin to his mouth and drinking, then he held it out to William. William smiled and shook his head. Hakeem shrugged and set the sheepskin down at his knee.

"If the Sheik was killed by another tribe, will there really be a war?" William asked.

"Yes," Hakeem replied, keeping his eyes on the fire with a solemn focus.

"What will we do then?"

"We will pray," Hakeem said in a soft voice that showed he knew if war did erupt it would take more than just words to save them.

Despite the anxiety caused by talk of war, William felt the soft light from the fire soothing his eyes into a drowsiness he knew would soon make him join the chorus of snoring riders. Just as he was about to close his eyes, Hakeem rose to his feet and walked back to his blanket, taking the mangled loaf of bread and the sheepskin with him.

William lay on his back and exhaled slowly, wishing he had thought to take his blanket. He struggled to keep his eyes open as he looked at the stars, the thought of war being the only thread keeping him from plummeting into the dark abyss of sleep. He could see the wind pulling thin sheets of sand across the sky, obscuring the stars only for a minute before unveiling them again. With the image of the caravan in his mind, the last thread of William's consciousness made a gentle tick as it snapped, and he began floating silently through the air beneath him as he entered the strange land of dreams.

# 9

WILLIAM TURNED TO HIS RIGHT AND STARED at a barren stretch of land. He could see the side of a man and a legless horse in a distant mirage. He looked ahead and continued scanning the desert as he had been for the last couple of hours, which seemed to pass quickly because of the silence and his own random thoughts. The land around him bore hundreds of hills that resembled small dunes, and he supposed they must be just another day's ride from the real desert. A faint crack from a rifle sounded to William's right. He turned his head toward the noise as he brought his horse to a stop. He listened intently, hoping his tired mind was not playing with him. To his momentary relief, a second shot echoed into the silence, coming from the same direction.

He urged his horse toward the rider he had spotted moments ago, his mind already picturing an arrow in a man's back. As he rode over the top of a hill, he stopped his horse and looked down at the pan-shaped valley below. There, Hakeem and the rest of the riders gathered in a circle around the bodies of two dead men that lay close to one of three small campfires at the center of the valley. Forming a triangle around Hakeem and the other riders were three tents. Their blue cloth looked faded from a layer of dust that coated it and the center posts pointed crookedly at the sky. Around the camp, several more men lay scattered on the ground in a way that made it impossible to tell who had died first.

William rode down into the camp, and the stench of decay washed over him like an invisible wave of curling fumes. When he reached the rest of his group, William dismounted. He had come too late to hear Hakeem's orders, but after a quick glance at the men scattering around the camp, he decided to do the same and see what he could find. He walked closer to the fire pit where the two dead men lay, his steps growing slower as he neared because of the smell of rotting flesh. He took a quick glance at the dispersing men and saw them spread around the camp to search the area on their own to see if one of the dozen or so bodies was the Sheik or the previous owner of a valuable souvenir.

William felt his camera case tapping gently on his thigh with each move of his legs and thought that his days of taking pictures of men strewn dead and tangled in lattice works in the muck weren't as far behind as he'd wished.

He stopped at the edge of the fire pit and looked down at the two tribesmen across from him. A breeze fluttered their dusty robes like the feathers of a dead bird. One of them lay on his back with his rifle clutched over his head. William's gaze moved on to the man's eyes, frozen in their twisted expression of fear. In between his eyes protruded the back end of an arrow whose black fletching fluttered in the gentle breeze.

William looked at the other tribesman, this one on his side, with his head bent toward his chest and his arms grasping his stomach, gnarled like the fingers of a pianist trying to reach a difficult chord. The sand underneath was stained reddish brown. William wondered what these two would tell him about their attackers, if only they could speak. This thought was interrupted when footsteps crunched the sand behind him. He looked over his shoulder and saw Hakeem walking towards him with his camel following behind. William turned back toward the tribesmen and Hakeem stopped when he stood alongside him.

"The Bedouin warriors are known for their skill with a rifle," Hakeem stated as he looked at the dead tribesman who held his weapon above his head. "And yet there is not a single bullet shell on the ground. They must have been ambushed during the night," he added after a pause, a mixed frown of curiosity and disgust on his face.

"Is the Sheik here?" William asked, looking up at his fellow riders wandering the camp, then back at Hakeem.

"We have not found him yet, but alive or dead, he can't be far from here," Hakeem replied, a sigh of frustration filling his voice as he looked up at the ridge of a dune.

"Hey," a rider shouted behind them. William and Hakeem looked at a tent at the edge of the camp where the shout had come from. Suddenly, the criminal who had been hiding among the caravan burst out of the tent, screaming as if his hair had been lit on fire while he ran for one of the surrounding hills.

William, Hakeem, and the other men scattered around the camp watched the criminal run, dazed by what they were seeing. One of Hakeem's guards burst out of the same tent and chased after him. Another one joined the chase, his yell waking the others from their momentary stupor. Hakeem darted from William's side to help capture the criminal. Everyone had assembled around the man, except William, who watched from afar.

When the men surrounded the criminal, they tried to catch him, but he jumped between their legs and wiggled his way out of their grip like a slippery serpent slithering for its life. When, at last, the men tackled the criminal and piled on top of him, William realized he should be there helping them. As he reached them at the edge of the camp, he stopped at Hakeem's right side and looked down at the struggling criminal, whose head was the only part of him not buried underneath the bodies of the riders.

"Get off of him," Hakeem ordered when the criminal's face started turning dangerously red. The men did so, leaving the criminal to stagger to his knees, out of breath. And still he wouldn't yield. With a burst of speed, he reached for the sword handle sticking out of a guard's belt, but a heartbeat later, Hakeem's blade was already at the man's throat.

The criminal grimaced because the sword had cut him even though it was pressed softly to his neck, and slowly brought his hand back to his side. William noticed something different in the criminal's eyes. They did not burn with the same hatred he'd seen outside the caravan camp. Instead they quivered in fear like a child about to be beaten for a second time. The guards drew their swords and held them at their sides to deter the criminal from making another attempt to escape. He bowed his head in submission and Hakeem lowered his sword.

"Who attacked you?" Hakeem asked.

"If I go back, my family is going to die for what I've done," the criminal said, his face grimacing as he fought back tears. When he spoke, William thought that his voice sounded like a man who had once been kind.

"Who attacked you?" Hakeem repeated, forcing himself to ignore the criminal's grief and the possible truth in his words.

"I don't know," the man replied, shaking his head as if he had been forced to eat something unpleasant and was being offered another spoonful. Hakeem stepped forward and kneeled close, not to comfort him, but to get a better look at his face.

"What did they look like? Who were they?" he asked quietly, but no less intense.

The criminal stared at the ground near his knees where his tears began to fall. The only thing leaving his mouth was his shaky breath. Hakeem looked up at a guard standing to his right and nodded. The rider took a step forward and kicked the criminal in the face. He yelled out as he was knocked on his back. Hakeem stood up and walked to the left of the man, who writhed on the ground with both hands covering his bloody nose.

"Who were they?" Hakeem asked, his voice sterner than before. The criminal continued grunting as his body twisted in pain. Hakeem placed his foot on the criminal's chest and pressed down to keep him still. The man curled toward his stomach and let his head fall back against the sand in pain. Hakeem placed the blade of his sword against his throat and began applying pressure. The criminal grimaced again and turned his head away from Hakeem.

"Stop," the criminal gasped in a voice muffled by the hands he held over his nose. Hakeem took the blade away but didn't lift his foot from the man's chest.

"Tell me who attacked you," Hakeem demanded in a calm voice.

"Demons," the criminal gasped as he turned his face back toward Hakeem, blood seeping through spaces between his fingers pressed over his broken nose.

"Demons?" Hakeem said in disbelief.

"Warriors from hell. Invisible in the dark. All I could hear were the screams as they killed everyone. The screams," the criminal said, his eyes darting from face to face of the men standing over him.

"How did you survive?" Hakeem asked, his voice full of doubt.

"I hid under a blanket in the tent," the criminal explained, glancing briefly toward the tent he had run out of.

"Where is the Sheik?" Hakeem demanded, pressing strong on the man's chest.

"I did not see him. I do not know where he is," he said, choking on his own breath.

"Did you kill him?" Hakeem asked, wondering if the criminal took his revenge on the Sheik during the chaos of the attack.

He didn't get an answer. The sudden neighing of horse came from the other side of the dune they faced. Hakeem looked up and everyone followed his gaze. The dusty silence that followed sent a sinking feeling in the stomachs of every man there.

"Get to the horses," Hakeem shouted as he turned around and started running back toward the horses, where most of the men had left their rifles.

William darted for the horse he'd left across the camp. The criminal, abandoned by the dispersing riders, scrambled to his feet and ran over to the tent he'd used for shelter. Before William reached his horse, the others had already grabbed their rifles and scattered around the camp, some using the tents for cover while others kneeled or lay on their stomachs in the open because there was nothing to hide behind.

When William reached his horse, he kneeled near its belly and left his rifle hanging in its case at the horse's shoulder. He wasn't going to kill anyone, even if it was in self-defense.

When the last pair of footsteps faded, the camp became dead silent once again. William looked underneath his horse's belly searching for Hakeem. He found him crouched with several other riders near the three fires at the center of the camp. Above his right shoulder he held a British army pistol ready to be lowered and fired.

"Who are you?" a voice echoed behind one of the hills surrounding the camp. The voice was faint and pronounced every word slowly. It was an Arab voice but spoke English almost better than Hakeem. Hakeem remained silent. William looked up at the surrounding dunes but saw no one. "Explain yourselves or be shot," the voice echoed.

Hakeem saw no arrows aiming at him and yelled back, "You first."

His men aimed their rifles at the surrounding ridges. A shot shattered the silence followed by a cry of pain. William looked around to see who had been wounded. One of their men who was standing near a tent dropped his weapon and collapsed, pressing a hand against his right arm. It was the man Hakeem called Fudail. William's horse began shifting on its legs and making unsettled grunts with the onset of panic, as did the other horses and camels gathered at the center of the camp.

William glanced at the dunes that surrounded them. They were barren like before, with nothing behind them but the dusty blue sky. He looked back at Fudail, who was sitting with his head bowed, rocking back and forth in excruciating pain. William took one last glance at the ridges of the dunes. When he saw no one there, he jumped out from under his horse and darted across the camp to where Fudail sat.

Hakeem turned to look behind him when he heard footsteps and watched with dread as William ran. Fudail, who was pushing himself with his legs closer to the tent, motioned for William to go back to his horse. William ignored the signal and continued running, since going back now would be too risky. When he reached Fudail, William picked up the rifle he had dropped. He instinctively pulled the bolt back and pushed it forward, sliding a round into the chamber. After loading the rifle, he slung it over his right shoulder and crouched closer to Fudail to get a better look at his wound.

A stream of blood was running down the man's right arm and dripping off his pinky like water from a sink faucet. William motioned for Fudail to take his hand away so he could see if the bullet had passed all the way through or would need to be pulled out later. The man obeyed and William ripped away the fabric that covered his shoulder. Fudail hissed in pain.

"I'm sorry," William said and continued tearing away the cloth a little more carefully. He looked at the back of the arm and saw an exit wound.

"You'll be fine," William said as he leaned back on his heels. Fudail nodded in relief, bowing his head. William looked over his shoulder. Hakeem and the others who were still kneeling at the center of the camp.

The distant voice broke the silence again, "Explain yourself. We will not miss."

The criminal chose that moment to burst out of the tent and run as fast as he could toward the dunes, his panicked footsteps and shaky breaths filling the almost heavy silence. A second shot cracked from the ridge and the criminal fell to the ground and rolled onto his back. The top of his skull was missing and his brains spilled out onto the sand. Several men looked at Hakeem with eyes that urged him to be more careful.

Hakeem realized he had no choice but to obey the invisible voice, otherwise he and his men could be lying dead like the criminal.

"My name is Hakeem. I am the leader of a caravan that is passing though this area," he yelled. The men around him flinched and the booming sound of his voice echoed into the distance.

"Why are you here?" the voice asked.

"We are looking for the Bedouin Sheik who came to us for help," Hakeem yelled again.

All remained silent. A moment later, the dunes encircling the camp rose in a wall of dark blue. William counted close to a hundred men, each carrying a rifle aimed at Hakeem's search party. Hakeem's men didn't bother taking aim and a few stood up, abandoning their cover. The two groups stared at each other, motionless. A man dressed in white emerged from the wall of rifles and began walking down the hill where Hakeem first heard the horse's neighing. The man's robe was spotless, and the way he walked made his arms seem like they were stiffly pinned to his sides. Hakeem stood and slowly tucked the barrel of his revolver under the belt around his stomach.

The rest of the riders stood as well. When the man entered the camp, he walked past two riders with a cheery spring in his step and continued straight for Hakeem. Hakeem started walking toward him, leaving the men who protected him behind.

"That is far enough," the man said when the distance between them reached about ten feet, and they both stopped.

The man in white had a gray beard descending from his wrapped head. Only his face and beard were exposed. His robe was the kind of white worn by saints and it hung on his shoulders like the cheeks of a starving man. He looked around at the bodies of the dead Bedouin. His attention seemed to be drifting away from the fact that there were a hundred men waiting for the order to lower their rifles trained on every man and beast in the camp.

"I have told you who I am. Now tell me who you are," Hakeem said in Arabic as the man's eyes perused the dead bodies around him with morbid curiosity. The man snapped his head back toward Hakeem like he had shouted at him.

"I am Prince Abdul, the son of the Bedouin Sheik," he replied in English, his voice sounding proud in its own soft volume. "I am here in search of my father," the man continued like he was dictating a letter. "If he is dead, as we have come to believe, we will bring him back to our tribe and bury him." Neither his face nor voice appeared saddened by the possibility of his father's death. This seemed peculiar to Hakeem. Abdul turned and looked at the fire pit near his feet then back at Hakeem.

"I believe it would be right to assume that you have yet to find my father or any others who are alive," the Prince said blandly. His choice of words seemed foreign to Hakeem. Had he grown up reading English books?

"The man you killed was the criminal your father was looking for. He was alive during the attack... we had been interrogating him," Hakeem said, nodding in the direction of the dead criminal.

"Oh," Abdul said, showing a kind of expected disappointment as he looked at the criminal's motionless body. Then his eyes began to drift to the other riders.

"Although... " Hakeem started in a hesitant voice and the Prince turned his attention back to Hakeem. "We have not been able to find your father but there is a good chance that he is not far, if he is still alive."

"Undoubtedly," the Prince replied and looked past Hakeem at the rest of the little search party. The man seemed rather disinterested by the Sheik's fate. Taking a deep breath, Hakeem frowned at Abdul, wanting to ask a relevant question.

The Prince, however, spoke first. "Has anything been found that could help us identify who attacked my father and his men?"

"We did find something. But I do not know if it will help," Hakeem replied. Abdul's gray eyebrows lowered into a frown, the first facial expression he had made. Hakeem turned to one of his men and asked him to bring forth his camel. The man nodded and went off to get the animal. Hakeem looked around at the rifles still aiming at him and his men. They weren't exactly a sign of full cooperation.

"I'm sorry, but my men are tired from travel and their nerves are... a little unsteady," Hakeem said while scanning the ridge with his eyes.

"Oh, how rude of me. I shall call them off," Prince Abdul said before raising a hand above his head and turning in a full circle to signal his men to lower their rifles. The warriors did as instructed and began walking down toward the camp. Abdul's eyes found William and Fudail, still crouching behind the tent.

"I am sorry about your man," he said turning to Hakeem, "but it was a precaution that had to be taken. I hope you understand."

Hakeem nodded just as the rider he sent to get his camel returned and reached into one of the bags to pull out one of the arrows.

"This is an arrow we found that killed one of your father's men," Hakeem said as he handed the arrow to Abdul. While the Prince's eyes were focused on the arrow, Hakeem observed his face carefully and noticed it turn sour with disgust. Hakeem dismissed his man, relaying a silent message to return the camel back to the other animals. As he left, the rider gave a short scowl at Abdul, who was too busy studying the arrow to notice.

"Do you know who this arrow belongs to?" Abdul asked at last.

"No," Hakeem replied, noticing the blue robes of the warriors entering the camp from behind Abdul's back.

"If only we knew which tribe made arrows with black fletching," Abdul said wistfully with his eyes still on the arrow.

"The criminal's family? What will happen to them?" Hakeem asked, remembering the dead man's words.

"They will be punished," Abdul said calmly. "It is the Bedouin law that if a man kills another, the murderer's family must pay the price also."

"The price is death?" Hakeem asked.

"It is the law," Abdul replied. His voice feigned displeasure as if some power from above was forcing his hand, but his eyes revealed something else, a joy almost, at the thought of carrying out the family's execution.

Hakeem looked away from Abdul, at the Bedouin warriors walking past him. As they entered the camp, his men looked uncertain whether to trust them or be on guard.


William and Fudail watched as the whole camp was overrun by the tribe's warriors. A few of their group started talking to the tribesmen, then handshakes and even a few hugs of relief were exchanged. Fudail watched one of Abdul's men separated from the rest and walked toward him with his rifle slung over his shoulder. As he reached them, he stopped and looked down at Fudail from behind a covered face.

Unexpectedly, the man bent down and extended his hand. Fudail seemed hesitant, but then he lifted his good hand and they shook. Behind the Bedouin's face covering, they saw his eyes squint in a smile. All was forgiven. Having cleared that misunderstanding, the warrior gave a nod of respect before walking back to his comrades and disappearing among them.

"Do you think he is the one who shot me?" Fudail asked with a sensitivity foreign to him.

"I don't know," William said, his eyes still staring at the spot in the crowd where the warrior had vanished. The two of them looked up to see Hakeem walking toward them.

"How is your wound?" Hakeem asked as he stopped at their feet.

"It hurts, but I am all right," Fudail replied, looking at the makeshift tourniquet William had managed to tie up around his wound.

"Can you still shoot your rifle?" Hakeem asked, sounding hopeful.

Fudail grunted, then took the rifle from William and placed the stock against his left shoulder. With his wounded arm he tried to bring the sights of the rifle up to his eye. Little by little the front sight rose from the ground. Fudail's face tightened the higher he lifted it but when the sight was halfway up to his eye, Fudail gave a grunt of pain when his arm suddenly gave out and the barrel plunged into the sand.

He looked up at Hakeem asking permission for a second chance. Hakeem nodded for him to try again if he wanted to. This time lifting the rifle was harder and the sights lifted several inches short of the first attempt before his arm gave out again and the rifle fell, proving he could not shoot it. Fudail tightened his face to lift the rifle for a third time.

"All right, that's enough," Hakeem said, stopping Fudail from making the wound worse.

"I am sorry." Fudail was looking at the ground.

"You should be proud. You received a wound in battle. A great honor," Hakeem said and Fudail looked up at Hakeem with a slight joy in his eyes.

"What do we do now?" William asked.

"We are going to continue searching," Hakeem replied.

"What about us?" Fudail asked, since Hakeem sounded like they weren't included.

"Do you know how to get back to the caravan from here?" Hakeem asked.

"I know the way," Fudail answered, not sounding excited about returning to the caravan just because of his wound.

"Good. You and William are going back to the caravan," Hakeem said. William wasn't particularly happy about the news either.

"Go back to the caravan? Why can't I stay here and continue the search?" Fudail protested. William looked up at Hakeem with hope.

"You need to take care of that arm. If it gets infected, it will have to be cut off. Also, the others need to know about our progress," Hakeem said, putting a swift end to Fudail's protest.

"How long will it take us to reach the caravan?" William asked Fudail, feeling nervous about the journey, since it would be just the two of them this time.

"The rest of the day," said the guard. "We should get going now so we reach the caravan before dark."

"Good thinking," Hakeem nodded.

"Hakeem! Hakeem!" Abdul's soft voice called from near the center of the camp. Hakeem gave a soft grunt under his breath and left William and Fudail to prepare for their journey back to the caravan.

As Hakeem walked away, William turned to Fudail and said with a sigh, "Well then, let's get going." He slapped his knees and rose to his feet, excited that he would spend the night in his tent. He left Fudail to get the horses that had remained on the other side of the camp.

He wondered whether they would be able to find the caravan on their own. What if they strayed off course and got lost in the desert? And William was the only one out of the two able to fire a rifle. He was not that good of a shot; he was good at aiming cameras, not rifles and would barely be able to defend them if they were attacked by thieves or worse, the men with the dark arrows.

When William emerged from the other side of the crowded camp, he saw his horse standing with its side facing him while it sniffed one of the tents. He took the reins, gathered Fudail's horse and began walking back to where he'd left the wounded man. Back at the tent, Fudail pulled himself slowly onto the saddle of his horse, while William grabbed the man's rifle and slung it over his shoulder before pulling himself onto the saddle of his own horse.

After saying goodbye to Hakeem, William and Fudail led their horses up one of the dunes so the guard could get a good view of the desert and figure out which way to ride. When they reached the top of the dune the desert showed itself, kilometers of sandy land and William wondered what it would be like when the caravan reached the scorching sands at the desert's heart. He imaged himself riding over soaring dunes, hundreds of feet tall, even though he was surrounded by small, unimpressive ones. He didn't care what he saw. All he cared about was reaching the true desert and feeling its vast emptiness.

"There, that is the direction we need to take," Fudail said, pulling William out of his daydream.

William turned to his left and saw Fudail pointing to the south. They rode down the dune into the vastness of the desert and William felt an overwhelming feeling of smallness come over him. With it came a kind of peace in knowing that his trial in the desert would come another day. They rode side by side in silence, keeping their thoughts to themselves, if any managed to survive the serenity of the desert.

It did not feel like long before the sun was beginning to level with the horizon and the sky changed from blue to deep purple. All this time, William had thought about the caravan only a handful of times and he hadn't realized how much he'd missed his tent, the people, and the chess games with Hans and Alexander.

A wind with a monstrous roar swept the desert and obscured the few stars in clouds of dust. Without the caravan's camp in sight and nightfall approaching faster, William began to doubt they would make it in time.

"Do you think we will reach the caravan before nightfall?" William voiced his thoughts, leaning close to his companion because of the roaring wind.

"We are not far. We should be there before midnight, I promise," Fudail shouted back, his response calm and precise, just as the man hidden behind his shaggy beard.

Even though it was becoming darker, William trusted Fudail enough that he knew they would arrive at the caravan before midnight. He didn't know why he trusted Fudail, but he did. The day before, he would have thought Fudail was lying if he said the sky was blue and now he was following him in the dark back to the caravan. This was a warrior's trust, one tempered out of the flames of life and death encounters.

It had been a while since they had last spoken when William and Fudail made their way up the side of a small hill. As William neared the top he saw Fudail standing next to his horse and staring at the land in front of him. When William's eyes beheld the view his breath was stolen. The fires of the caravan below illuminated the dark stretch of land like countless fireflies. He jumped down from his saddle and stood next to Fudail, who seemed to notice that the sight captivated William's attention. William looked as if he were in love with each and every one of them.

"Let me take your horse back to the caravan," Fudail offered, extending a hand to William who considered the prospect for a moment before handing the reins and nodding in gratitude.

# Caravan

He kept watching as the guard walked down the hill toward the caravan, slowly blending with the shadows until his shape disappeared into the darkness like a rock slipping farther into the depths of a lake. William sat down and crossed his arms over his knees, hugging them to his chest to keep himself warm from the chilling breeze.

When Fudail entered the caravan, several people tending to the fires noticed him and, curious to hear any news about the search, surrounded him and started asking questions. They noticed his wound and asked about how he got it and what had happened during the search. Fudail was excited to be at the center of attention and took his time telling them what he knew. Naturally, he also got a little carried away, sometimes exaggerating certain details about the journey. He felt elated telling about their little party being surrounded by not one hundred but five times as many Bedouin warriors. And how, when they had been searching the desert, they found the dead tribesmen pierced by dozens of arrows, with their hands and feet cut off and taken as trophies.

As William watched the fires below, he could hear the faint voices of the gathered crowd filling the golden-brown air above the camp. The longer he sat on the hill the colder he became, and the warmth of his tent became even more tempting, but he decided to stay for a while longer so that he could get his nightly dose of coldness before going to bed. After a while, he noticed that the fires were beginning to dwindle and decided to go head to his tent since he had stayed longer than he wanted to and his eyes were beginning to feel droopy.

He rose and as he walked down the hill he tucked his hands in his pockets to protect them from the cold that nipped at his ears and numbed his nose. The wind roared violently, now that it was late, flapping the tents around him into a swaying dance. When he entered his home away from home, feeling its warmth and comfort, he fell to his knees and collapsed onto his chest. Within several deep breaths, William was asleep.

# 10

WILLIAM OPENED HIS EYES. He laid perfectly still, covered in his blanket. The tent was glowing fluorescent with the light of day, filling the space with a cozy warmth comparable only to the womb. Outside, he heard the pleasant hum of chattering people, something he had missed during the search. He sat up, feeling refreshed and alert from a full night's sleep without the cold keeping him awake. A breeze played with the flaps of his tent, allowing him small glimpses of the world outside. Several people were walking past, one was leading a camel, another was carrying a heavy looking roll of carpet over his shoulder. William rubbed his eyes with his hands and stood. His aching legs made him think about the search for the Sheik and the long, quiet ride back. The memories seemed like a distant world compared to the caravan—one scattered with dead warriors, where a tribe leader was hiding from his mysterious attackers.

He folded his blanket and thought it would be a good idea to find Hans and tell him about the search. William knew how excited the German would be to hear a story from outside the safety of the caravan. Once the blanket was folded, William stopped outside his tent, watching the busy people walk past. He felt like the only person in the camp who wasn't busy selling something or carrying merchandise.

The caravan may have been smaller than Nador but it had a market of its own that was much larger than the one he'd seen in the city, even on a day when the flow of people was slow. It was a market brought to life by the nature of the people, to give and to be given to. He heard the sound of wings fluttering over his head and looked up.

A crow flew over William's head before spreading its wings and gliding gracefully in a low sweep to his right then landing on the ground behind a tent, perhaps to eat a piece of forgotten bread.

William walked into the path in front of him and turned left, joining the busy flow of people and animals that swept in all directions. The people, the smells and groans of the animals, the sound of a dry-sounding drum banging under a performer's tapping hand—all of this reminded him of the festival in Nador. His childlike curiosity about the world around him seemed revived, but a strange, ominous feeling came with it, slipping past his conscious thoughts and looming in the background like the beating of the drum.

He thought about Fudail and how the man's wound had separated the two from the search party. He wasn't blaming Fudail for getting wounded, of course, but something about walking through the camp created an itch, even though on the surface of his mind, the waters were calm and drifting with fog.

When he reached the entrance of Hans' tent he opened one of the flaps and took a quick peek inside. Hans sat on a small stool with his back facing him. His head was bowed and his back was arched. One hand held a book open for him to study while the other was thoughtfully scratching his chin. At his feet lay a small chessboard with several pieces on it. William saw an opportunity he didn't want to miss and stepped into the tent, his grin widening as he entered.

He stopped when Hans was just at an arm's reach and raised an open palm to slap him on the shoulder, but stopped when he saw the pages in the book Hans was studying. Both pages were printed with diagrams of a chessboard and several oddly placed pieces. Below each diagram was a small text explaining the purposes for certain moves and how that would affect the positions of both players.

William was so captivated by the book that he almost forgot he'd wanted to surprise Hans and looked down from the book to the board on the ground. The pieces were placed on the same squares as the diagram in the book. William's grin was replaced by a concerned frown when he realized the book Hans was reading was a manual of some kind that he hoped would give him a definitive edge in their next game, ending the succession of fateful draws.

He nearly flinched when Hans suddenly brought the hand scratching his chin down to the board at his feet. It hovered above one of the pieces and a frown covered his face as he reread the instructions in the book. He quickly drew his hand back to his chin as if to rethink what he was doing and continued scratching. He brought his hand down to the text at the lower part of the page and quickly swept his finger from left to right.

As Hans read the text, he lifted his hand from the book and lowered it to the chessboard. His fingers pinched the top of a white bishop and carried it to the other end of the board with the tender hand of an artist making the final stroke of a painting.

Checkmate.

William bit his tongue and slapped Hans' shoulder. "My, it's been a long time," he said in a voice just under a shout to add to the well-intended scare. Hans continued to look down at the board, unaffected.

"Why, what a surprise to see you here. I thought you were still with Hakeem and the others," Hans said blandly as William walked around him to a small stool placed coincidentally across from him, perhaps to simulate their next match. William grinned as he sat down and studied Hans' observant gaze pointed at the board.

"When did you know?" William asked.

"I could smell you," Hans said as he closed the book and placed it on the ground. William bowed his head and smelled his shirt. He smelled like the underparts of a goat and made a note to bathe soon, if not in water then in fragrant oil.

"Tell me what happened with the search," Hans asked as he looked up at William curiously. William's smile widened because Hans appeared unbothered by getting caught studying a book on chess.

"If you haven't heard already, then I'll tell you that we were almost ambushed by the Bedouin," William said.

"They wounded Hakeem's man?" Hans asked.

"Yes. They managed to take a shot at us without us seeing them first," William said.

"How far away were they?" Hans asked, showing the interest William had anticipated.

"Around a hundred yards maybe," William replied, considering the distance.

"Outstanding," Hands said, slapping his knee in admiration. He paused for a moment in thought then asked, "Do you know if the Sheik is alive? I heard there might be war if he's dead."

"We don't know if he's alive. No body turned up while I was there but Hakeem must be close to finding him. He has to be alive," William said quietly and almost to himself. He remembered what Hakeem had said about the caravan being caught in a war as he looked down at the chessboard.

He could feel Hans staring at him and looked up. The German didn't look frightened by the idea that there could be war in the camp, and William smiled but just to show him that he wasn't worried. But Hans must have seen through him because he didn't smile back.

"You're going to need more than a book to be the champion of the caravan, let alone beat the man waiting for you in Yemen," William changed the subject as he rose to his feet and started walking to the entrance of the tent.

"You're laughing now, but when I crush you on our next game, don't expect me to wipe your tears," Hans declared with a smirk as he turned around in his stool. William laughed as he said goodbye, assuring his friend that their next match would be soon.

Outside again, William walked back to his tent to get his camera. He hoped that taking some pictures of the caravan would take his mind off Hakeem and the Sheik. He looked at the people who passed him as he walked down the path, the thought of war looming in the back of his mind.

He imagined the people, tents, and animals all wiped out by the guns and blades of another tribe, incinerated by the blazing fire of hate. This was a cloud of grim possibilities. Everything beneath it was impermanent, as William often forgot life was.

When William went inside his tent, he was more than ready to enter the trance that overcame him whenever he took pictures and clear his mind of the cloud swirling in his head. He grabbed his camera and tripod and started walking to the entrance of his tent but stopped at the swaying flaps.

He looked down at the camera in his hand, but something about it didn't feel right. Normally, when he held his camera it was like holding a rope that connected him to the life he had lived. This time he felt like he was holding the murder weapon of a crime not yet committed. Its weight was uneven, cold, and lifeless.

Why did he feel this way? It didn't take him long to bring the source of it out of the dark recesses of his mind, and what he found both surprised and horrified him. By working for the *London Dove*, he was betraying the caravan in the way only foreigner could. Suddenly, it became harder to breathe. He was taking pictures of the caravan for a country that wouldn't care if the whole camp was burnt to the ground and all its people and animals hacked to pieces.

He was betraying the way of life that he wanted to become a part of by giving vain people living lavish and isolated lives a glimpse into a world they hadn't earned the right to see. The thought of staying in the caravan and becoming "one of those pathetic sympathizers," as Reginald had cheekily put it, shot a dose of loyalty to England into William's system, but it quickly wore off and the feeling that made it seem like he was suffocating returned.

The decision he had made at the hotel in Nador to survive the desert was more than it seemed. It was a promise to pay the price of living in the desert and all his effort to fulfill that promise would mean nothing if he made the caravan appear to be something it was not—a romanticized fascination spoken about over tea then quickly forgotten.

By traveling in the caravan, he was doing Hakeem an injustice, but if he left, he would have wasted the money Reginald gave him and without earning more to pay Mrs. Eldrich what he owed her. After realizing his dilemma, he noticed that the feeling was still there. He knew something had to be done to resolve the issue, but that was for another time. He had a job to do and whether he wanted to do it or not, he had to. He had signed a contract and that had the same weight as a promise.

William forced himself to step outside and was struck by a sudden rush of lightheadedness. The sun stung his eyes. The crowds were too loud, the air too hot. He took a step backwards while shielding his eyes from the light that came from the whole sky.

Slowly, his hand lowered as his eyes adjusted to the brightness of day. He stood outside his tent with his camera at his chest, squinting at the crowds of people walking by. He looked at them like a man about to commit a murder against his will and felt just as excited to do the deed. He considered not taking the pictures, but he forced the thought out of his mind.

Against every instinct in his body, William's right foot moved from the ground and stopped short of its usual stride. He took another step, and another, until he found himself standing in the middle of the crowd. The murder victim. The wondering glance of a passing face fell on him and he looked at the ground crowded with feet. He followed the flow of the crowd so as not to attract attention to himself, letting it take him wherever it wanted to.

At first, William thought walking along with the crowd was going to be the equivalent of petting a lamb before slitting its throat, but contrary to his expectations, it actually helped him forget about the camera hanging around his neck. Slowly, his pace returned to its normal stride and his chin rose from the weight of guilt that had pinned it to his chest. William followed the crowd to the center of the camp, where the people were busy gathering water from the well, selling goods from improvised shops, cleaning camel skins to be sold, and selling meat and cooked food.

He spotted his first victim, an old man sitting behind a table displaying several kinds of silk scarves and rolls of cloth. The table was placed underneath an awning the man had created by lifting a section of his tent's cloth and using two posts to hold it up. When the man noticed the stranger staring at him, William walked closer to the table and asked the man if he could take a picture of him and his shop.

The man was no fool. He agreed to be a model only if William bought a scarf first. Considering the exchange fair, William agreed. He didn't really care which scarf he bought; he just wanted to take the picture and leave. With shaky hands he looked through the merchandise and picked out the first scarf that caught his eye, a bluish green piece that resembled a peacock's tail, embroidered with gold colored leaves and stems that weaved and arched like the vines of Eden. He gave the man the money he wanted, stuffed the scarf into his pocket and began setting up his tripod and camera, catching the attention of many with his three-legged contraption.

Once the camera was ready, William focused his eye to the lens. The man sat with a thick-cheeked smile that reminded him of Gabriel. A small number of people huddled around William to see how the strange magic of picture-taking happened. William didn't mind the watchers standing behind him, whispering in each other's ears as if admiring an avant-garde artist painting in public, but he didn't want them there either, they got in the way of the little peace of mind he had managed to hold onto.

William took a succession of photographs as quickly as he could while making sure that each picture was perfect, then he thanked the man for his time and left, almost grateful that he would never see the photographs he had taken until they were processed in London.

As he walked away, William couldn't bring himself to take another picture—he wouldn't. He decided to walk back to his tent and pack up the camera and tripod. But that didn't make the feeling of dread go away. He needed to clear his head and decided to walk out of the camp. He took the less-populated paths to avoid being seen as he always did in times of shame. As he emerged from the tents at the edge of the camp, William heard a pounding noise coming from the hills in front of him. He stopped and looked up.

A rider was taking the slope of a dune at a dangerous speed, galloping on the back of a horse. His knees were hugging the horse's belly and his back arched forward as the animal's kicking created a constant drum roll. As William watched the rider slowly get larger, he wondered if the man was delivering some urgent news from Hakeem. The man rushed past William with a gust of wind that flapped his clothes. William spun around and watched him enter the path he had just come from then quickly disappear behind a tent.

William ran after him. In the path ahead, handfuls of men and women were running in the same direction. He continued on and quickly realized that the every person he saw was running toward the caravan's well. Like a frenzied stampede, people poured into the paths, and a deafening roar filled the air.

The closer William came to the center of the caravan, the more crowded the paths became, choking the flow of people so that they were forced to move forward at a teeth grinding crawl. The path turned left, leading William to the open area around the well, where everyone had gathered. William spotted the rider still on his horse near the well with the crowd eagerly jostling at his ankles. The messenger was surrounded on all sides by people hungry for news.

The rider raised a hand over his head for the people to quiet down so he could speak to them. The voices dwindled until only a few mumbles lingered in the dust-filled air.

"I have been sent from Hakeem. He is riding back now," the rider shouted, his voice echoing in the open area now quiet enough for everyone to hear him. He took a moment to clear his throat, dry from the desert ride, and wiped the sweat on his brow with his arm. Someone at the rider's knees handed him a curved clay pot filled with water that had a wide mouth and a long, heart-shaped handle. The rider lifted the pot up to his mouth with shaky hands and drank quickly, spilling a good amount of the water down his neck. "And along with him is the Sheik," the rider said in a gasp then brought the pot of water back to his mouth and drank again. The stomachs in the crowd turned. When the rider brought the pot down, he turned to the crowd, panting, and yelled in a trembling voice, "He is alive."

# De Collibus

The entire crowd burst into an roar, and William stood with a smile of relief at the cheerful people around him. While the crowd was celebrating, the rider dismounted and stepped into the crowd, where people were offering him food and water for riding through the desert to bring them the good news. The crowds began to move away from the well at a slow, but joyful speed, and the paths became easier to walk through. William felt that a weight had been lifted off of his chest because of the news, but the threat of war was not completely over, since the tribe who had attacked the Bedouin Sheik remained a mystery.

William walked away from the well and separated himself from the crowd, entering a narrow path leading to the edge of the camp. He wanted to feel the sun's warmth before the cold of night arrived. When he emerged from the path, he walked a little away from the tents. Normally, at this time of evening there would be a few people standing at the caravan's edge to watch the sunset. Unlike those other evenings, today William was the only one to witness the horizon darken with the setting of the sun and the beginning of uncertain times.

# 11

As the sky put on a silent performance for William, thoughts concerning loyalty to Reginald turned over in his head. Behind him he could hear the wind blowing softly against his shoulder, ruffling his shirt, and chilling the sweat on his back. On the outside he looked as calm and serene as the land around him, just a man enjoying the sun setting over a distant emptiness. Inside, he felt as if he had drunk a mixture of poison and medicine. The chaos in his head was both the problem and the solution. He felt like a stuffed doll being fought over by two crowds. A crowd of Londoners gripped his ankles while his wrists were manacled by the people of the caravan in matching strength, pulling hard enough to rip a hole in the universe, but going nowhere.

Only now was he realizing that what he had felt earlier was his left hip tearing open, exposing a plume of white stuffing. This tug-of-war had been going on much longer than he realized. It had started the day he stepped off the boat in Nador. The problem was that he didn't know which side to tell to let go: the one at his ankles or the one at his wrists. He was afraid he might make a mistake and end up on the wrong side forever, so he kept quiet and endured the growing pain.

But if he didn't choose one side or the other, the rip in his side would widen until he was torn in half, neither side gaining or losing him, only holding their portions of the soft doll, realizing they had accomplished nothing in all their struggle. Each second he waited, a thread snapped like the string on an instrument tightened to reach a pitch too high.

"Could it be that bad? Being ripped in half?" William whispered, looking at the heavens. He felt a change in the air and turned around to see who had interrupted his thoughts. To his surprise, Nadia was walking in his direction, her eyes thoughtfully staring at the ground and unaware he was standing ahead of her. Finally, she looked up and a surprised smile covered her face she ran to him.

"I thought you were still with Hakeem's search party. When did you get back?" Nadia asked as she stopped in front of William.

"Last night. Fudail and I rode back together, but we entered separately," he explained.

"I see." When William looked in Nadia's eyes, they had such an effect on him that he didn't even remember a country called England. All he could see was the green of the forest and all the possibilities it hid.

"What did you see when you were in the desert?" Nadia asked with unveiled curiosity.

"We didn't see much other than some of the warriors who'd ridden with the Sheik," William replied, instantly regretting his answer because he knew it would lead to talk of the dead.

Naturally, his shift of expression caught Nadia's attention. "If you saw the warriors, why didn't they return with you?"

William bowed his head and tried to think of a way to change the subject but she'd learn the truth when Hakeem returned anyway, and he'd appear a liar.

"They were all dead. Killed," William replied.

"All of them? How? Who would do such a thing?"

"All of those that traveled with the Sheik. We don't know who did it, but we found black arrows with their bodies," William said, realizing his mistake too late.

"Black arrows," Nadia mumbled quietly, looking at the horizon with a far-away expression.

Thinking he would cheer her up, William also told her about the Sheik's son and his warriors, who were very much alive.

"What were they like?" Nadia asked.

"I only saw them for a little while because Hakeem had us ride back to properly bandage Fudail's wounded arm. But the Prince seemed a quirky fellow. I don't think Hakeem liked him very much." William expected to get a laugh out of Nadia. Instead, her eyes turned thoughtful again.

Finally, William asked, "what are you thinking about?"

"It's strange," Nadia said, more to herself, focusing on the ground near her feet.

"What is?" William genuinely thought he'd scared her.

"I... No. I'm sorry. It's nothing," Nadia said hurriedly and turned to walk away.

"Don't go" He took a step towards her, "Tell me, what it is?"

Nadia faced him and took a deep breath. "There is a story I was told as a little girl, about a dangerous man who led an army in the desert attacking anyone who attempted to cross the great sands. His warriors used arrows with crow's fletching. I guess your words reminded me of this story, but it's not important," Nadia said, her voice sounding less worried.

"No, it's interesting. Tell me more," William said gently, an inexplicable feeling tugging at his heart.

She looked strangely at him for a moment, surprised he wanted to know more then said, "Ok, I will tell you, even though you are a foreigner." She smiled then her eyes went blank as she remembered how the story began.

"A few centuries after the holy wars, a falling star landed in the desert and tunneled deep into the earth. While sinking further down, the rock split in half," Nadia said, moving one hand to the right and the other to the left. "The rock tunneled deep enough into the earth that it formed a spring, and over the centuries an oasis was created. The oasis was sought by many astrologers who had heard about the star and the earthquake it had caused. But it was never found.

"Stories about the fallen star spread throughout the Mediterranean until it was impossible to trust any one story completely. The story that became most widely known said that inside the rock was the glowing spirit of a demon cast from the sky. It had been imprisoned inside a crystal globe at the center of the rock. If a human touched the crystal, the demon would enter their body and steal their soul.

"Many years after the story was forgotten, a battle was fought between two tribes that had been at war for many years. One army wore black robes and carried black flags. They lost tragically at the death of their general, and the soldiers fled into the desert. After many days of wandering the sands, the army found an oasis. The same one that the fallen star had created.

"When the men reached the place, dirty and exhausted, they heard a crazy laugh coming from inside a deep tunnel. Most were frightened, some decided that the voice might belong to one of their comrades who had lost his mind with exhaustion and had ran into the tunnel. They couldn't let him die.

"Led by a low-ranking soldier, they ventured into the tunnel. Following the echoing voice of their comrade, which laughed and and giggled at them, they went deep under the ground. Finally, after hours of walking under the desert, the soldiers found a round boulder that glowed bright from within.

"Out of curiosity, one of them struck the stone with his sword and the boulder fell apart to reveal a small crystal globe that shone too bright for their human eyes. Most were momentarily blinded, but their leader stepped forward and touched the globe. The light suddenly vanished, and the leader fell to the ground, dead. The soldiers rushed to his aid, yelling his name, but he did not move. Then, to their surprise, his eyes opened, glowing with the same light the globe had emanated. The demon now lived in him.

"According to the story, the glow in the man's eyes would eventually fade, but the evil inside him would exist forever. Even if his body died, the demon would return to the crystal, waiting for his next victim.

"When the soldiers realized their leader was alive, they swarmed him, but the instant they touched him, their voices were gone, along with their souls. The men who had remained at the oasis were deathly afraid and some ran away, but those who remained were forever changed, turned into soulless creatures, thirsty for blood."

Nadia looked at William, searching his expression for any reaction, then continued. "When the last man in the army was touched by the demon, humanity was wiped from their midst. They belonged to the demon now, and he gave them eternal life in exchange for their souls. As long as their bodies were unharmed, they would continue to exist. Led by their leader, the Desert King, this demonic army roams the desert, killing everyone they meet. According to the story, the Desert King is determined to keep the Sahara pure, and is always ready to recruit valiant men to fight for his cause." Nadia fell silent when she finished the story. She looked shaken, and though William understood how she could connect the dots, he didn't want her to feel afraid. Besides, old stories were most usually myths with little truth.

"I can see why you're frightened, but this Desert King is just a myth, Nadia, a story from long ago," William said, hoping to erase the fear from her mind.

Suddenly, a horn interrupted the short silence, coming from the other side of the caravan. Both of them looked at the tents. "It must be Hakeem," William said with a hint of excitement as people poured into the streets and followed the horn. "Come on." William said as he started walking toward the tents, his pace quickening to a run.

As William and Nadia entered the caravan, the horn sounded a second time but because the excited voices dominated the air as well as the streets, it was barely noticeable. The paths were stuffed with people hurrying to see what was happening. Men, women, and children sung various songs that reminded William of celebrations and weddings. Drums and tambourines joined in the noise, making everything else impossible to hear. William looked at Nadia. She was smiling like the rest of the people but wasn't singing.

"What are they singing?" he yelled out, but his voice was drowned out in the roar. Nadia frowned slightly and pointed to her ear. "The people, what are they singing?" William bellowed even louder this time.

"A very old song of welcome," she yelled back, her voice barely audible above the chaotic celebration.

"I like it," William shouted as he nodded his head and turned back around to the flowing street ahead of him. When he and Nadia neared the front of the crowd facing the desert, they saw a long line of riders descending carefully down the side of the hill overlooking the caravan. The women around William began yelling the high-pitched call of celebration he'd first heard back in Nador, then their voices wavered into a single harmonious note.

As Hakeem led the group into the caravan, trailed by the blue-robed warriors, he held an open hand over his head and smiled at the people as they cheered around him. He looked like a victorious general entering the capital city after winning a war without firing a shot. Close behind him was a stretcher with an improvised canopy carried by four tired-looking men.

William couldn't see the Sheik, but the man must have been close to death when Hakeem and the warriors found him. The men who rode past sat straight in their saddles like soldiers in a military parade, their faces coated with a layer of dust and eyes empty from the long journey. The warriors looked down at the people with a curious stare as if they had never seen a caravan before. The cheering of the crowds only began to soften as the last of the Bedouin warriors entered the caravan.

At the very tail of the procession, William spotted a tribesmen he thought he recognized—the man who wounded Fudail. William couldn't resist the feeling of protection wash over him as this man passed. He watched as the warrior disappeared among the crowds who were happy that the tribe leader had been brought safely back and were more than ready to get a good night's sleep without any surprises.

When only a handful of people remained, Nadia bid William goodbye and hurried on before her mother saw them together. Left on his own, he started down an empty path, with the thought in his mind that somehow he would find a way to make his life in the caravan possible.

# 12

THE SUN WAS SHINING DOWN ON THE CAMP with the heat of a furnace. Under these conditions, no one dared venture outside. The paths were nearly empty, making for a rather peaceful atmosphere. William had left his tent to get himself some water from the well because his tongue felt like a piece of driftwood and because he wanted to get a taste of what the real desert's heat would be like.

As he walked to the well, his shoulders felt oddly heavy and beads of sweat trickled down his back with the tickling slowness of an insect. The path William took wound among the tents instead of going straight to the well, and before the last bend he heard the faint voice of a woman coming from not too far ahead.

*It must be a hot day indeed. I'm hearing angels' voices.* When William turned the corner, the smirk on his face widened and he came to a stop a stone's throw away from the well. The angelic voice he had heard belonged to none other but the girl who had been visiting his dreams. Under the coolness of an awning that had been built over the well, Nadia was busy telling a story to a curious group of boys and girls sitting on the ground near her feet. She didn't notice William step out of the pathway, and continued telling the story, using her hands to help communicate her lessons to the children who would giggle and listen intently.

The story she told interested William even though he heard only a half-dozen words. Something in the way she spoke though made the whole world new and interesting. He wanted to hear more and decided to go join the group of enchanted children. First, he took a quick look to his right and then his left to make sure Nadia's mother was not posted somewhere he couldn't see, ready to shoo him off with a slap to the back of the head like some pest.

She wasn't.

William began walking towards the children as quietly as he could so he wouldn't distract them. He saw Nadia reach towards the sky and spread out her fingers to resemble a tree. The children giggled and Nadia continued telling the story. As he always did when trying to blend in, William put his hands in his pockets and slowed his pace, but with each step he took he only grew more self-conscious, which wasn't helping him sneak into the group of children. When he was a couple of steps away, those at the back of the group turned around and saw him.

William instantly stopped walking. Nadia looked up and the rest of the children turned around and stared at William with their bright innocent eyes. He looked at Nadia. She seemed slightly bothered that he'd interrupted the story, but the blush in her cheeks was a sure sign she was happy to see him as well.

"Please, continue," William said when neither Nadia nor the children would take their eyes off him. A moment later, the children faced Nadia in unison, and slowly, the spell she spun returned over the minds of her young audience. William, not wanting to distract the children again, walked in a wide arc around Nadia and the children to the other side of the well so that he could get his drink of water and leave. But, being curious by nature, the children looked at him with fascination, deaf to Nadia's words. There might as well have been a giraffe walking behind her.

When she noticed the children weren't paying attention, she stopped mid-sentence to look over her shoulder and there he was. Nadia frowned, though William couldn't really understand why. He had certainly not chosen this time of day to get thirsty on purpose. Since no other wells existed in the camp, anyone could walk by in search for water. It had just happened to be him.

Nadia turned around and continued telling the story from where she had left off, her suddenly sharp voice snapping the children's attention back to her in an instant. William shrugged to himself and continued walking around the well until Nadia's back was blocking him from the children's sight. He relaxed when he was behind Nadia and bent down to pick up the bucket and rope to pull water from the well.

A moment later, William dropped the bucket down the well. It made a splash as loud as if he had jumped in. He felt a change in the wind followed by the sudden urge to cringe. When he looked up, he saw Nadia glaring at him with eyes hotter than the sun and the children peeking curiously at him from behind her dress. With one arm down the well, he stared at Nadia with frozen eyes.

"You're being distracting. Go away," Nadia snapped. A few of the children started giggling, which only heated Nadia's temper.

"I'm sorry," William said, feeling bad for disrupting Nadia's class, and he began pulling up the bucket of water as fast as he could.

Nadia's face softened a little and she turned around to continue telling her story, which had an important lesson for the children to learn. When the children's giggles died out, Nadia continued her story.

The bucket of water arrived at the top of the well, and William, not having any dish of his own to pour water into, drank straight from it. His thoughts turned to the Sheik, and as he brought cupped handfuls of water to his mouth and drank in thoughtful silence, a frown appeared on his face.

He hadn't heard much news about the Sheik since Hakeem had arrived with him last night, and this made him even more curious. After sipping his final handful of water, William stood and walked away from the well, unnoticed by the children, who were now fully captured in the dreamwork of Nadia's storytelling.

William walked down a path that would take him to Hakeem's tent the fastest, braving the heat a little while longer to feed his curiosity. Shortly after leaving the well, he spotted his two friends, Alexander and Hans, walking toward him, apparently choosing the same path to stretch their legs.

"Hallo, William," Hans said as he and Alexander started walking alongside William in the direction from which they had just come.

"Good day Hans, " William greeted, sounding like he had more important things on his mind.

"You look like you're in a hurry. Where are you going?" Alexander asked, seemingly curious.

"I'd like to have a talk with Hakeem," William answered, his eyes pointing straight ahead.

"Ah, serious business. Then we won't bother you. Take care, my friend," Alexander said and began to turn around.

"Listen, William, I think the time has come for you and me to settle something—something important," Hans said, drawing Alexander back into their three-man march.

"What are you talking about?" William asked, surprised by the concern in the German's voice.

"I am talking about the chess game that you owe me. When will we finally see who's better, huh?"

"We'll have to do it some other time, I'm afraid," William said as the group took a turn in the bend.

"Tomorrow at noon?" Hans asked hopefully, watching William's face for any hints.

William thought that over. This game had to happen at some point. Better sooner than later. "That's all right with me."

Hans stopped walking and held out his hand as if to confirm the deal, while Alexander watched along side him with an amused twinkle in his eyes.

"I will see you tomorrow at noon," Hans called out after William who had shaken his hand and hurriedly walked away. "Everyone in the caravan will be there. It will be great," he added in excitement, raising his voice to a shout as William disappeared behind a tent and continued walking to Hakeem's tent.

When he arrived at his destination, William stopped, surprised to see no guards standing at the entrance. At first, he thought that Hakeem was not there, but a gut feeling pushed him to walk closer and maybe peek in the entrance. Seeing that the least he could do was check, he stepped inside.

The scorching heat outside was suddenly replaced by a chilling darkness. The two guards who normally were posted outside Hakeem's tent were now standing on either side of William, showing all signs of readiness to protect their leader from the intruder. Hakeem was walking from one end of the tent to the other with a book spread open in his hands and, unlike his guards, paid no attention to William. Finally, he stopped, looked up, and said, "Please, come in," then his eyes returned to the book.

William took a handful of steps forward and watched as Hakeem moved the tip of his finger across a page in the book he held, right to left, so probably the book wasn't written in English. William thought he'd ask Nadia about it the next time he saw her.

As Hakeem finished the last words, he slowly moved his head up toward William but kept his eyes on the bottom of the page he was finishing. Once Hakeem finished the last word on the page, he quickly closed the book, making a heavy thud and looked up at William.

"How can I help?" Hakeem asked as he took a seat on a low stool and tenderly placed the book on his lap.

"This might sound strange, but I've been wondering the Sheik," William said cautiously, taking a few steps closer to a stool opposite Hakeem.

"Yes, of course," Hakeem nodded, sounding as if he had been answering that same question the entire day, and extended his open hand to the stool William had been eying. "But first, please sit."

William sat across from Hakeem and waited.

"My doctors say the Sheik will live, but seeing that he needs treatment, we will have to stay here until his heath returns and he can go back to his tribe," Hakeem said.

"I understand," William sighed, happy to hear that the tribe leader was alive, but sad that they had to put a pause on their journey for as long as was needed. "I'm glad you found him alive."

"As am I. Finding him was a sheer miracle. He was so close to death and the doctors say that the desert would have killed him if we had found him just a day later," Hakeem said thoughtfully.

"Has he said who ambushed him?" William asked.

"No, but he has been mumbling quite a bit," Hakeem said as he straightened his back and stared at the book on his lap.

"Only mumbles," William repeated to himself, seeing that there wasn't as much news as he'd hoped.

"Yes. The sick tend to say odd things, and the Sheik's been chased in the desert almost to death. Madness is sometimes inevitable in tough circumstances... How else to explain his mumblings? Children's stories of ghosts and such..." Hakeem said, though William hardly caught his last words.

"What stories?" William asked, wondering if this had anything to do with the one Nadia had told him.

"It doesn't matter. The Sheik is hardly alive, and we can't hold onto his words of nonsense," Hakeem said, putting an end to William's questions.

But William's curiosity had only been fed a morsel to nibble on, and it began to sniff the scent of a feast. Why Hakeem insisted the tribe leader had only mumbled nonsense? Why did Hakeem so protective? There was a short moment of silence. Both of them knew there was more to it than what was said, but neither dared speak.

"In that case, please excuse me. Thank you for your hospitality," William said as he rose to his feet.

Hakeem followed suit then bowed his head slowly. William did the same, hoping no one would suspect that he knew the leader wasn't being entirely truthful. A moment later, he stepped out of the tent and into the bright sun. As William's eyes adjusted to the light, his mind was suddenly cast into a tempest of the kind of thoughts best kept where they came from.

As William took a path that would lead him back to his tent, he wondered if Hakeem was keeping something from him. *Is the Sheik actually alive or did he die? Is Hakeem keeping it a secret? Why? To buy him enough time to figure out a plan? Whatever he's up to, it's something he doesn't want known so it'd be best to keep your mouth shut unless things change.*

By the time he reached the entrance to his tent, William's thoughts had got too muddled by the heat for them to continue productively. He looked up at the pale sky and closed his eyes. As the sun warmed his face he pictured himself in the desert, alone in the vast silence and the heat, where only the truth existed.

# 13

WILLIAM OPENED HIS EYES AND LOOKED AROUND his tent, expecting it to be daybreak. It was cold and he couldn't see anything but darkness. He could feel beads of sweat running down his forehead and his heart was pounding in his chest like a drum. He thought he had woken from a bad dream, but no frightening images came to mind. He stared up into the dark ceiling above him, hoping tiredness would return and he would fall asleep again.

A while later his heart had calmed, but his mind was wide awake. He felt like he'd drunk a cup of coffee. William sat up and stretched his hands toward his toes. As he straightened his back, he decided to go outside and test whether his attempts to adjust to the cold had done him any good. If the cold of night still pierced his body as usual, he would run back into his tent where he would lay in boredom until sunrise.

He didn't know where he was going to walk, but he decided to surrender to the restlessness inside him and let it take him where it wanted to. William wasn't really afraid of getting lost among the tents, because he had walked the paths so many times since camp was first erected that he could navigate them blindfolded.

Whisking the blanket off his legs, William rose to his feet. Even if he took his camera now, it wouldn't serve him in the darkness, so he decided to leave his camera behind at the back of his tent where it had laid for the last two days, unused and uncared for. The instant he stepped outside, he felt the cold breeze numb his face and freeze his lungs. He instinctively crossed his arms and hunched his shoulders to protect himself from the cold. He stood still for a few moments, looking down the different pathways that branched away from his tent, wondering which one to take.

Instead, a gut feeling made him look up at the sky. Among the stars, the moon was shining above a distant hill, casting a silver light over the camp and the surrounding hills. The shadows of the tents seemed like ghostly creatures in the darkness. William felt an odd kind of joy in knowing that he was the only one in the caravan to see the moon shining at this very moment. His gaze fell on one of the hills, the same one Hakeem's rider had come from with news of the Sheik being found. He felt a gravitational pull he couldn't describe and surrendered to it.

Turning to walk in that direction, William could hear the tents around him flapping in the gentle breeze. The chilled sand under his feet made soft puffs of ghostly white dust as he walked. He neared the caravan's edge with a smile on his face because something floating in the silence made him happy: a calm joy that made this moment seem different than the other moments of silence.

When William reached the perimeter of the caravan, he stopped and looked at the hill in front of him. It was a black heap of earth crowned by the moon and the stars. Then he noticed a light in the corner of his eyes. He turned to examine it and stared at what appeared to be a small flame in the distance. Could it be the campfire that he had noticed the day he met Nadia?

William was surprised to see it again, because he had thought that the person who had created it the first time had moved on. Apparently, though, the traveler had stayed. William knew it was the same fire, because he started feeling the same ominous weight lower onto his shoulders and was reminded of the image of the witches and the bubbling cauldron. He wondered who was camping outside the caravan and, more importantly— why. His mind felt clouded like a mountain covered in fog, but a part of him wanted to go there and meet that lone traveler, whoever it was.

He started making his way to the base of the hill, glancing at the fire every couple of steps. Then up the slope he went, and though his legs were beginning to tire, he reached the top and looked at the sky. It was filled with a soft shade of pink that complemented the pale color of the sand in a surreal color scheme.

Down at his feet, the wind was growing stronger, sweeping away the dirt on the crest of the hill, whisking it into the air in front of him where it swirled like cigarette smoke and faded into nothingness. William kneeled and took a handful of soil from the ground before rising back to his feet. He looked at the white grains in his palm and felt it with his fingertips before he slowly loosened his grip, and it slipped through his fingers. The sand was carried away by the wind before it landed on the ground and vanished like the mists of sky-high waterfalls.

As William watched the wind carry the grains of soil away from him, his focus shifted to the caravan below. The camp, situated in a large circle, mesmerized him with its hundreds of tents and an even larger number of people and animals. Slowly, his hand lowered to his side, almost instinctively. He wondered how long it would be until he reached Yemen and what it would be like taking the boat back to England.

Initially, he had welcomed the idea of returning to his cozy apartment, kissing Mrs. Eldrich on the head and seeing the smile on her face as he handed her the money he owed. It was a pleasant thought, but as he considered the life to which he was going to return, his spirit saddened. The very thought of leaving the caravan, having to say goodbye to the nomad way of living, to his friends, to the desert, made his stomach turn.

He knew that the misty streets of London, walled off on either side by endless rows of buildings, were someone else's home. The home of a lonely man who had felt imprisoned there with nowhere to go and nothing to see. He would be indistinguishable in a city full of people just like himself. No longer unique. No longer a foreigner.

The more he thought about London, the more a quiet dislike for the city entered his mind until William admitted to himself that he actually dreaded having to return there and continue living just as he used to. Living in a cell-like apartment, a prisoner serving a life sentence to the warden of his own limiting beliefs about the life he was capable of living. He could not go back.

This conclusion felt strange echoing in his mind but like a boy discovering his desire for girls for the very first time, a voice deep in his subconscious told him that what he was feeling was normal. The caravan had become his home now a place where, even though he was a foreigner, he felt accepted. This truth seemed to set him free.

But what of that feeling of betrayal he had felt when taking pictures of the old merchant? He wished the feeling would go away, but the more he tried to push it out of his mind, the stronger it became. William knew that if he didn't put an end to it, that feeling would forever stay a burning ember inside him, slowly eroding the good in him until bitterness took its place. He knew that he could not be attached to his old home while living as a free man in the caravan. The rules weren't written that way. He had to make a decision and stay with it no matter what happened.

But William didn't want to break the promise he had made to Reginald and Mrs. Eldrich; that would be stealing, and William was no thief. He thought he could send his camera back to London, but where would he find a city with a post office? After pondering this for a while, he decided that if he didn't find an opportunity to get the camera to London any other way, he would simply wait until the caravan reached Yemen and then send it with a detailed note to Reginald regarding Mrs. Eldrich, then return to the caravan.

William liked the idea because he would not be stealing from Reginald, he'd be paying Mrs. Eldrich, and even the photographs would still be published in the newspaper. At least he wouldn't have to take any more pictures. Feeling especially victorious for the early hour of the morning, William decided to make this his plan unless some other problems came up that he hadn't considered.

Soon, the sun began to rise. When it was halfway over the horizon, William felt its warmth touch his face. He decided that he should start making his way back to the caravan to get his morning meal. With the thought of food in his head, his stomach grumbled and he took his first step down the hillside.

As William walked closer to camp, he noticed one or two people walking down the paths at the perimeter, setting up shop for today's customers and starting a handful of fires. By the time William got close to the center of the camp, orange light peeked over the crest of the hills and covered the tents and paths. Walking toward the bread maker's tent, William noticed a large crowd crammed together down one of the pathways, the people talking quietly to each other.

Abruptly, he changed his course and noticed Hans with eyes glued to the crowd ahead. William quickened his pace to catch up with his friend and hopefully learn something about the commotion that was stirring.

"Good morning," William greeted as he caught up with Hans and matched his pace.

"Do you know what's going on?" Hans asked nodding toward the crowd.

"No. I was hoping you did," William said, disappointed.

Hans frowned, then shrugged. "Then it looks like we are going to have to find out for ourselves."

The murmurs of the crowd were not very coherent but William could hear people talking about the Bedouin Sheik. He and Hans stopped walking when they couldn't push their way forward any longer and saw Hakeem's head rise above the people when he stepped onto a stool. The voices quieted. When Hakeem looked at the crowd, the silence became heavy, almost ceremonial, matching the solemn look in his eyes. From where William stood, he could see a trace of sadness on Hakeem's face, a look he had never seen there before.

"I am here to tell you something I think you all deserve to know," Hakeem said softly. Even though he spoke in a soft voice, every person could hear him. He paused and swept the crowd with his eyes. "The Sheik died last night," Hakeem announced. The people stood in silent shock, saddened at the loss of the tribe leader after so much hope and effort had gone into his rescue. "Since there is no reason for the Bedouin warriors to remain here any longer, they are going to leave tomorrow morning," Hakeem continued with a blankness in his voice he probably used to hide his own sadness. He was about to step down from the stool when he turned back to his audience and said solemnly, "I am very sorry."

When Hakeem's foot landed on the ground, the crowd exploded into a frenzy of sadness. The women cried out in lamenting wails of loss and the men had drawn, solemn faces of emptiness. William and Hans simply looked at each other.

Hans could see a sadness in William's eyes that was deeper than the crowd's roar because he had saved the man's life. When William looked back at the crowd, the people were starting to disperse, many with comforting arms around each other's shoulders.

To William, this didn't feel right. Just yesterday, Hakeem had assured him the Sheik would live. William had known the caravan leader had offered him half-truths, but this was too much a lie to cover. He stepped forward in the dispersing crowd to try and catch up with Hakeem, his mind so clouded by drowsiness and determination that he forgot to say goodbye to Hans.

"Hey, where are you going?" Hans called out when William started walking away from him.

"There is something I need to do," William yelled back without stopping. "I'll see you at noon."

William followed the path leading to Hakeem's tent, certain he would find the man there, but not so confident that he would get any answers. From afar, William spotted Hakeem and his men enter the tent, and he quickened his pace.

This time the guards remained outside. William expected them to stop him, and prepared to push his way past them, but that had turned out to be unnecessary. The guards simply eyed him with curiosity as he nearly stumbled through the entrance from his own momentum.

Hakeem was at the back of the tent, pacing back and forth nervously with a frown on his face and his eyes lowered at the carpet. He turned in William's direction, and greeted him with a frown, perhaps realizing that William had seen into his lies and was here to ask questions.

"What is going on?" William asked in a frustrated voice.

Hakeem started rubbing his hands as if to get rid of some filth that had become a part of his skin, his mind reluctant to give an answer good enough to satisfy William's curiosity. When William saw Hakeem remained silent, he knew his instincts had been right. The caravan leader continued pacing in silence and the frown on his face became tight as if it were painful.

"Hakeem?" William insisted, calling his name for the third time.

"William, I am sorry I had to hide the truth from you, but it just had to be done. No one could know," he stated as he looked up at William. The man's voice carried the same apologetic tone it had earlier when he had delivered his message to the people outside.

"Know what?" William asked, his voice slightly louder, because seeing Hakeem act this way made him wonder if something had gone seriously wrong.

"The last words of the Sheik," Hakeem said softly, continuing to wring and rub his hands nervously together as his eyes inspected the various patterns of the carpet.

William didn't know what to make of that but decided it would be better to have the man sit down. He walked to a short stool in the center of the tent as if inviting Hakeem to talk with him. Just as the previous day, they took their seats opposite each other. For a moment, they sat there in silence, one of them preparing what to say while the other waited quietly. Hakeem's eyes darted around the floor at his feet as he struggled to come up with the right words to begin with.

"What did he say, exactly?" William prompted with a hint of cautious excitement. "Did he say who attacked him?"

Hakeem brought one of his hands up to his jaw and covered his mouth as he rubbed his beard and brushed the hairs back and forth. William was beginning to worry Hakeem wasn't exactly in his right mind when the tent's entrance opened. He looked over his shoulder and saw one of Hakeem's guards with a hand on his sword and a worried frown on his face. Hakeem waved the man off and he left reluctantly, shooting William a warning glare.

William turned around and looked back at Hakeem. He decided not to speak, wanting to give Hakeem enough time to explain himself. Hakeem brought his hands down and continued wringing them, only a little less nervously.

"The truth can be scary sometimes, and the Sheik's last words can bring terror in our hearts, should people care to believe them," Hakeem said at last, his voice shaky with a mixture of embarrassment and fear. William didn't know what to say to that, but he had certainly not expected Hakeem's next words. "The Desert King," the caravan leader said as he looked up at William. "Those were the last words the Sheik ever uttered."

"The Desert King?" William frowned, remembering Nadia's story.

"You have heard the legend, then?" Hakeem guessed, obviously relieved that he wouldn't have to recount the story himself.

"Yes, but he couldn't mean that literally, could he?" William asked, his eyes searching Hakeem's for some kind of answer, but the Arab was diligently staring at the ground. The longer Hakeem remained silent, the wilder William's thoughts became. Finally, he voiced the question that bothered him most. "Hakeem, the Desert King is just a myth, right?" But he got no answer, and each passing second troubled him even more.

"I think you should leave," said Hakeem, suddenly rising to his feet. "You know what I know, there's nothing else to discuss here."

The Arab's voice sounded louder and resistant now, but William sat still looking up at him inquisitively. A moment past during which the two men eyed each other, then, seeing that this would get him nowhere, William slowly rose from his stool and walked to the tent's entrance. William wasn't sure what he should do from then on. Could he even trust Hakeem?

"William," Hakeem called out, and William turned around to see the caravan leader standing in the exact spot he'd left him. "Not a word about this conversation."

William appreciated Hakeem's concern for the people, even though the same couldn't be said about his honesty. He gave a small nod and walked out, past the guards and into the morning sun, realizing he had been given more questions than answers. He stood a few feet away from the tent's shade and looked around as if noticing certain things for the first time.

For one, he could sense a strange feeling around the camp. Apparently, the others did too, as he saw them walking in small, scattered groups, some talking with each other while others walked silently.

Somebody cleared their throat behind William's back, and he turned around. Hakeem's guards stared at him with a cold look in their eyes, a signal for him to leave. William ignored them. Instead of leaving right away, he looked up at the noon sun, feeling that more odd events were still ahead in this day already so full of surprises.

# 14

THE SKY WAS CLOUDED AND DUSTY, slightly dimming the light of day. A crowd of people, both young and old, stood under a large canopy of awnings, eager to watch an event that there had been much gossip about. Under the center of the canopy was a simple square table made of wood. The people in the caravan were sure that if such a popular match was to be decided on a chessboard, then it must be on one worthy of the occasion and thus provided one of their own. The arena was set for the chess match to begin, but the contestants were still missing.

Most of the crowd had been standing for a long time already, and some were becoming impatient. As the crowd waited for the match to begin, they chatted with one another as any large group of people would, and the noise grew until a low, unwavering murmur hummed in the air beneath the awnings.

Suddenly, the nervous expectations of the people were heightened when the murmuring loudened at the edge of the crowd. The disturbance seemed to be growing as it neared the center and people stepped aside. The crowd started cheering when they saw William and Hans, with Alexander walking between them like a referee at a boxing match, making their way to the table. As the applauding slowly quieted, Hans made his way to the chair nearest to him and sat down, his eyes on the chessboard eager to get this over with. While Hans took his seat, William walked around the table and gave an open-handed wave and the most charming smile he could muster.

The people applauded him as appreciation for being a part of the excitement. When Hans saw William win some of the crowd just by charm, he smiled as well. He wasn't going to give up his title as champion unless it was pried from his cold, dead fingers. As William took his time getting in his chair, Hans observed him with a relaxed smile, confident that, unless William had read the same book he had, today would be the day the chain of ties would be broken.

After a bit of healthy politics, William took his seat across from Hans and adjusted his position by scooting the chair closer to the table. While the two of them turned their eyes to the game, Alexander took his seat on a nearby stool, where he could observe the game from a distance and prevent any unfair play. By the time William was comfortable in his chair, the voices in the crowd had started to soften, along with the last faint jingles of wagers being handled. When silence filled the canopy, each pair of eyes focused on the chessboard.

William extended his hand to Hans to shake before the match began, but the German looked at him as if to say, "A handshake? This is war, you idiot." The hope in William's eyes began to evaporate as his hand continued to hover over the board. Hans, seeing that he was the reason the game was being held up, calmly leaned forward and smacked William's hand away from the board as if it were a mosquito.

The spectators gasped and booed, and Hans suddenly realized he had made a mistake. He wasn't playing only for himself now, there was the crowd to consider. William seemed to know this already and moved his hand back over the board to give Hans a second chance. The crowd quieted down again, then erupted in applause when, after a short pause, Hans took William's hand and shook it.

Finally, the match was ready to begin.

William, who was in command of the white pieces, knew Hans' strategy by now and was certain the German was going to try to crush him with sheer force by bringing his most powerful pieces out and playing very aggressively to gain a swift checkmate. To prevent that kind of play William decided to use his first move to get an early start in creating a defense that could hold off Hans' anticipated assault on the white king. It didn't take much time for William to come up with a plan, and shortly afterward he made his first move. Just as expected, Hans brought one of his knights right in front of his pawns.

As the game continued, William noticed Hans had improved his style of play and wasn't making as many mistakes as before. Both sides of the board were becoming more developed with every move, and the crowd grew more mesmerized by the surprising moves that took place on the board. Alexander's reporting, "Hans takes knight," or, "William exchanges bishops," was only adding to the excitement. After a long sequence of cunning moves, it became obvious that Hans was having trouble getting around the defense guarding William's king. For what seemed like an hour, he sat with one of his elbows on the table and his chin cupped in his hand. Although he appeared to be staring blankly at the board, the German's brain was actually hard at work.

Hans was busy sizing up William's defense when he felt a sudden rush in his stomach. He realized that the move that would end the game in his favor was right in front of him and had been there since the very beginning of the match. It was daring, and everything would come crumbling down if it failed, but it was still an option that had a sliver of a chance of working. After calculating the move he was about to make, Hans focused all his efforts into concealing his excitement by covering his mouth and looking at squares of the board.

When his turn came a move later, the German brought his hand down from his mouth and adjusted himself in his seat before pulling on the ends of his shirt. The crowd watched closely as Hans leaned closer to the table, picked up his queen, and moved it to a square on the far corner of the board, putting William in check.

"Check," Alexander reported, and whispers filled the tense air under the canopy. Seeing this as an opportunity to take Hans' most powerful piece, William disregarded the bells in his mind and eliminated the black queen. A swell of excitement came from the crowd when Alexander reported, "William takes Queen."

He checked Hans' expression, and the smirk he saw made him realize he'd just fell into a deceitful trap. The German made his next move by bringing another piece from the rear of the board up close to William's line of defense but out of danger. What was this strategy? Had Hans picked it up from the chess manual he'd been reading or did he make it up on the spot? Whatever the case, William feared that an unexpected checkmate was only a move away.

William looked up from the board that presented him with a problem, and saw that the grin on Hans' face had grown larger. After glancing up at Hans' taunting eyes, he looked back down at the board and started planning how he would escape the trap Hans had sprung on him. When several minutes had passed, William realized that there was no way for him to avoid losing the match. His stomach turned into a knot of regret, and the more he stared at the way the pieces sat motionless on the board, the more it seemed as if they were mocking him.

Seeing that nothing could be done about the trap he'd gotten himself into, William decided to take his mind off the square with Hans' piece. Instead, he would attack. When William changed his focus, he realized that Hans' aggressive offence had left the black king open, which meant that William could turn the game in his favor depending on the next move he made. Making a conscious effort to appear gloomy, William planned carefully then brought his queen to a square that put Hans in check. This was surely the end of Hans' aggressive assault.

"Check," Alexander reported.

Murmurs and whispers followed. Hans moved his king out of danger, dismissing the move as a last attempt from William to fight back. But William was prepared. He took one of his rooks that had gone neglected in the game and placed it alongside his queen.

"Check from William," Alexander chimed again.

More gasps and whispers. As Hans was about to calmly move his king out of harm's way, he slowly began to realize that the squares where he could shelter his king had run out.

Curious murmurs began to rise from the crowd, and Alexander stood up from his chair to take a look for himself.

"Checkmate from William," Alexander shouted so everyone would hear. The crowd remained silent. When William looked up, he saw Hans frowning at the board. The German still thought that there was some way for his king to escape that Alexander had overlooked. But Alexander was correct. Hans looked up at William with a wild glare in his eyes, glanced down at the chessboard, then back up at William.

"Why you…? How did you…?" Hans stuttered as if he were betrayed at a trial. "You bastard," Hans shouted finally.

William, who could not prevent himself from smiling, saw the face of Satan flash across Hans' eyes just before the German jumped over the table with the agility of a cat, taking both William and his chair to the ground. The crowd started laughing, and some even began to cheer while William swatted Hans' hands away from his throat, his uncontrollable laughter limiting his ability to do much else. When his attempts to get a hold of William's throat showed no results, Hans decided to try a different tactic.

"Hey!" William gasped when Hans slapped the side of his head. Another slap followed, then another, and William realized this was getting out of control. "Get him off me, Alexander! Get him off," he yelled in a surge of real panic. The crowd burst into a roar of laughter while Alexander made his way to his brawling friends.

"This is for my queen," Hans growled before reaching down and pinching him on the ear with the sting of a crab's pincer.

"Hey! Stop it, Hans!" William shouted out as he felt the blood in his ear rush away in a tingly pinch.

As Hans pinched William's ear and continued slapping him with his other hand, William caught a glimpse of Alexander coming to his rescue but lost sight of him in the chaos of slaps. But when William caught another glance of Alexander he saw him standing idle an arm's distance away from him. "What are you waiting for? Get him off me!" he cried out to his fellow countryman, no traces of laughter left in his voice. Still the slapping continued, but now he could hear Alexander chuckling lightly where he stood with his thick arms crossed over his chest and a broad smile on his face.

"What's the matter with you? Get this monkey off me," William pleaded. Alexander, whose reply was yet another chuckle, bent down and grabbed hold of Hans from under his arms as if he were a child and pried him off William.

Finally, William got the chance to rise to his feet and Alexander stepped between the two friends. William pressed both of his hands against his cheeks, which felt like they had been stung by a swarm of bees, and looked at Hans, who stood a few feet away dusting off his pants.

The crowd had largely dispersed though a handful had remained to see Hans get his revenge.

"Damn you, Hans," William choked out at last. "If every man was such a sore loser as you there would be much fewer people."

Hans chuckled and walked past Alexander. William opened his arms to embrace his friend, but then, as Hans opened his arms, William slapped him across the face, making him twist back to Alexander with his hand over his cheek and eyes squinted. Alexander gave a light hearted chuckle, slightly afraid that he would have to pry Hans off William a second time, Hans throwing fists instead of slaps. Hans smiled as he turned around to face William, his hand still pressed against the side of his face.

"I'll admit I deserved that one, you lucky bastard," the German said with a little chuckle as he faced William.

"No, you earned it," William retorted with a smile. "Come here, you old dog," he said as he stepped closer. Hans hesitated, expecting another slap was in the making, but William was genuine this time.

As they exchanged a friendly embrace, William noticed a familiar face in the dispersing crowd. Nadia was standing a little distance away, staring curiously at the great canopy of awnings.

"I will be right back," William said, tapping Hans on the shoulder, and going in her direction.

"Who is she?" Hans asked as he and Alexander watched William walking towards the woman.

"I don't know, but she's pretty," Alexander replied.

As William walked closer, Nadia kept staring at the awning that flapped in the breeze.

"I'm afraid you're too late; just missed the excitement," William said, motioning to the scene of the match he'd just won.

"What happened to you?" Nadia said when she noticed William's pinkish cheeks.

"Oh, this is the result of winning a chess match," he shrugged nonchalantly while bringing one of his hands up to his cheeks.

"Who did you beat?" She stepped closer and gently touched his hot cheek.

"That little man in the red over there," William answered as he turned around and pointed to Hans, who was standing in the shade of the awnings where he'd left him.

When Hans realized William was pointing at him, he smiled and waved, Alexander towered over him. Nadia covered her mouth to hide a smile she couldn't hold back.

"Come, let me introduce you to him. We're good friends," William said to Nadia while motioning with his hand for her to follow him and walking to where Hans and Alexander stood. They had only taken a couple of steps when William stopped her and said in a concerned voice, "You better wait here a moment." Nadia had no idea what he meant and looked after him with a perplexed expression.

"No, she looks more like a gypsy," Hans was saying just as William reached them.

"Listen, you two," William said in a hushed but firm voice, interrupting something Alexander had been about to say. "I'm going to bring her over here and introduce her to you."

"You know her?" Hans asked with surprise in his voice.

"Yes, and I want the both of you to act like the gentlemen you are already," William said as he buttoned up the two top buttons of Hans' red shirt, which were unbuttoned to help relieve him of the heat, covering up a little burly patch of orange chest hair. "So please stay here and don't try to impress anybody," William said as he finished the last button on Hans' shirt and took a step back like an artist stepping back from a painting to see if it had improved after a couple of additional strokes.

"What's that supposed to mean?" Alexander said.

"It means act gentlemanly," William said as he turned around and waved for Nadia to come to him.

"Gentlemanly?" Alexander asked, looking down at Hans.

"Don't look at me," Hans shrugged.

Nadia had stopped walking a couple of feet away from William's friends and now stood with them in the cool silver shade of the awnings.

"Nadia, meet Hans and Alexander," William said as he turned around to the two men. "Alexander, Hans, this is Nadia." Each of his friends placed one hand over his chest and bowed while sweeping the other hand out in front of him, looking like two jesters meeting the queen.

"It is nice to meet you," Nadia said, smiling with a slight laugh in her voice, charmed by their gesture. From the other side of the abandoned canopy a woman gave a screeching cry.

When they turned to see what was happening, a woman who was standing near a small group of people suddenly fell to the ground and didn't get up. People who stood nearby rushed to her and more people began to pour into the area surrounding the woman, hiding her from sight. William ran out from underneath the awnings and into the open, where the woman lay face down in the dirt.

As he walked farther into the thickening crowd, Nadia, Hans, and Alexander followed closely behind him. When William reached the inner circle that had been formed around the fallen woman, he looked down at her. She lay motionless on her side with one arm stretched out in front of her, carrying the weight of her head. She wasn't old, but she looked as if she had died of a sudden sickness. Her eyes stared blankly upward at the golden-brown dust clouds in the sky.

Near her head was a shattered pot filled with water from the well. A drop of blood slowly spilled from the corner of her mouth, then ran across her pale cheek toward the ground before being absorbed quickly where it landed. William could tell that the woman's death was the work of something far more sinister than a disease or an ailment. He looked behind him in the crowd to see Hans and Alexander, having lost their cheerful expressions to a feeling of suspicion and fear. Nadia stood next to them, her eyes glued to the dead woman in deep sadness.

A few moments later the crowd stepped aside to let Hakeem and an elderly man who was carrying a small bag walk into the circle around the woman.

"Make room," Hakeem yelled, motioning for everyone to step back. They were standing so tightly, even if the woman was still alive, she would suffocate. As the people stepped back, widening the circle around the woman, William noticed a tight nervousness in Hakeem's posture. He'd looked the same way that morning when he had told him about the Desert King.

The elderly man, who turned out to be Hakeem's doctor, knelt down beside the fallen woman. He dropped his bag on the ground and placed two fingers on the side of the woman's neck to see if she was alive. The crowd turned dead quiet, collectively listening for the woman's pulse. The doctor looked up at Hakeem and shook his head.

"She is dead," he declared, and the people began talking quickly but quietly amongst themselves.

"How?" Hakeem asked, his voice seeming to be the only one not touched by the reeking hand belonging to the hundred-handed monster of the mind called fear. The voices quieted to hear the doctor speak.

"I think it is some kind of poison," the doctor said as he rubbed the silver, goat-like beard that grew under his chin. The whole crowd burst into panicked conversation, everyone asking questions no one knew the answers to.

Hakeem motioned for them to settle down, then called one of his guards and gave him whispered instructions. By the subtle widening of the guard's eyes, William could tell that the message was best kept from the ears of the crowd.

William carefully observed the silent exchange and noticed that the guard was doubtful of Hakeem's orders. Nonetheless, the man nodded, turned around and pushed his way through the crowd, then disappeared among the tents.

Everybody seemed to wait in hushed silence, desperate to know what was going on. It was then William realized that the caravan leader was sweating under the pressure of everyone's expectations. After all, he had probably traveled this route for years—how often did such tragedies occur?

Finally, Hakeem looked up at the crowd. In his eyes William's saw a calm and reassuring look that seemed to belong to someone else, not the disturbed caravan leader from a moment earlier. The silence was fractured by a sickly cough that came from the crowd, but it went unnoticed. With this calming look that seemed to affect both his own heart and the hearts of the people, Hakeem gave one last glance to William before he turned around and walked through the crowd where he had entered, leaving the doctor behind with the woman.

After Hakeem left the crowd with the memory of his look that spoke volumes, the people continued to stand for several moments. A few people stepped forward to help the doctor carry the woman out of the street and to a tent where she could be taken care of before burial. Many moved away and dispersed, happy to get away from the unseemly sight.

William looked around to find Nadia and spotted her walking away from the place where the woman had died, glancing over her shoulder with a drowsy sadness. Soon, he lost sight of her, but noticed his friends were still there. He didn't have any answers for them but intended to find as much as he could. It seemed like another visit in Hakeem's tent was in order.

After saying goodbye to Hans and Alexander, William followed the path to Hakeem's tent, while the evening sun and the brown dust clouds overhead cast a strange light over the whole camp. Something poked his mind, urging him to search for a connection, however minimal, between the Sheik's death and the woman's. He found nothing that could possibly link them together, even though his gut told him otherwise.

At Hakeem's tent, the two guards stepped aside for him to pass, accustomed to his strange audiences with the leader. William couldn't help but wonder which side of Hakeem's personality he was going to encounter this time: the charismatic leader or the human.

Hakeem was standing at the tent's center with his hands laced together on the cloth wrapped around his waist. In continuing his vow of silence that he had taken when he walked away from the people, Hakeem sat down on one of the two stools that were in the tent. As he sat he pointed with an opened hand for William to take the stool across from him.

"It pains my heart to know an innocent woman has died today," Hakeem said a moment later, his voice heavy and solemn.

"Who do you think poisoned her?" William asked shortly after he sat down, going along with Hakeem's game of forgetting the past.

"It could be anyone in the caravan. A murderer or an accident. I do not know," Hakeem said with a fateful sigh.

"That man you sent away—what did you tell him?"

"A measure of safety that needed to be taken." This was a fraction of an answer, but William decided not to pressure the caravan leader. He knew how elusive Hakeem could be if pressed too far.

In that moment, the same man they'd been discussing stepped into the tent, standing with his hands resting on his knees and his breath heavy. William started to rise, thinking Hakeem might want to take care of this business in privacy, but the caravan leader placed a hand on William's shoulder, pushing him gently back down on his stool.

"Please, stay," Hakeem said, and William nodded. Then the leader turned to the guard. "Tell me what news you bring," Hakeem requested.

The man glanced between the two, as if to ask whether a foreigner could be trusted. "Go on," Hakeem confirmed, dismissing the silent question.

The man obeyed. "The well, it is..." he burst out then stopped, hesitant to speak the words.

"It is what?" Hakeem prompted impatiently, a frown appearing on his face.

"The well has been poisoned," the man said at last.

Hakeem and William exchanged a glance as strings of fear started pulling at their minds. The Arab had crossed the desert many times and knew there were many dangers to be aware of. The one thing he feared the most was what anyone who crosses either a sea of water or land fears: dying of thirst.

"You are certain?" Hakeem asked, unable to hide his emotions.

"We checked several times, and the doctor is sure it is poison," the guard nodded.

"We can't clean out the well," Hakeem thought aloud, while the other two stared at him. "I want you to send a group of men to the next well in our journey and check the water there. If it is good to drink come back and report to me. If not move on to the next well and don't stop searching until you find fresh water," the Arab ordered said, and William noticed he had regained some of his composure. The man nodded and vanished, ready to follow Hakeem's orders.

Meanwhile, Hakeem rose to his feet, and William did the same, knowing that there was work to be done. "I must take care of this," Hakeem said, clearly dismissing William.

"Is there any way I can help?" William asked when they reached the entrance.

"No. I have enough men. Just stay away from the well," Hakeem said before patting William on the shoulder and stepping back.

Outside, William didn't know what to make of the unearthly gloom above that drifted silently in the sky. With a new awareness, he began making his way through the paths back to his tent. Inwardly, he analyzed Hakeem's distinct personalities in light of the last events: one confident, one fearful.

When he arrived at his tent, the air, too, seemed to be scented with fear, and, standing there, William began to feel that life as he had come to know and understand it was all about to change.

# 15

ON HIS WAY TO BUY A LOAF OF BREAD the next day, William walked past the poisoned well. In his mind, he could still hear the dead woman's last scream as her body collapsed on the ground. Two of Hakeem's men were guarding it now allowing no man, woman, or child to drink from the poisoned water. It was a wise choice. William could already feel his throat tighten with thirst.

*I wonder if I could slip past them fast enough and get a drink. If the water isn't poisoned I'll live; if it is, well . . . oh listen to yourself, William. You're sounding like a mad man. This will all be over when Hakeem's men return with the water and then you can drink to your heart's content, drown if you like, but until then don't think about water. It will all be fine.*

He shook his head, thinking he would have to buy water too, or he wouldn't be able to eat any bread without his tongue sticking to the roof of his mouth.

A squeaky wagon wheel interrupted William's thoughts, and he turned around at the sound. What he saw was not at all what he had expected. A line of Bedouin cut across the intersection where he stood, much like a lazy river of blue robes, horses, and broken hearts.

William took a step back. Prince Abdul was riding at the front of the line on a white horse, expressionless as usual but colored with an aura of responsibility now that he was named the Sheik. The warriors behind him stared at the ground in mourning. A handful of them wept silently, hiding their faces behind dark veils.

They marched like an army retreating from battle, tired and saddened by their losses. The squeaking sound became louder as the men moved forward, and William spotted the wagon carrying the dead Sheik moving slowly among the procession of warriors. The body was covered with a pristine white cloth, a custom of the desert people.

124

# De Collibus

As the wagon moved past William, his mind was flooded with thoughts about the old Sheik and how they'd come to know each other. William remembered the ring that sat on his little finger; having worn it since it was given to him, he had nearly forgotten it was there. He brought his hand up to his chest and looked down at the ring. The stone set in the gold band was smooth like glass, light on the surface and darker inside, like the sea. It reminded William of the soothing fountain he had found back in Nador. He could almost feel the water chilling his fingertips.

Looking up, William watched as the wagon disappeared behind a tent along with the warriors that had marched behind it. Aside from the small amount of dust they raised, there was nothing left of them now other than the memory of their company. William sighed and, along with everyone else who had stopped to watch the procession, continued walking down the path that would lead him to the bread maker.

Everyone he passed along the way looked nearly as thirsty as he did. Their pace was slow, on the verge of sleepwalking. Their eyes stared emptily at the ground ahead of them and their crackled lips unconsciously hung open. William noticed An elderly man lying at the edge of the street. his hands were held out in front of him as if he was crawling, but they were frozen still. William knew the man had died from poisoning when he saw the way his eyes stared blankly at the ground near his face and a drop of blood that darkened the dirt near his mouth. William stared at the elderly man, his feet forgetting where he was walking but still carrying him for ward at a drowsy pace.

He wondered why no one seemed to care that the old man lay dead in the path like a stray dog. Less than two days ago, there would have been a crowd of people surrounding the body like pigeons around breadcrumbs, but now the body lay abandoned. William felt as if he was walking through a strange dream in which the world had lost its sense of humanity and he was the only one possessing it, but too weak to speak and helpless to change the world around him.

He struggled to bring his eyes back to the street ahead of him. His neck felt weak and his stomach quivered at what he might find next. Thankfully, the few people that he met were all alive, thirsty and exhausted, but alive.

Without any sign of warning, the ground underneath his feet began to teeter back and forth like the deck of a swaying ship. *I am going to faint,* he thought as his eyes became sensitive to the brightness of the soil. He stopped in the middle of the path and spread his feet to steady himself. The fluids in his brain were swishing around like water in a bathtub.

William tilted his head back and looked at the sky. His lips were dry and parched like those of everyone else who couldn't drink. His mind was stilled by what he saw. The sky was mud-washed. A golden halo around the sun was dimmed by dust that floated freely and silently. William imagined what it would be like to fly in the clouds, where the only sound he could hear would be the whistling wind in his ears. He began to fall backwards, but staggered and stopped his fall. He was back on earth like a bird with a broken wing.

The sound of people talking happily in the path ahead of him made him wiggle a finger in his ear. When laughter was added to the cheerful banter, he looked to see what was going on. A small gathering of people stood in a circle around a short, elderly woman. William squinted his doubtful eyes. When he looked closer, he noticed the elderly woman held a large bouquet of flowers close to her chest as if it were a baby. She and the people surrounding her looked like they were from another dimension, a hiccup in the universe that shouldn't be there.

William walked closer, almost unaware that his feet were moving, with his back slightly hunched forward and his head lowered, as if about to receive a punch he couldn't block. As he neared the group, he discovered that the people surrounding the old woman were buying the flowers she cradled near her chest. Slowly, the group thinned as each person walked away with a colorful flower.

Smiling at the woman, William passed by her and took a sharp turn down an abandoned alley. He found it strange that he saw no one here as this alley was usually brimming with people, but shrugged it off. The heat kept the people in their tents.

Then he heard it.

A growling noise was coming from behind him. William stopped and listened while he looked over his shoulder. He heard footsteps mixed with grunts and his suspicious awareness grew. A woman screamed. William turned around and ran back into the path where he'd seen the flower woman. His legs felt like they were made of sand he wasn't sure he would reach her in time.

When William arrived at the bend in the path, he saw a man with a face concealed by a turban furiously tugging at the old woman's hands that held onto a pouch of coins she'd earned selling flowers.

"Hey!" William shouted as he ran toward the woman and the thief, surprised his voice didn't fail to leave his lips. The thief, clearly not expecting company, gave a last tug at the pouch, ripping it open. The coins scattered as the woman fell on her back, and the thief, seeing he had no time to gather the coins, darted away from the woman and ran down a path to the left. As William chased after him, he forced his lungs to work harder and quickened his pace, but the thief was much faster. Soon William lost sight of the thief, and came to a stop at the mouth of the path. It was empty and there was no sign of the man. He'd never find the thief now.

William turned to the old woman, now kneeling in the path, picking up coins and sniffling. He walked toward her, and the woman glanced up in fear.

Seeing that he wasn't her assailant, she wiped away her tears. When William reached her, he kneeled in front of her and started collecting her coins in his palm. William continued picking up the coins in silence until he thought it best to see if the woman was all right.

"Are you ok?" he asked in a soft tone, looking up briefly. The woman didn't speak english but she nodded and her face relaxed a little, but still the tears continued to flow.

William looked back down and continued collecting coins, all the while thinking that the woman looked different than the Arab women traveling in the caravan. Her skin was lighter and her eyebrows were dark and thick. She reminded him of the gypsies he had photographed during the war.

He remembered that everything they owned was piled onto an ox cart; anything they didn't need, they abandoned or burned. In the photograph, the gypsies were looking over their shoulders at him, a mixture of injustice and fear written on their faces. The grandparents sat on the back of the wagon with the grandchildren on their laps. A little girl clasped a dirty doll to her chest and a little boy held a badly tarnished wooden sword at the side of his mud-streaked legs and round-top boots. The adults walked at the side of the wagon or sat on piles of boxes and furniture. The photograph never made it in the newspaper. "Not enough glory in it," William's commanding officer had told him when he saw the picture.

When the coins were placed back in the torn pouch, William and the woman rose to their feet. For a moment they stood there silent; William unable to come up with the words to say goodbye and the woman not quite sure how to thank him. Then she wiped away a stray tear from the corner of her eye and looked up at William.

With a nod and a smile, William walked away, hopeful that he would buy his loaf of bread soon. He was disappointed he couldn't catch the thief, but what could he do about it now?

"Stop," the woman said when he'd taken a dozen strides. William turned around and saw her running towards him, surprised to feel her strong embrace as she pulled him in for a squeeze. "Thank you," she said and promptly let go of him. He smiled instead of speaking, mainly because he didn't feel he should be thanked. The woman stared at him for a moment while she made up her mind.

"Here," the woman said staring at him and bringing a handful of flowers up to her chest. "Choose one and it is yours." A girl's smile was frozen on her face as she waited for William to pick a flower. He leaned closer to examine his options and noticed that each flower had a distinct personality, yet only caught his interest.

"I will take this one," William said, pointing a finger at the flower he wanted.

"Good choice," the woman smiled, pulling out a flower with deep purple petals speckled with dark spots. At the center was a bright yellow circle of pollen. "This is a desert flower, very hard to find," the woman said as William took it from her. "It only blossoms right before the rainy season and is a symbol of good luck. I picked it myself," she stated proudly. William brought it to his nose and took a small sniff. The scent was barely noticeable, but rich in complexity.

"Thank you," William said.

The woman smiled and bowed her head, and William returned the gesture before continuing on his way. He kept staring at the complex colors of the flower, smelling it again as he walked. Just like the woman, the flower seemed to come from another dimension.

He hadn't considered this before, but now he realized that the woman's clothes and her youthful smile resembled those of Nadia, he thought it would be a good idea to give the flower to her to help bring back the light in her eyes. Perhaps, even if only for a minute, he could help her forget about the sickness in the camp.

With that thought in mind, William changed direction and chose a path that would lead him to Nadia's tent. It looked like all the others in the alley, except for one thing that William had never noticed before. Near the flap three small bells were sewn into the cloth, so that when anyone entered or left it would jingle. William slowed his pace when he realized this was the handiwork of Nadia's mother. How would he call Nadia when her mother could come bursting out instead?

And still, his hand reached out and pulled the bells. What had he done? *What if her father comes out to see you holding a flower in your hand like an idiot? He'll kill you. Even if he's only three feet tall and missing an arm, he'll strangle you,* William thought. His ears strained to make out a sound coming from inside the tent. It got louder. When the flaps opened, William took a step back and saw Nadia's face, sad and exhausted, much like his own.

"Hello, William," Nadia said, a trace of joy stirring in her voice. She looked down at the flower in his hands and smiled.

"It's for you," William handed the flower to her. "It's a desert flower. It can only be found right before the rainy season," he explained, as if speaking from experience.

"Where did you find it?" Nadia asked with a slight frown.

"I didn't. A woman gave it to me in exchange for a favor." *How odd that she would frown,* he thought to himself, observing her face with interest.

"Oh, I see," Nadia said quietly. "Did you hear about the group Hakeem sent to the next well?" she asked as she ran her fingers along the fuzzy petals.

"I did. I hope they bring some water back with them." William observed Nadia playing absently with the flower. Was she thinking about the caravan? The deaths? Though the flower had brought her a moment of joy, it didn't help her forget about their situation.

William wanted to tell her that everything was going to be all right, but could he predict the future?

A faint horn echoed in the silence. William and Nadia looked at each other, then followed the direction of the sound. A moment later, a multitude of excited voices entered the air as people began filling the streets.

"What is that?" Nadia asked.

"It must be the group returning from the next well," William said as he looked back at Nadia with a dreamy smile. "Let's see for ourselves."

He hurried toward the perimeter of the camp along with the rest of the people. His legs felt heavy, but his excitement pushed him forward. All around him, the people's eyes looked crazed with hope. They helped each other down the path with arms around each other's shoulders. A person fell down unconscious and was left behind in the stampeding crowd. Every path pointing east was overflowing with a river of dirty robes and forgotten sandals. The excitement was contagious.

When the crowd reached the perimeter, they began to cheer as they made way for a man and his horse.

William and Nadia stepped to the side and the rider galloped past them without stopping or paying attention to the people. But William had seen the man's face, exhausted and mangled by a terror that he seemed to be riding away from. A bit of that terror rubbed off on William. The rider didn't slow down for the people, and the cheers quickly died out when the crowd sensed panic in the air.

"What's wrong?" Nadia asked as William looked down the path where the rider had disappeared.

"I'm not sure," he muttered, looking back at her. The people around them slowly dispersed, worried and confused. More than anything, they felt their hope drain away because water wasn't coming soon.

With nothing else to do, William and Nadia starting walking to her tent, each of them lost in thought. What would they do now if water wasn't coming? They couldn't stay at the poisoned well, but where would they go? But most importantly, what had happened to the men searching for fresh water and why had only one of them returned?

"Thank you for the flower," Nadia spoke after a while, looking up at him with her brilliant green eyes.

"Oh, you're welcome," William said, almost startled by her voice, having nearly forgotten she was still there. The flower brought back thoughts of the thief he had chased away earlier. Could he be standing in the crowd now, waiting for the people to disperse to exact his revenge? William looked around, searching every man's face for eyes the same as the thief's.

Still a long distance away from Nadia's tent, the two of them stopped and faced each other. It could have been the mutual silence, but exhaustion and not wanting to have to battle Nadia's mother from chasing him with a spear were probably among the reasons why they didn't go together any further. Nadia looked at the flower in her hands while William glanced from each passing face to the next. Both waited for the other to speak first so they wouldn't be the one to say goodbye, but no words came out.

At last, Nadia's soft words broke the silence. "Goodbye, William," she said, and continued walking down the path leading to her tent.

William was too tired to speak. Instead, he waved at her turned back, and considered his options. A sudden pain in his stomach almost made him double over, probably because he had eaten nothing since the previous night. The thought of skipping the bread and returning to his tent to rest taunted him... but no. *I won't become like the others,* he thought, *weak and hopeless.* His stomach growled to remind him why he had left the tent in the first place, and before exhaustion's temptation could grab a hold of him, William started walking down toward the bread maker's tent.

The air in the caravan had become deathly quiet now that people were returning to their tents. In the silence of his own footsteps, William imagined a second pair running up behind him and putting a blade in his back or slashing his throat. It was an image that he felt belonged in the dark streets of Nador more than it did in the caravan, yet here it was. He'd always imagined the caravan to a be safe place, but now his hair stood on end while walking down the empty paths, even in daylight.

When he arrived at the open area that served as their market place, the same area where he had taken pictures of the old man and his scarf shop, William stopped. The baker's tent looked abandoned. Gone was the smell of bread and the cloth so often used to shade the baker's busy customers had been lowered in haste.

*Too many people are getting sick. Something has to be done,* William thought as he felt the emptiness around him. He considered speaking with Hakeem, offering his help... then he imagined Hakeem receiving the news from the rider and decided now was not the right time. Instead, he decided to pay Hans a visit and see if he knew anything about the group that had gone out for water.

As William made his way to the German's tent, he only met a handful of people, their sickly faces filling him with more of the same grimness he had felt at the baker's tent. After taking several different paths, he reached Hans' canvas home and walked inside to find his friend sitting on a stool at the back holding a wine bottle to his mouth. William stopped halfway in the entrance. Hans' gulps continued without any sign of stopping, and a frown of disbelief appeared on William's face. When Hans brought down the bottle he jumped.

"Hey, William," Hans said, happily surprised, as he wiped his lips with the back of his hand. A sharp fermented smell filled William's lungs.

"Hans, is... is that wine?" William asked as he stepped fully inside the tent. Hans looked at the bottle with a strange gaze, then adjusted it so he could read the label and held it perfectly still with a studying frown.

"I am not sure. It's in French," he said with a groan as the barely sober part of him realized the pit it was falling into.

William took several cautious steps in Hans' direction, not because he was afraid the German would do anything foolish; he just didn't want to distract Hans from being himself. Hans looked up at William and extended the wine bottle up to him. The label was in English. William took the bottle and read the label, fighting off the temptation to drink. He could hear Reginald's voice echoing, "Do you take to the bottle, William? I recommend you try it sometime; I can't get enough of the bloody stuff."

"Don't you hate the taste of wine?" William asked as he handed the bottle back, thinking he'd heard Hans say so on a previous occasion.

"Yes, I can't stand it," Hans replied as he lifted the bottle to his mouth and took a charitable swig. As the bottom end of the bottle rose above Hans' head, William sat down on the ground and noticed a small photograph laying near Hans' pillow.

The photograph was an olive-green color and contained three people standing against a white background. Two men, one around forty and the other half that age, stood side by side, each with a hand on the shoulders of a young boy of around twelve, smartly standing in front of them. The father and the oldest son wore brass-buttoned uniforms with caps cupped underneath their arms, bearing proud looks on their faces. The boy's undeniable confidence singled him out as a young Hans. William thought it strange that Hans had never mentioned his family and he guessed that this was his. The German made a loud hissing noise as he brought down the bottle and cocked his head quickly to the right. William looked up at his friend, trying to keep a neutral expression on his face.

"Why the wine?" he asked as Hans wiped his lips then looked down at the bottle and up at William.

"I can't drink water, so I bought some wine. Besides, this can't be poisoned, can it?" Hans replied with a confident voice that slowly turned doubtful.

"That's true," William said, wondering if Hans saw him looking at the photograph. The German was looking at the bottle with concern in his eyes.

"You don't think it's poisoned, do you?" Hans said as his stomach began to feel strange.

"I doubt that," William said.

"Are you sure?" Hans brought the neck of the bottle close to his nose and sniffed the wine with eyes that stared over William's shoulder in deep concentration.

"Your wine isn't poisoned, Hans, your brain is," William declared. Hans kept on sniffing.

"Here, you smell it," he said at last, thrusting the bottle in William's general direction. The wine swished inside the bottle as it traded hands and William held it up to his nose. He took a sniff of the sour liquid and scrunched his nose. Hans' face twitched as he leaned closer.

"It smells fine. Here," William said and handed the bottle back to its owner.

Hans took it back and frowned. "God have mercy on the poor bastard who poisons a bottle of wine," he said as he examined his warped reflection in the emerald glass of the bottle as if after a good shave. William smiled and leaned back on the central post. "Were you in the British army?" Hans asked after a moment, his voice solemn and strange.

"Yes," William muttered, an admission of shame, but his eyes kept staring forward.

"You fought Germans?" His voice bore the innocence of a child's questions that would make any adult feel a little uncomfortable.

"Yes," William said again, the pain in his stomach intensified.

The look in Hans' eyes changed. He didn't seem to look so drunk and imbalanced any more. His gaze was steady, looking right into William's soul.

"And you?" William asked to break the uncomfortable silence.

"I did not go. I couldn't because my mother was sick at the time. I was the youngest and had to stay to watch over her," Hans said, his eyes returning to the bottle.

"Your family, what were they like?" William asked quietly.

The German was silent for a moment, breathing heavily. "My father was a quiet man. He didn't talk to Meinhard and me a lot until we were grownups; he didn't take what we said seriously. My mother was kind to us. She always gave us dessert if we ate our vegetables and was there to listen to what we had to say." Hans stopped speaking when a memory, one he had not thought about in years, made him burst into wheezing laughter that sent his head back with his eyes squeezed shut. As he brought his head down, he gave a high-pitched sigh that spoke of good times.

"One time, when my brother Meinhard and I were little, we went for a hike in the mountains around our village and found a hill with a muddy slope. We decided to do a little competition to see who could make it to the bottom first. Meinhard won the first time, so I decided we should do a rematch. We spent the whole day on that hill.

"When evening came and we were walking back home, we saw a farmer driving a wagon. He laughed so hard at us, dirty as grave diggers, I thought he was going to fall off his seat. Meinhard asked him why he was laughing, but instead of answering, the farmer asked us which hillside we had been rolling on. We told him and he started laughing even harder. When he caught his breath, he told us that his cows had been pasturing there the day before." Hans burst into a roar of drunken laughter, "We were covered in Scheisse." William chuckled with him, silently imagining the picture.

"What about you? Do you have any brothers or sisters?" Hans said and took another drink from the bottle.

"No, just me," William said.

"Your parents—what are they like?"

"I didn't see my father much as a child. He was either working in the factory or drinking at the pub. But my mother was kind to me," William said.

"Where are they now?" Hans asked.

"My mother died when I was very young and my father—the last time I saw him was shortly before the war," William said as he counted the years.

"I'm sorry."

William stood. "Don't be. Thanks for... the conversation." Hans nodded but stayed seated. "Will you be all right?" William asked in a serious tone, wondering if his words would reach Hans' sober self that was busy drowning in wine.

"I can handle myself," Hans slurred while motioning toward the flap of the tent. William nodded and started to leave. When he caught a glimpse of the camp outside through a brink in the cloth, a part of him hoped Hans would call him back. Instead, he heard a sliding noise followed by a soft thump. Hans had slid from the stool and was now lying on his side, fast asleep, while the remaining wine spilled on the ground in a growing pool of red. With a rhapsody of snores, Hans pulled his legs into a fetal position.

William's smile broadened. Shaking his head, he stepped outside the tent and looked around with squinted eyes. He thought it would be a good idea to go back to his tent and rest before going out to look for something to eat once it cooled down.

When William neared his tent, he slowed his pace when he saw a man carrying a rifle standing by the entrance. He approached the man slowly from the side. The man was staring ahead of him as if waiting to be spoken to. He stood several inches taller than William and the knuckles gripping the rifle across his chest looked as defined and hard as his face. When he heard footsteps, he looked straight at William.

"Hakeem wants to talk to you," the guard said.

"Why?" It was strange that Hakeem wished to speak with him now.

"Follow me. I will take you to him," the guard said, ignoring William's question and started walking straight toward the mouth of a narrow path from the tent.

William remained where he was, but when the guard was about to enter the alley, he ran after him to catch up, noticing they were going to a part of the camp which he had only visited a number of times.

It was a long walk until the guard stopped. "We stop here," he struggled to say in English and turned his back toward a tent to stand guard. "Hakeem is waiting," the guard said as he pointed to the entrance of the small tent to his left.

William studied the guard's eyes. They were half open and had a cold emptiness inside their dark brown color. He moved closer to the tent, keeping his eyes on the guard, then slowly pulled the cloth back and entered.

He was instantly blinded by darkness. The tent constituted a single shadow at first, but slowly, shapes began to appear. William thought that extra cloths might have been placed outside to keep the heat out, but it seemed to serve another purpose. He noticed three candles placed around the tent, marking out the space it contained. It was much smaller than Hakeem's, and not that much larger than his own.

"Come, William, we need to talk," Hakeem's voice spoke to him from somewhere near the center.

A moment after, William spotted a shadow sitting on a small stool where the voice had come from. He walked across the tent to where Hakeem was sitting and noticed the caravan leader's face was disarranged by strange shadows that cast odd shapes up to his forehead. By now William's eyes had adjusted to the darkness, and when he reached the center of the tent he sat down on a stool across from Hakeem. The figure of a man stood behind Hakeem, a colorless shadow. Then he heard something move behind him.

He turned around and saw another man standing right behind him, still and breathless. When William faced Hakeem, the leader was staring at him with an empty look in his eyes.

"Why am I here?" William asked, his soft voice sounding like a shout in the cave-like silence. Hakeem brought his hand over his mouth and coughed several times.

The cough sounded painful and dry. "Because I need your help," Hakeem said as he looked up, the painful look fading from his face.

"Why do you want my help?"

"Because I trust you. I don't know why, but I do. You are a good man, William," Hakeem said, his voice sounding tense from the pain in his throat.

"I'll help. What do you want me to do?" William said. "Did you see the rider arrive?" Hakeem asked and William confirmed. The Arab was about to speak when footsteps walking past the tent's entrance disturbed the silence. A faint cough reached their ears, then the passer's footsteps were gone. "The group I sent out was ambushed," Hakeem said, and William imagined the men's dead bodies scattered on the ground like the warriors in the Bedouin camp. "The man you saw was the only survivor. They were killed with arrows. Black feathers." Hakeem's voice bore a preacher's hatred.

"Is the water in the next well safe?" This seemed to be the most important information now.

"I do not know, they were ambushed before they tested it. I don't know what to do," Hakeem said, and coughed a few times, turning his head away from William and covering his mouth with his sleeve. When he turned back William felt as though a needle had stuck him in the back of the neck. "What is it?" Hakeem asked when he sensed the fear in William's gaze. William's eyes lowered to Hakeem's wrist.

The man looked down. A few drops of blood had turned the blue of his sleeve into black. William's eyes glanced at Hakeem's face. He was deathly pale and a fateful sadness filled his eyes, the look of a man who knows he is fatally ill and can't do anything to change his circumstances.

William knew what the blood meant. Slowly, Hakeem turned his wrist toward his knee and looked back at him. The look on his face seemed the same as it was when William had entered. Calm and focused.

"What should I do?" Hakeem asked, feigning calmness to mask his dread of a slow death. William looked down at the ground and thought about what he would do if he was in Hakeem's place.

"Send another group to the well. They won't be expecting us to go back a second time. We need clean water, so a wagon with barrels and sheepskins has to go as well to bring water back to the caravan. We'll need more men too," William said.

Hakeem nodded with a determined frown. "I like your plan. I will be sure to use it when the right time comes," Hakeem said. His eyes drifted to the darkness below him. "The right time," he repeated wondering when that time would come. For a moment, William and Hakeem stared at each other with the same thought in their minds and the same unsettled feeling in their hearts. Hakeem rose slowly from his stool and William did the same. Then the Arab walked past William and toward the tent's entrance.

"Do you know when you will send the next group to the well?" William asked as Hakeem's robe faded in the darkness. The leader turned around, his hands behind his back.

"I will know soon. I have to gather my men and inform them of the change in our plan. We will work as quickly as we can to get water," Hakeem said in a reassuring tone as William walked toward him. "You will be among the first to know when the men are ready. Be safe," Hakeem said to William, placing a firm grip on his shoulder, and smiled at him.

William tried to smile back as genuinely as he could. But being this close to Hakeem, he could see the pain in the man's eyes that darkness couldn't hide, which, he began to realize, was why this tent was chosen instead of Hakeem's. The Arab patted William on the shoulder twice and William stepped out of the tent.

On the walk back, William hoped that Hakeem would send him to the well along with his men so he could do something to help get water. He thought about the riders who were ambushed and wondered by whose hand they fell. Remembering the helpless feeling he had experienced when seeing the slain Bedouin warriors in the desert, William imagined Hakeem's men being picked off with no target to fire back at, and the screams of their last man echoing in the empty dunes like a call for vengeance.

135

# 16

WHEN HE LOOKED UP AT THE SKY, the sun was shining like a pearl behind the dust clouds. The evening air was cool but only a handful of fires illuminated the camp, since many of the people were too weak to build one. William walked down an empty path, his footsteps sinking into the sand making the only noise. As his mind considered Hakeem's plan to send a second group, his mouth chewed on a piece of bread his hand had plucked from a loaf near his chest. He glanced over his shoulder at the long path behind him, thinking the thief might be following. To his relief, no one was there.

He heard the groan of a camel somewhere in front of him and stopped as if he had walked into a wall. His jaw lowered, like the feeling of hope in his stomach, and the loaf of bread rolled out of his fingers and landed on the ground. In front of him, a thick crowd of people, animals, and wagons, probably numbering half the caravan cut across the path ahead. The silence was shattered when he heard a woman scream, the pleading scream of a woman about to lose her dignity to a desperate man.

A couple of people ran around the procession, but they weren't able to stop them. William took a closer look at the wagons and the loaded camels. Among other belongings he noticed neatly folded tents ready for travel. With disbelief, he ran up to the crowd and a few people followed behind him, pleading and screaming for the others to stay; many stood watching from the sides with a detached gaze.

William reached a wagon and hurried to keep up with the rolling wheels. "What are you doing?" he asked a man slouched on the back of the wagon.

"Leaving," the man replied, showing indifference to the shock on William's face. Obviously, not everyone had been privy to this planned departure.

"Leaving? Where?" William asked, his voice slightly louder.

"To Yemen. I'd come if I were you. Come with us and you will live. Stay and you will die," the man said with the blandness of a priest quoting scripture.

Deep down, William knew the man was right, but it didn't have to be like this. "Listen to me. Hakeem is sending more men to the well. Everything will be all right in just a few days. Stay. Stay and we will all live. No one has to die."

His words fell on deaf ears. "We are not going back. If we stay another day, we will all be dead," another man chimed in from the bed of the wagon. He stood up and yelled to the assembled crowd: "Save yourselves!" Behind him, William could hear a baby crying and a family arguing over who should stay and who should go.

"If you abandon us, our blood will be on your hands. All of your hands. You'd have murdered us yourselves," William said, his voice just below a shout as he spoke with indignant rage at the men sitting on the wagon.

"No matter. We have made our choice. We are leaving," the first man said.

William stopped walking. His legs couldn't take another step out of disbelief at what he was hearing. Around him, people were weeping; others stood with cold eyes and still mouths and even stiller hearts.

"Damn you, then," William shouted at the wagon that drifted away. *I can't believe it; they're abandoning us. They're...*

William's thought was interrupted by another, more troubling one. "My camera," he gasped, fearing that his only chance to send his camera back to England had just slipped through his fingers.

He turned around and started running toward his tent, panic filling his chest like seawater in the hull of a sinking ship. His legs burned and his lungs struggled to suck in another breath, but he continued to run. When he entered the tent he rushed to the back where he had last seen his camera and groped in the darkness with his hands. The camera and its case were gone.

Vanished. William sprang to his feet and ran his hands through his hair as a panic-driven headache threatened to split open the side of his head like the rifle stock had on the first day he entered the caravan. Pacing the tent, he puffed his cheeks to let out a breath, desperately trying to remember where he had put the camera. He remembered seeing it but couldn't remember where. It was as if his memory was a piece of film missing several frames that had been cut out and the ends taped together.

The camera's leather case was vivid in his imagination. It was in his hands, but then, where had he left it? He bent down and whisked his blanket up in the air. The soft thud he was hoping for didn't come. He spun around as his eyes moved from one corner of the tent to the next. He rushed to his suitcase and threw open the top half. The camera wasn't there either. He rose and started pacing back and forth, combing his hair nervously back.

Suddenly, William spotted a dark shape the size of the camera case lying in the left corner of his tent. He fell on all fours and snatched the camera from the ground where it had laid untouched for the last couple of days. He panted as he turned it around in his hands, barely believing he had found it.

As he rose to his feet, a white rectangle captured his gaze in the darkness. A small paper lay face-down at the edge of the suitcase, tucked into his clothes.

His breath calmed and his hand slowly lowered into the darkness to pick up the paper, forgetting the group of people that was walking farther and farther away. As he straightened his back, William flipped the paper around so that the front was facing him. A series of words were scribbled there in blue ink: "The London Dove." A soft smile appeared on his face as he remembered the day he'd stood in the foggy London street looking down at this note in desperation.

To know that one day a delivery man would carry his camera to the *London Dove*'s doorstep filled him with a sad excitement for not finishing the job himself. He folded the small note and tucked it inside the camera case then glanced over his right shoulder at the short table near the entrance of his tent. In a moment of mental clarity William remembered that Reginald wouldn't know who to pay when the camera returned to London. He would have to instruct Reginald about paying Mrs Eldrich. But he would have to hurry. If he took too long the leaving crowd might be gone by the time he returned, the thick darkness obscuring their path.

With great haste he scribbled down a note with Mrs Eldrich's address and the details of her payment and he tucked this note into the camera's case along with the other one.

William kneeled in front of his suitcase and pushed the clothes over to one side, revealing the envelope containing the little money he had left. He plucked the envelope from the suitcase and ran out of the tent. As he ran to the edge of camp, his lungs began wheezing from the strain he had put on his body.

The paths near the perimeter of the camp were congested with people. Many of the men were talking loudly with each other, and the women and children were crying. A few people were scrambling to take down their tents and gather their belongings to catch up with the rest of the deserters, and an equal number of people were trying to stop them.

When William emerged out of the camp, he slowed down to a walk and searched the gray hills with his eyes. The deserters were gone but the panicked voices they had left behind loomed in the cold air at his back. The horizon was dulled by the clouds that dimmed the retreating sun.

He looked to his right. The land was empty except for the caravan's remaining tents that stretched away in a long line. Turning his head, William looked at the flat plain to his left. Something was moving in the distance; a long procession of dark figures crawling farther away from the caravan.

William ran in that direction, his camera case bouncing on his hip. The dirt around his feet was thrown into the air when the wind raced across the flat plain, hitting him like the shockwave from an artillery shell. The wind pushed on his shoulder, making it difficult to hear or keep a straight line as he ran. It bit at the tips of his ears and he shrugged his shoulders. That didn't help much. The cold wind found other ways into his shirt.

As William reached the group of deserters, now a good distance away from camp, he stopped at the front of the crowd. People, animals, and wagons passed by him and the wind created a howl that added to the panic in his veins. His eyes jumped from one person to the next, looking for the face of the person he would trust to mail his camera back to London.

Everyone ignored him as if he didn't exist and moved past him without so much as a glance. They were leaving and there was nothing he could do to stop them. He stood in the middle of the moving column, his camera held to his chest and his feet constantly shifting to his right or to his left. *No, not that one or that one. No. No. He looks too old. He doesn't look trustworthy. I don't like the way he looks.*

William examined one passing face after the next, and always found some reason why each person was not meant to send his camera back to England. He looked toward the newly assembled caravan and saw the end of the crowd crawling closer to him. He was running out of time. On a whim of desperation William rushed over to a man riding a camel, paying no attention to whether he looked trustworthy or not.

"Hey," William shouted as he waved at the man to get his attention in case the wind drowned his voice. The man stopped out of curiosity, examining William from head to toe. William grabbed onto the side of the camel's saddle. "Are you going to Yemen?" he asked, the wind forcing *him* to squint.

"Yes," the man confirmed as he leaned down to William, his right hand keeping the cloth wrapped around his head from getting blown away.

"Good. Can you do something for me? I'll pay you," William shouted.

"What is it?" the man asked. The wind suddenly became louder as the last people moved on without them, leaving them exposed to the wind.

"When you reach Yemen, go to a post office and mail this for me," William said as he raised his camera up to the rider and nodded to see if the man understood. The man took the leather case with a frown and turned it around in his hands to get a good look at it.

"Mail it where?"

"To London. Here," William said as he handed the envelope containing the money up to the man. "Use this to pay the post office and what is left is yours."

The rider took the envelope and looked inside then back at William.

"Why do you want me to do this?" the man asked, not appearing to care that the crowd of people was getting farther away from him.

"I have a promise to keep," William yelled. The man looked back down at the money, then at the camera case, then back at William.

"I will do it," he said at last, nodding solemnly.

"Thank you," William shouted back, smiling.

"Good luck," the man said and tapped his camel on the shoulder.

William stepped back and the camel trotted away, carrying its owner toward the rest of the deserting crowd. William watched them until he couldn't see them anymore. The wind blotted out any sound and allowed him to think clearly. Even his mind felt silent.

He felt freed.

His chest felt lighter; breathing seemed easier. That man was taking his camera, the pictures he had taken on his journey, and everything he used to be, to Yemen—to be shipped to England. He thought about Mrs. Eldrich and the promise he had made to her. He would have loved to give her the money himself, to pinch her round cheeks and stare into her grayish blue eyes. The thought that he might never see her again saddened him a little but one little regret was nothing compared to the life he would live once the caravan continued to Yemen.

He was standing in the middle of a land as bare as his loyalty to the *London Dove*. William put his hands in his pockets and started walking back to the camp, his eyes looking down at the pale dirt under his feet. When he looked up at the remaining tents, the relief that had settled over him began to slip away. He knew that when the caravan found clean water they would start to travel, and they might even catch up with the ones who had deserted them.

Of course, all of that might have just been wishful thinking, but the prospect of getting water soon made him forget about the grim situation of the caravan and also gave him hope that everything would be all right. The wind slowed down when he entered the camp. On his way back to his tent, William felt confused.

Mixed feelings churned in his heart. Half of him felt happy that he would never have to return to England. The other half felt sad that the caravan had been split in two, its people poisoned and a few already dead. Despite the contrasting feelings of freedom and despair, the camp looked beautiful to him. It always would.

By the time he reached his tent, darkness had fallen. There were no fires and no moon. Inside his humble abode, he lay down on the blanket and closed his eyes, hoping the next day would bring good news of clean water— and with it, hope of continuing their journey through the desert.

Long after people had returned to their tents and given into sleep, William found himself lying on his back, his eyes staring up at the dark canvas above him with melancholy. His head dug into the side of his leather suitcase, his neck felt stiff, and his back was glued to the ground from exhaustion and weakness.

His face carried a gentle frown, and though his mind was hard at work, William couldn't place his finger on what was wrong. This time he was certain it was not the feeling of restlessness he'd experienced a couple of days earlier. It was different, a feeling tinged with the fear of a forgotten memory. Or was he just frustrated that he couldn't go to sleep? He couldn't tell.

# De Collibus

William decided a quick walk to stretch his legs might be the straw that would break the camel's back, as far as getting a decent night's sleep was concerned, and rose to his feet. He didn't like the cold that greeted him outside but staggered forward anyway. The cold air stung his nose and ears like needles, and William quickly brought his hands up to his face to keep it warm. Uncontrollable shivers ran down his body, and he considered going back inside.

*Relax. The cold will make you strong*, a voice whispered from somewhere inside him. It wasn't at the front of his mind or a conscious choice of words. He wasn't even sure it was him that spoke. The words came from the abyss where thoughts and memories often drift and lay forgotten for ages.

Before going on his nocturnal strolls, William always looked down the barely visible paths around him. That night, the darkness was so thick he couldn't tell the hour. The tents were triangular caves leading into another dimension, all without clear color or shape. Every pathway led in a dark and uncertain direction that could take him anywhere. Large areas of the camp were empty now without the tents of the deserters.

Judging by the heaviness of his eyes, William knew he only needed to walk a short distance for the night air to silence his mind. He staggered forward into the dark, deciding to start walking before he surrendered to the thought of his warm blanket. He hadn't gotten far from his tent when his eyes became heavier. His mind, though, became more active, like a tropical jungle whose creatures stay silent during the day only to come alive when darkness falls, sounding off every wail and screech to assert their presence in a world ruled by sound. He didn't try to stop his mind from thinking, because it helped distract him from the cold.

As his thoughts wandered to uncharted territory, William fastened his pace. His mind had become too alert to sleep, and his attention slowly moved away from the cold that stung his nose and ears and toward the troubling feeling that lured him out of his tent in the first place. All of his senses were put on hold while his mind worked feverishly. It was as if he were sleepwalking with a mind dreaming of the warmest and grimmest thoughts in his imagination in order to tickle an answer out of his own frustrated conscience. What had kept him awake?

*Was sending the camera back a mistake? No. I did the right thing. What could it be then? An overwhelming sense of freedom? Not that either. Think, William, think!*

William felt as if the solution was right in front of him but he just couldn't grasp it; too far out of his reach and taunting him in the darkness. Suddenly, his eyes blinked with renewed sight. The dark path in front of him revealed the shape of the well as a lonely shadow. It was unguarded. As he walked closer to the well, William looked around. He didn't know what part of him had led him here, but he knew it was not by accident. Most certainly fate didn't have a hand in it either. When he reached the stone wall surrounding the well, William looked down into it but saw nothing in its depths.

He closed his eyes as if to say a prayer. His mind felt empty, preparing to be filled with clear, cool water. Water. That word, whispered from the part of him that exuded calmness, echoed through his mind like water dripping in a deep stone cave. Suddenly, his eyes opened and stared at the darkness below him with a fire bright enough to illuminate it.

William frowned. The thought hovered in his head like a vulture over the carcass of some unfortunate beast, circling above but reluctant to swoop down and land. *What is this feeling? A suspicion or the truth?*

He stepped back from the well and walked around it, dragging a hand over the wall. At his slow pace, he reached the other side of the well with the right amount of time to let the thought in his head fully develop. William stopped and looked across the well. In the distance, a flickering yellow light drew him out of his own mind. The light flickered between the sides of two tents. Clearly, fate had presented him with the answer he'd been searching for.

*The person camping in the distance must have poisoned the well. It's a strong accusation, but who else could have done it?* He had to share his suspicions.

Pushing away from the well, William realized there was just one person who could help him. On his way to Hakeem's tent, his walk turned into a run and he was surprised he was able to navigate the paths as if it were daylight. When he spotted Hakeem's tent, he slowed down but didn't stop. One guard sat on a short stool underneath the awning. A torch roared nearby. When the guard saw William's shadow near the tent, he jumped to his feet. He grabbed the torch and held it out to see better in the darkness.

"Who's there?" he demanded in a loud voice. Strengthened by fear, his other hand slithered toward the sword at his belt.

William stepped into the light.

"Why are you here?" the guard asked as he recognized the man before him.

"I need to speak with Hakeem," William said stopped in front of the guard, taking note the man wasn't holding a rifle.

"It's night time. He's asleep."

But William wasn't about to give up. "It's urgent," he said hardening the tone of his voice.

"Hakeem isn't seeing anyone now. You can come back in the morning." The guard nodded to the darkness past the awning.

"I can't do that. I need to speak to him. Like I said, it's urgent," William took a bold step toward the entrance.

But the guard, perhaps anticipating his thoughts, moved in front of him. "No," he said with a scowl of warning.

The sound of a cough came from behind the guard and the two men looked to the entrance of the tent. The torchlight revealed Hakeem standing there, holding a ghostly white cloth over his mouth to cough into. He motioned for William to enter and stepped back into his tent. Glancing at the guard, William followed after Hakeem, momentarily getting hit by a thick fog that hung in the air like the steamy gray mist of a bath house.

Several sticks of sweet-smelling incense gave rise to thin trails of smoke that smelled of jasmine and cinnamon and attempted to cover the smell of sickness. Hakeem was barely visible and stood as a gray shadow over the dark table at the back of the tent. There was no doubt in William's mind that the group of deserters had kept him up.

The crisp sound of tea being poured into a cup entered the clouded air, Hakeem wanting to give his mouth a taste other than that of blood.

"You're dying," William observed in a whisper.

Hakeem ignored him, or at least appeared to, and the tea continued to spill into the cup. When the cup was full, Hakeem picked it up with both hands and held it up to his chest. He turned around and walked over to a short stool near the center of the tent, releasing a short groan as he sat. Only then did he turn his attention from the tea warming his chest to William.

"Why have you come to me?" His voice was tired; the man obviously yearned for solitude and rest.

"I have something important to tell you,"

"Important? Uh, uh... what do you mean?" William stepped into the fog and sat down on the stool across from Hakeem. The bags under the Arab's were darker than before and sweat glimmered on his forehead.

The incense served its purpose from a few feet away but up close it wasn't hiding much of anything. For a moment, there was dead silence. The tent's wooden frame creaked when the wind swayed it left to right, making it seem as the ground was shifting beneath them.

"Are you aware that a small camp has been set up to the west?"

"No," Hakeem answered and a frown appeared on his face.

"It's been there for several days now. At first, I thought it was a traveler, but why weren't they moving on? Tonight is the third night I saw it, and, something feels wrong about it. The woman died the same day when I saw the fire for the second time," William said.

Hakeem appeared deep in thought. "You think the person who made the camp poisoned the well?"

"I couldn't know for sure, but yes, I think that," William confirmed with a nod.

Hakeem grimaced. He brought the white cloth up to his mouth and coughed into it. Even hearing him cough was painful. They were the struggling exhalations of a windpipe choked by poison, sounding more like the whining of a dog than a human noise. As he brought the cloth away, he looked at it for a moment before stuffing it under his leg with painful stiffness.

"I will send a small group of men to examine this camp. They will talk to the occupants and search the camp. If nothing seems suspicious, we will let them go," Hakeem said.

William thought this was an urgent operation and pressed on. "Can you send them now?" Hakeem paused for a moment considering the question.

He nodded. "I can have five men ride out in a half hour."

"Good."

"I want you to lead them," he said, which surprised William.

"I... I will," he said at last.

Hakeem nodded and a grunt escaped his lips as he rose from his stool. "I will send my most trusted men. Fudail is one, but I have to check who else is well enough to ride with you," he said as he walked through the cloud of incense to the entrance of his tent.

William stood as well but didn't follow him. The Arab pulled one of the flaps a few inches open and peeked outside of his tent. Letting go, he looked back at William as if checking for something he thought he'd forgotten. "They will be ready for you in a half hour. Wait for them at the well."

When William nodded, Hakeem pulled back the cloth and motioned for the guard to come to him. Hakeem gave his instructions in Arabic then let go of the flap.

"I better get going then," William said as he walked to Hakeem.

"My men will bring an extra horse and a rifle for you."

"I don't need a rifle," William protested, knowing how useless they had been on their last expedition.

"Your horse will carry one anyway," Hakeem said, disregarding William's personal request. "If you need to do something to clear your conscience before you ride out, I suggest you do it now while there is still time. Be careful, William, and I will see you when you return."

Hakeem sounded as if speaking from experience. He pulled the flap back so William could leave, and a gust of icy air blew in and mixed with the incense. William walked out of the tent and into the cold air outside.


As William walked away, Hakeem peeked through the flap of the tent and watched the foreigner become part of the darkness the torches could not fight off. When William dissolved into the darkness, he let the cloth drop like a theatre curtain and stepped back into the tent.

He hoped this new mission accomplished something before it was too late—for him and for the others.


After leaving Hakeem, William walked back to the well. He was prepared to meet the men, but could he lead them into the camp that had filled him with an ominous curiosity? He leaned both of hands on the wall of the well and slouched his shoulders. His eyes stared calmly but alertly into its unfathomable depths. A soft smile appeared on William's face, and he felt a calm happiness mingle with excitement. He was happy to be free, to be living his life the way he wanted, even if it meant living a dangerous one. It was his choice and that mattered more to him than how he felt.

He looked up at the tents surrounding the well. They looked ghostly. In a deeper part of his mind, William felt that something larger was going to happen as a result of the expedition, though he didn't know how or when. As he looked at the grey tents around him, he knew that the caravan was going to be the canvas of a painting made with dark strokes from the bush of fate. Fate... he didn't believe in it, but a part of him wanted to recognize that what was about to happen was orchestrated by something larger than the caravan, larger than the desert, larger than the earth itself.

William knelt on one knee and sank his fingers into the soft, white soil. It felt cold and powdery on his skin. He scooped up a small handful and rose to his feet.

He stared at his palm and brushed away some of the sand, so that only a small lump remained, light and soft in his hand. There was nothing impressive about it, but William found himself amazed by a simple thought. A teasing of one's mind. Despite its innumerable varieties, textures, and colors, the earth consisted of one thing—dirt. It was the simple truth.

William extended his hand with a smile on his face and, clenching his fist, turned it downward. Three white trails of sand slipped through his fingers and trickled to the ground, and when it was all gone, William brought his hand to his side.

There was no sound. No whistling caused by a distant breeze. Nothing but silence. His head was bowed slightly from drowsy relaxation and his eyes stared at the dirt, waiting for the sound of footsteps to interrupt the silence.

# 17

WILLIAM'S EYES WERE CLOSED. His breaths were soft and slow as the velvet curtain of sleep was lowering over his mind. His forearms held his weight on the wall of the well and his head was bowed toward the poisoned water below. He blinked his eyes open when he thought he heard a noise and straightened his back. He glanced over his shoulder at the path he had taken from Hakeem's tent. He felt a finger with an icy touch poke his chest. Standing in front of him were seven shadows belonging to Hakeem's men and their horses. The man to the very left yawned and scratched the side of his ribs.

"Weren't there supposed to be five of you?" William asked with a slight frown.

"Could not come," Fudail's voice came from the far right.

"Why? What happened to them?" William hoped they had not all been killed by the poison.

Fudail shifted on his feet and kept silent. "Hakeem told us not to—"

"They're sick?" No one corrected him. "I see. You all know why you are here?" William asked. All three of them nodded. "Good, then let's get going," William walked toward Fudail, who was holding the reins to the extra horse.

The men pulled themselves up onto the saddles. As William took his place on the horse's back, he looked over at Fudail who gave him a curt nod. A nod that placed all his trust in the Englishman.

William did the same, but the weight of being a leader was heavy on his shoulders.

"How's that arm?" he asked Fudail.

"I can shoot if that is what you are asking," the man replied in a slightly cold tone.

"Good." William looked down at the saddle and saw the standard British army rifle that hung near his right knee. *I'll carry it but only to make them trust me,* he thought as he stared at the golden glimmer of the rifle's stock.

He turned to look at the men that constituted his little army, all three awaiting to hear his orders. In the darkness, he could hardly see their faces, and still, he could tell that one of them looked around Hakeem's age. His jaw was hidden beneath a coal-black beard and he had a long, curved nose that looked like an eagle's beak. His eyes were permanently squinted, an after effect of having spent his life traveling the desert.

As if in contrast, behind him was the youngest man William had seen under Hakeem's command. He looked just under twenty years old, without so much as a wrinkle on his face or a hair on his cheek.

William rode his horse in front of the others, and they followed behind him down a path that would take them to the west edge of the camp. As they passed by the tents, the whole caravan appeared empty and cold. No fires were burning, no people walking. More dark land opened before them, and William felt that the brush of fate was about to touch the canvas of their lives.

As they trotted out of the camp, William turned around in his saddle. He glanced at Fudail, but the man was looking at the hills to his right as the tents behind him gave way to open land. William kept his gaze ahead. The lone campfire they were out to investigate had vanished behind the hills, so he used them as his compass. His body felt light—too light, as if he were leading himself and the others into some surreal dream. Every bone in his body told him to turn back and try to convince Hakeem that what he had felt was just a distant suspicion. But no. This was just the voice of fear whispering in his head. He ignored it and kept riding.

The sound of the horses' hooves was lost to whistling gusts of chilled wind. William's horse turned its head away from the wind and announced their presence by giving a wavering neigh. Like the many men driven mad by the howling gusts, William began to lose his grasp of time. Soon, they were riding over the crest of a medium-sized hill when William spotted a shadowy tent and a dark fire pit a little distance away. He stopped his horse and motioned for the others to slow down.

Looking back, William saw the silent caravan in the distance. It was a sea of shadows, a reservoir of inky black water in a plain of gray sand. He turned around and looked down at the small camp before him. There was one tent, oddly shaped, and of cloth so dark it blended in with the night sky. *They must have seen us coming and ran for it*, William thought when he noticed there were no horses or camels around the camp. Fudail and the other two men arrived on either side of William's horse, any sounds they made getting stolen by the wind.

Getting off his horse, William landed softly on the ground, followed by the other three. He looked around, and motioned for them to gather closer.

"Here's the plan," William said as the men huddled together. "One of us is going to stay here and watch the horses while the rest of us go down to the camp." After a short pause, everyone nodded. "Who wants to stay with the horses?"

The youngest man nodded quickly.

"Good. You will stay here." Then he turned to the other two. "We will go down to the camp. You," William pointed to the older man, "will look for my signal and stay a little way behind to make sure nobody comes or goes while Fudail and I take a look around. Does everybody understand?" All three nodded in unison.

"All right then, get your rifles," William ordered and walked back to his horse. As Fudail and the older man went to grab their rifles, William stopped at the right side of his horse and looked down at the weapon hanging from his saddle. He unhooked the sling from the pommel and took hold of the rifle. He turned it on its side, feeling its weight in his arms. His eyes closed and his head bowed. His mind began to drift into the land of memories better left untouched.

A hand slapped him on the shoulder. Fudail stood looking at him with a frown, his eyes filled with worried curiosity.

"I was thinking," William said as if to answer Fudail's look of suspicion. The man, always saving his words, took his hand away and stepped aside but continued staring at him.

William stepped forward confidently to hide his exhaustion and began making his way down the hill, with Fudail and the older man following close behind. With each step William took, his heart pounded a little harder in his chest, but despite the fear he forced himself to keep moving until he reached the bottom of the hill. There, realizing the hill wouldn't cover them any longer, he bent his knees and hunched his back, making himself harder to spot in the swirling dust. The two that followed him did the same.

When they were halfway to the tent, William waved behind him. The older man stopped and kneeled, watching as William and Fudail slowly lost their forms in the dust-filled darkness.

His hands were sweating on the hardwood of the rifle, and his nose caught the scent of smoke. William walked past the smoldering fire with his eyes staring at the entrance of the tent, its flaps swaying back and forth in the wind. He heard a heavy thud behind him and turned around. Fudail stood cringing in fear with his hands near his head. His rifle lay on the ground near his feet where the dark shape of an iron kettle was knocked over on its side. William raised his index finger, signaling him not to move. They stared into each other's eyes while their ears listened for any movement inside the tent. Several seconds passed with just the wind flapping their clothes and swirling the dust that loomed in the air.

Fudail knelt down and carefully adjusted the kettle into upright position then picked up his rifle while William turned around to face the tent. The pounding in his chest began to quicken as he focused his eyes on the dark cloth before him. He took a crouched step forward, his foot falling quietly on the soft white sand. Fudail followed close behind him, glancing to his left and right. Each time the wind swayed the tent's flaps, William tried to peek inside. But the wind was dying down, giving way to silence. In these conditions, every noise—the movement of cloth on skin, shaky breaths, soft steps—stood out twice as much.

William slowed his pace and stepped to the right of the entrance, while Fudail took the left side. William placed his hand on one of the flaps glancing up at the other man's shimmering eyes, which stared into the dark entrance with a mixture of eagerness and fear. Fixing his grip around the handle of his rifle William began pulling back the flap. The inside appeared dark at first, but as he pulled back the cloth, he saw a source of dim, yellow light. William jerked the flap down and stepped back. He closed his eyes and exhaled through his nose. When he realized it was a candle that had frightened him, he reached over to the flap again.

This time, knowing what to expect, he pulled the tent's flap higher than before. A yellow candle was flickering at the back of the tent, illuminating the small table where it was placed. William looked at Fudail motioning forward, a signal that he was going to enter the tent. The other man nodded and took a half-step closer. William placed his left foot inside the tent and slowly shifted his weight forward. He could almost hear his heart beating in his chest. His other foot followed with Fudail close behind.

The interior of the tent remained half-hidden in darkness. William stepped forward, making his way toward the candle. He held his breath, fearing he might step on somebody, inciting shouts and gunshots. But nothing happened. When he reached the table, William spotted a small metal lantern. He grabbed its iron handle and lifted it. It made a gentle squeak as it shifted under its own weight. He glanced quickly around the dark tent. All was still and silent.

When William brought the lantern into the circle of light, he opened the small door and placed the candle inside.

Outside, a faint noise sparked Fudail's attention and he turned around to take a look. He pulled back one flap and peered into the darkness. The black fire pit and the kettle were just where they had been. Nothing moved in the shadow of the night. Dismissing the sound to his imagination, the guard stepped back inside the tent. William had set the lantern on the table; his head was bowed and his eyes staring at something in his hand.

Fudail moved swiftly away from the entrance and looked over William's shoulder. An arrow lay in the open palm of his hand.

The feathers belonged to a crow.

"The Desert King?" Fudail said in a gasp.

William kept silent and continued staring at the arrow with a slight look of disgust across his illuminated face, but Fudail's attention was caught by an object at the ground near William's feet. A short, curved bow, designed for both strength and mobility on horseback, lay next to a leather quiver stuffed with arrows.

William examined the tip of the arrow in the light of the lantern. It was shaped like a diamond and glimmered in the darkness as William spun it with his fingers, his eyes studying the fine lines of its two-edged blade.

"Do you think this tent belongs to one of the men who killed the Sheik?" Fudail asked, claiming William's attention.

"I don't know," William said thoughtfully. "Let's take this arrow back with us and show it to Hakeem." He started walking toward the entrance. "It's time to go anyway. Whoever made this camp couldn't have left more than twenty or thirty minutes ago." Enough time to ride to the caravan and back, he thought, lifting the lantern from the table.

"I agree," Fudail nodded and walked outside.

William opened the lantern door then bent down and blew out the candle. In the sudden darkness, he struggled to see what he was doing, so he followed the sliver of night light that came through the flaps. When he stepped outside, a gust of wind roared in his ears. The air around him was blue and dusty. Dawn was coming sooner than he thought.

A few feet away, Fudail's figure looked like a fuzzy shadow in the gloom, his head and shoulders blurred into an arch and his legs combined all the way down to his ankles. William hurried past the dead campfire. When he caught up with Fudail, he could see the dark figure of their third companion walking toward them with his rifle held across his chest. The older man fell in step alongside William toward the base of the hill.

"Did anyone come or leave?" William asked.

"No," the man replied confidently.

"Good."

"Did you find anything?" the man asked, glancing back at the tent.

"This." William held the arrow up in front of him so the other man could see it.

A frown furrowed his face, then sad recognition settled there instead. William brought the arrow back to his side, seeing no need to explain, and the three of them started heading up the hill. They were halfway to the top when a panicked scream pierced the roaring of the wind that came from above. It was the voice of their youngest comrade.

The three men hurried up the hill as quickly as their legs could carry them. The young man shouted again and Fudail held his rifle at the ready. Finally there, William noticed the shadows of two men struggling on the ground behind the horses.

One of the shadows jumped to its feet and darted down the other side of the hill; the other stayed on the ground, grunting and cursing. William ran to the young man to see if he was injured while the other two chased after the fleeing shadow.

But the assailant didn't want to leave any survivors. As he reached the edge of the hill, he stopped and drew out a dagger from his belt, preparing to throw it at Fudail, who was gaining on him. A gunshot roared, casting the hilltop in a brilliant gold light before growling in the emptiness of the surrounding hills. The dagger fell to the ground and a moment later, the man fell backwards over the side of the hill. William looked to his left, where the gunshot had come from. His older comrade stood with his shoulders shrugged up to his ears and the rifle trembling in his hands, still aiming at the spot where the man had fallen out of sight.

William looked down at the young rider who lay on his back with his hands held above his chest, panting heavily. His eyes reminded William of a look he knew well because it had once been his own. The look of a soldier huddling in the corner of an empty trench with his knees pressed against his stomach and his rifle hugged against his chest while his friends over the top died in a drumroll of artillery.

"Are you wounded?" William's voice came out gentle and understanding.

The young man shook his head stiffly. William tapped him on the shoulder then walked to his horse. He put the arrow in the saddle bags then walked to the edge of the hill where the assailant had fallen. He stopped and looked down to the bottom. Gunpowder poisoned the air. The man lay on his side where he had stopped rolling, his arms reaching out on the ground in front of him. William started walking down the side of the hill, hoping to learn something about the man. Halfway down the slope he looked out and spotted the caravan in the distance. The camp looked just as cold and dark as before, although now the sky above a shade brighter.

When William reached the bottom of the hill, he walked to the body of the dead man. A long black robe covered him from head to toe, leaving only his eyes visible. The memory of Nadia's story came to his mind—of soldiers dressed in black wandering through the desert. He was tempted to believe the legend but decided that any kind of man could wear black. William's feet stopped near the man's hands. A pool of blood had spilled on the ground near his chest, turning the pale sand dark. His eyes were open, but lifeless.

William crouched over the body and pushed the upper shoulder back, making it roll over on its rear. One lifeless arm flopped out, the body resembling a crucifix. William leaned closer and began checking the man's pockets. Once upon a time, he'd been disgusted by Fudail looting another dead man in the desert, yet here he was, doing the same thing except with only a hint of remorse.

Not surprisingly, the man's pockets were empty. William grunted in frustration but decided to check the folds of the robe as well. He lifted the black cloth which felt light to the touch, but suddenly stopped. Something was tucked right at the man's chest. A different kind of fabric that felt coarse. He pulled it out—a small, triangular cut of light blue cloth that looked somehow familiar.

Spreading out the cloth with a sudden whip, William began kneading it with his fingers. It was rough, like the kind used for tents or camel blankets but he couldn't tell where he had seen the likes of it before. It certainly appeared to have been cut from the corner of a much larger piece. William put it in his pocket for further investigation. Finally, he bowed his head and took a long look at the man. He wondered how a living being, with thoughts and aspirations of its own, could so quickly turn into nothing.

The sound of footsteps, followed by the neighing of horses, came from behind him. William looked over his shoulder and saw Fudail and the others descending, dark shadows on the ghostly pale slope.

"Find anything?" Fudail asked as he stopped at William's side.

"No," William lied. He didn't know if the piece of cloth was important. Not until he remembered where he'd seen it.

"What do we do now?" the young rider asked when the horses came to a stop on the other side of the body. His voice had regained most of its natural calmness.

"We'll go back to the caravan and tell Hakeem about what happened here," William replied, a sense of determination filling his voice.

"What about him?" Fudail asked, nodding at the dead man.

"We'll take him back with us."

No one said a word of protest, but William had the feeling that neither of them wanted to get in close contact with the corpse.

He walked toward the man's head and Fudail to his feet. They reached down and picked the man up, William from under the arms and Fudail grabbing the legs, then hefted him up onto to the young rider's horse, as it was the closest. With a bit of struggle, because the body weighed a lot, they adjusted him behind the terror-stricken youth.

The man's arms dangled halfway down the horse's right side as they reached toward the ground and his legs stuck out stiffly from the horse's other side. That was the best they could do.

Fudail nodded to William, then his gaze quickly moved to his stomach, his expression suddenly different. William glanced down. A large crimson circle stained the part of his shirt that covered his stomach. Now that he was looking at it, he also became aware of the wet feeling of the blood soaking through his shirt and sticking to his skin. It must have happened while carrying the body. Unconsciously, he touched the stain then examined his fingertips. They were red with blood. A look of guilt filled his eyes, even though he hadn't been the one to pull the trigger.

William lifted his head when he heard Fudail's feet treading on the soft sand as the Arab walked back to his horse. That stain seemed to mean something to the men because their expressions changed. Did they, like him, feel sickened by the death of the man?

*I am unclean,* William thought as he stared at the blood. He'd need to change his shirt when he got back to his tent.

He glanced up at the youth for a second then started walking back to his horse at a brisk pace. He pulled himself onto the saddle and started riding in the direction of the caravan. The entire time it took them to get back, William couldn't help but look at the black camp in the break of morning and hope that the streets would remain as empty as they had been when they left.

# 18

IN THE EARLY LIGHT OF DAWN, FOUR HORSES and five men, counting the dead one, neared the caravan's perimeter. William's back was hunched, and his arms were folded over his stomach in a futile attempt to hide the blood staining his shirt. Although an occasional person could be seen walking among the tents ahead of them, William and his company kept to the blue shadows so they wouldn't bring attention to their presence.

As they entered the path that would take them to Hakeem's tent, a shadow came toward them. William clutched his shirt tighter, but even if he hadn't, the man would have hardly noticed anything. He slipped past William's left knee without looking up at him.

Ahead of them, a group of people were coming their way and William groaned inwardly. He squeezed his hands into fists and slouched his back as he prepared himself to go through another round of examination. Determined to keep his eyes on the back of his horse's neck, William hoped the stain would go unnoticed. But as the footsteps got louder, his eyes disobeyed and glanced down at the nearest person.

It was Nadia.

Her eyes were looking straight ahead, unaware and uninterested by the riders. William turned his face aside, hoping she would keep walking without noticing him, and as she did, his shoulders relaxed. Then the footsteps stopped.

"William?" Nadia asked from the back of the horse.

He considered pretending that he hadn't heard her, but what good would that do? He stopped the horse as she came around to face him and looked down at her with a surrendering gaze. His mouth wouldn't let him speak.

The riders, too tired to move on without William, stopped as well and waited.

"What are you doing here?" she asked, roaming his face with her curious eyes. Even when she glanced down at his awkwardly folded arms he said nothing. All he could do was stare helplessly into her now frowning expression, drowning in guilt.

"Are you all right?" Nadia demanded when she saw the sick look on his face and took a step closer. William kept quiet, but when she glanced down at his arms covering his stomach, he knew he couldn't keep his secret any longer.

"William, what is it? Did you drink from the well?" Her voice sounded concerned as she leaned up against the side of the horse. William felt ashamed for his cowardice and wished she hadn't seen him. Nadia looked down at his forearms. They were streaked with dust, drenched in sweat, and slightly pink.

Suddenly, Nadia grabbed William's wrist and yanked it away. He didn't try to resist, revealing the full picture of his bloodied shirt. Nadia gasped loudly and stepped away from the horse, her frightened eyes staring at the red blotch on William's shirt. She started talking to herself in Arabic, then looked up at William, her eyes hoping for an explanation.

"What is this?" She asked in a gasp of panic that stole the strength from her voice, but he kept looking down at her in silence, his eyes half open and blank.

Nadia glanced behind him to the line of horses and saw the dead man's arms hanging over the side of the last horse.

"That man, is he dead?" No reply. "Did you kill him?" She demanded looking back at William and grabbing his free hand. "Answer me!"

"No," William said at last, but her eyes told him what he already knew—she didn't trust him. She let go of William's arm as if he was contagious. "I am not a killer," he said in an empty voice. His eyes were not pleading for understanding. Instead they looked down at her, knowing that there was nothing else for him to say, nothing else he could say, that would make her trust him.

William looked up at the path ahead and flicked the reins of his horse. His horse started trotting forward and Fudail and the others followed him to Hakeem's tent.

As they rode away, Nadia watched his horse ride down the path with a sad stillness on her face until the rider at back of the group disappeared behind a tent. William tried to put Nadia out of his mind and instead focused on the job he had been sent to do, which was still a long way from being finished. The handful of people they passed on the way to Hakeem's tent looked at him worriedly, but he didn't care to hide the stain anymore. Five minutes later, the four of them stopped outside the leader's awning, carefully watched by a different guard holding a torch that illuminated the ground separating him and the horses in golden orange light. William slid off the side of his horse but motioned for Fudail to stay with the others. Then he took the arrow he had found in the dead man's tent and walked underneath the awning where the guard straightened his back and brought his rifle closer to his side.

"Is Hakeem here?" William asked urgently.

"Yes," came the stern reply.

"Can I go in?" The guard hesitated for a moment but nodded when he saw the arrow in William's hand.

William took a handful of steps toward the entrance, but just as he was about to pull the flap aside, he noticed something strange in the shadows near his feet. A piece of fabric was missing from the bottom corner of the flap. He kneeled by instinct and he obeyed his inner voice. As he kneeled he caught the attention of the guard and the riders waiting outside the awning. He reached down to examine the cloth when a pair of sandals stepped onto the ground in front of him. William looked up.

Hakeem stood over him; a bloodied white cloth clenched tightly in his hand covered his mouth. He was wheezing like a whining dog. The skin of his cheeks was nearly as pale as the cloth pressed against his mouth. Hakeem looked from William to the riders, then at the guard who was standing watch at his tent, before returning to William, who was still kneeling in front of him.

"You have come to report?" Hakeem asked in a barely audible voice that tried to conceal his sickly appearance. William nodded.

The Arab coughed twice then stepped back into his tent. William rose to his feet and followed him inside. The strong smell of incense disoriented him at first but he quickly regained his senses.

"The man you brought back with you... is he dead?" Hakeem asked as he turned to face William, neatly hiding the bloodied cloth in his interlaced fingers in front of his belt.

"Yes," William replied without much shame in his voice.

"Why?" Hakeem asked, glancing down at the dried blood on William's shirt and then locking eyes again.

"He attacked us," William reported, his voice maintaining the lack of emotion it seemed to possess when he spoke to Nadia. Hakeem nodded and walked over to the table at the back of the tent. William watched him pour a cup of tea and bring it to his mouth. A faint slurp entered the incense-fogged air.


His mind churned as the hot tea warmed his chest and removed the taste of blood from his mouth.

"Tell me what happened," Hakeem said as he turned to face the Englishman, his movement causing a slight stir in the fog.

"I met the men at the well," William began as he walked to Hakeem. "From there we made our way to the camp in the west, which was made up of one tent large enough for one person, maybe two. I had one man stay behind to watch the horses while I led the rest to the tent to see if anyone was around. When we were around halfway to the tent, I told the other man to stay behind to make sure no one would come or leave while Fudail and I searched the tent. I saw no animals so I didn't know if the person who had made the tent was gone. When we searched the tent, I found this." William lifted the arrow into the dim light and Hakeem watched it with interest. His hands came up to take the arrow, but he had recognized the fletching even before his fingers wrapped around it.

"There was a bow and a quiver with twelve more arrows just like this one," William continued as Hakeem examined the arrow with shaky fingers.

A look of realization flashed across his face. Hakeem turned around and hurried to the right side of the table. William saw him kneel in front of a chest he'd seen but never really noticed before. An iron screech came from Hakeem's knees. The screech was followed by the sound of papers rustling and small pouches of jingling coins being shoved to the side of the chest. Hakeem froze. Cloth ruffled in the silence as Hakeem rose to his feet. In Hakeem's hands were two arrows instead of one. One taken from the dead man's camp, the other from the back of a dead tribesman.

"They are identical," Hakeem gasped, shaking his hands like he was begging God for mercy. William looked down at the arrows Hakeem was holding and couldn't tell which one he gave to Hakeem.

"Do you think it is real?" William asked, almost as an afterthought. Hakeem looked up at him with his sickly eyes in a moment of confusion.

"If what is?"

"The Desert King and his army—are they real?" William repeated.

"Why do you want to know this? You are a foreigner," Hakeem said in an advising but concerned tone.

"Because our lives depend on it,"

There was a short silence.

"If the Desert King is real... *if*," Hakeem stressed, "then we are all as good as dead." William stared in Hakeem's dark eyes as a heavy silence filled the incense-clouded air. "Now, did you find anything else that could tell us whether that man had anything to do with the poison?"

William didn't like the swift change of subject. Was this Hakeem's own fear? That they had no chance of survival?

"No. Just the arrow," William replied. "Wait," He reached into his pocket. "There is something I forgot to show you. Here, look at this," William said as he handed the small cut of cloth to Hakeem.

Hakeem set the arrows on the table and took the cloth tentatively, not sure what to make of it. After a couple of moments passed in silence, Hakeem looked up to William with a puzzled gaze.

"What is this?" he asked.

William wasn't sure what to tell him. "I don't know, but I found it on the man and thought it might be important, so I took it."

The Arab grunted. "I do not know what this cloth means," he said and handed the cloth back to William, who tucked it into his pocket. "That man out there, do you think he is one of the Desert King's men?" directing his eyes to the entrance of the tent then back at William. William nodded, not knowing what else to say. "Then we must hope that he is not," Hakeem said with a fateful sigh.

His face tightened in a painful grimace. He brought his hands to his stomach and bent low toward his knees. William thought he was going to die and he stepped closer to help him but Hakeem raised his hand for William to stay where he was. William obeyed but kept looking at Hakeem's face, hoping he would be able to recognize the signs of the pain getting worse. To his relief, when the moment passed, Hakeem grunted and straightened his back.

"If the dead man didn't poison the well, then who did?" Hakeem asked in a voice so tight it sounded more like a hoarse whisper. He bent down again, his body shaking with painful coughs.

"You need help. I'll go get the doctor," William said and started walking toward the entrance.

"No. Stay," Hakeem choked out between the coughs.

William stopped in mid stride and looked behind him. Hakeem had not moved, but his body had curled on itself, and the pain he felt on the inside was now freely seeping through to his eyes with a tenacity second only to that experienced in torture chambers. William knew he had to get the doctor, but instead he walked closer to Hakeem.

"Since you have proven yourself a good leader I will have you lead a group of men and wagons to the next well," Hakeem said when William faced him. The thought of him leading a large group of men through the desert both excited and terrified him, but the well was the caravan's only hope for survival. William hid his doubt behind a calm look and nodded.

"Good. This relieves me a little. I am glad," Hakeem said in a calm voice. Hakeem straightened his back and patted William several times on the shoulder with a smile of gratitude. William smiled, the fear that Hakeem would not live to see the return of his group adding a sad tinge to his smile. "I will have the news spread among my men that a group is going to the next well. They'll be ready around noon. A man I know, but who is not under my command will go with you. He has crossed the desert more times than I have and he will lead you and the men to the well when everything is ready,"

William could do nothing else but agree with that plan, and since a lot had to be done in preparation, Hakeem walked him out. Outside the tent, Hakeem began speaking to the guard in Arabic, while William looked around the camp, admiring the sunlight that was beginning to illuminate the tents and paths and warm the air. As he placed his hands in his pockets, he remembered the piece of cloth. He turned and looked at the the flap of the entrance. Kneeling slowly, William grabbed the tent's cloth and pulled it into the light of a flickering torch posted to the side of the awning.

When Hakeem had finished giving his orders and the guard had bolted to do what was asked of him, the Arab turned around and took several steps closer to William. Hakeem's eyes weren't the only ones watching William with interest. Fudail and the two riders who'd remained outside with the dead man now stared at William as well. They were so drawn by William's focus on the cloth that they began walking closer to get a better look themselves.

Hakeem kneeled next to William and stared at the flap he held in his hand. The corner was missing, cut by a dull knife that had left many of the naked threads frayed. William's face was thoughtful and calculating, too busy to notice Hakeem's eyes staring at him.

Holding the flap with his left hand, William reached into his right pocket and pulled out the piece of blue cloth he'd found tucked in the dead man's robe. As he brought it closer to the flap, it became obvious the piece belonged in that corner. He heard several voices begin speaking worriedly in Arabic, but he didn't turn to see who was there, too fascinated by his own find. The piece of cloth fit exactly with the design of the flap, the spots where the embroidery trailed off it continuing perfectly onto the flap.

William had been right in his suspicion and that brought a small smile on his face. But that wasn't a good sign at all. It meant that the dead man, or someone else entirely, had been able to walk into camp and reach Hakeem's tent, guarded as it were at all times, and cut the piece of cloth. What if it had been Hakeem's throat instead?

"Why do you think that man cut a piece of cloth from my tent?" Hakeem asked when he noticed William's half smile, his voice showing the kind of concern any man would if he were in the same situation.

"Someone wanted to know which tent was yours," William concluded looking up at him. Hakeem stared at the cloth with a fearful anger in his eyes.

"Leave us," Hakeem snapped at Fudail and the others who were now standing under the awning. They looked at each other for a second, then briskly walked back to their horses.

The sound of Hakeem's voice didn't bode anything good.

"William," the Arab said in a growl, rising to his feet and pointing a finger at William. "If this is some kind of game you're playing I'll-"

"This is no game," William interrupted facing Hakeem at his full height. "You asked me to report to you and I told you what I know. I've told you nothing but the truth." He didn't bother to hide his disappointment at Hakeem's mistrust.

The Arab's shoulders sagged. "I am sorry...," he said and bowed his head. "I am angry and frustrated. Half of my people are sick and can barely carry their belongings to the next well. Every time we get close to finding a solution, what do we get in return? A question!"

Hakeem avoided eye contact with William out the frustration and embarrassment. William, on the other hand, stood in front of Hakeem, still and silent.

"I feel like a ball of yarn that some wretched cat is toying with. A cat from hell," Hakeem muttered the last part to himself. "I had one responsibility—to keep those who joined my caravan safe and alive." The painful cough suddenly overtook his lungs and didn't stop for several seconds. "Now look what I have done to my people," he said at last, his tone turning sorrowful and tense from the pain in his chest. William wanted to comfort the man, but he didn't know how. The only thing he could do was listen. "I poisoned them," Hakeem said finally, his eyes wandering over to the men gathered around their horses. A few people were talking with them about the dead man.

William kept looking at him.

"*You* didn't poison them," he said, trying to bring some sense back into Hakeem's poisoned mind.

"If I didn't, then who?" Hakeem said, his voice nearly raised to a shout. "Some ghost? A demonic spirit? Some ancient myth they call the Desert King?" Hakeem shouted as he stepped out from under the awning, grabbed a handful of dirt and threw it into the air above his head, crying out in frustration as he did. As the powdery sand floated back to the ground, Hakeem panted in anger, his fists clenched near his sides so tightly that his shoulders were pulled up near his neck.

The people that had gathered around the horses were now staring at him, having heard his plea for liberation and relief. Hakeem didn't pay attention to them; his mind was too clouded with anger to see the ground at his feet. He bowed his head and his shoulders rose and fell as he took slow deep breaths.

"I killed us all," Hakeem said in a hopeless tone. "I killed us all..." He mumbled hopelessly again and again, his voice growing weaker with each repetition, like a man about to fall asleep from having too much to drink. And then, Hakeem's words turned into a slur, he suddenly staggered forward barely keeping his balance.

"Hakeem?" William's words went unheard. The Arab began to walk away from the tent, tripping over his own feet. "Hakeem?" William shouted, not hiding the worry now naked in his voice.

Hakeem exhaled all the air in his lungs before falling flat on his chest. The crowd, staring at their leader in a daze, shouted in fear. William darted to Hakeem's side just as the guard was returning from his errand.

William was the first to reach the fallen leader. William fell to his knees and rolled Hakeem on his back. The guard kneeled at Hakeem's side, paralyzed at the sight of a small drop of blood trickling from the corner of his mouth. The caravan leader continued mumbling and throwing his head from side to side in delirium. William looked at the guard who was staring at Hakeem fearfully.

"Go get the doctor," William shouted to the guard. "Go!" The man didn't move or respond, his eyes staring at Hakeem as if looking his own demise in the face. William jumped to his feet, leaving Hakeem on the ground where he kept mumbling as his mind slipped farther into unconsciousness. He took hold of the guard's robe and  pulled him close to his face.

"Go get the doctor now or Hakeem will die. And if he dies, we all die, understand?" William said in a slow clear voice that the guard would understand even if he only spoke Arabic. The guard looked at Hakeem then back at William. He nodded his head nervously as his resolve returned to him and backed away from William in the direction of the doctor's tent.

With the guard gone, Fudail hurried toward William, who noticed that the people kept their distance from Hakeem, some covering their mouths in horror.

William turned back to Hakeem. He had stopped mumbling and the coldness in his face made it seem as if he had stopped breathing as well. William dropped to his knees and lowered his head onto Hakeem's chest, keeping his ear pressed over the man's heart. He heard a faint thump, and a long moment later, there was another one. It wasn't much, but all was not lost.

Hakeem's face seemed purplish and his eyes were closed as if he were sleeping. A small trickle of blood kept falling from his mouth onto the ground near his left ear. William heard footsteps approaching from behind, and thinking the guard was returning with the doctor, he turned around.

It was not the guard. Fudail was approaching, along with the other riders, their faces mangled by fear.

"Is he dead?" Fudail asked as he kneeled on the other side of Hakeem.

William shook his head. "No, but he won't be alive much longer if the doctor doesn't come soon."

A crowd of people was beginning to surround them, making the air tense and suffocating. Where was that guard?

"I'll go get some wine," Fudail said, leaping to his feet.

"Good, but be quick," William advised as Fudail ran away. Within seconds Fudail had disappeared into the flow of people coming out of the paths. They surrounded Hakeem and William, forming a large circle around them. Everyone seemed to have heard the news and more people than William thought now poured into the small clearing before Hakeem's tent.

He could hear panicked voices and feared the crowd might end up cutting the air Hakeem had a hard time breathing in anyway. Seeing that the crowd was growing thicker, William shouted and waved for the people to stay back and keep their distance. A moment passed, but the approaching wall of people stopped.

William's eyes searched the crowd for the guard and the doctor. What was taking them so long? He turned back toward Hakeem. When he looked at the man's face, William felt his blood chill in his veins. The leader's cheeks were beginning to turn a dark purple that looked deathly cold. He placed his hand underneath Hakeem's nose and waited for a warm draft to tickle the hairs on his hand. There was nothing.

At last he heard shouts from the crowd and looked up to see the people parting to let in the guard and the doctor. The doctor was an old man. Obviously, he could not run as quickly as the guard but still he made an effort. Clutched in the doctor's frightened hands was a bag hastily packed with medicine.

"Here," the guard said as he pulled the doctor to Hakeem's still body. The doctor moved to Hakeem's body, too slowly to satisfy William. *He's going to kill him*, William thought as the doctor took his time kneeling.

"Is he dead?" William asked hurriedly. The doctor looked up in confusion. He didn't speak English, and William was too anxious to remember any Arabic he'd learned. "Ask him if Hakeem is dead," William said to the guard, while pointing at the doctor. The guard, obviously out of his stupor, kneeled quickly at Hakeem's side and talked to the doctor in their language. The doctor said something and the guard looked at William.

"What'd he say?" William demanded, barely giving the doctor a chance to finish talking.

"He doesn't know," the guard replied.

William began to think the man the guard brought back was no doctor at all and that Hakeem could die because this man didn't know what he was doing.

"Tell him that if Hakeem dies, he dies with him," William said to the guard kneeling across Hakeem's body. The man hesitated, glancing from Hakeem to the doctor several times.

William glanced at the guard's rifle abandoned in the sand above Hakeem's head. In a sudden sweep, William snatched the weapon and loaded a bullet into the chamber as he rose.

The guard rose to his feet to stop him, but William met the man with the rifle aiming at the center of his head. The guard must have seen William's determination in his eyes, because he slowly squatted back down to the ground beside the doctor. William remained standing. The doctor glanced fearfully from the rifle's barrel to the guard.

"Now tell him what I said." There was a moment of silence that was filled with gasps from the crowd surrounding Hakeem. The guard still appeared hesitant. "Tell him now or I'll kill him," William threatened, turning and aiming the rifle at the doctor. The old man flinched, and a wave of gasps and whispers came from the people that enclosed them.

When the guard realized he had no choice but to comply, he relayed William's words to the doctor, and a verbal battle ensued. William understood none of it. The crowd around him looked terrified. Were they more concerned about the rifle in his hand or about Hakeem's fate? Finally, the doctor pressed his ear against Hakeem's chest. He remained in that position for quite some time, then looked up at William and shook his head nervously, fearing a bullet awaited him.

"Ask him what he means," William said. The guard spoke nervously to the doctor to figure out what he meant by shaking his head.

"He can't tell if there's a pulse." the guard said after frantically conversing with the doctor.

"Tell him to try again," William said, motioning to the doctor with the barrel of his rifle. The guard didn't waste time and turned to the doctor.

William could hear the sound of footsteps approaching. He hoped Fudail was returning with the wine and turned around, but the sight he saw confused him.

He saw Hans walking toward him with a furious stride, his cheeks and the ridge of his nose was reddened as if he had been lying out in the sun too long. Was that from yesterday's wine?

William looked back down at the guard and the doctor and hoped Hans would leave him alone, even though he knew he wouldn't.

When Hans reached William, he was about to yell at him for aiming the rifle at the old doctor but lost his words when he glanced at Hakeem who lay on his back with blood still trickling from his mouth and bleeding out onto the dirt.

Hans turned back to William.

"What on earth are you doing?" Hans demanded as he closed the final distance between them.

"Not now, Hans. I know what I am doing," William replied coldly, glancing at Hans before returning his eyes to the old man. The doctor was terrified by the sight of the rifle pointed at him, even though William's finger wasn't on the trigger.

Hans took a step closer, ending up just behind William's shoulder. He calculated the situation, but no matter how he looked at it, everyone seemed terrified by William and what he might do next. Had he caused Hakeem's present state? Hans looked at the doctor who scrambled to save Hakeem.

"Lower your gun," Hans said in a soft but firm voice.

"No," William replied, shifting his feet in the sand, clearly, his nerves were beginning to snap like strings on an old violin bow. Several seconds passed, and Hans realized the rifle would have to be pried from William's hands so his friend wouldn't do something he'd later regret.

Throwing his arms around William, Hans held on tighter than the iron brackets on a wine barrel, making the rifle point toward the sky. He struggled to take William to the ground, and both of them tried their best not to lose their balance, waltzing stiffly away from Hakeem and the doctor.

Below the surprised faces of the doctor and the guard, Hakeem still went without breathing.

Suddenly, Hans slipped his foot behind William's and brought him down on the ground with a heavy thud. The rifle fell from the William's grasp hand and landed on the ground an arm's length away. But Hans wasn't finished. Tucking his chin into his chest, he tightened the death grip he had on William. William felt as if a stone slab had fallen on his chest. Hans dug his feet into the ground and began pushing William forward in the dirt.

William found it hard to breathe, and his eyes started to tingle with the onset of lightheadedness. As he tried his best to catch his breath, he saw the guard and the doctor working on bringing Hakeem back to life.

The crowd watched in surreal shock, following with a held breath everything that was happening in the clearing. William kicked the ground with his left heel to try and push himself onto his side, but Hans held his position, unmoving like a mountain.

As their struggle continued one grunt, cuss, and elbow to the ribs at a time, four of Hakeem's men, who had been sucked into the crowd, rushed to go help their leader. A small group began to gather around Hakeem with the doctor and the guard, all trying to help revive a man who looked as good as dead.

William wanted to be right there as well, but his attempts to escape Hans' grip failed miserably. He looked down by his feet and he could see the guard's rifle he had taken beginning to slip away from him on the ground as Hans pushed him farther away.


Alexander had noticed small groups of people gathering in the early hours of morning and followed them, curious to see what had happened this time. He pushed his way to the front, but what he saw there, in the clearing before, stunned him. The caravan leader was lying on the ground, motionless, surrounded by his men. A little ways to the side, two men were fighting ferociously, and what a surprise it was when he recognized their faces: Hans and William.

Being no doctor, Alexander couldn't help Hakeem, but he sure could break up the fight between his friends. He pushed his way through the last few people before him and ran to where William and Hans were rolling in the dirt.

William was rocking his back from side to side in an attempt to get free from Hans. A moment later he had gained enough momentum to flip Hans on his back, clearly taking the German by surprise. Hans wasted no time trying to gain back his advantage and quickly wrapped his legs around William to keep him within striking distance. While William was trapped by Hans' legs, Alexander grabbed him underneath the arms and began tugging him away from Hans.

When William felt Alexander's arms wrap around him, he let go of Hans to get free from Alexander. The instant William's hands reached Alexander's arms, Hans sat up in a jolt and struck William square in the jaw with a fist like an iron skillet. William's body slumped back into Alexander's arms who laid him on the ground. Hans rose to his feet, panting like a wild bull.

"Jesus Christ, what happened?" Alexander asked as he looked up from where William lay in the dust.

"He aimed a rifle at the doctor," Hans said calmly.

"Why?"

Hans shrugged his shoulders.

Both of them looked to where Hakeem's men had gathered. "Is he dead?"

"I don't know, but if he is, things won't be good," Hans replied, still staring at Hakeem. Hans' words echoed in both their minds like a whisper in a network of stone caves.

"What about him?" Alexander nodded toward William and Hans followed his gaze.

"He'll live."

"No, I meant what should we do with him?" Alexander asked in a stern tone.

Hans exhaled loudly while he wiped the sweat off his forehead with the back of his wrist.

"Take him to his tent and stay with him while he gets to his senses," he replied after a moment of thought.

For a short moment Alexander and Hans stared at William. Finally Hans shook his head in disappointment and began walking toward the crowd. Alexander nearly didn't notice Hans walking away until he was almost gone. He turned around as if suddenly remembering something.

"What should I do if he tries to leave his tent?" Alexander asked Hans.

"Knock him out," Hans said, walking backward for a few steps, then turning around to continue walking. Since the people Hans neared didn't want to see him knock out another person, they parted like the Red Sea.

Alexander turned back toward William. He didn't like the thought of knocking William out if he tried to leave his tent but what choice did he have? William wasn't thinking straight and if he left his tent he would only cause trouble. It was up to him to make sure that William stayed in his tent until his head cleared and he started acting normal again. Alexander sighed in acceptance of whatever would happen when William awoke, and picked him up.

# 19

WILLIAM GASPED AS HE SAT UP ON HIS BLANKET, eyes wide open and chest pounding. Hans' face, the last thing he remembered seeing, glowed in his mind like the memory of a terrifying dream, but he was unable to remember exactly what had happened. He remembered an old man looking up at him in terror. But why? It didn't make any sense.

The very possibility of him being the cause of the man's fear sent a wave of remorse washing over him. William heard a crunch near the entrance to his tent and looked up. Alexander was slouched forward, sitting on a stool, his elbows on his knees. In his right hand he held a green apple with a white bite mark. William looked at his friend, searching his dark eyes for a clue about what had happened, but Alexander's gaze retracted as he looked down at the space between his feet.

William quickly brought his hands up to his eyes and rubbed them with a sigh, as if that would help him retrieve the memories. He didn't know what, but as the pounding in his head suggested, something had gone wrong.

Alexander calmly took another bite from his apple.

"What happened?" William groaned, rubbing his eyes.

"Hans knocked you out," his friend replied with a mouthful of apple. Somehow, William already knew that was true, but to hear it spoken to him and have all doubt erased caused him to wonder what else could have happened.

"Why?" He looked at Alexander, bracing himself for the truth.

"You were aiming a rifle at a doctor." Alexander replied before taking another bite from the apple.

Suddenly, the memories of rummaging around the small camp, the dead man, Hakeem's pale face, and the quivering doctor came flooding back to William in a dizzying rush that filled him with a mix of shame, repulsion, and the determination to make things right.

"Hakeem," William muttered as he stood up and walked to his suitcase at the back of the tent where he changed into a clean shirt nearly identical to the one stained with blood.

Alexander rose as well, moving his tree trunk of a body in front of the entrance where he stopped and crossed his arms.

"What are you doing?" William asked as he pushed the last button through his shirt.

"I can't let you leave," Alexander said, the expression on his face as cold as stone. William continued walking calmly toward him.

"Why?" William asked.

"Because Hans said I couldn't let you leave. You might end up doing something you would regret. Again."

Though William saw concern in Alexander's eyes, he also knew that his friends knew nothing of what was really happening around the camp.

"That doctor is a fool, and if Hakeem dies, he should be held responsible for doing nothing to save him. Now enough of this nonsense. Let me go see Hakeem; there's something important he wants me to do." With that said, William attempted to walk past Alexander.

A moment later, a head-splitting pain fell on William's temple, though the force was not enough to knock him out.

"Hey!" William shouted as he brought his hands up to his head. "What's the matter with you?"

"Hans told me that if you—"

William pointed a tense finger at Alexander "Don't you listen to a damn word he says! That idiot doesn't know the half of it. Now, move aside and let me pass."

Finally, Alexander stepped aside, and, with renewed determination, William rushed out of the tent with Alexander on his heels.

William walked out of his tent and stepped into a world as blindingly white as a painter's canvas, stunning his vision right away. William squinted and held his hand up to the sun. Today, for the first time in a week, the sky was clear. Not a single cloud of rain or dust.

He hadn't taken a step in the direction of Hakeem's tent when he saw a short man standing in front of him. The man, who was clenching a piece of paper close to his chest, opened his mouth to speak, then closed it fearfully, then opened it again like a fish recently pulled out of the water.

"What is it?" William snapped at the trembling messenger as Alexander stepped closer behind him.

"Hakeem," the man gasped and winced as if anticipating a punch him in the face.

Feeling guilty, William nodded, encouraging the man to relay the message he was carrying. On the inside though, he was afraid.

The man spared William the pain of suspense by extending his shivering hand and holding the crumpled paper out. As William took the paper, the man quickly pulled his hand back and watched William's face with curiosity.

The note contained several short lines written in barely legible writing.

"Hakeem's alive?" William asked the messenger.

The man started speaking in Arabic so fast, William only made out a couple of words, but they were enough to put him at rest. At least for the moment, Hakeem was still alive, though unconscious.

William looked back at Alexander then turned to read the paper in his hands.

*William, I have already asked a lot of you. For that I am grateful. I ask of you one last thing, not for me, but for the caravan. Follow my orders as clearly as possible. Lead the group that is going to the next well. Gather enough water for everyone then return here as safely as you can. My men will be waiting at the well at noon. The doctors say I only have a few...*

A sudden seizure seemed to have shaken Hakeem's hand at that point that the writing became unreadable. It regained some clarity several lines later and looked to have been written painfully slow in order to be clear.

*I need you to accept. The people need you to. Lead them, William. Lead them.*

William slowly lifted his blank eyes from the paper and stared at the ground near the messenger's feet. He knew that he was going to accept. Not fulfilling a dying man's last wishes wasn't the kind of thing William did, but he tried to convince himself that he had the choice to decline if he wanted to.

"What does it say?" Alexander asked from somewhere behind him.

"Hakeem wants me to lead a group that is going to bring fresh water from the next well," William replied slowly as he realized that his time to see the true desert had come.

"Are you going to do it?"

"Yes, I will," William said as he folded the paper, a kind of smile appearing in his eyes.

"I'm coming with you," Alexander declared, but William shook his head.

"No. I can't let you come with me, it's too dangerous. Stay here and keep an eye on Hans," William said as he placed the paper in his pocket. Alexander nodded even though he wanted to help on the expedition to the next well.

"What time is it?" William asked, hoping Hakeem's message wasn't too late. Alexander reached into his pocket and pulled out a small round watch.

"Ten to noon," he replied.

"Good. I can still catch them. Goodbye, and stay safe," William said as he started down the path that would take him to the well. The further he got from Alexander, the more his pace quickened until he was running at full speed, leaving his friend and Hakeem's messenger standing outside his tent.

As William ran down the narrow path, everything felt like it was happening in a split second. One minute the path was long and wide, the next it was windy and narrow. He thought about the desert and how today he would see what he had longed to see since the hotel owner in Nador told him he couldn't: the endless horizon of a wasteland belonging to no one but the man brave or witless enough to stand under its blistering sun. He could feel himself getting nervous. Worms of fear wriggled in his stomach and his legs were just strong enough to carry him down the path. His head felt detached from his body, like it was floating on its own, and the brightness of the sand under his feet made him feel like he was going to faint. *I have never felt more alive,* William thought as a dreamy smile formed on his face.

William ran out of the path and into the open space surrounding the well, stopping when he saw the group of twenty men that he was going to lead. Most were sitting on the ground or on empty barrels, while others were loading the wagons with large, wooden barrels and countless sheepskins that they would fill up and back to camp. He noticed that, along with the wagons, a dozen camels were loaded with large barrels tied on either side of their backs, making their bodies look disproportionately large compared to their skinny legs.

But something else caught William's attention. The men that weren't loading cargo were carefully running smooth stones along their blades, cleaning the barrels of their rifles, or slinging bandoliers across their chests. Only a few of them glanced at William, staring at him as he drew near. Fudail noticed him as well and made his way eagerly toward William, swiftly moving around the barrels that still needed to be loaded onto the wagons.

"I see you are going to lead us after all," Fudail said once he reached William, a hint of approval in his voice.

"Yes, I am," William said softly as he scanned the men sitting in front of him, examining them carefully as Fudail looked at him with eyes expecting to be given an order.

"There are only a few barrels left that need to be loaded, then we will be ready to leave," Fudail reported as he nodded toward the wagons circled around the well.

"How's Hakeem?"

"He is alive, but he is walking closer to the edge," Fudail replied in the soft voice of a priest. William looked down at his shoes, imaging Hakeem lying in his tent, attended by the same doctors who had taken care of the Bedouin Sheik. He could picture his face pale and purple as he had last seen it. He hoped that rest and care would help Hakeem regain some strength.

"Our guide is over there," Fudail nodded toward a man to his right. "He knows the way to the well and he will lead us there."

William looked up and saw a bony-looking man sitting quietly on the back of a camel that was resting right at the mouth of a path leading away from the well. The man looked like he could be the Bedouin Sheik's father. The tested look in his eyes revealed why Hakeem trusted him. His camel's seat was decorated in the traditional way of the bedouin, and its neck and head were covered in a spiral of bright orange and blue beads, a symbol of status not gained by staying inside one's tent.

*Excellent. That lowers our chances of getting lost,* William thought as he examined their guide.

"Tell the men to gather their things. We will leave as soon as the wagons are loaded," William said, looking back at Fudail who nodded and rushed away, stirring up the men from cleaning their swords and rifles, patting some on the shoulder as he shouted instructions.

In an instant the men, camels, and wagons were being maneuvered in a narrow file that coiled around the well like the tail of a serpent. Because of the whirlwind of motion, clouds of dust rose into the air so thick that it became hard to see the men scrambling in the growing gloom as they grabbed their weapons, loaded the last barrels and skins, and pulled themselves onto the wagons in a lively storm.

Searching the procession, William considered which wagon should go first so he could climb on it. He examined the lot and found a sturdy contraption lead by a pair of healthy brown horses. The guide and his camel were waiting just beside it.

William walked toward the wagon while observing their guide bring a match up to a narrow smoking pipe that was clamped in the corner of his mouth by a pair of old, dry lips. The man's thick, dark eyebrows did a perfect job of protecting his eyes from the blinding light of the desert. Currently, they were pushed down in study of the smoke he blew from his mouth, enjoying each puff with the caution of a ritual.

And indeed, William considered it that: a quiet reflection on the moments in life worth remembering before one is too desperate to think rationally and ends up charging across the minefield between them and what they want to accomplish, willing to throw it all away.

The guide looked up into the dusty air as if contemplating a thought or an idea, letting the chaos of the moving wagons and men slip from his mind. His eyes looked straight at William, and the man smiled, his yellow teeth contrasted with his dark skin. William smiled back at the guide, grateful for the times he had gone to the dentist as child, and then pulled himself onto one side of the wagon seat as one of Hakeem's men, a tall, lively fellow, occupied the other side and took the reins.

"William," a woman's voice shouted, and William turned in his seat. A feminine figure was running in his direction, but a shawl wrapped around her face obscured her features. When she drew close, she pulled away the fabric.

After their last encounter, William had thought he wouldn't see Nadia again or at least for a long time, but there she was, her half-covered face looking up at him from the wheel to his left.

Her face was covered in dust and her lips chapped from the heat. "Where are you going?" she asked as she placed a hand on the wagon wheel near her chest.

"To the next well. We'll try to gather water and bring it back here," William replied, searching her flushed face for a sign that he'd see her again.

"Oh." Her tone had softened. "I thought… never mind." He was curious to hear what had made her run so fast, but now was not the time.

"Is there any news of Hakeem?" he asked, worried that she had been sent to him with the dreadful news.

"Some say he's alive; others say he is dead. I don't know what to believe anymore," Nadia said, looking up at him with eyes that wanted nothing more but to be taken away from the turmoil of the caravan.

"Don't believe the rumors. If he is dead, we will know. Did you hear about the people who left?" William asked.

"Yes, I did. They are cowards to abandon us and let us die like starving dogs. I hope the Desert King killed them all," Nadia said with the resentful frown of a child.

"You should have gone with them," William said frankly. She looked up at him with shocked eyes that calmed as she realized he was right.

"Promise me you will be careful when you are gone," Nadia said as she looked down at the rings covering her slender fingers, hiding the sadness that suddenly took over her face.

"I promise," William nodded. For a moment both of them remained silent, staring at the rings on her fingers as the men prepared to leave.

"Here, take this," Nadia said as she lifted a hand up to William. Inside her palm was a thin silver necklace coiled like a gray snake. "It is for good luck," she added, her voice nearly lost in the chaotic roar of yelling men and screeching wagons.

"Oh, I nearly forgot. I have something for you as well," William said hastily, as he reached into his pocket. He brought out the blue scarf he bought from the old man and gave it to Nadia.

"You can have it if you like it; if not that's fine," William said as Nadia took the scarf and he sat back in his seat. As Nadia admired the beautiful designs, a smile entered her eyes.

"I like it." She nodded in joyful admiration and looked up at him.

As they stared into each others eyes, the sound of the group's movement ceased and a heavy silence entered the dusty air without them knowing.

171

The men were ready, and the guide was tapping the shoulder of his camel, urging it to rise up. The animal gave a reluctant groan as it leaned forward on its front legs and used its back pair to push itself off the ground.

Fudail approached William's wagon with heavy steps. "The men are ready. We can leave now," he said as he stood next to Nadia.

"Then we shall. Tell the guide to lead the way," William said with a newfound charisma in his voice

The Arab nodded and started walking away, but suddenly turned, looking straight at Nadia with recognition before continuing to his own wagon. Before William could say a word, his wagon started forward in a sudden jolt when the driver whipped the reins on the backs of the horses. That was the sign for the entire line of wagons and camels to unravel from around the well and follow William's lead toward the mouth of a path.

William looked over his shoulder at the place where Nadia was standing and waved back to her. As she disappeared in the clouds of white dust, her soft figure's silhouette waved back at him. When he couldn't see her anymore, he turned around and saw the guide speeding his camel towards the front of the group.


They were well on their way when William turned to look behind him at the camp that would soon disappear in the distance. The dozens of tents looked almost abandoned, as if they were one with the white dirt of the flat plain they sat on. As he looked at the camp, slowly slipping behind the ridge of a small hill, William soaked in every color he saw, just like he had done when he first saw the caravan back in Nador. When the hills finally obscured his view, William turned around in the seat of his wagon, promising himself that the next time he laid eyes on the camp he would be returning with barrels and sheepskins full of clean water.

In the empty land ahead lay nothing but green patches of shrubs and bushes scattered randomly among the soft hills. The air above was hot and thick with white dust. The bright desert sun forced William to look down and protect his eyes from the sharp glare that filled every corner of the sky.

As the wagons traveled farther away, the heat and their soft rocking movements caused William's mind to fall into a kind of dreamy sleep. His head slumped forward and his chin almost touched his chest. He lost all sense of time and as one moment slipped and morphed into another; everything seemed like one long blur.

Sometimes hours felt like minutes, other times minutes like hours. Several times he would wake and look around to see if they were getting close to the desert. Each time he looked, the white hills appeared more like golden dunes and the air became hotter in his lungs.

William was woken out of his trance when the wagon suddenly stopped. He looked up and saw the guide and his camel had stopped as well. William stood up in his seat and looked behind him, his back hunched from drowsiness. All the wagons waited and every man's eyes were locked on something behind William's back.

William glanced once more at the guide. The man, just like the rest of them, was also staring ahead him, the narrow smoking pipe hanging loosely out of the corner of his mouth. William's eyes darted back to the guide when he saw him taking the pipe from his mouth.

"The Bahr Almawt," the guide said in a low, gravelly voice as he pointed his smoking pipe to the desert in front of them.

William looked ahead of him. What he saw was perhaps the most frightening thing he'd ever seen—more frightening than being face to face with a starving wolf whose teeth, drool, and eyes were filled with the primitive force to kill, to want to kill for no other reason that killing is its nature.

Beginning a few feet in front of the horses that pulled his wagon was a change in the sand's color. It became charcoal Black and continued all the way, even beyond, the wavering horizon. There wasn't so much as a single shrub, and the land seemed as flat as the surface of a frying pan. The only thing differing from the black sand were small areas of white powder scattered over its surface as though a lousy chef had sprinkled salt over a cut of meat. William imagined the white spots to be the eroded bones of men and beasts who had died of thirst.

"Is that the desert?" William asked of their guide.

"In my language we call this place the sea of blood," the man replied around his pipe. "Those sands have soaked more blood and powdered more bones than any plague or war." Then the guide answered the silent question that was bothering William and perhaps every man in the group as well. "The Sahara is a vast place, and this is just a part of it. We only need to go a little ways in to reach the well, though that too will require time. If we try going around, there won't be anyone waiting for us when we get back."

"How long will it take us?" William asked, squinting at the sun.

The guide appeared to be thinking, calculating every aspect of their journey. "I do not know. If it were just riders on horseback, it could take several hours, but with the wagons it might take us two days just to get there." His gaze pointed forward.

William noticed a growing feeling inside of him that threatened to overwhelm his mind. What would it feel like to see the real desert beyond these black sands?

Dread is what he imagined most vividly. Dread that he was not strong enough to cross because he was a foreigner. He felt his sides tighten at the thought of dying from the heat and thirst.

The guide tapped his camel's shoulder and the animal started ahead, leaving the soft and seemingly pleasant sand behind and trotting onto the hot, sizzling dirt ahead. For a moment, the group watched, reluctant to follow as the guide began to lead his camel into the black sand with ease.

William sat back down on his wagon and motioned for the driver to get going. The man flicked the reins of the horses, lurching the wagon onward. A roar of groans and grunts came from man and beast alike as the line of wagons began to stir forward. When William's wagon crossed from the golden sand to the dark one, he felt as if the gates of hell had been opened for him to enter. He could almost hear the corrupted souls, who had faithfully stirred the coals of hell since Lucifer was cast from heaven, laugh at him in a taunting chuckle.

As the group moved farther into the black sand, desperation seemed to fill the air around them. Having drunk water days prior, their throats felt thirstier now when there was no shade to cover them from the blazing sun. With every breath William took, he could feel the hot air filling his lungs, drenching him in precious sweat, slowly and carelessly giving up all the water he had left in his body.

Soon enough all of William's thoughts seemed to circle around the heat that scorched his neck and shoulders with hands made of embers. The wind was stagnant here, making their slow and painful journey even more miserable. The men kept their heads down so as not to succumb to delirium from the heat and would only look up to see if they had changed direction.

William heard a sound that stood out from the drowsy creaking and swaying of the wagons behind him. The sound very similar to a sack landing on rocky ground. He looked behind him.

A camel walked by the side of the wagons and, a little distance behind it, its rider lay on his side, motionless. William recognized the stillness in the man's body.

He was dead. He had fallen victim to the desert. The camel moved along, leaving its owner's body behind. Tragic as it was, there was no going back. This journey wouldn't have mercy on anyone. William could feel tremors up his legs with that realization. He pushed it all away and sank in the seat of the wagon like a man taking his last breath.

Shutting his eyes, William hoped and prayed that he would not fall so deep into the pit of sleep that he, too, would surrender to the desert and become one of the many other claimed souls. He promised himself that no matter how tired or beaten down he felt, he would not let himself fall asleep. The sound of the wheels rolling over the rocks made the urge to sleep and avoid the heat in unconscious bliss the devil's torment. When William found himself breaking his promise, he would pinch himself on the side of his leg to wake himself up, only fending off the desire to sleep for a little while at a time before eventually giving in again.

Looking at the man beside him, William could tell that the sun and the desert was affecting him the same way because his eyes were twitching wildly as his mind teetered on the edge of sleep. William nudged the man with his elbow, and the driver straightened his posture, trying his best, as the rest of the men were, to stay awake.

William saw that he wasn't the only one who was succumbing to the heat. His eyes slowly turned to their guide. Since the old man had no one to keep him awake, William feared that he could have wandered off in his sleep. The thought that their guide had fallen asleep and had been leading them in circles made his fingers tense and frightened him into staying quiet. William stared at the guide's back, his mind somewhere other than the present moment.

In his mind, William wondered how long it would take for a man to die of thirst. And then he heard a sound.

That dreaded sound.

The sound of a sack landing on the rocks. He stiffened every tendon in his neck to stop himself from turning around and continued looking straight ahead as beads of sweat ran down his face. He already knew what the sound meant.

Death was drawing a check mark in the empty square before a name on his list as he carried on with his work, so concerned with numbers, numbers, numbers...

# 20

WILLIAM'S EYELIDS SLOWLY OPENED AND CLOSED as he numbly stared at the desert, the pause between blinks getting longer each time. His chin began to bow to his chest like a withering flower. A man shouted behind him in an off-key pitch, and William slowly lifted his head and turned to look over his shoulder, both damning and thanking the man for waking him from his daydream.

The shouting intensified as more men joined in. Their faces looked crazed with joy. Some of them hugged each other while others stood up in the wagons to get a better look at what was ahead. William turned around. Had he missed something in his half-sleep?

He squinted his eyes and stared hard at the rippling horizon where blue dunes hovered above the heat waves. William smiled and turned around to look at the men with the same crazed joy in his eyes. Someone fired a rifle and his shot was followed by several others, sending gray plumes of smoke into the hot air.

Straightening his back, William watched as the dunes moved slowly toward them. It was a victory of a kind, although one that was marred by the thought of the last group, who must have celebrated as they did now only to meet their end at the hands of hidden enemies. And what about the two dead men that already lay abandoned in the land of black? It seemed like that thought had been hovering over the entire band of wagons because none of them rejoiced as they crossed into the golden sands that stretched before them.

With the lighter sand, the temperature visibly lowered. Almost as a sign of welcome, the desert sent a wind that chilled their sweaty clothes. William looked up at the sky, considering how much longer it would be before dark. The sun, that had showed no mercy to them all day long, was only a handful of hours from kissing the horizon and shrouding the world in darkness.

Ahead of him was the desert he had longed to see and traverse. Dunes nearly as large as the buildings in London formed both wide and narrow valleys littered with rocks. To capture the moment, William closed his eyes and bowed his head in a strange kind of worship.

He had arrived, and even though this wasn't exactly how he'd imagined it would happen, William was grateful the dunes had granted a humble traveler like him an entrance into their majestic palace. In the recesses of his mind he could get a glimpse of the desert silence, sensing it like the sweeping beam of a lighthouse signaling him from a foggy coast. It was there, coming and going in his focus yet seemingly ungraspable.

He dreamed of feeling the empty vastness of the desert surround him, but that would have to wait for another time. He had a job to do, and the caravan depended on how well he did it.

When the time came, if it came, he would return to the desert and spend as much time in pure silence as he wanted. If the desert's silence was all his imagination made it seem, it might make a monk out of him.

The group was ascending a wide slope of sand, and beyond it William could see the tips of rolling dunes. When the guide reached the top he stopped his camel and everyone else trotted to a stop. William followed the guide's gaze down to the bottom of the slope which descended slowly to an open area surrounded with tall dunes.

At the center was the well.

It had a short wall built with black stones probably cut out of the desolate desert they had passed through, making it easy to notice against the golden sand.

In the back of his mind William had expected to find the well surrounded by the men who went before him, each with a carefully aimed arrow at his heart. But the well stood alone and the smooth sand around it didn't have so much as a footprint. Yet William knew that the ambushed group had soaked the sand with their blood. He could not see their bodies but he could sense that this was where they had met their end. It weighed on his mind to know that the ground he would walk on hid the bodies of men killed by the bowstrings of myths.

William looked at the guide, whose head was tilted back with eyes staring up at the sky. His mouth gaped slightly open. William frowned and looked up as well. Several clouds carrying rain in their gray pillows of mist were floating gracefully toward them. The sun was slipping behind them silently, sending out bright rays of light like bronze fingers reaching for their hold over the sky. The light had dimmed and a soft coldness entered the natural shade.

With the sun gone, William looked over his shoulder. Every man in the line of wagons was gazing up at the clouds in silent awe. The moment felt hallowed, created by the hand of chance and blessed by minds of thirsty men to be something belonging to the divine. A blessing to a band of weary pilgrims searching for redemption.

From the corner of his eye, William saw the guide's camel move forward and watched as it trotted down the slope. The driver sitting beside him drove the horses forward and the whole column began to move down the other side of the slope. The men kept quiet and alert, frantically looking around. They could not afford to make a mistake now because more than their lives depended on it.

William instructed the driver to circle the wagons around the well like they had back at the caravan. When the last wagon stopped, the men hopped off their places like sailors off a capsizing ship and began unloading skins and buckets in a silent frenzy of grunts and heavy breaths. William, who'd been the first to jump off the wagon, made straight for the well. Upon reaching it he placed both his hands on the black stone wall and looked down over the edge where he saw a small silver circle of wavering light surrounded by darkness.

So that was it, the well they had longed to find. Two questions still circulated in William's mind: was the water clean? And what if this was a trap?

He looked up at the surrounding dunes with a brief scan. They reminded him of the hills that had surrounded the camp of the Bedouin Sheik, except these were actual dunes, not small hills. As he swept the last dunes, William pushed away from the well and walked back to the wagons. He was happy to see that every man was busy: some were taking off the tops of the barrels, others were tying long ropes to buckets, and still others were preparing the skins to be filled.

William bent down and picked up a bucket tied to a long length of rope and started walking back to the well where some men were already lowering buckets to get water.

By the time William reached the well, the men were already filling the barrels with water. As he slung his bucket over the wall, ten others made their way in and out of the darkness simultaneously. William pulled his heavy bucket up, hearing the dripping and splashing of water along with the grunts and breaths of the men around him. When the bucket arrived at the top, he turned around to hand it to the man behind him.

"Wait," Fudail shouted from a wagon opposite the well. The whole group stopped and looked up. "We need to test the water first," he shouted as he stepped down from the wagon and walked toward William. William nearly stopped breathing. He feared they forgot to bring a doctor. If they did not have one, their journey would be useless.

"Is anyone a doctor?" William shouted, glancing from face to face as he clutched the bucket in his arms. The men looked at each other and the silence stretched on. Fudail made his way around the well and stopped in front of William, looking down at the dripping bucket of water.

"How are we going to see if the water is good?" he asked as he looked up at William, feeling the temptation to drink build inside of him.

William didn't know. He looked up at Fudail and bit his lip, hoping to come up with something.

Frankly, William was tired. Physically, too, but mostly he was tired of the way fate seemed to throw an obstacle in his way every time he tried to make progress. He wasn't playing the game any longer. Now was the time for action, even if it meant getting a little reckless.

"I'll do it," William said, looking back at Fudail with a smile of excitement on his face.

"Do what? Drink?" Fudail asked with a doubtful frown. He shook his head. "You're insane."

"Maybe. But if I get sick, we'll know it's not good, and if I'm fine we can fill the water barrels and be on our way." It sounded like a plan, though it could go horribly wrong. Fudail looked angry and probably thought the thirst had mangled William's brain, but what else could they do?

"No, that is a bad idea. I'll get our guide; he'll know what to do."

As Fudail began turning around, William lifted up the bucket to his lips and drunk the water. He didn't care that Fudail and the others watched in silent horror. He took gulp after gulp of the water, slowly raising the bottom of the bucket above his chin as streams of water trickled down his throat. William brought the bucket down and gasped for air.

"You fool! You drank enough to kill you this instant!" Fudail shouted, suddenly waking from his momentary stupor.

William's eyes were half open with satisfaction. "Exactly," he said with a careless smile as he felt his body welcome the cold, sweet water. He felt the stares of the men strengthen as they waited for his body to turn stiff and drop dead.

"How do you feel?" Fudail said in a soft voice.

"I feel... I feel fine," William replied, noticing no change in his body, except now his thirst was satisfied.

"Drink some more," Fudail urged, and William lifted the bucket up to his mouth a second time, drinking desperately.

"Well?" Fudail demanded.

William lowered the bucket and beamed. "It tastes good."

"Give it to me," the Arab said and took the bucket from William like he was going to show him how to drink it the *right* way. He brought it up to his mouth and drank several gulps. When he brought the bucket down, his face looked pleased.

"How is it?" William asked.

"You are right. It is good to drink." Fudail's smile now matched William's. The whole group began cheering and lifting their buckets to get their fill.

They would need their strength and their senses if they wanted to fill up the barrels and leave before sundown.

As William stepped closer to the well and lowered into the darkness, his smile was uncontainable. They had taken another priceless step in getting water back to the caravan.

Soon after everyone had gotten enough to drink, they began drawing water from the well. Two-man teams were in charge of pulling up buckets and passing them down the line of men leading to the wagons, refilling them as quickly as they could. As William pulled up bucket after bucket and passed it to the man behind him, he saw Fudail walking around the well and organizing the men who were moving too slowly or taking too many sips of water.

At one point it began to dawn on William that this whole process was taking a lot of time. Filling the bucket, passing it full, then receiving it empty and lowering it back into the well was a lengthy process. Would they be able to fill up all the barrels before darkness settled? The men seemed to have reached the same conclusion because everyone was now working at speeds difficult to obtain in usual situations.

But fast speeds also meant getting tired more quickly, and that meant slowing down the whole line. William couldn't let that happen. When he felt his arms straining so much that he thought he'd drop the bucket, he switched with the man behind him so that he would not slow down the process.

The only man who wasn't working in the line was the guide who stood on top of a dune overlooking the well, cradling his rifle in his hands while scanning the surrounding dunes. Down below, William worked alongside the others, passing buckets of water as quickly as he could. Little by little the men's clothes became drenched with a mix of water and sweat that began to chill them with the onset of evening. Every passing second seemed precious, since the sky was filling with more rain clouds that shut out the light, meaning that dark would arrive earlier than expected.

For every gallon poured into the barrels, the desert around them turned a shade darker and a degree colder. Water was getting spilled in the haste of motion and tiredness was beginning to settle over the group and slow their speed. But though their fingers were beginning to get numb and their clothes were entirely soaked no one stopped. They couldn't stop.

The cold began to set in as a sign that the day was drawing to a close. The men had already filled up all the skins, and when the last barrel got a final bucketful of water, no one wasted time when loading the buckets into the wagons and hammering the tops back on the barrels.

William was busy loading up sheepskins onto the back of a wagon, grabbing two at a time and handing them to a man standing in the wagon bed above.

A tiredFudail approached, his eyes following William's arms. "All the barrels are full and loaded. Only a few skins remain and then we can leave," he reported as he bent and picked up a pair of skins.

"Good," William said, taking the skins from him and passing them on to the man standing in the wagon. "I need to speak with our guide. You make sure that everything is ready so we can leave as soon as I return."

Fudail gave an eager nod and ran off to organize the men and wagons in preparation to leave while William helped load the last of the sheepskins and started walking toward the guide who was still keeping watch from the top of the same dune. As he weaved his way through the busy swarms of men loading the last of the skins, William felt pleasantly surprised that he had made it this far in their mission without being killed or getting lost. A task his former self never would have thought possible to achieve.

"We are going to leave soon," he told the guide upon reaching him. "Do you think we can go back tonight or should we stay the night?" In all honesty, William dreaded the first option as much as the second.

"If we leave now, we can make it back around midnight. Although if we stay here it would be safer. It is your choice, not mine," the guide said while his squinted eyes swept the tops of the dunes.

"The sooner we get the water back to the caravan, the better for everyone. There are women and children that need it desperately. We really have no choice but to travel through the night," William heard himself say. On the inside though, he wondered whether this was the right choice at all. What if they got lost in the darkness and didn't end up bringing water to anyone? If they stayed the night though, it might be too late.

The guide's silence showed he was indifferent to William's decision. He didn't even nod before making his camel ride down to the circle of wagons. William headed in the same direction and saw Fudail emerging from the wagons as the guide trotted past him.

"Everything is ready," Fudail said as he joined William.

"Good. Tell the men to get in the wagons; we're leaving."

Fudail nodded before running off to give the order.

With hurried strides, William and the rest of the men took their places, some in the wagons, others on camels that staggered to their feet with the weight of two smaller barrels and a handful of sheepskins on their sides. When William pulled himself up onto his wagon, he felt that the easiest part of the expedition had been completed and the hardest, most dangerous part still lay ahead of them.

The guide kept at William's side, ready to take them back. William looked at the men behind him, and they stared at him with a fearful eagerness and determination to return to the caravan.

William turned around and looked up at the guide. "Lead on."

The guide nodded and the camel started toward the slope overlooking the well. William's driver whipped the horses with the reins and the wagon began rocking forward, followed by the long procession behind them. As they reached the peak, William turned around and took a last look at the lonesome well. Its sturdy wall was the only sign that humans had ever been to this part of the world, a sign he was grateful for.

The well soon disappeared from his gaze, and William's attention turned elsewhere. Ahead of them lay the golden sands that had turned dark gray with the setting sun. The clouds above contributed to the gloom, gray and foreboding. They reminded William of the day it had rained in London, dark like water tinted with ink.

But that wasn't why his mind was anxious, and he guessed that the men he was leading felt it too as their eyes roamed the desert in fear of an ambush. William certainly felt the suspicion creeping just under the surface of his mind.

The group moved at a slower speed now that the weight of their precious cargo strained the animals. With rifles at the ready, the men who were not responsible for driving the wagons carefully watched the dunes. Darkness settled shortly after sunset making the men more anxious to shoot at anything and break the silence that toyed with their sanity. Waiting for a shot to be fired plucked at their nerves like a toddler slapping his hand on a piano.

A strong wind came over the desert and covered them in a strange fog until it became impossible to see the entire column of wagons. Suddenly, the ground beneath the wagons turned harder, a sign that they were nearing the Bahr Almawt. Even here, in this hard terrain, the wind managed to hide the rumbling of the wagons in its constant roar. The gusts grew stronger by the minute, carrying news of the inevitable. A sandstorm was brewing.

William kept his head low and his eyes staring at the dark shadows between his knees, trying to protect his exposed skin from the grainy sand peppering the side of his face and ears like pins and needles. All he could hear was the relentless booming wind and an occasional neigh of irritation from the horses. He hadn't looked up at the guide since darkness had fallen, too afraid that he would see nothing but whirling clouds of dust. But he had to keep track of the man, lest they lose sight of him.

Gathering up his courage, William lifted his head. The sand hissed on the right side of his face. He squinted his eyes and held his hand up to shield them from the storm. Panic pounded in his head. All he could see were the dark backs of the horses pulling his wagon, the shape of their heads softened by the gloom. The guide was nothing but a vague shadow moving in and out of his vision—but he was there. With a sense of relief, William brought his head back down and closed his eyes, hoping that the guide will still be there the next time he looked up.

As the wagons swayed from side to side in what William sensed was the Bahr Almawt's dark sea of rocks, the wind continued to scratch away the skin at his neck and hands and sent chills down his spine. The farther they traveled into the Bahr Almawt, however, the sandstorm began to calm, and to his surprise the wind suddenly died out. Every sound created by the wagons and animals was naked without the wind to cover it. Sand no longer scraped his skin. Instead, a thick cloud loomed in the air.

They rode on for hours after the wind had gone silent, and when the ground became soft again and changed back to pale sand, a round of cheers came from the men behind. William felt the fear in his chest turn to excitement. He turned to the driver next to him and smiled with a quiet laugh of amazement.

In his mind he could picture the faces of the people when the wagons entered the camp: smiling faces, weeping with joy and gratitude. He realized that they would be able to continue to Yemen and leave the mysterious force that had harassed them in just a handful of days.

When that thought faded, William began to realize what he had done. He had traveled through the Bahr Almawt, seen the true colors of the desert, filled the barrels with water and was now heading back to the caravan that was only a kilometer away. In truth, though, he realized that he'd only seen a glimpse of what the desert really meant and was longing to return to that silence he craved.

With the column of wagons slowly moving through the valley ahead, William looked up at the nearby hills. He imagined their silvery peaks as mighty waves during a storm and the wagons below as merchant vessels sailing fearlessly through the rough waters of the sea.

He heard the guide's camel groan and looked up slowly, somewhat irritated that his dreaming had been cut short. To his surprise, William saw the guide had stopped in front of his wagon and the man kept deathly still.

"Stop the wagon," William said to the driver. "Something's wrong."

When the horses halted, William stood on his seat and turned around. Waving both of his hands in the air, he shouted for the column to stop, then jumped off the wagon and walked over to the guide . The man kept his eyes focused on the horizon, his mouth open in terror.

"What is it?" William asked following the direction of the man's gaze.

The guide raised his right arm and pointed to the horizon with an unsteady finger. William didn't see it at first, but then fear and confusion filled his core. A dim orange light lined the horizon and the bottoms of the clouds, illuminating them with a gloomy shade of golden brown, the kind of brown that fills the sky when a city is being ravaged by flames. William thought that the sun was rising, but knew that sunrise was still a long way off.

"What is that?" William asked as his worried glance returned to the guide's terror-stricken face.

"The caravan," the guide blurted out in a gasp. He turned his camel around and toward the wagons.

"Hey," William shouted at him, but the guide continued down the line, now illuminated by the glowing horizon. When the man passed the fifth wagon, William heard a faint whistling sound.

183

The guide suddenly fell off his camel and lay still on the ground, his frightened animal continuing on without him. William started running toward him, thinking the man had fainted from fear or exhaustion. The others, confused and momentarily stunned, stayed near the wagons and watched silently.

When William reached the guide, he fell to his knees and pulled the man toward him, but the guide only slumped over on his back, deathly still. William felt a warm liquid on the palm of his hand, right at the man's chest. As he brought his hand up in front of his chest, he began wondering what the faint whistle had been.

From the glowing horizon, clusters of rifle fire suddenly broke out. William jumped to his feet and looked in the direction where he heard the gunshots. He noticed the light at the horizon had grown much brighter—so much so, that it partially illuminated the plain before them. He raised his hand and looked at it. Blood was dripping down from his palm to his wrist. His stomach tightened and a nightmarish unease filled his lungs with poisoned gas. The same uncleanness he felt at the dead man's camp filled him once again.

There was another faint whistle behind him, and William spun around in fear. A rider standing close to the dead guide fell to his knees with his hands wrapped around the fletching of an arrow sticking out the front of his chest. Another man fell as an arrow struck him in the throat; he gargled on his blood writhing on the ground.

William bolted toward the wagons, where the men began to take cover. Snapping sounds came from the ridges on either side of the them, and when he saw a man slump over the side of a wagon William realized what it meant: a tight bowstring striking the frame of a bow. He kneeled at the side of the wagon taking cover in the shadow cast by the burning horizon. As he crouched, an arrow punched into the wood just behind his head. He looked around briefly before jumping to his feet.

He put his hands near his mouth and shouted in an unrestrained cry of terror that trembled in his chest and mouth, "Ambush!" A bright flash from a rifle blinded William's eyes momentarily and the violent punch of the rifle in the silence made his ears numb to all sound except his own shaky breaths. William crouched down at the wagon's side and looked up at the ridge to his left. It was gloomy and orange, but barely visible.

The screams produced by the wounded men split the darkness like a ghost wailing in pain. Some of them were close to him, others farther away. William was beginning to realize that their attackers used the wounded men as bait to draw the others out from behind their cover, only to be struck down with an arrow through the heart.

A man rushed out from around the wagon in front of William to take cover by his side only to drop dead on the ground when an arrow passed through his chest and plunged into the wagon, speckling William in a mist of blood. William started backing away from the man, fear paralyzing his limbs. Another arrow struck the wagon's side, inches from where William crouched.

William dropped down on his chest and began crawling towards the front of the wagon. A gunshot from the seat of William's wagon flashed the sand around him in orange light. As he reached the front wheel of the wagon, the screams of the men who were being picked off with systematic accuracy chilled the blood in his veins. William looked down the line of wagons and counted only a handful of men crouching near the wheels. Most lay in the sand, dead.

He spotted something moving on the hill to his left. A long row of shadows was descending the hill with swords drawn to finish them off.

William jumped to his feet and ran to the spooked horses at the front of the wagon. When he reached them, he saw the silhouette of a man riding toward him with a short bow raised to shoot. A man in the back was killed suddenly by a whooshing arrow and his rifle landed on the seat beside William. He picked up the rifle and aimed it at the archer. The weapon felt heavy and William's fingers were clumsy on the trigger, but he put the moving silhouette in his sights and pulled hard, expecting for the recoil to punch him in the shoulder.

Click.

The rifle was jammed.

On instinct, William pulled back the bolt. It was frozen still. He frantically rattled the bolt back and forth to get it free, but it wouldn't budge an inch. William looked up from the rifle. The rider had drawn his bow and was about to get within firing distance. William grabbed the barrel of the rifle in his hands and raised the stock over his shoulder like a club. The rider loosed his arrow. It whistled past William's neck and punched into the wagon behind.

He chose that moment to leap toward the horse and simultaneously hit the rider in the chest with the iron stock of the rifle. The man fell over the side of his horse, landing with a hard thud a couple of feet away from William. The horse continued riding down the line of wagons. From the corner of his eye, William noticed a handful of scattered shadows running closer to the wagons and away from the orange gloom.

The fallen rider scrambled to get on his feet but William dashed toward him. The man was almost standing when William swung at the man's head with the rifle. The man caught the stock near his face and jerked William forward, bringing both of them to the ground. The rider pulled a dagger from his waist and brought the blade down on William's chest. William reached for the glimmering dagger just as everything suddenly went black from the blinding flash of a rifle. He felt the rider's arms fall in his hands and they weighed like an elephant. The tip of the dagger trembled as both men pushed with all their might, but William's arms were failing and the blade slowly lowered to his chest.

William heard footsteps all around him as a multitude of shadows rushed to the wagons and fought his remaining men. But William's focus was at the dagger that was about to cut him open. Then a bright flash and a deafening bang shook his chest. William felt the rider's hands relax on the handle of the dagger and slump over William's left shoulder.

For a moment, William stared at the rider's empty eyes and covered face that lay next to him. His own hands were the only ones holding the dagger now, and they shook like he was being electrocuted. William looked in the direction where the shot had come from. The driver of his wagon stood a few feet away, trembling, with a rifle still aimed at the dead man. William stared into the man's terror-filled eyes, a look of horror having twisted his face into a wince of disgust.

As William and the driver stared at each other, the shots and screams coming from the other men in the group were becoming less and less frequent as more were felled by the arrows and blades that seemed to appear out of the darkness.

An arrow whistled over William and punched the driver in the chest, passing swiftly through. The man staggered backward a few steps. The small wound in his chest began to trickle blood onto his white robe like wine pouring from an invisible pitcher. He looked down at his chest with an expressionless face before he dropped on his back.

William scrambled to his feet and rushed to the horses tied to the first wagon, glancing briefly at the wagons now swarming with black robes. When he reached the horses, he began undoing the harnesses that held the animal closest to him. The horse neighed as it moved forward freely and started to slip past William when he jumped onto its back and grabbed two handfuls of its thick mane to keep from falling off.

A moment later the horse was galloping at a wild speed toward the light on the horizon, throwing William up and down as it pummeled the ground with its front hooves. An arrow whizzed past the side of William's head and landed in the dirt ahead of him. He ducked and hugged himself closer to the horse's neck.

When William had gotten a good distance away from the ambush, he could hear the rumbling of thunder echo in the clouds, mixing with the roaring wind that had started once again. Little drops of water began ticking on his arms and face, becoming more and more frequent as he rode on. Within seconds, the sky was pouring down rain that brought with it the damp smell of smoke.

Finally, he reached the hill that overlooked the camp and urged the horse toward the top. The sky was bright above and when William finally looked down, he thought that a crack in the earth had spilled a lake of lava and smoke.

His heart stopped pounding in his chest. The whole caravan was a sea of burning coals engulfed in flames. Amongst the flames the shadowy figures of people running and fighting danced on the ground and on the few remaining tents like a Renaissance painting of hell. All around the edge of the caravan, hoards of people fled and were cut down in droves by horsemen hacking at the shadows on either side of their horses at will.

The screaming, the neighing of horses, the striking of one blade against another overwhelmed William's ears in a roar that crippled his mind with overpowering terror that shook the deepest part of his core. He closed his eyes and looked away. He wanted to run as far as he could from the caravan, but the memory of Nadia waving to him as he left the camp appeared in his mind like a vivid dream. He turned back to the flames below with a sad look in his eyes. He knew he would have to ride through the chaos if he wanted to find her. If he could find her.

He battled the fear of riding into the camp, and a moment later he kicked the horse with his heels. The animal dove over the edge, galloping down the hill with the speed of a swooping eagle. He rode past a small group of fleeing people near the bottom of the hill. As he neared the burning tents, William heard the vivid screams of the people as they ran in panic through the disfigured alleys.

He entered the camp and was momentarily enveloped in the roar of chaos. Many rushed past, screaming as they fled. Shouting Nadia's name, William quickly became a part of the turmoil and confusion. The air he breathed was hot from the flames that roared at him and damp from the rain that fell from above.

Among the shadows swarmed men in black robes, seemingly invincible in their swift attack. They raised their blades to every man and woman who came in their path. Some stood and fought. Others ran for their lives. Those too weak to fight back were killed in cold blood.

The soldiers in black swept through the caravan like a flood of murky water, leaving behind nothing but burning tents and corpses. Every soldier ran wherever his blood-thirst took him, taking what lives he could with either his sword or his bow, never stopping or slowing down, never heeding or hesitating in the devil's work of war.

As William approached the poisoned well, the Desert King's men—for he didn't doubt that's who they were—stormed past him as if he didn't exist. One man on horseback was firing arrow after arrow with deadly accuracy at a group of fleeing people, hitting every person he aimed for. The camp was engulfed in the flames of hell, with demons running rampant in the crumbling haven of the caravan.

He found no one at the well though people were running past in futile attempts to escape. Holding onto hope that despite everything Nadia could still be alive, William decided to look for her at her tent. He rode away from the well and back into the chaos, hoping that his memory would lead him where he wanted to go. Starting down a path that looked like the fire hadn't yet reached it, William rode on.

Just as he entered the path, an arrow struck the horse in one of its hind legs. The horse dropped from underneath William and sent him flying through the wet, smoky air. He flew several feet before landing hard on the ground with enough momentum to send him rolling in the dust. When his body hit a tent post, William grunted and looked up to see the horse limping as it struggled to stand, a wall of flames behind it. An arrow passed through its heart and the animal fell to the ground, writhing in pain until it breathed its last.

William stared above the dark corpse of the horse as the soldier who had killed it ran toward him, drawing a curved sword from his waist, The flames of the camp glimmered off the round iron shield on his left arm. William jumped to his feet and ran down the path.

The soldier bolted after him, and more soldiers joined in the hunt much like hounds after a hare. William took turn after turn and ran among the fleeing crowds, hoping to lose the men who were chasing him. Each time he glanced over his shoulder, the soldiers seemed to gain on him. He broke away from the fleeing people and turned down another path. Behind him, the soldiers were almost an arm's length away.

A large street with hundreds of people opened up ahead, each of them running frantically. William hoped he could lose the soldiers in the crowd.

Entering a street, he took a sharp right turn.

In front of him the ground trembled as a massive horse charged at him in a frenzy of fear. Before William could step out of the way, the horse's muscly chest slammed into him and he was thrown backward into the air across the mouth of the path he had come out of. He landed on the ground, unconscious.

When the Desert King's men arrived at the edge of the street they turned to the right and kept running, leaving William lying with his face in the sand, to carry on with the greedy slaughter that raged on, in the flames and the rain.

# 21

THICK PLUMES OF SMOKE SPIRALED INTO THE SKY. Down on earth, the ground was black, burnt from the fires that had illuminated the night. The camp was as empty as the desert surrounding it, kept barely alive by the few sounds of burnt tents flapping in the wind, the wheel of an overturned wagon squealing as it slowly turned round and round, the booming gusts of wind in the distance. A burning wagon roared furiously when the wind fanned its flames, and a cloud of smoke drifted over William's motionless body, enveloping him and stinging his lungs.

He coughed several times, making the first human noise in the camp since the night before. His eyes squinted in the blinding light of the sun that had chased off both the shadows and the rain. Pushing to get on his hands and knees, William turned over to sit down.

His mind whirled with images of the night before. The wagon that still burned in front of him made the air he breathed hot in his lungs. William rose to his feet and his head instantly stood out from the smoldering ruins of the camp. As far as he could see, there were burnt tents, overturned wagons, dead bodies and piles of possessions scattered in unrecognizable heaps.

William staggered as his breath managed to escape him. The once lively caravan now looked like the bottom of a waterless sea scattered with wrecked ships. Hundreds of crows circled above the tents and swooped down to feast on the slain. He started to feel dizzy, and the light stung his eyes. Turning around with a staggering step William saw the full scale of the devastation. The sight of it made his head spin.

He fell to his knees, holding himself up with one hand on the ground as the other covered his mouth. His body surged forward, and he vomited. For several moments he stayed kneeling, looking at the vomit puddled on the ground between his hands. He threw up again and felt his stomach tighten.

The acidic taste in his mouth made him cough again, then he stood up and looked at the camp around of him, feeling weaker but slightly better. His dream of forever staying with the caravan was destroyed by the flames. William felt utterly alone, but this was not the same loneliness he had sought in the desert. That was peace; this was emptiness. This was the chaotic silence in which fear breeds like bacteria in an infected wound.

Could he find Nadia's tent now? Could she still be alive in this wreckage? He stared sightlessly at the disfigured camp around him and listened to the smoldering flames. Then came a different noise.

William spun around with his fists clenched in front of him. Across the path, a lone camel scrounged noisily in the wreckage of a collapsed tent. There was a loud clang when the camel knocked over a cooking pot with its nose. The empty saddle on its back suggested that its owner was most likely dead. William lowered his fists and straightened his back.

He turned back around, knowing he would not last long on his own. The nearest city was on the other side of the Bahr Almawt and the amount of food he could scrounge in the caravan would probably last him a day.

Soft footsteps came from his left and William saw in the corner of his eye a dark figure step into the path.

His head turned instinctively. Though bloody, this face he would recognize anywhere.

"Fudail!" William shouted as he ran to him. The man stayed where he was and watched William running toward him. He held a sword streaked with blood, the sleeve of his left arm hanging open from the slash of a blade that ran along the length of his arm but had stopped bleeding. "How did you survive?" William asked as he stopped in front of him.

"I escaped the ambush and rode here, looking for Hakeem, but the attack had already begun. " Fudail said, as if reporting.

"Hakeem, is he alive?" William asked.

"Before I reached Hakeem's tent, I saw one of the doctors and he told me that he had died just before the attack."

William looked down at his feet. In a way, he felt relieved that Hakeem hadn't seen the destruction of his caravan but it saddened him know that the earth had been robbed of another good man.

"What do we do now?" Fudail asked, as if looking to William for guidance.

William looked up, considering the question.

"I need to find my friends," he said, shutting the thought of finding them dead out of his mind. They *had* to have survived.

"What about supplies?" Fudail asked.

"You look for supplies. We'll meet at the north end of the caravan in two hours. If I'm not there, go without me," William said as he started moving back toward the path where he had woken up. Fudail gave a nod and ran off in search of food.

William turned around and bolted down the path as quickly as his legs could carry him. But given the journey from the day before, his speed wasn't impressive. He felt weak and his body ached.

When he ran past the camel, now chewing on a piece of cloth, his footsteps slowed down. He stared at the animal for a moment and realized that if he rode it around the camp, he would be able to search much faster. He hurried back and stepped into the half-collapsed tent, taking the camel's reins and leading it outside.

Making a clicking noise with his mouth, like he'd seen other riders do, William motioned to the ground, hoping the camel would kneel and let him climb on its back. This must have been a tame animal, because even though it groaned, it also kneeled. William pulled himself onto the camel's back and at his clicking noise the animal staggered up to its feet bringing William high above the ground.

The height of the camel gave William a wide field of vision over the wrecked tents scattered around him. He patted the animal's shoulder and the camel started trotting down the path at a speed much faster than William could have managed with his own two legs. With a tug of the reins, he steered the animal to the left of the path, deciding that checking out Hans' tent first would be a good place to start his search. His last resort would be to look among the dead.

As the camel bounced him down the path, William's eyes took in the devastation around him. The caravan had been destroyed, its people slaughtered in the paths. William's heart thudded in his chest. He wouldn't choke his fighter instincts any longer. He wouldn't be weak and submissive. He would fight back, for freedom.

When he reached the remains of Hans' tent, he stopped the camel near the entrance. The contraption was burned and barely standing. He saw nothing moving but the tattered cloth swaying in the breeze and inside, nothing resembled a corpse.

"Hans!" William shouted at the top of his lungs. His voice was swallowed up in the spaciousness of the camp. There was no response.

William turned the camel and began riding down a different path hoping it would lead him to Nadia's tent. As he rode across the camp, he thought about what he would do if he didn't find anyone. He had two choices. First, he could search for Hans, Alexander, and Nadia until he had to meet Fudail, and would leave without them. Second, he would let Fudail leave without him and continue searching. He didn't like either option, but he decided he wouldn't choose either one until his time ran out.

He was riding across a large intersection that he thought had been near Nadia's tent when he noticed something in the path to his right that seemed to scream his name even though the camp was still and silent. He slowed down the camel and looked at a motionless figure lying in the abandoned street. It was a woman wearing a beaded dress. Several crows cawed wickedly as they pecked through the dress at the woman's back.

William felt a rush of revulsion fill his lungs. He shouted at the crows and rode toward the woman. Reluctantly, the scavengers flew away to feast somewhere else. When he reached the motionless figure, William slid off the saddle and fell to his knees at the woman's side.

For a moment he was perfectly still, as if he knew the woman was sleeping and didn't want to wake her. He looked at a hand reaching above the woman's head. The dusty fingers were decorated in small brass rings and the wrist was delicately small. William knew who it belonged to.

A frown of sadness appeared on his face. His eyes turned to the back of the woman's head and looked at the small beads woven into the cloth of her scarf. Tears blurred his vision like the heat waves rippling on the desert horizon.

William moved his hand to the woman's shoulder and put his hand around it. It felt soft in the palm of his hand. Soft and cold. He tightened his grip and turned the woman onto her back.

Nadia's eyes were closed. The glowing green light wouldn't shine in them again. Her face looked silver and her lips pale. The forest of her eyelashes was riddled with pebbles of dirt. William let out a shaky breath as his eyes began to sting from the tears that fell freely over Nadia's still face. He bent down and wrapped his arms around her shoulders and lifted her gently onto his lap, where he continued to hold her.

Her head lulled back, exposing her throat to the sky. He lifted her head back up with his left hand so that her face looked up at him. His eyes began to squint and a sad smile pulled the corners of his mouth toward his ears. He bent down and hugged Nadia's still body to his chest. His mouth pressed against her cold shoulder and he took shaky breaths through his nose. He squeezed her tightly and closed his eyes, knowing that when he let go, he would never see her face again. The tears dropped from his eyes and landed in the absorbent sand below. His hands moved closer to the center of her back as he hugged her tighter to his chest. He wished he could make her a part of him, even if that part of him was dead inside.

"William!" a voice screamed in the distance. It sounded like Fudail, but it was hard to tell. William ignored it and continued to hold Nadia in his arms. She had left him too soon, again.

"William!" the voice shouted as the sound of running footsteps grew louder behind him.

It was Fudail's voice and it trembled with intense fear. William's face tightened. He knew the time to say goodbye was coming, but he didn't want to say those words. He couldn't.

"William," Fudail ran up behind him. "They are coming back. Around twenty or thirty of them at the east side, on horses," he yelled, a little out of breath. "Come. We need to go," Fudail said as he grabbed William's shoulder. "We need to go now."

As if in a trance, William ignored the man and continued to hold Nadia's body in his arms. Fudail gave a sigh of frustration and started running in the direction he had come from. As his footsteps faded away, William's arms slowly lowered Nadia to the ground.

"Don't worry about me. I'll be with you soon. I love you," a silent voice whispered inside William as he let go of Nadia and her back returned to the ground.

"William!" Fudail shouted as he ran back to him.

When William laid Nadia on the ground, he remained kneeling for a moment, staring at her pale face. "Goodbye," the same whispering voice said just before Fudail grabbed him for the shoulder and yanked him away from the woman who had brought so much joy in his life.

William didn't resist when Fudail turned him around. The Arab, ever so faithful, grabbed the reins of the camel and lead it at a quick pace down a path leading to the west. William ran to catch up with him, turning to look over his shoulder.

Nadia's body lay still in the empty street, the only speck of color in a sea of charcoal and ashes, slowly moving away from him as he walked. William heard a horse neigh in front of him and turned around. Three horsemen blocked the path ahead. Fudail and the camel stopped in their tracks.

William looked at the riders, their faces covered in black cloth so that only their eyes were visible. A bow rested on the thigh of one rider. The other two had drawn their swords and their polished shields looked like silver mirrors in the blazing sun.

To his left, Fudail was slowly edging backward as if stepping away from a sleeping animal. When his foot landed in the sand, the horsemen kicked the horses with the backs of their heels and started racing toward the them.

"Run!" Fudail shouted as he let go of the reins and bolted towards William who spun around and followed. Near Nadia's body was a small path that branched off to the left and they took it.

The path was narrow and windy, offering very little opportunity to lose the riders, but they couldn't turn back. William looked over his shoulder and saw the three horsemen riding in a single file, the one with the bow riding in front. William quickened his pace. His legs were burning with cold chills, and he was beginning to lose speed. Over his shoulder he saw the archer draw his bow and aim at him.

On instinct, William ducked and veered to the right. The arrow whistled past his left shoulder and sank deep into Fudail's left calf. The Arab shouted and grabbed his leg as he limped forward. William ran off to help him.

"Go," Fudail shouted as he waved down the path.

With nothing else he could do, William obeyed and kept running. Over his shoulder he saw the riders hurry past Fudail, one of them sweeping a blade toward his neck. The rider's blade severed Fudail's head from his shoulders in a clean swoop and Fudail's headless body fell limp to the ground.

William felt bile rise in his throat but he hurried on even though his strength was beginning to leave him and his lungs gasped for air that was too thin to breathe. Behind him, the pounding horse hooves closed in on him. They seemed to be pounding just behind his heels. When he glanced over his shoulder, William expected to see the rider drawing his bow. Instead, the man was crouching on the saddle of his horse. William veered to the left, but the solder had anticipated the move.

Springing from his horse with the swiftness of a panther, the rider wrapped his arms around William's shoulders, his momentum knocking both of them off balance as they stumbled inside the remains of a half-burnt tent.

As soon as they hit the ground, William wriggled to his back to protect himself. But the soldier had something else in mind. The last thing William saw was the rider's fist falling on his face and everything went black with a painful thud and a slow, tense exhale.

# 22

A LONG TIME PASSED BEFORE WILLIAM REGAINED consciousness. He felt disoriented by the constant swaying of his body.

Where was he?

Slowly, he opened his eyes to thin beams of light slipping through the threads of a woolen sack. The tips of his fingers were pulsating from a rope tied around his wrists. He wiggled his toes and realized his ankles were also bound. The sounds he heard were faint at best: horses neighing and wagons creaking. As he came to, his mind restored the images he last remembered and a terrifying thought made his blood turn cold.

*Why am I being taken?* Indeed, why hadn't they just killed him, like they had Fudail? Like Nadia? Like everyone else?

Was he taken hostage? But who would they want ransom from?

Or was he being led to his execution? This option seemed somehow more than plausible. He imagined the soldiers were gathering him along with the rest of the survivors for a mass execution that they would relish. After all, hundreds of victims were hard to come by. It would be the perfect dessert for the six course meal of destruction they had wrought on the caravan. He couldn't tell if there were any other survivors, though, so why go to all this trouble just for him?

The swaying suddenly stopped, and everything became deathly still. William's breaths sounded shaky in the sack. Voices and footsteps moved close and a latch gave a short squeal. Unable to see anything, William could only go by the shouting he heard. It certainly sounded as if the soldiers were busy unloading and stacking bags of grain on the ground. He felt strong hands grab him up by his shoulders and feet.

Every muscle in his body ached. Obviously, the soldiers weren't going to go out of their way to make his execution comfortable. All around him

William heard muffled footsteps mixed with grunts, thumps, and even screams. He realized he must not be the only survivor as the soldiers threw him to the ground and his head bumped into something soft that grunted. A patch of grainy sand was sticking to his neck, which meant they were nowhere around the caravan. How long had he been unconscious?

The sound of a blade being pulled out of its sheath suddenly caught his attention as footsteps walked over to him. A moment later, he felt the rope around his feet loosen as a blade cut it away and a pair of hands grabbed him by his arms and jolted him to his feet.

A loud puff of air reached his ears as the bag was whisked off his head, leaving him squinting at the blinding light that stung his eyes. Before his sight could adjust, a hand grabbed him by the elbow and led him forward at a hurried pace that made it nearly impossible to keep his balance. As William stumbled at the hand of the soldier, he heard a multitude of voices drawing near. He looked up with one squinted eye and caught a glimpse of a crowd of men sitting shackled together in a maze of tangled chains and locks. There must have been four hundred of them. Behind them, a camp of thousands upon thousands of black tents continued all the way to the horizon and possibly beyond it.

William was ruthlessly shoved to the ground where he landed face first. Sand got into his eyes and stuck to the inside of his mouth. Blinking furiously, he looked behind him and saw the soldier kneel at his side and cut the ropes the bound his hands with a sudden slash before he stood him up and pushed him the rest of the distance to the crowd, where he forced him to sit.

The soldier shackled William's hands and feet to the chains crisscrossing on the ground. In that moment, he felt hatred, deep and insatiable, toward this man, and he hoped the soldier will look up and see that hatred in his eyes. But he didn't. When the shackles were locked around William's wrists, the soldier stood up and walked back to the wagons, where more prisoners were being unloaded and added to the crowd.

Four wagons were lined up in a row. Most of the men getting pulled off the wagons looked docile and dirty. Few resisted, but none went willingly. Because new men were constantly getting shackled to the network of chains, William was now around twenty feet deep into the mesh with triple the number of chains and locks around his feet.

His eyes turned toward the edge of the crowd of prisoners and froze when he saw two of the Desert King's soldiers dragging a man by his feet, away from the crowd, while he kicked and screamed at what he surely knew awaited him. A long slash in the man's arm had covered his robe in dry blood; the injury must have happened during the attack. When the man was about thirty feet away from the other prisoners, his cries were quickly put to an end by a quick thrust to the chest with a lance.

William felt sick and disgusted at the same time. Could these men truly be so cruel? A cold feeling of dread entered the pit of his stomach as he started to feel as if he were existing in a living nightmare. To his left, William saw the same kind of selective process being carried out as two soldiers took another man out of the group to execute him. That man was also wounded. The soldiers threw him to the ground, and knowing what would follow, William turned away and closed his eyes. The man's voice fell silent a moment later.

More men were added to the crowd of prisoners and William listened as those who were wounded were put to death a little distance away. The soldiers left the bodies of the dead to bloat in the evening sun and returned to the crowd to pick off the injured with a ruthless apathy.

At last, this whole process ended and the wagons began moving. Upon reaching the edge of the camp, they circled back and drove off in the direction they had come from, finally disappearing over a dune. Once the wagons were gone, hundreds of voices filled the air all around William, as the chained men talked to one another about everything from the attack on the caravan to how hot the shackles were around their ankles. Mixing with the murmurs of the crowd was the trampling and neighing of the soldiers' horses as they circled the prisoners to make sure no one escaped. If any hope remained, they sought to destroy it with a show of force.

William had been sitting, shackled, for several hours when he began to sense the panic that had filled the air finally settle. If he was going to be executed, it would happen another time. William felt, as did most of the men, that their captors had other plans. He looked at the faces of the men sitting around him. Their eyelids were half open with exhaustion and their faces were covered in dust. Not far away, one of the men was sobbing uncontrollably. Dark stains of sweat covered their robes around the armpits and backs because, even though it was evening, the lack of shade or water made it seem twice as hot.

One of the men sitting in front of him had a large portion of his chest covered in blood that had soaked through his white robe. He was taking long heavy breaths that seemed to help cope with the pain of his wound. William dreaded seeing him get dragged away and killed. He looked up from the man's bloodied chest, his eyes lingering on his bowed head. The man was in his forties, and most of the hair on his head had retreated from the top. He had a bony face, and wrinkles divided his forehead into small sections. Instead of being fearful of death, he looked calm and ready for the fate that awaited him when the soldiers noticed his bloody clothes.

Out of the corner of his eye, William saw a man standing above the crowd. At first he took him for a prisoner who'd undone his shackles, but no. The man was a soldier. Over his right shoulder, William saw more soldiers scattered throughout the crowd with their heads examining the men at their feet. William looked back at the soldier to his right who was slowly making his way in their direction.

Even though the soldier didn't seem to notice the other man's wounds, fear began to race through William's mind like an untamed stallion. He couldn't bear to see another man get dragged from the crowd and killed in cold blood. He looked away from the soldier, hoping the man would keep on walking and search somewhere else. William slowly lifted his head and, despite the risk of calling attention to himself, looked straight at the approaching guard.

With his gaze William followed the soldier as the latter walked through the crowd of men, stepping over shackles and chains as he inspected those who looked up at him. When the soldier was almost within touching distance, William turned his eyes toward the wounded man in front of him. The man's body appeared stiff as a statue, to move now would only call unwanted attention. But the soldier walked past them, looking over the man's head and continued his inspection further into the crowd.

"He's gone now," William whispered, facing the wounded man.

"But he will be back." The man's eyes were staring over William's shoulder with an empty, fateful gaze. "And when he comes back, he will find me." He sounded defeated, almost on the verge of surrendering.

"Don't talk like that. We'll find a way to get you out of here," William said as he leaned forward to get a closer look at the shackles around the man's ankles. He grabbed the metal contraption and rotated it around the man's leg to examine the lock. It was the size of William's hand and its weight seemed to be made up of the grief of the hundreds, if not thousands of people it kept shackled.

"Why do you think they kept us alive?" William asked after a moment passed.

The man let out a low grunt that didn't seem to care much for talk. His eyes silently followed the wandering soldier as if he were waiting for death do its worst.

William continued studying the lock for several minutes. He wanted to beat it with something until it gave way, but the noise would surely attract the guards' attention and they couldn't risk that. It soon became obvious that unless he had the key, it would be impossible to unlock anyone's shackles

"The lock is strong. I can't unlock it without the key," William said at last and sat up straight.

"That's all right. If I can't escape, then use my death to free yourself," the man told him.

"What do you mean?"

"When the soldier comes back and takes me, steal his keys," the man explained, nodding toward the soldier.

"What if they see me?" William asked, but he knew the answer already. This plan was going to get him killed.

"Then you will die too," confirmed the wounded man in a rather calm voice.

That didn't calm William one bit. He looked away and scanned the crowd, realizing that if there was an opportunity to escape, the chances of living to see it through were low, and many would have to give their lives for such a plan to work. As William considered all possible ways he could snatch the keys, he noticed something odd. The crowd consisted solely of men. Some were old and others were only boys, but all were men. He even recognized a few, having helped them with their tents or bought bread from them.

"Where are the women and children?" He asked, his gaze returning on the man's face. But he felt dread build in his stomach. The man kept his tongue. "What's the matter? You only speak when you have something hopeless to say?" William sounded bitter, but he couldn't help it. He'd lost so much to these desert barbarians.

"They killed them and took us," the man said, emotion choking up his words. William clearly remembered the children Nadia had been teaching at the well and he couldn't bring himself to imagine all of them dead—lifeless just like she was.

"Why?" he heard himself say in a softer tone as he looked up at the man before him.

"They couldn't use them."

"For what?" William asked.

"To be soldiers. Killers for the Desert King," the man said resentfully as he nodded toward the tents behind William.

"How do you know this?"

"It is what has always happened to the men taken by the Desert King. It always has and always will, so long as there is a king to lead these soldiers."

The other men around them appeared to be listening in to this conversation and some shifted uncomfortably.

"But why did he attack us?" William kept asking, unable to understand.

"We were in *his* desert. His temple. Dirtying it just by breathing the same air and walking the same sands. The truth, a myth, or a lie, believe what you want, but this is what I know."

William looked toward the edge of the camp and his eyes wandered onto the scattered bodies of the dead men. He stared at the corpses with empty eyes, wondering whether he would end up next to them.

Perhaps, sick though it sounded, in that moment the dead were better off than the living. They were at least free in spirit, and William realized he would rather be in their place, roaming the desert plain forever, undisturbed by anyone.

But no. That train of thought had a demonic feel to it, and William couldn't allow himself to entertain it any longer. With a hand he wished he could place over his heart, he promised to himself that he would always cherish his life and the life of others. No matter how hard, ugly, and cruel things became, he promised that he would never choose to die if he could prevent it.

With this rebellion against all thoughts of surrendering and accepting the eternal bliss that came with death, he felt his determination to escape regain its strength, even though the odds looked slim at best. As he stared at the bodies of the dead prisoners and thought about what awaited him, he kept his eyes open and patiently waited for the opportunity of escape to come his way.

# 23

THE SOLDIERS CIRCLED THE PRISONERS more cautiously now that it was night. William sat with his hands resting on his knees, his back straight as the men tried to get some sleep. Everything appeared calm, but the soldiers and the men continued shooting glances at each other. William had been following one of the torches making its way around the crowd when he looked down at the wounded man in front of him. He was sleeping with his head resting on his arms, which were crossed on top of his knees. The rhythmic motion of his chest was a sign the man was still alive, but how much time did he have left?

"Are you all right?" William whispered and tapped the man on the arm.

"I don't know," he replied without lifting his head.

William looked over his shoulder, making sure no guard had seen him talking. The torch he'd been following was well out of earshot. He turned back.

"We need to get you out of here or you're..." William's words died out when he realized it was the man's life he was talking about—and he didn't know half of what that man was going through. "I'm sorry for what I said earlier," William said.

The man kept silent, and William's chest tightened by a feeling that resembled hopelessness. Until then he hadn't stopped to consider whether they would escape whatever horrible fate awaited them. But if he lost hope, if they all did, there truly would be no life left for them. He wouldn't allow that to happen. He couldn't. He knew that if he didn't do something to give the man hope, he would surrender like the men who died crossing the Bahr Almawt.

"What is your name?" William asked the man, even though he knew he was risking punishment if a solder saw him. If he was lucky, he'd only receive a few quick lashes with a whip. But he also knew that men who caused trouble or tried to fight back were hauled off into the camp and weren't brought back.

"It doesn't matter," the man said softly and William released a frustrated sigh. But he was determined to get the man talking.

"Do you have a family? Are they alive?" William asked, leaning in slightly closer.

"I have…" The man paused as soon as the words left his mouth. "I had a wife and a daughter," he corrected himself.

William covered his mouth in both shock and shame. He knew that he was touching on a painful subject for the wounded man and almost all of the rest of the men around him. Whatever he said now, he knew it had to be said carefully.

"I'm sorry," William said in a soft voice. "When do you think the wagons are coming back?"

He received no response, not even a shrug or a grunt. The man didn't want William's help, that much was obvious, but William couldn't stop thinking about the family the man had lost.

In the distance, a golden light appeared around the base of a dune. William straightened his back with momentary excitement until he realized what it meant—more prisoners were being brought to the camp.

A faint neigh carried by the wind reached his ears. All around him, those who had heard the sound lifted their heads and looked toward the slowly approaching light. Then the light doubled and tripled. They heard the rattling of wagons. One by one, more heads straightened up to see what they could in the torch light.

"Look," William said, tapping the wounded man on the arm. Murmurs rose in the crowd followed by the cracking of whips. The man lifted his head and followed William's gaze into the darkness over his shoulder. "Survivors from the caravan?"

"Looks like it," the wounded man responded as the four wagons came to a stop at their side of the crowd. The patrolling soldiers ran to the wagons, roaring torches in their hands, to oversee the process of unloading prisoners and selecting the wounded.

With no soldiers left to guard them, William considered using the arrival of the new prisoners as a diversion. Perhaps, if he could manage to free himself from the shackles, he could make it out of there.

Shouts and grunts stirred the silence as prisoners were dragged off the wagons and piled on the ground like sacks of wheat. Their shadows danced in the torchlight as, one by one, they were taken to the edge of the crowd and shackled with the rest. One of the prisoners suddenly pushed a guard to the ground and bolted blindly into the darkness, away from the camp, with a bag still over his head and his hands tied behind his back. William felt the urge to stand and cheer for the man, but that would mean they would both be dead within seconds.

The darkness quickly swallowed the man, but the soldiers weren't going to let him get away. A group of five guards swarmed after him, though

William realized they were too late. The driver of the first wagon stood in his seat and shouldered his rifle. He took careful aim in the darkness and a moment later a bright flame shot out of the rifle, casting hundreds of shadows on the ground below.

In the silence that followed, the men around William held their breath to see if their fellow had made it out of the rifle's range. Then the soldiers emerged from the darkness, dragging the prisoner by the arms. The cloth bag over his head was splattered with blood.

All hope for escape seemed lost. If darkness itself couldn't help that man save his life, they were all doomed.

The unloading resumed, followed by the cracking of whips as the men were driven like cattle. They grunted and yelled as they were forced forward in a frenzy of fear, some stumbling and tripping over each other. Instead of a helping hand, they received a sequence of lashes before they were roughly yanked to their feet and pushed forward.

A sudden cry for mercy split the air. The process of selecting the wounded had begun.

William's stomach lurched.

He looked back to his wounded companion and noticed something had changed in the man's eyes. Something only the screams of the dying could inspire in the living. Where indifference had been only half an hour ago, now there was a twinkle. A revival of the will to live.

Over the man's shoulder, William saw the silhouettes of those unlucky souls selected for quick execution. Some went down fighting, some went quietly, but all were dead in the end, killed like sick calves that had lost their worth.

William averted his head and stared into his companion's eyes. He didn't want to witness this barbaric manslaughter and have the images poison his mind for the rest of his life—however long it was. The last agonizing scream pierced the air, and William looked down at the ground, sweat glistening on his forehead. The killing had stopped, at least for a while.

On the ground, the rusted chains crisscrossed in a multitude of directions, resembling the tangled branches of some mythical vine that clutched the dusty legs of the prisoners. William stared at the chains with a pondering frown while his companion briefly scanned the crowd. When the man's gaze turned to the soldiers, William heard the man whispering to himself and he lifted his head in confusion.

"There are more of us than there are of them," the man said, looking straight at William.

"What are you talking about?" he asked, still unable to understand.

"Look," the man said in a hushed tone, glancing briefly on either side of him as he leaned closer. "There are more prisoners than there are soldiers. We outnumber the guards by two to one easily." Traces of hope seemed to blossom in his voice.

"But there are thousands of them," William said, looking at the camp of tents that stretched to the horizon.

"Yes, but we don't need to kill them all. We can eliminate the guards quietly and escape before the rest realize what's going on."

It sounded like a plan that could go horribly wrong if anybody in the camp heard any sound of commotion out here. But it was better than nothing.

"Our numbers are our only advantage," William said thoughtfully, more for his own sake, as he analyzed the situation.

"Exactly," the man whispered, and though he was clutching a hand over his chest, he appeared to be more lively than before.

"But our numbers do us no good if we aren't free," William observed, looking down at the chains. The man followed William's gaze.

A sudden uproar of screams came from William's right. He looked up. A large group of prisoners were yelling at the nearby soldiers who responded with whipping and quick strikes with the stock of a rifle. The guards backed off and a stare-down ensued. The prisoners slowly resumed their places, glaring at the soldiers with pure hatred.

But William saw something else as well. Something mischievous, even secretive. Had they, blessed be their souls, been able to snatch a key or a dagger during the short skirmish of insults and were simply playing along to hide their excitement? As the soldiers walked back to where the new prisoners were being shackled to the wide network of chains, William's heart filled with dread.

He knew that someone was soon going to start searching the crowd picking off the men who didn't pass the criteria they were going by. William looked at his companion. Perhaps he was thinking the same thing.

"They're going to come back for you; you know that, right?" William said, studying the man's face for a reaction.

"That doesn't matter. If I die knowing my death helped free these men, then I will go willingly." He looked determined too.

That also put a lot of pressure on William who felt anxious about stealing the soldier's keys. Could he actually do it? Even if the alternative was death— or something more sinister? He found himself staring blankly at the ground, thinking of how best to snatch the keys, when he saw a yellow light cast a bright circle on his knee. William turned to his right and there he was; a soldier stood in the crowd with a torch over his head, examining the prisoners.

William's heart began to pound with a mixture of excitement and anxiety similar to those evoked when standing on the edge of the steep cliff and looking down at the rocks below. Slowly, he tapped his companion on the knee and the man looked up.

Upon seeing the soldier, the man gasped, then screwed his face in determination. The man nodded to William silently, then slowly moved himself so that his back faced the guard. But that had been a mistake.

The movement, however subtle, had caught the guard's eye, and he started walking in their direction, his cold stare staying on William's companion so he wouldn't lose sight of him among the hundreds of other sweaty robes. As he neared, the soldier turned and waved at two guards to join him.

William kept quiet, hoping that the soldiers would pick some other unfortunate soul and leave his companion alone.

"Get ready. Act fast," he heard the man say in a hushed voice as the torches illuminated William's frightened face.

The soldier who had spotted the wounded man first placed a firm hand on his shoulder and pulled him back with a sudden jerk, exposing him into the light of the torch. William sprang to his feet and swung at the soldier striking his jaw with enough force to knock him down. The prisoners around them quickly enveloped the fallen guard with their hands, grabbing onto his legs and arms and pummeling him with fists.

One of the other soldiers raised his rifle into the air and fired, scattering the prisoners around the fallen soldier who stood up and walked toward William.

William hadn't moved an inch, glaring furiously at the pure evil before him. When the soldier reached him, he grabbed William by the shirt and head-butted him, knocking him to the ground. The prisoners sitting behind William caught his fall and lowered him to the ground with the grace of angels.

The two guards finally reached William, unlocked the shackles around his feet, and put new ones on his wrists while he watched in a daze. He glanced past them at his wounded companion, who sat with his legs hugged close to his chest hiding the dry blood on his robe, his face turned away from the soldier who had discovered but forgotten about him.

When they were done, the soldiers yanked William to his feet and pushed him toward the end of the network of prisoners while their comrade followed furiously behind. The clanking of the chains and the murmurs coming from the prisoners helped William recover from his momentary daze. He didn't know what the soldiers intended for him, but whatever it was, it couldn't be good.

He planted his feet in the ground and began thrashing from side to side. None of this worked, and they neared the end of the iron prison at the same steady pace despite his struggling. The chained men and William himself assumed he would soon meet his end. He could feel his death getting nearer to him, like a shadowy hand creeping over the side of his bed with pointy fingers spread wide and that made him struggle even harder. As the threat of death loomed over him, William threw himself from side to side, kicking with all his might, but the guards seemed unshakeable.

William looked back, but no one was going to defend him. Just like he had done, the men were averting their eyes, thankful someone else was going to be executed. He understood them all too well. There was nothing they could do to help him.

The soldiers walked around the network of prisoners toward their camp which continued into the far and unseen darkness. William looked at the tents, both relieved that he would not die right away and terrified of what might wait for him instead. Maybe they had something special in mind for the rebel.

This camp seemed about as large as the caravan's had been. Even the paths looked similar, but they were used by hundreds of armed soldiers instead of women, children, and cheerful merchants. Their small group turned onto what appeared to be a main street lined with rows of black tents where soldiers ate their dinners out of rough iron plates, using their portion of bread to sop up the last drop of soup. Ahead, William heard a loud grinding noise and, through the crowd, caught glimpses of a soldier sitting behind a large grinding stone that he spun by pedaling with his feet. All this motion sent sparks from a sword's blade into the open street where the soldiers walked.

William began to realize that the camp, which he had thought was asleep during the night, was in fact a beehive of activity.

In the midst of it all, he noticed a strange odor in the air that reminded him of dye mixed with vinegar. It sickened his stomach which rolled with unease. William glanced up at the covered faces that walked passed him, searching their eyes for any sign of life. Every pair of eyes he looked at shared the same look, one completely void of expression or emotion. The look of a true killer. A silent conscience behind them, always ready to act on command and wet their blades with blood.

By now they were so far down the street that making a run for it would surely cost William his life before he could take all of six steps. The soldiers kept dragging William, making a right turn at a large intersection, and led him to the front of a huge tent surrounded by soldiers and illuminated by torches. Two men guarded the entrance, rifles thrown across their chests. When the small company neared the tent, the two guards stepped aside and let them pass.

Inside, William expected a banquet table lined with every torture tool known to human kind, spread in a long, organized row. Instead, a few scattered torches cast light over the lavishly decorated black silk, embroidered with golden threads, that made the interior. The black rugs covering the floor where divided in two by a long red carpet that reached all the way to the back. The soldiers on either side of William stopped at the entrance, while the third one continued walking down the red carpet.

William followed the soldier with his eyes and caught a glimpse of a pillow-cluttered throne positioned on a raised platform at the back of the tent. Someone was sitting in it, but the soldier's back hid him from sight. To William's left, a small table held a crystal bowl with vines of green and red grapes spilling over the side like the mangled stomach of a warrior fallen on the battlefield.

Looking down at the carpet, William wondered if his blood would soon turn it any darker. When his eyes moved up, he saw the soldier halt at the foot of the throne, bow, and began talking. The conversation between the soldier and the man sitting on the throne was a one-way conversation. The soldier did all the talking, energetically waving his hands and pointing in outrage back at William, who hung on the shoulders of the two soldiers at the entrance, while the man on the throne sat patiently, tapping on the thick armrest with his fingers. When the soldier stopped talking, the silence in the tent became heavy. The throne gave a gentle creak and soft footsteps fell on the carpet. William kept looking until the outline of another black robe emerged from behind the soldier, although the man's face and body remained hidden. The guard stood deathly still. William sensed movement but couldn't see what had caused it. Then liquid splashed onto the carpet, and the soldier's body fell hard on the ground, his severed throat spitting up a stream of blood to the beat of his rapidly failing heart. Finally the face of the one who stood before them was revealed.

The man was dressed in a black robe embroidered with hundreds of golden stars like it was an ancient map of the sky. He was tall of stature and slim, not a frame strong enough to carry a gluttonous belly. His head was covered in black cloth but his face was visible. A black beard grew from the man's narrow chin, streaks of gray running down its full length. His hands looked wrinkly, with blue and green veins crossing over the knuckles and his right hand trembled as it clenched the dagger which had slit the soldier's throat.

The man lifted his eyes to William, who expected to see glowing fires in their midst, but nothing seemed unusual, except the unquenchable desire for blood. There was no mistaking this man. He was the Desert King.

The Desert King stepped lightly over the dead soldier and started walking toward William, stopping an arm's distance away from him. From this close, William saw his face clearly. His cheeks were sunken and ashy. His nose was long and his bushy eyebrows almost obscured his bright hazel eyes. The Desert King gazed into William's eyes, as if searching for a sign of fear. Instead he found disgust and hate. Suddenly, his eyes smiled as if to say, "Ahh, another one who has heard of me."

He looked up at the soldiers on either side of William and spoke to them in a language William didn't understand. In that moment, the Englishman wished to be anywhere but here, at the mercy of this monster.

Then the man turned back to William and opened his mouth. "You tried to escape...," the Desert King said in the same unfamiliar language, but this time it penetrated William's core and the words gained a meaning he understood. "Now you will pay."

The two soldiers suddenly jerked William out of the tent and dragged him into the street. Before he knew it, he was being led across the wide path and into a smaller street. He struggled against the soldiers now that his fear had resupplied his strength. This street was empty, giving William hope that he could manage to escape if only he could get his hands free. As he threw himself from side to side, the soldiers took him farther down the path. It was darker here, the fewer torches spread further apart. The soldiers turned to the right side of the path and stepped inside a small tent where, William was sure, this time he would see that fine torture table.

A sole lantern illuminated a large iron cage that nearly took up the left half of the tent. The soldiers threw William to the ground inside the cage, slammed the door, and locked it. And then they were gone.

William slowly rose to his knees, slightly confused as to why he was still alive. He grabbed the bars and looked at the entrance. Why was he brought here? The black flap swayed back and forth from a gentle breeze, but gave him no answer. The ground outside was dark and the air silent. William turned away and examined the ground he was standing on.

To his surprise, there was sand beneath his feet. Sand. He fell to his knees and began scooping out handfuls of sand in delirious excitement, like a dog digging in a garden. He could easily escape this prison! How stupid were...

Suddenly, his fingers struck the bars at the bottom and his body tensed under the weight of defeat. Escape was impossible.

In utter frustration—though it had been foolish to expect such an easy escape—William kicked at the sand, filling the hole he'd dug out, then walked to a corner of the cage where he tried his best to make himself comfortable while he waited for the soldiers to return.

He wondered how his end would come. *A blade? A thumbscrew? Poison? Or something much worse, much slower?* But no one came.

As he sat looking at the entrance of the tent, William thought about Nadia; the pale color of her face as he held her limp body, the rings on her fingers he'd dreamed would hold his hand one day. He thought about Hans and Alexander. The thought of them being dead made his blood boil and his heart pound for vengeance, even though he didn't know if they had been killed. He felt utterly alone in the dark, a feeling he hadn't felt since the war, and one that he feared wouldn't go away as much as the thought of what was going to enter his tent.

# 24

WILLIAM LAY ASLEEP ON HIS SIDE in the corner of the cage. Night had yet to lift, and the lantern continued to illuminate the tent. The shadow of a head and shoulders crept closer to William and divided his figure in half with its darkness. It lingered over William's back, watching him take slow, deep breaths.

"William," whispered a tense voice, but the Englishman kept sleeping. "William," the voice repeated a little louder, and slowly, William stirred out of his sleep. He opened his eyes and blinked in the light. Hans was crouching on the other side of the cage, with a sword in his hands.

"Hans, you're alive!" William shouted in joy. Hans grimaced and quickly waved for him to quiet his voice. William nodded and crawled closer. "How did you get here?" he asked as he grabbed the bars, the chains around his shackled wrists jingling against the iron.

"Someone stole a key and unlocked everyone's shackles by passing it around. When I was handed the key I unlocked mine and went to look for you," Hans said, holding up a large metal ring that had a key swinging from it.

"Good work!" William exclaimed in a whisper, a broad smile on his face. "Is Alexander with you?"

"No, I didn't see him. He must be in the crowd somewhere," Hans replied, slightly out of breath.

"How many of the men are free?" William asked, adjusting his grip on the bars separating him and Hans.

"Nearly all of them," the German said, glancing at the entrance of the tent. "We decided to free everyone first before we make a run for it."

"How did you find me?" William asked, knowing he wouldn't be able to backtrack his way to the crowd if he had to.

"One of the prisoners told me that the men who caused trouble were put in cages near the east perimeter of the camp. I knew that's where I would find you if you weren't in the crowd. You're the first one I've found so far," Hans replied with a smile. William chuckled softly. He felt as if he was dreaming, but hoped that he wasn't.

"Well, don't waste any time. Get this door open and let's get the devil out of here."

Hans smiled wider as he rose to his feet and walked to the door. William stood up and followed him from the other side of the bars. With the sword safely rested against the cage, Hans placed the key in the lock and turned it to his right.

The lock didn't budge.

A frown appeared on Hans' face as he stared at the key in his hands. He shook the key in the lock, making the lock's mechanisms rattle loudly.

"What's wrong?" William asked as he pulled himself closer to the door.

"I do not know."

"Is it broken?"

"I am not sure." Hans continued rattling the key from side to side and still the key wouldn't turn. He stopped after a sweaty minute and looked up at William.

"What is it?"

"I think I have the wrong key," Hans said, horrorstricken.

"I thought all the locks could be opened with the same key," William said in a panicked voice.

"I thought so too." The frown on the German's face deepened, but he appeared thoughtful rather than panicked.

"What are we going to do?" William asked, fear climbing up his chest.

"I will find a way," Hans whispered decisively as he looked up at William, his eyes seeming to apologize for what he was about to do. Hans took the sword from where it rested on the side of the cage, and headed for the entrance.

"Where are you going?" William asked.

"I'm going to find the right key," Hans said as he took a quick peek outside. His head suddenly jerked away and he rushed to the back of the tent.

"Someone is coming," Hans said while falling to his knees and lifting the tent's cloth. "I'll come back for you," he promised and crawled out of the tent.

Alone again. William hated everything about this situation. He looked at the entrance in dreadful anticipation. The sound of footsteps became louder the closer they came, and so did the pounding in his chest. A moment later, a soldier entered the tent and two more followed close behind. The second one carried a chair with shackles built into the armrests and the front legs. The third soldier, the tallest one William had ever seen, held a large wooden chest beneath his stomach. William could see why they had chosen him for the job. William looked back at the chair.

*Torture.*

As the first soldier walked over to the cage to open the door, the one carrying the chair set it down with its back at the tent's center post and its seat facing the entrance, and the tall soldier placed the chest opposite the cage. The lock clicked and the hinges whined as the door swung open. The first soldier entered the cage calmly and grabbed William's shackled hands before pulling him to the door then pushing him toward the center of the tent.

William's foot caught on the steel lip beneath the cage door and he fell clumsily to the ground. The tall soldier slapped his hands on William's shoulders, jerked him to his feet, and shoved him in the chair with strength forged by routine and extra portions of barley. William pushed himself up in an attempt to stand, but the soldier struck him in the jaw with a fist of stone. William fell back into the chair, his head resting on his chin.

After that, meeting no further resistance, the soldiers closed the shackles around William's ankles and locked them. His wrists were taken out of the shackles and locked onto the arms of the chair. His head swayed side to side as it lifted, and his vision cleared as lost memories of the past returned. William lifted his eyes to the men standing above him.

The soldier who had pulled William out of the cage was unlocking the chest while the others stood guard on either side of the tent's entrance. The lid creaked open and the soldier pulled out a short length of rope with two loops tied on the ends along with a short, straight rod that could be slipped through the loops and twisted.

Next came an iron mallet that was set to rest on the ground next to the rope. The soldier then removed a knife with an elegantly curved blade whose needle thin edge glimmered in the lantern's light. It joined the mallet. The man looked over his shoulder at William, calculating which tool of punishment brought the most terror in William's heart.

He brought his hands up behind his head and undid the cloth that covered his face. His skin was dark and silvered with smooth scars that speckled his cheeks and the top of his bald head, cutting across his face and head like the rivers on a coastal map. The look in his eyes was cold and empty. His eyebrows were thin and arching like a pharaoh's. The soldier picked up the rope and the rod and walked to the back of the tent, keeping his eyes locked on William's.

William didn't blink until the soldier walked around him and disappeared from his sight, so he strained his ears to hear the soft noises that came from behind him. One end of the rope landed on his shoulder, and the soldier's hand slowly pulled it across his neck, making sure William felt the rough grain of hemp scratching across his throat. The soldier pulled the ends of the rope behind the post and put the rod through the loops and then began twisting the rod.

The rope began to tighten around William's throat, cutting the flow of air to his lungs. His breath choked and he grimaced as he struggled to keep his windpipe from collapsing. The soldier's hands began to slow when the rope tightened in a neat coil, but he continued to twist the rod like he was squeezing the water out of a wet cloth.

William couldn't breathe. His stomach began to feel cold and his body started twisting and thrashing against the shackles in a primal seizure of panic. He closed his eyes and leaned his head back against the post, hoping to loosen up the rope as it creaked under the straining force of the soldier's twisting hand. None of it helped. William could feel every bit of the grainy rope cutting into the soft skin at his throat.

Still no air.

William began squeezing his fists to the point of trembling, and blood rushed to his cheeks and throat in amounts that made the drowning feeling even stronger. The soldier grunted and his own face tightened as he applied more pressure to the rope. William's head was starting to lull forward as his grasp on consciousness began to slip.

But the soldier wasn't going to let the fun end so quickly. Wanting to keep William conscious for what was going to happen next, the brute loosened the rope and William gasped as precious air entered his lungs. He coughed and inhaled, half-conscious as his chin bobbed near his chest. On a wheeze he exhaled, slowly lifting his head.

The soldier struck him in the stomach.

William's brain screamed, but his mouth was silent as his body curled toward his knees. He was suffocating even though the rope was no longer squeezing his neck. He barely noticed the soldier's legs move back toward the torture chest and kept his eyes on the ground. He didn't want to know what was coming next in this sick man's play of pain.

The skin around his throat was painfully hot from the countless microscopic incisions created by the rope, but that thought failed to register as the soldier stepped into his field of vision, stopping in front of the chair. William stared at the soldier's boots, speckled with drops of dry blood, but with the corner of his eye he noticed the object in the man's hand.

The soldier took a step to the right.

William felt a dull point of cold iron touch the top of his hand. He glanced up. The soldier was fixing a rusty square nail that could probably split a large bone in half, while the mallet rested at his side. William wanted to scream, to call out for help, for this to end. But he didn't. He couldn't give them that satisfaction. He would deal with the pain the way he always did; quietly and internally.

He began shaking his hand in a futile attempt to stop the soldier from nailing it to the armrest.

The tall guard suddenly joined them and grabbed hold of William's hand, leaning all his weight on it and pinning it to the chair as if it were set in cement.

The cold tip of the nail touched the center of his hand again, sitting neatly between the bones of his third and fourth fingers. The soldier raised the mallet and leaned forward to bring it down on William's hand. William gasped.

# De Collibus

A horn blasted in the cold air outside, suddenly interrupting the soldier's train of thought. The mallet hovered above the soldier's head, ready to drop. The horn sounded a second time, followed by footsteps that rushed past the tent. With a frown and a grunt, the soldier tossed the mallet near the chest and walked outside the tent to see what was happening, giving William a glimpse into the path. Hundreds of soldiers were now swarming in the torchlit path carrying rifles, swords, and shields.

Still locked in the chair, awaiting his fate, William wondered whether this was the sign of the prisoners' escape or if the Desert King had ordered them to be massacred. Either way, his hand wasn't getting nailed to the armrest. For the time being, he could breathe a little easier, though he also realized he could easily be killed on the spot for the soldier's convenience. After all torture is hard work. The tall soldier let go of William's hand and said something to his comrade who had carried in the chair earlier. The smaller soldier replied calmly and nodded in William's direction.

The tall soldier nodded, then kneeled at William's right leg while his comrade walked to William and began unlocking the shackles around his wrists.

He wasn't going to taste death yet. His heart quickened as both excitement and dread washed over him. The voices outside started shouting, and he could hear footsteps running down the path. He kept watching with a still body as his ankles and wrists were set free, trying his best to look docile and cooperative. When all his limbs were out of the torture chair, the tall soldier jerked William up to his feet.

William felt the urge to spring up, slit their throats, and escape. But he had to calculate his plan thoroughly because he knew if he hesitated the soldiers would show him no mercy. When his old shackles clapped around his wrists, the tall soldier grabbed him by the arm and led him to the cage. William took a step, realizing that now was his only chance.

He twisted out of the soldier's grip and swung the sagging chains up at the man's head. The chains struck the giant hard on his forehead and blood ran over his blank eyes before he fell to the ground with a heavy thud. But William was not done yet. He looked up to see the other soldier's hand moving toward the hilt of his sword and rushed forward, tackling the man to the ground while the sword was only half out of its sheath. William landed on top and straddled the soldier, pinning the man's arms to the ground.

On the ground just beyond the soldier's head he noticed the torture knife that lay forgotten by the chest. Could he grab it? Lifting up his body would release the soldier's hands, but William decided to take the risk.

He reached for the knife and the soldier drew his sword. Before the soldier could maneuver the sword, William grabbed the knife by the handle and stabbed the soldier in the neck, sliding it down to the hilt. The soldier began wheezing as his body relaxed and then became completely still. For a moment William remained sitting on the soldier's stomach, staring at the handle protruding from the man's neck. William took his hands away from the knife handle and rose to his feet, his shaky breathing the only noise in the silent tent.

William reached down and grabbed the soldier's abandoned sword and slowly approached the entrance of the tent. He carefully pulled back the flap. The street was swarming with soldiers that would know he was a prisoner the moment they laid eyes on him. He let go of the flap and stepped back into the tent.

He didn't care for the blood-soaked robe of the dead man, but he could certainly make use of the other guard's clothes. William didn't think the tall man was dead, but though he appeared completely unconscious, William still kicked him in the ribs to check. Nothing. Not even a grunt.

With the thought of the third soldier returning, William knew he would have to hurry. William rolled the man onto his back, grabbed the keys for the shackles and freed his hands. They jingled loudly then hit the ground with a heavy thump, coiling like an iron snake. William kneeled by the soldier and began undressing him. Though this man was rather tall, William thought it better to be seen in a robe that didn't fit him rather than one covered in blood.

Soon he put the robe over his clothes, but the belt required more work and William's hands were shaking uncontrollably. After several unsuccessful tries, he finally managed to fasten the belt, then took off the soldier's headdress and put it on in a clumsy assembly. While the clothes fit him loosely they did the job of keeping his identity hidden.

William walked to the center post and opened the little door to the lantern before blowing out the candle with a quick puff of air. In the dark, he turned around and made his way to the entrance. Rifle fire and the roar of combat filled the silence at the edge of the camp, where the prisoners were shackled. He peeked through a small slit in the cloth at the street overflowing with soldiers.

Hoping that his disguise was good enough, William stepped out of the tent into the crowd of soldiers and started jogging away from the tent, against the flow. He kept his eyes to the ground praying no one would notice the white skin around his eyes. A soldier ran into him, nearly knocking him off balance. At the impact, something landed at his feet, but the soldier didn't notice and kept running down the path with the others.

William looked down at his feet. In front of his toes lay a rifle. A British army bolt-action rifle. He picked it up and felt its ominous weight in his hands. Everything else around him seemed to disappear as he stared at the glimmer of flittering torchlight on the smooth black barrel. The distorted flames brought up the temptation to take the delicious opportunity fate had given him. An internal struggle ensued, where, like a priest tempted by a notorious harlot, William labored to decide whether to do what he knew was wrong but felt so right, so necessary.

Resistance proved useless against the thirst that had taken over his mind. With the rifle safely clutched in his arms, William made his way up the path, feeling the harlot's clutches embrace him passionately. The farther he ran, the less dense the stream of soldiers became as more of them rushed to the edge of the camp where a battle with the prisoners had erupted.

In a matter of seconds, he was all alone on the street. William quickened his pace. At the intersection he reached, William took a left turn into the wide street he'd traversed before getting thrown in the cage. Earlier it had been crawling with soldiers. Now it was empty and abandoned.

There were no torches, no soldiers, no movement but his own. The sky was filled with clouds of dust that hid the moon. In this darkness, William could see only a dozen steps in front of him. His feet crunched the sand quietly, allowing him to hear the sound of the fighting getting louder. The occasional pops of rifles had turned into clusters. The single scream in the clashing of weapons was becoming a continuous roar of pain, fear, and violence.

Ahead of him in the street, William recognized the large tent surrounded by torches. No one stood outside to guard the entrance. Everyone was busy putting down the prisoner outbreak—and who would dare consider the thought that a prisoner might come looking for Death itself?

William's pace slowed to a walk as he approached the entrance. A gust of wind made the sand around his feet hiss and swayed the tent's cloth, giving him a glimpse of the brilliant light inside. He fixed his grip on the belly of the rifle and took a couple of steps closer. The flaps shifted and showed him the long line of red carpet leading to the back of the tent before closing down again.

Calmly, William placed the stock of the rifle against his shoulder and raised the barrel in front of him. Like a lion approached by someone other than its trainer, the torches on either side of him roared as the end of his barrel poked through the flaps of the tent. Half of the rifle disappeared inside followed by William's hand and his shoulders.

In an instant, he was covered in the warm light of numerous torches. The throne at the back of the tent was empty. For a moment, William stared at it, wondering if he had missed his chance. His rifle began to lower in disappointment.

Glass clinked together at the table to his left. William turned. The Desert King was standing at the table, his back to the entrance as he poured himself a glass of wine. He said something in Arabic, quietly and most likely to himself. He lifted the rifle and aimed at the Desert King's back.

The Desert King spoke again in the same soft tone and turned around, his fingers wrapped gently around the fragile glass. He stopped when he took in the sight of William. His eyes lowered to the rifle and a dark, sinister smile split his sunken face. What might have been pride or daring confidence filled every aspect of his smile; a defiant grin that recognized the blue eyes behind the headdress as belonging to the man who had heard the legends and wanted to put a stop to them.

Every inch of the Desert King smiled with the deep pleasure he received from each death he caused. William's pain, the prisoners' pain, it was like food to him.

His eyes seemed to say, "Are you the one I've been waiting for all my life? The one whose soul burns with revenge so strong he could truly bring my end? Are you really the one?"

William pulled the trigger.

The rifle punched him in the shoulder at the release of a deafening roar. The Desert King staggered backwards, the smile long gone from his face. His eyes and mouth were wide open at the realization that death would come by the hand of a foreigner. The wine glass slipped out of his hand and landed softly on the ground.

The Desert King looked down at his chest where his black robe was beginning to glisten in the light, now that blood was spilling out and soaking his robe, painting the intricate patterns of golden stars and moons red.

William pulled back the bolt. A cartridge spun out of the chamber and landed on the red carpet to his right. He pushed the bolt forward and took aim. The Desert King looked up as William pulled the trigger a second time.

The rifle shattered the silence with a grotesque punch. The Desert King staggered back two steps and bumped into the table of wine and fruit. His left hand knocked a bowl of fruit to the ground as he tried to get a grip on the table and straighten his posture.

But the daring smile had disappeared, and now William saw the eyes of a dying stag staring back at him, frightened and surrendering.

William pulled back the bolt and pushed it forward before taking aim again. Then he pulled the trigger a third time. A red mist shot forward from the Desert King's chest, and he slid off the edge of the table and onto the ground with a sequence of soft thuds. William lowered the rifle and stared at the Desert King with a calm, tired look in his eyes.

The man who'd terrorized the desert lay on his side, his eyes staring sightlessly at the carpet in front of him where his blood continued to spill forth in a widening pool of shimmering red.

The gun smoke whirled in the air like the incense William had seen in Hakeem's tent. Instead of smelling of jasmine and cinnamon, the air was sour and putrid. The depthless gaze of the Desert King had drawn him in and lost him in a space as vast as the sky.

A pair of footsteps darted past the entrance of the tent before fading into the silence. William looked behind him. The flap didn't stir. Enemy or friend, he'd have to find another way out.

He hurried toward the throne, walked behind its back, and kneeled by the cloth of the tent preparing to leave. Before he disappeared into the night, William looked over his shoulder at the long red carpet leading to the tent's entrance. The table was a mess of scattered fruit and spilled wine, and the Desert King lay on the ground, pathetic in his dead state and absent of the glowing spirit which might not have ever lived in him. The tent was silent. Nothing moving. Nothing living.

William reached down and lifted the black cloth, ducked his head, and stepped outside. He stood up and took a step forward. All he felt was his legs giving out, and his body collapsing to his knees.

The sand was whooshing at him as the wind gave rise to a sandstorm. He felt sick. He was too tired to lift his head, too frightened to stay where he was. He straightened his back and set the rifle down. He was done with this tool of killing. William tore off the headdress and threw it to the ground in front of him rejecting it. The wind chilled the blood smeared on his forehead from the last man that wore it. He undid the belt and took off the robe, feeling like a sheep that had disguised itself in the coat of a wolf in order to avenge its flock, greying its once pearly white fleece and growing a jaw meant for tearing flesh instead of vegetation.

He coughed several times and stood tentatively, then darted away from the tent toward an empty path that he hoped would lead him to the edge of the camp. Though he tried to keep his wits about him, his mind felt fuzzy with the thought of killing not one, but two men—possibly three.

Didn't killing belong to the old William? Before the William who took baby pictures and charmed Mrs. Eldrich? Had he really changed at all from the lessons life and the desert had taught him?

William didn't know where he was going. He was following the general direction of the path without paying attention to his surroundings. Then the path ended and he lifted his head. Ahead of him was the desert, vast and open. Dark dunes seemed to peak in between dust clouds created by the rising storm.

He realized he was on the opposite end of the camp from where the fighting was taking place. If the soldiers had not killed the last escaping prisoner by now, there must only be a handful left.

Beneath the dominating roar of the wind, he could hear the nearing sound of a horse's neigh. William turned to his left. A white horse rode toward him with a dark figure on the saddle. Instead of running, William stayed still. Now that he had done what he needed to do, the thought of dying didn't bother him as much. The horse rode straight toward him and neighed as the rider, hidden by the sandstorm, pulled on the reins.

"Climb on," Hans said while motioning to the back of the saddle.

"Did you find Alexander? Is he all right?" William asked, making no move toward the horse.

"Yes, during the fighting. If he's still alive he should meet us at the caravan." Hans was yelling now because the wind was growing stronger. The horse took a few steps forward and Hans pulled on the reins, steering it back to William.

William nodded as he stepped toward the horse's side.

"Hurry up!" Hans shouted, his gaze moving beyond William toward something else that was closing in on them.

William looked over his shoulder and saw a dozen figures emerge from the path, barely visible now in the gloom. As Hans turned the horse to the desert, William pulled himself onto the saddle. The soldiers opened fire on the ghostly white horse and several bullets cracked past William's head. Hans spurred the horse forward with a kick of the heel and the stallion raced away from the camp, hiding the two friends in the dark of night and the gloom of the building storm.

# 25

THEY RODE THROUGH THE WINDY NIGHT, rested for a couple of hours in the morning, then continued for the rest of the day. Meanwhile, Hans was trying to hide his frustration. When the Desert King's men were taking Hans to their camp, he had memorized the dunes and rock structures they passed so he could make his way back if he escaped. Even though he knew he was close to the caravan, the camp managed to hide from him. Hans feared that they had gotten lost in the darkness.

Ahead of them, a large slope rose out of the desert floor with a peak that would give him a good view of the area. As the horse began ascending the slope, Hans thought about William.

The Englishman had kept silent through the journey and Hans was beginning to worry. Had he picked up a burden too heavy for him to carry that had shattered his soul? Was this quiet withdrawal William's way to pick up the pieces? Hans wanted to shout at his friend, to get a reaction out of him, so he could get his emotions out of the way and return to his normal self.

Then he rebuked himself. If William was going through a rough patch, perhaps he needed some time to think it over first. When and if he was ready to talk it out, Hans would do his best to listen.

As the horse neared the top of the dune, the desert revealed itself in the late evening sun, and the wind strengthened. Hans stopped the horse at the top and looked around, hoping to get his bearings. Ahead lie the vastness of the sand ocean. To his right, however, was a different sight. The caravan looked like an endless forest, ravaged by a fire that had turned the ground into ash and charcoal, sparing nothing from its hellish roar. Now all was quiet.

He glanced behind him.

William's head was resting on his shoulder, his eyes closed. He was asleep, but not because of drowsiness. It was the kind of sleep summoned to forget one's shame. Hans sighed, calming his urge to shake William out of his trance and looked ahead. He tapped the horse with his heels, and the animal slowly began to descend the dune down the other side.

Hans steered the stallion toward the plain that had once welcomed their camp, where numerous tents stood in the evening light as relics of a time long past. Now they were just the possessions of the unfortunate dead. When they reached the perimeter, Hans slid off the saddle and landed on the ground near the horse's shoulder. He looked up at William, who had hunched forward in the saddle, his eyes still closed and his hands resting on his thighs. Hans took the reins and lead the horse through the sea of carnage. He did not fear the threat of the Desert King's men. He could feel the place was empty.

Hans walked farther into the maze of tents, some half-burnt, but most completely destroyed. The wind whispered to him as it swept down the abandoned streets and through the holes torn and burnt into the tents around him. Hans looked back at his friend, and though William's eyes were now open, they were staring blankly at the horse's saddle. Did he know where they were? He closed his eyes and Hans sighed.

When they emerged from the path and into the open area surrounding the well, Hans exhaled a breath that carried all of his worry away. There, sitting on a short wooden barrel with his eyes staring at the ground was Alexander. He'd also brought a horse he'd stolen from the camp of the Desert King.

Alexander saw them too and jumped to his feet. Walking at a brisk pace, he led the horse behind him.

"You made it," Alexander said as he hugged Hans. "I was beginning to think that you had been killed or gotten lost."

"I am glad to see you are alive too," Hans said with a smile on his face.

Alexander looked up at William, who sat slouched in the saddle, and his smile disappeared when he noticed the blood on William's hands where they rested on his thighs.

"Is he wounded?" Alexander asked, a note of panic in his voice.

"His body is fine," Hans said, and Alexander frowned in confusion. "It is his mind," Hans tapped the side of his head then pointed at his chest, "and his heart that's bleeding."

The two friends looked up at William with concern. He sat with his shoulders slumped forward, his chin resting on his chest, his eyes closed and relaxed.

"What are we going to do with him?" Alexander asked.

"We are going to let him heal, but for now let's take him down and get a fire going. We need to make camp to spend the night. Tomorrow we will decide what to do," Hans said as he moved closer to William's horse.

Alexander nodded, tied his horse to a nearby beam, and left to gather firewood and whatever food or drink he could find. Hans pulled William off the saddle and half-dragged, half-carried him to the well. There, he gently set William on the ground with his back leaning up against the stone wall and his legs sprawled out in front of him. Hans knelt down and looked at William's blank face. The Englishman's eyes were closed, but they still bore that eerie touch of consciousness. He hoped William would say something and start acting normal again, but the longer the silence stretched, the more Hans realized that wasn't going to happen, at least not easily.

Hans took a last glance at his friend and was rising to his feet when he saw something glimmer around William's neck. He knelt back, moving closer to William. A thin silver necklace reflected a beam of dim sunlight. He didn't remember seeing it before and he brought his hand up to William's neck to take a better look at it. A hand suddenly clamped around his wrist.

William's eyes were staring at him, half open and weak. His wrist trembled from exhaustion but was strong enough to keep Hans' hand away from his neck. Hans saw a change in William's eyes. A cold emptiness had replaced the youthful brightness that had once filled his eyes.

A moment later, Hans' hand was free, while William's flopped heavily to the ground near his thigh. Hans sighed. He knew that though William appeared as if his emotions were gone, there was a storm whirling inside his mind and heart.

As a friend, the best thing he could do was keep his mouth shut and be ready to listen.

"Hey, Hans," Alexander shouted from the mouth of a nearby path.

Hans looked over to see Alexander smiling while he held a minuscule barrel above his head. He nodded, but discretely pointed toward William and waved for Alexander to stay back. Alexander nodded in return, slowly lowered the barrel and continued scavenging for firewood and things to use.

When Hans turned around, William was staring blankly at the ground near his thigh.

"She was special, Nadia. Unphotographable. She couldn't be frozen in a picture, forever captured and confined to one roll of film. She was everything I feared to be. Completely free. Now what is she?" William asked of nobody in particular, his bloodied fingers playing with a small pebble in the sand. "Gone," William answered his own question.

Hans wasn't aware that his friend had gotten so close to the gypsy woman, and now received a real glimpse of the pain in William's heart. He realized he couldn't shake him out of his sadness, though he wanted his cheerful friend back.

"While I was in France," William started again, "I heard there was a platoon leaving the trenches to do some reconnaissance around a farm where a German sniper had killed several of our men." A twitchy smile of embarrassment appeared on his face as if his ear was being tickled with a feather. "I went with them," he admitted and began nodding as if agreeing with his own memory.

"We arrived at the farm when night fell. The barn we checked first, and it was empty. The Boche must have heard us, though, because shells began exploding in the field around us. We waited in the dark, listening to the bombs going off. Some landed closer, some farther away. It went on for so long, I thought it would never end.

"When the last bomb hit, I was sure there was going to be another, but the barrage had ended. One of our men shouted that the Germans were outside the barn. Through the wooden planks, I saw a shadow run past," William waved a hand quickly from right to left. "I scrambled for my rifle and took a shot where I saw the movement. The footsteps stopped, and I crept outside to see if I had killed a German. It was a little girl."

William turned silent, a sad frown playing on his face as he looked at his feet. "She was lying facedown in the mud with the back of her head missing. The men, they told me it was an accident. No one could've known who was outside the barn. No one had to know what I'd done. But I took a life and there's nothing anybody can do about it. I got away with murder." William's jaw clenched as he looked up at Hans. Silence enveloped him again, then his gaze returned to his feet.

Hans realized that William was losing hope, now when the past was catching up with the present. But he didn't want to see it happen in front of him. Sure, that had been a horrible thing that William had done, and Hans understood why it haunted his friend, but William had been at war. It was by no means a justification; it was an explanation as good as any.

"Nadia could be alive," Hans said at last, hoping that would bring a spark of life to his friend's mind. "She may still be out there somewhere, as alive as you and me. You took a life; now use this as a chance to save one. We can look for her."

William continued staring at his feet, silent as the camp around them.

"What if she saw you here, sulking?" Hans said, taking a different approach.

"She can't see me though; she's dead," William said in a softer voice.

Hans, thinking William was projecting the past onto the present, decided that it was the time to shake his friend out of the spell he'd put himself into and straighten him out.

"You want her to be dead," Hans declared. "You want her to be dead so that you can have something to cry about." William kept his eyes glued to the same spot on the ground. "I lost my father and brother to a war I couldn't fight in. You don't see me sobbing and groaning like a child, taking for granted the life that had been pried out of my family's hands."

The silence stretched, endless like the desert, and that spiked Hans' aggravation to a new level.

"You have no love for life," he said as he rose to his feet. "You don't care about Nadia or me or Alexander. I risked my life for you. We almost died trying to save you when we could have left you behind to die. We should have. You don't care for anybody but yourself. You're a selfish pig." Hans stood above William, panting and unable to say another word because the anger he felt was out of his control.

William slowly lifted his gaze.


Alexander, humming a cheerful tune under his breath, stepped out from behind a burnt tent carrying a bundle of firewood in his arms when he saw William, finally awake from his stupor and glaring up at Hans. Seeing a storm brewing, Alexander laid the wood he had gathered on the ground in front of his feet, not taking his eyes off of his two friends. This time, if they were going to fight it would not be over a lost chess match or something trivial. They would be defending their pride.

"How could I have called you my friend?" Hans scorned, and Alexander realized the German was losing control to anger. He didn't know what had sparked this confrontation, but suddenly, William tackled Hans by the legs. They tumbled to the ground and landed with William on top of the German.

They stared at each other, neither willing to throw the first punch. They didn't hate each other, but disappointment and frustration was putting their friendship on the line.

William grimaced and punched Hans in the jaw harder than Alexander had ever seen him hit before. The blow knocked the German's head back and, a moment later, Hans responded with a heavy fist that brought blood to William's mouth.

Alexander grunted in frustration of his own, feeling tired of breaking these two off. This time though he sensed that if he didn't do something soon, things wouldn't be good. He ran to the well where the two men were trading punches that drew blood and spattered their knuckles in red. He grabbed William and threw him to the ground with the strength of a bear. With rage still clouding his mind, William jumped to his feet and began walking over to Alexander.

"Stop!" Alexander shouted, standing between William and Hans. "I'll fight you both if I have to, but you will stop this nonsense this instant."

The commanding tone behind Alexander's words seemed to penetrate William's deranged mind and he stopped mid-stride. He shook his head as if to clear his thoughts and stood for a moment, panting in exhaustion. Alexander heard a footstep behind him and quickly turned around, expecting to see Hans charging at him to push him out of the way so that he could continue fighting William.

The German was kneeling a few feet away, spitting blood. Slowly, he lifted his gaze and rose to his feet, taking a few calm steps toward Alexander who cautiously stepped back. Hans stopped his advance and lifted his hands at chest level to show he'd had enough. Then, silently, he made his way to

Alexander, and, upon reaching him, pulled him in for a hug that conveyed the apology words could never express.

"This has got to stop between you two," Alexander said at the awkward hug, but he patted Hans on the back nevertheless. The German nodded silently and pulled back, his eyes searching for William's.

"I didn't mean what I said," Hans stood before William. "I needed to provoke you out of this hopeless stupor you were in. I didn't know what else to do, I just... I just couldn't bear to see you like this."

William nodded and looked down at his feet, knowing that he should be apologizing too. His knuckles were reddened with the blood of his friend, and a bead of sweat made its way to the edge of his eyebrow.

"I am sorry, too, for hitting you," William said, wiping his forehead with a hand and looking anywhere else but at Hans. "But you were wrong. You thought I was making things up, but I wasn't. I saw her... Nadia... dead in the mud, just like the little girl..." His gaze returned to his friends and a sad realization dawned over them; Nadia had died.

"I'll get the fire going," Alexander said after a while, and William was grateful that at least one of them carried a clear head on his shoulders.

While Alexander worked on the fire, Hans and William silently unsaddled the horses and created a space to camp for the night.

Later, as the sun was setting behind the surrounding hills, William, Hans, and Alexander found themselves sitting silently around a small fire that offered them heat to fight off the cold. Each nibbled on a piece of bread, part of a loaf that Alexander found while looking for wood. Hans had been staring at the flames with tired eyes, his mind as still as a peaceful pond.

"What now?" he said, as if expecting the others to have a plan worked out. William and Alexander turned to him. "Where do we go from here?" Hans clarified, his eyes still glued to the fire. Both Englishmen remained silent. Neither of them knew the answer to that question.

"The caravan is gone," Hans added. "The nearest city might be hundreds of kilometers from here. We have nowhere to go." Finally he looked up at Alexander. There was a short moment of silence.

"What about Yemen?" William voiced a thought that had been churning in each of their minds. "If we travel to Yemen, you can play your chess champion and you can buy a ticket back to England," he said, looking first to Hans, then to Alexander.

They considered the plan, each of them separately. William expected to meet resistance or doubt from his friends, but to his relief, Hans turned to Alexander and asked, "What do you think?"

"It sounds like a good idea. What about you?"

"I want to go to Yemen, too," Hans said and nodded.

"Then we head east," William said without taking his eyes away from the fire crackling in front of him, the short pauses between cracks and pops making the silence feel heavy. "Let's use the morning to gather supplies— everything that might prove useful on the way. But for now, let's get some rest. We have a long road ahead of us."

William scooted down and lay on his side, covering his body with a half-burnt blanket he'd found earlier. Alexander and Hans did the same, slowly drifting off while the fire, fighting a hard battle against the cold wind, crackled gently in its pit as it covered the camp surrounding them with a soft golden glow.

# 26

WILLIAM OPENED HIS EYES. HE WAS LYING on his side with his hands cradled by his chest. His eyes stared calmly in front of him. What he saw was as cold as the air.

The sky was painted dark blue with the coming of the sun, the earth a depthless black. Center posts stood like trees knocked sideways from an artillery barrage, trailing with shreds of burnt cloth. His sleep had been dreamless, a dark reserve for his conscious mind to draw back into and hide like a turtle in its shell. A still escape that sheltered him from the cold as he slept, protecting him from the whistling wind and the rest of the outside world.

William rolled over onto his knees and stood. The others seemed to be asleep and he decided to leave them at peace for a while longer.

The fire had gone out completely, another spot of black in the burned camp. William felt a shift in the air, a presence observing him discreetly. He looked down and saw Hans staring at him with a curious frown. He took a step closer to Hans and kneeled, resting his hands on his knees. This close William could see the cuts and bruises on Hans' face and felt instant regret in his stomach.

"I am going to see what I can find. When Alexander wakes up, search with him until noon and then meet me at the east end of the camp with the horses," William said.

Hans nodded. "Will you be all right?"

"I'll be fine," William said, more out of consolation than truth. With a smile that wrinkled the corners of his eyes, he patted Hans on the shoulder and rose.

He spotted the mouth of a path flanked by crooked tents that would take him to Hakeem's tent, if the paths hadn't been drastically changed by the fires. As he walked toward the tents, he could feel himself becoming alone in the dark, the cold stinging the cuts on his knuckles. He looked down and became more aware of his feet treading softly on the white dirt and the sound they made. As he entered the path, he tucked his hands into his pockets.

When walking through the caravan, either early in the morning or late in the night, it was normal for William to feel excited about his life with the caravan or worry about getting water to the people. Now, he felt neither of these. Making the decision to still travel to Yemen, though on their own, had revived a piece of his soul. The cold reminded him of his days when he practiced getting his nightly dose of cold to prepare himself for the desert. The days when he thought he was weak. Unworthy of the desert.

When he spotted Hakeem's tent some time later, William slowed his pace but didn't stop. The blue cloth blended in with the retreating darkness. Though parts of it were ripped to pieces and charred by the fire, William hoped that what he was looking for would still be inside—and untouched.

The posts that held up the awning stood crookedly like the legs of a baby giraffe standing for the first time. As William neared, he remembered that day back in Nador when he'd come down the mountain and walked through the caravan for the first time, looking for the leader who would grant his request to join this new, exciting world.

There were no guards to stop him now as he freely walked inside the tent. The place was empty. The crack of dawn was visible through a side of the tent which gaped wide open, burnt away and left jagged by flame. The putrid smell of death was largely gone, now that the wind could freely pass through the holes in the canvas cloth.

William stopped and looked at what remained of Hakeem's abode. With gratitude he noticed that the back of the tent was almost completely intact, though Hakeem's table was knocked over.

As he walked to the back of the tent, William felt ash, pieces of wood, and burnt cloth making the once-soft carpet under his feet uneven. He stopped when he saw that the chest he'd seen Hakeem open wasn't much more than a pile of smoldering embers. Not far from the table was a map of the Sahara. He'd found what he was looking for. He picked it up and held it so that the light from the rising sun illuminated its markings. The upper half of the map showed a sliver of the Mediterranean painted in bright blue. The edges of the coast were riddled with hundreds of dots and small texts in Arabic that named cities too plentiful to see in a lifetime of wandering.

At the very left of the map was Morocco with its mountain range running along the edge of the desert like a wall protecting the coastal cities from the desert heat. In the center of the map was the Sahara, painted in bright orange, featureless and unoccupied.

William considered where they were on the map. If he were right, they were somewhere near the Libyan and Algerian borders, but it was impossible for him to tell. On the right of the map was the Red Sea, its top half branching out like the pincers of a beetle. At the bottom of the peninsula lay Yemen, with the Red Sea extending up from its left.

He stared at Yemen, wondering how long it would take them to get there. How silent the journey would be. No crowds. No music. Just him, his friends, and the silence of the desert.

Even though the edges of the map had been badly burnt and it bore no markings that indicated the location of any wells, he decided to keep it. With the map rolled in a neat scroll, William tied it with a piece of cloth he ripped off the tent's side.

For one thing he was glad—Hakeem hadn't died there. Perhaps they'd taken him to the doctor's tent, where he'd breathed his last before destruction descended over his people. And even so, William could feel some part of Hakeem's presence watching him, and he felt ashamed that he'd failed to bring water to the caravan, failed to save his leader and failed to protect all those innocent souls who'd died a death they didn't deserve.

"I am sorry," William said, his voice just above a whisper.

He raised his head and looked about, feeling a change in the air. An invisible hand seemed to cover a brave heart and bow to him in forgiveness.

Hakeem had been a man of honor, just, and caring. He always held the lives of the people above his own. He was a true leader and a real man and William admired that about him. He knew the man had experienced real fears and doubts, yet possessed the calmness not to let them control him.

The memory of Hakeem's poisoning was blurred by a lack of sleep, guilt, and rage. He felt ashamed when he remembered aiming the rifle at the doctor and making the already tragic situation worse with the threat of violence—and regretted it.

With a soft goodbye, William made his way outside, his feet crunching the flaky ashes he stepped on. The cool sand outside was soft on his feet and quieted his footsteps. The sky had brightened a little and an orange tinge arched across the horizon.

Turning right, William took the familiar path that would lead him to his tent. When he reached he reached the place, William stopped and looked at the home he'd lived in. The center post was knocked slightly off balance and the cloth was riddled with large holes like the tattered sails of a sinking ship.

Even though it was not the best, he felt proud that this was his tent and that he had learned how to pitch it on his own through trial and error. He smiled when he remembered what he'd had to give up for this tent and how he'd shivered that first night after he'd failed to set it right.

He stepped inside.

The holes in the cloth became circles of soft blue in the dark. He grabbed hold of the center post and started walking in a circle, testing it with his weight. William stopped when he faced the back side of the tent. He let go of the post and searched for his suitcase in the dark. It was missing. Someone must have taken it during the chaos, though he wondered why anyone would need it.

Resigned that he was destined to remain with his dusty, blood stained clothes, William stepped out of the tent and looked on either side of him, deciding which direction to take.

The camp was bright enough for him to see, and the sun was sure to rise in a handful of minutes. He started walking to the left when a beam of orange light landed on the white sand at his feet. William looked down at it as he walked, watching it grow brighter as the sun rose behind him.

First, he decided to search what had been the main streets of the caravan where the markets had flourished, hoping he would find some merchandise that lay untouched by the flames and rain. He remembered how crowded they had been—crowded with people shouting out prices of lamb and fresh milk, bargaining, and playing games where small sums of money could be won and lost.

All he could hear now was cloth flapping in the wind.

When he had searched the various tents that remained in the main streets, the sun was nearing the center of the sky and William thought it was time to head to the meeting point he and Hans had agreed to.

William gathered all the provisions he had found in the middle of the street and realized he had a small treasure to carry. He had found two large sheepskins with goat's milk. He'd also found one containing water, but left it behind for fear it was poisoned.

He also found several cuts of dry meat that looked and smelled good and a sharp knife, as well as a wicker basket with dates and a bottle of wine with half the contents missing—a last resort if the goat's milk ran out and they hadn't found a village or a well. A rifle and two belts of ammunition. A pair of silver chalices and a box with precious-looking stones that would prove handy if they had to bargain their way into or out of something. And finally a red sack with seven loaves of bread.

He felt proud at how much he had gathered and thought that if Hans and Alexander had found as much provisions as he had, there would be little fear of starving in the desert.

William laid everything, except the rifle and the two sheepskins, in the center of a large cloth and tied the ends together with a small length of rope. He slung the rifle and the sheepskins over one shoulder and the makeshift bag over the other. The weight made him lean forward slightly but it was worth it.

Lifting his head, William felt a strain on his neck, but he started walking down a path that would lead him to the eastern side of the caravan. He quickly realized that the weight of the supplies was making his steps fall short, but he pushed onward. After a dozen steps a drop of sweat dripped from his forehead and stung a cut on his cheek.

Unconsciously, his mind drifted in another direction as his feet stepped carefully over debris, bodies, and what else. He remembered looking at Fudail with disgust when the man had taken a dagger off a dead Bedouin. Yet here he was, carrying a sack of provisions, a rifle, and two sheepskins that had once belonged to the people of the caravan without a hint of remorse on his face. The thought put an eerie smile on his face that quickly vanished when he realized that there was more truth to the joke than he wanted to think about.

As he walked down the path, William realized this would be the last time he would walk through this caravan. He lifted his head, even though the movement strained his neck, and looked at the tents he passed. They were covered in a thick layer of dust, and most of were half burnt or lying on the ground where they had collapsed. A gentle breeze sung through the holes in the tents and William listened to the quiet song of the wind. It was as if the caravan was saying goodbye to him in its own subtle way.

When he reached the east side of the caravan, William looked about and spotted Hans and Alexander sitting in the saddles of their horses a short distance away. Behind them stood a camel and two goats, one of which bleated when it noticed William staggering their way and moved a few steps to the side.

At the goat's warning, Hans and Alexander looked away from the caravan and saw William toting the bag of provisions over one shoulder, his face beaded with sweat. They dismounted and ran over to help him carry whatever he'd found to the horses.

"How did you do?" William asked as Alexander took the bag from his shoulder.

"We did all right," Hans answered with a smirk as he took one of the sheepskins from William and looked at the camel and the goats. William smiled, happy to know that his friends hadn't changed since he left them that morning.

"Tents?" he asked, hoping he would not have to spend the rest of the journey sleeping under the stars.

"Yes, we found two that were untouched," Hans nodded as Alexander set down the bag of provisions near the camel's side.

"How much food and drink?" William asked while he watched Alexander put the camel to its knees so that they could load the provisions onto its back.

"Not a lot. It seems you did quite well though." Hans said as he brought the sheepskin to his mouth and took a drink.

"Enough to last us around a week or two; longer if we ration it," William said.

"Good," Hans said and wiped his lips.

"If we don't find a village or a well by then, we'll have to—" William stopped talking and raised his eyebrows at the goats as if they could understand human speech.

"I hope we find a village before then," Hans winked and set down the sheepskin to help Alexander load the supplies onto the camel's sides.

When the camel was loaded, Hans climbed onto its back while William and Alexander mounted the horses. Ready to leave this place, Hans and Alexander started trotting away at a slow pace, but William turned back and looked at the caravan for the last time. He felt as if he was leaving behind a physical piece of his life that he would never be able to get back after the desert swallowed it up, as it did all things.

William heard Hans' faint voice shout his name and turned around in the saddle. His friends had become small dots climbing the hillside. When he saw Hans sway on the camel, he smiled and looked back to the caravan. He soaked it all in, hoping the very image of the camp would replace the part of him he was leaving behind. He absorbed every tent, every smell, every memory, knowing that this part of him, however small or large it may have been, would remain in the past. After taking a last look at the caravan, William turned the horse around and rode to catch up with his friends.

# 27

ONE MONTH LATER. WILLIAM'S HEAD SWAYED side to side on his chest as his horse slowly sank one hoof after the other into the dry sand. Through their journey, the animal had thinned out, and its bones protruded sharply underneath its warm hide. William's grip on the reins was loose as he continuously fell in and out of a heat-induced sleep that wet his back with sweat. He'd wrapped a length of white cloth over his head, but under the desert sun, even that wasn't helping.

Hans' camel gave a long groan of discomfort, and William's eyes blinked open. They instantly saddened when he saw the same view of the last thirty days. Empty desert. The palace he'd longed for had become his prison; the silence his torment.

The sweat on his face had made a thick layer of dust stick to his skin, hiding his eyebrows and lips in a pale mask. His eyes were like sapphires set into a marble statue and his lips were as dry as tree bark. William's stomach ached from hunger. His last meal had consisted of a handful of bread crumbs that he had pinched from the sack that had contained their bread. The last liquid he remembered touching his lips was a drop of sweat since the sheepskins they'd filled up at the wagons where the ambush happened were long gone.

Alexander's horse had died several days earlier and had they been this hungry then they would have eaten it.

"William," Hans called from the back of his camel.

William looked up at the sun and his eyes twitched uncomfortably. He didn't hear Hans. He was occupied with the heat and the emptiness in his stomach.

"William, we need to rest. We can't go on like this any longer," the German was saying, his voice shaking from hunger though slightly louder than before.

But William was lost in the light of the desert sun. Its brilliant glare stung his eyes, but he didn't mind. It was the purest light he'd ever seen.

"William, he's right. We need to rest," Alexander joined in, perhaps the most tired of the three since he had to walk now that his horse was dead.

William pulled on the reins. He closed his eyes and sat for a moment with his neck arched back, feeling the sun on his face. He opened his eyes and looked over his shoulder. Alexander had stopped walking a couple of feet behind the horse. Hans sat on the back of his camel with a cloth covering his head. Because of the dust, he looked like he was a part of the saddle and his once groomed beard had been replaced by grayish moss.

"We'll stop and rest here for a while," William said, nodding slowly. His voice sounded relieved but his face bore a slight look of annoyance because to him stopping meant surrender.

He dismounted with the speed an old man, the speed at which most things were done lately. When his feet landed on the ground, William stared at the side of the horse's saddle. He couldn't help but wonder if this would be the last time he would make camp in the desert with his friends before they joined the many swallowed up by the sands.

Hans' camel gave another groan as it kneeled onto its front legs before leaning back. William looked up just in time to see Hans jump down onto the sand. In William's mind, they were waving the white flag, but he was not afraid. He had done his best leading their small group, and now was the time for the world to forget he had ever existed.

William grabbed the reins and turned the horse back to Hans and Alexander to help them set up camp. Instead of unloading the camel's supplies, as they'd been doing, this time they kept the camel as it was and created a makeshift awning by draping a large white cloth over its back and pounding two long posts into the ground on one side to hold up the cloth.

While William and Hans were putting together the awning, Alexander made a small fire in front of it to create the illusion that they were still fighting back, still surviving. Assembling the awning took longer than it should have, but they were in no rush. When it looked the best it could and Alexander's fire was crackling on some dry branches he'd gathered from dead bushes they'd passed earlier in the day, the three men sat down and rested their backs on the side of the camel's belly. They didn't talk as much as they used to, because it made their mouths dry and words only became necessary when something important had to be said. Days spent in silence allowed them to know what the others were thinking, because each one was acutely aware of his own thoughts.

They had been sitting for a while, as if waiting for something to arrive, when Alexander suddenly crawled out from underneath the awning. William and Hans continued staring at the wavy horizon, their minds so tired that when Alexander's footsteps were gone, they forgot that he had left. When

Alexander ducked his head and stepped under the sagging cloth of the awning, William and Hans stared with dead hope at the bottle of wine he had brought.

Alexander sat down cheerfully even though their situation was grim. Once he had made himself comfortable against the camel's side, he wrapped his fingers around the cork and began pulling on it. The cork squealed before making a loud, hollow pop. Alexander tossed the cork into the fire and handed the bottle to Hans.

As the German took his fill, William turned back to the crackling fire, disappointed that its flames would not cook them anything to eat today. He thought about Nadia, whose face his mind had reconstructed down to the last eyelash. Now it was a clear image in his brain, and he could nearly sense the soul behind the rainforest green of her eyes. In a way, he considered her death a mercy. It had been fast and clean. She didn't have to suffer thirst or hunger, or the pain of seeing the children killed in cold blood.

Gentle footsteps crunched the ground to William's left. He turned and stared at the direction of the noise. The head of a goat appeared from behind the camel and looked at William with a squinted eye and an odd, black-lipped smile. With each step the goat took, more of its body appeared. William watched the animal in disbelief as it neared the left post of the awning.

Alexander turned to hand William the bottle of wine but stopped when he noticed the goat walking toward the fire. The animal stopped just under the awning and looked at Alexander then at Hans, its senses calculating if they were a threat or not.

Even though the goat's ribs could be counted, to William it looked like a meal just waiting to be cooked. The goat seemed to be taunting them with its bulging eyes and thin lips. *We can have two weeks' worth of meat if we kill the goats, and the horse could buy us a month, or so. They could be our way out of here if we ration them,* William calculated, his stomach doing the majority of the thinking.

William's stomach grumbled, set off a chain reaction that spread to both Hans and Alexander. The goat heard the symphony of hunger and took it as a bad sign. Instead of taking chances, the animal slowly turned around and started making its way to the other side of the camel, where it had been lying peacefully before evoking thoughts of sizzling meat.

As the goat pranced away at a hurried pace, William, Hans, and Alexander turned their heads, following it with their eyes. When the goat disappeared behind the camel, William sunk onto his hands and knees and crawled out from underneath the awning, the other two close behind.

Clear of the awning, William rose to his feet and continued walking. Alexander followed. They stopped when they saw the goat circling toward the front of the camel at the same hurried pace. Suddenly, Hans jumped in front of the goat and aimed a rifle down at the animal's head.

"No, don't shoot Glenda," Alexander shouted as he ran toward Hans, who looked up with a confused stare.

"Glenda? You named the goat Glenda?" Alexander kneeled at the goat's side and began petting it.

"Wasn't that your wife's name?" William asked.

"Yeah, I did. You two haven't been exactly chatty, and I like to have someone to talk to," Alexander said, glancing back at William as he hugged the goat closer to his chest.

"Well, that's your loss. I am not going to starve," Hans said, raising the rifle back to the goat's head. The animal suddenly darted away from Alexander and the camel.

Hans followed it with the rifle sights, but lowered the weapon when Alexander ran after it yelling, "Glenda, don't go. It's safe here. Come back, I'm not going to hurt you."

The German glanced at William, who looked as confused as he was, then turned back to Alexander. The two of them ran after their friend who was now chasing the animal in a large circle.


He would catch that goat if it was the last thing he did. And he would protect it. Glenda was his friend, not dinner.

Alexander ran after the frantic animal, calling Glenda to come back. They were just about to make another circle when his foot caught on something hard and he fell to the ground, shouting in pain. Grasping the toes of his right foot, he quickly sat up and looked at the ground. It was covered in sand, but underneath the surface something glinted in the sun. Forgetting all about Glenda and the pain in his foot, Alexander moved closer.


William and Hans came to a stop just in front of Alexander and watched him dubiously as he began digging away handfuls of sand like a delirious pirate. At first, William thought that the heat and hunger were having their effects on his friend, but his worry disappeared when he saw a long, rusty piece of metal appear in the sand.

"Railroad tracks," Alexander gasped.

Hans turned to William with a smile that threatened to push his sunburnt cheeks into his eye sockets. Alexander swept away a little more of the sand, revealing the sister track.

"Look. They run east," he shouted as he straightened his back and pointed in the direction they had been riding.

William followed Alexander's finger. There was not a dune in sight, and the sand stretched over the edge of a horizon so wide, you could see in every direction at once without turning your head. In the distance, heat waves rippled like the stream of an oasis, almost cool and exempt from the heat of the desert.

The vastness he saw silenced the feelings of hope and replaced them with a stern message coming from a silent, internal voice: the desert is an unforgiving furnace where delusional hopes are more abundant than its sands. To give in to such hopes would only ensure that your bones would be powdered and forgotten in the pale sand.

William turned around and looked at Hans and Alexander. The cold looks in their eyes told him that they had come to the same realization.

"What should we do?" Alexander asked calmly, looking up at William with a hope he didn't trust.

Considering what provisions they had left, William looked back at the camel and his horse. Should they continue their journey following the tracks, or should they wait for the train to come? If trains still ran along these tracks at all, it might be days—or even weeks—before they saw one. Waiting, too, would not take them any closer to Yemen or to refreshing wells that might be just a kilometer away.

Neither option seemed acceptable because they both heavily relied on one thing William despised: waiting.

"It might be days, or longer, before anything comes along. We'll have better chances if we continue riding east once it's dark, staying close to the tracks." Looking back at Hans and Alexander, William saw their faces mirrored his own thoughts, even though they didn't like traveling at night. Still, he found it a blessing that they were willing to do it for the sake of getting one step closer to Yemen as well as food and water.

"What about the goats?" Hans asked with a hopeful look.

"Alexander?" William asked his fellow countryman, wanting to respect the man's feelings.

"Eat the other one. I don't like him; he looks at me funny," Alexander said with a childish dislike, looking back at the goats. Hans grinned and started walking back to the camel with a new sense of determination.

"How's your foot?" William asked Alexander.

"It's all right," Alexander said as he rose to his feet and brushed off some of the dirt, though it did little good since the color of his clothes and skin were hidden behind a permanent layer of dust. A gunshot echoed from behind the camel and the two friends turned toward it. One of the goats, which had obviously searched for refuge behind the camel, swayed on its feet before landing on its side with a soft thud. The camel gave a groan at the sudden noise but kept still while the other goat ran in frantic circles around it.

"Hey," Alexander shouted and ran to the fallen goat, William following close behind.

As they neared the camel, Hans walked from behind it with his rifle resting on his shoulder like a big game hunter having felled a prize-winning elephant. When Alexander reached the goat, he fell to his knees to examine the animal. It was dead.

"You shot Glenda!" Alexander yelled at Hans.

"Oops. They look so similar," Hans said with no remorse whatsoever. A smirk was playing on his face as he looked down at the goat.

William chuckled but looked away, a little ashamed that their life came at the price of Alexander's sadness. A moment passed and Alexander stood up. He was so dehydrated, his eyes couldn't expel any tears, but his drawn face was enough of a sign not to bother him. He crawled underneath the awning and settled there, drinking from the remaining wine and feeding twigs to the fire.

"I wonder what Freud would have to say about this," Hans chuckled to himself as he slung the rifle over his shoulder then picked up the dead animal.

While Hans gutted and skinned the goat, the air around them turned sour with a putrid smell so bad that William thought the goat might have contracted some horrible disease—but he was too hungry to care. He couldn't go another day without food.

Hans cut away all the meat that was good for cooking and put it inside a cloth to keep it away from flies and the sand. Then he and William took hold of the carcass and carried it as far away from their camp as they could. In less than an hour's time, the goat had turned into meat ready to be cooked, and they would have to prepare all of it so it wouldn't turn sour in the heat.

Three steak-sized cuts were already sizzling on rocks that Hans had placed in the fire, and the men sat underneath the awning watching it cook with a look of impatience on their faces.

William glanced at Hans who didn't hide his pleasure at hearing the meat sizzle. The German radiated happiness that soon the hunger in his stomach would be gone. Alexander was another story. He sat just inside the fire's range, his face turned away, but his eyes discreetly watched the meat sizzle. A mixture of disgust and resignation played on his features, and though William felt bad for his friend, he knew that once the hunger was gone, Alexander would feel much better.

It was nearly sundown when the meat was ready, and the cold of night was already beginning to settle in the darkening air. Hans, enthusiastic to finally sink teeth in his dinner, fished one of the pieces from the cooking stone with the tip of a knife and handed it to William. William grabbed hold of the meat and a few drops of juice dripped down his hands as he brought it to his mouth. There were opposite expressions in Hans' and Alexander's eyes as they watched him sink his teeth into the meat and rip away a piece big enough for him to chew.

"How is it?" Hans asked with delicate excitement, leaning closer while William chewed.

"It's good," William said with a grin on his face. The meat, despite its putrid smell, tasted better than some of the best mutton he had eaten in England, and satisfied the empty hunger in his stomach.

Hans fished another piece out of the fire and handed it to Alexander. The Englishman stared at the piece of steaming meat with disgust and couldn't bring himself to take it from the blade.

"I know you don't like it, but you must eat. You'll need your strength for tomorrow," William reminded him and nodded toward the piece of meat. Alexander's sad eyes looked from William to the meat.

Slowly his hands rose from his lap and pulled the piece away from the blade. William and Hans watched as he brought it to his mouth and took a bite. Alexander ignored them and took another bite in silence. Satisfied and relieved, Hans turned back toward the fire and took the last piece of meat for himself.

They ate in silence, each absorbed in their own thoughts and hopes for the future. When they finished their portions, along with the last of the wine, William and Hans took down the posts that held up the awning so that when they woke in the middle of the night they would be ready to leave. As usual, they used the awning as a blanket to keep them warm. The goat's meat eased their minds into sleep despite the arriving cold.


William opened his eyes to complete darkness. The air had turned frozen, but still smelled of their dinner. He knew he'd only been asleep for a couple of hours but though his body felt tired, his mind was alert. He looked up. A multitude of stars hung in the night sky, blissful and unbothered by the problems of man.

Next to him, Hans and Alexander snored quietly. Above his head, the belly of the camel rose and fell as the animal slept after a hard day of carrying supplies. William turned back toward the sky and focused on a lone white star. It shone brighter than the rest, and he tried to remember if it had a name.

A distance sound turned his attention elsewhere. He frowned at his imagination but listened closer. A faint puffing noise reached his ears, and William scrambled to his feet to look in the direction the sound was coming from. Far away, two small yellow lights were approaching at a speed far greater than it appeared. He watched them for several more seconds as if hypnotized. The puffing sound became louder until William's mind caught up with his eyes.

A train was approaching.

"Hans," William gasped as he patted Hans frantically, the tears in his eyes blurring the vision of the lights.

"What? What's going on?" Hans grumbled as he pushed himself up to his side.

"Look! It's coming!" William shouted, turning Hans' head who stared at the approaching lights with squinted eyes.

"Train!" Hans shouted as he rose to his feet next to William and whisked the blanket off Alexander to prepare to catch the train.

"Why are you—" Alexander said in a confused voice as he rose.

"Train! Look," Hans said and pointed to the approaching lights as William started to get the horse ready. Alexander straightened up, saw the lights, and joined William. The horse was already stumbling to its feet.

In the meantime, Hans tucked away the cloth into the camel's saddle and pulled himself onto the animal's back. He tapped the camel on the shoulder, rushing it to get a move on. It gave a loud groan and lethargically rose to its feet.

William and Alexander were up on the horse, pulling up next to Hans. They heard the train as clear as ever in the desert silence. It approached fast, and if they didn't hurry up, it would pass by them in a flash.

"Come on," William shouted as he kicked the horse with his heels and galloped in the direction the tracks lead to. The camel moved behind them at a slow pace that soon turned into a trot. William looked over his shoulder and saw the headlights of the train catching up with him.

He tapped the horse with his heels and the animal gathered its strength and kept going forward, Hans' camel chasing behind it.

Suddenly, the locomotive sped past William's horse creating a thunderous gust of wind. It was followed by several illuminated cars that rattled by. As the animals picked up speed, the passing cars began to slow. William looked over his shoulder to see the end of the train, but the darkness covered it like a blanket. Unsure how long the horse could keep up the speed, William listened for the rattling of the carriages over the tracks. Surely, when he couldn't hear it anymore, he'd be able to see a hand rail to grab onto.

He glanced over his shoulder again. Hans was barely visible in the darkness and slipping farther away. He turned around again and watched as each rail car passed in the dark. A few square windows were glowing with golden light that shined through the drawn shades, but most were dark.

With each car that passed the rattling began to soften. The last carriage was drawing near. Looking over his shoulder, William counted three cars behind him, but Hans and his camel had disappeared.

William watched as the first car rattled past him. Then came the second one. Finally, the third car slipped by and he urged the horse forward. Underneath two dim lights right at the car's doorway, Hans stood, ready to help pull them onto the train.

Slowly, William caught up with the car and steered the horse closer to the side of the rattling train. He let go of the reins and grabbed onto the iron rail. Hans gripped William's wrists while Alexander steered the horse away from the train and William's legs slipped off the saddle toward the center of the train. He looked down and saw the rail ties passing beneath his feet so quickly that they became blurred. He raised his left leg onto an iron stairway leading to the small deck where Hans stood, and pulled himself over the rail.

Standing on the narrow platform, William turned back to find the horse, with Alexander sitting in the saddle, pounding furiously at the sand to keep up.

When Alexander was within an arm's reach of the train, he let go of the reins and grabbed onto the rail. William and Hans grabbed onto his hands like he was a sailor about to fall overboard. As the horse veered into the darkness, Alexander pulled himself up.

The three friends hugged each other and laughed with excitement, knowing that wherever this train was going, it would take them out of the desert. Death by starvation, thirst and heat was no longer a real possibility.

They relished this small victory for some time, then, feeling the cold chill their excited but exhausted bodies, turned their attention to the carriage door. It was green and flanked by two square lanterns that gave off just enough light to see onto the platform.

The seams around the door were lined with golden light that seemed both inviting and intimidating. The idea of riding on a train after a month in the desert seemed so alien to them that the friends felt slightly out of place. Yet here they were. Their futures hidden behind the door, if they would only open it.

William looked at Hans with a nervous smile and took a step toward the door. The brass handle was clean enough to reflect their warped figures in its shiny surface. When he wrapped his fingers around the handle, the brass chilled his palm. William turned the doorknob, producing a gentle click, and the door opened several inches.

Pushing on it revealed the inside of the car, crowded with people in white robes sitting on rows of wooden benches that faced each other. Some were sitting on the floor, while others were standing.

They looked like a hundred fallen angels bearing the fingerprints of destiny over their robes, illuminated by three light bulbs that hung from the ceiling via metal dishes that swayed with the rocking of the train.

The passengers, one by one, turned to the door. The people's eyes hid whatever curiosity they had. Instead their gaze seemed to be searching for something deep in the eyes of the unannounced strangers. William took a hesitant step forward. Hans and Alexander followed then the German closed the door and the constant rattle of the train was shut outside. William took in the faces of the people, calm and sure of the future.

Several passengers, who were sitting on a bench to the right side, silently rose from their seats.

William nodded, unable to produce any words, and started walking toward the bench with Hans and Alexander on his heels. Within three steps, they had entered the crowd of passengers. Many of them couldn't move out of the way because there was no room for them to do so, and William was forced to slide awkwardly past them. William noticed a white goat near his side and heard a baby's raspy cry. He looked up to where the cry had come from. Sitting on a bench to the right of the car, a nursing mother held a baby with puffy cheeks and swollen-looking eyes to her chest.

The friends sat down on the benches, the wood creaking under their weight. As they took their seats, the eyes of the people left them and returned back to where they were before the strangers had entered. William looked at Hans and Alexander and smiled. They were safe now, though none of them had felt that way just a few hours earlier. William's smile became contagious, bringing wide grins on Hans' and Alexander's dusty and sunburnt faces.

William looked out the window to his left. The shade was lifted and he expected to see the desert, but instead, the glass reflected everything under the light of the swaying bulbs in a bourbon tinge and had transformed his own face into a mask of gold with long shadows under the eyes and cheekbones belonging to a man he didn't recognize.

He looked at his eyes and in them he saw the familiar spark of life that always seemed to fill them. It was still there, that sign of recognition that separated humans from other animals. They were the only part of him that hadn't changed, despite everything they'd seen. William smiled again, perhaps just to reassure himself that the reflection was really his, though he sensed the smile was only half-genuine and it faded quickly.

Across from him, Alexander slept with his head resting on the glass, and Hans' head had found a pillow in Alexander's shoulder. William grinned at his sleeping friends then looked back at the eyes in the reflection. Slowly his lids drooped and he leaned his own head against the glass. His eyes closed and he let out a deep breath. The last thought that entered his mind was: *What do I do now?*

William was nearly shaken off his seat when the train rattled violently from side to side at one of the track connections. He squinted as he looked at the inside of the car. Bright light was coming from the windows, all the shades were now drawn. He looked outside at the golden sands that slowly drifted away from him.

He lifted up his head from the window and looked around. The German's face was the first thing he noticed, grinning the way Hans always did when he had an amusing thought in his head.

"Did you sleep well?" Hans asked while Alexander snored next to him with his mouth open.

"Better. Yes," William answered as he straightened himself on the bench and his eyes adjusted to the light. He looked to his right and saw an Arab man sitting next to him on the bench, his eyes looking forward and his face content.

"I'm going to get some fresh air," William said as he patted Hans on the knee and rose to his feet.

He stepped in the aisle and made his way to the back of the train, making sure not to step on any hands or feet as he walked. Some people were still sleeping, though most were staring either out of the windows or at the inside of the car to help pass the time. Only a few noticed William. The baby was sleeping soundly in the mother's arms, who had dosed off as well. The goat lay to the left of the doorway with an observant look in its eyes.

When William reached the door, he pulled it open and stepped outside before closing it behind him. In front of him was a never-ending line of railroad tracks. He leaned on the iron rail and looked down, watching the rail ties passing beneath him. His ears tuned in to the rumbling of the train and the other sounds: some more distinct, like his breath, and some farther away, like the wheels squealing behind him. Surprisingly, he didn't feel sad for leaving the desert. He missed certain things, yes, but that was just the cousin of sadness.

His days in the caravan belonged to a time in his life when he had become so obsessed with the desert that nothing seemed more important than being lost in the silence and emptiness that the sands presented. That part of his life was over.

He felt grateful for everything that had happened to him. Every night in the cold, every person he had met and watched die. It was the reason he was stronger. William looked up at the desert and smiled. He had never believed he would live to see the end of the vast sand ocean, but here it was. This was the moment he had dreaded back when the caravan had been alive and going, yet here he was, welcoming it.

William had said goodbye to Nadia, to Hakeem, Fudail, and the caravan, quietly and alone, without complaint or wishing things were different. Now was the time to say goodbye to the desert.

He knew the end of this journey also meant saying goodbye to Hans and Alexander, but he'd worry about that when the time came. Right now he wanted to think about himself and where he was going to go from here. There was nothing keeping him in the desert, and he had no reason to go back to London. He was free to live whatever life he wanted, and he was ready to start over in a place where people didn't have to die before their time, where the land wasn't trying to turn you into a raisin, and everything you wanted— food, water, friendship—didn't have to be paid in blood and tears.

He figured that once Hans and Alexander went their way, he could even go to Egypt and open up his own photography studio in Cairo. He liked the idea, certain that he'd be making a lot more money working for himself than he would if he went back to England. He could buy a house and learn Arabic, or become a camel merchant.

Anything was possible.

His mind and heart brimmed with those possibilities, bringing excitement to his very skin. William felt eager to get working again and begin this new chapter in his life.

One thing was certain though, no matter how much his life changed, he would never forget his days in the desert and the people he met—and left—there. It had been a great adventure indeed.

Looking up at the long line of track they left behind, William felt renewed. He knew how he wanted to live his life. He looked past the horizon and pictured the dunes in his mind. Quietly, he said goodbye to the sands that had tormented and teased his soul, and now he was truly ready to begin anew. As he watched the train tracks below, William wondered whether long after this day was through he would once again venture across the dunes and stand in the silence, alone with his old friend, the desert.

# About the Author

ALTHOUGH BORN IN CALIFORNIA, ADAM DE COLLIBUS is a man of the world. In his early years he lived in South America, and his love of travel has led to him living and traveling in over seventeen countries.

Inspired by both historical and actual events during his travels, De Collibus was compelled to write Caravan, his debut historical novel. Adam De Collibus lives mostly in California where he spends his time writing, reading, and playing the piano.

CPSIA information can be obtained
at www.ICGtesting.com
Printed in the USA
LVHW090033300719
625828LV00004B/615/P